S0-AVZ-963

THE BIG BROADCAST

THE BIG BROADCAST

1920 - 1950

A New, Revised, and Greatly Expanded Edition of Radio's Golden Age

The Complete Reference Work

by Frank Buxton *and* Bill Owen

Introduction by Henry Morgan

The Viking Press
New York

First published in 1972 by The Viking Press, Inc.
625 Madison Avenue, New York, N.Y. 10022
Published simultaneously in Canada by
The Macmillan Company of Canada Limited
Printed in the United States of America

To the men and women whose
names appear on the following pages
with gratitude for their contribution
to the fabulous but faded sounds of
the age that produced
The Big Broadcast

Introduction
by HENRY MORGAN

The "radio" part of Radio City is the National Broadcasting Company, which is housed in the RCA Building in Rockefeller Center, New York. The building was finished sometime in 1933. Five minutes later the third floor of NBC was crowded with actors. A series of broadcasting studios ringed a large central lobby in which the actors congregated before, during, and after broadcasts. About thirty of them did ninety per cent of the work. The rest sat around waiting for lightning to strike. What they wanted was for lightning to strike some working actor so that a job would become available. They realized—but couldn't bring themselves to acknowledge the fact—that if a bolt actually struck Santos Ortega at the last minute the producer wouldn't rush into the lobby and grab Axel Ramsfutter, he'd look for and find Leon Janney . . . or Bud Collyer . . . or Luis Van Rooten. These were *real* (*i.e.*, working) actors, and a producer knew them and their work and the outsider didn't have a chance.

The system was simplicity itself. At WMCA, for example, a man named Charles Martin got the idea of doing a daily *March-of-Time* type of broadcast and sold the idea to the station management. All radio was live then and the time had to be filled one way or another, and Charlie's way was as good as the next guy's, or *sounded* as good. A little stock company of unemployed Broadway actors was hired at thirty dollars a week apiece. The company included Martin Gabel (a recent graduate of the American Academy of Dramatic Art), Garson Kanin, Alice Frost, and, quite often, one of the page boys (H. Morgan.) Since Mr. Morgan was already being paid eight dollars a week in his other job, there was no need to pay him extra to "act." At the network stations the actors worked for what they could get. There was no union, no hours. Hugh Conrad, a staff announcer at WMCA, doubled as the "Voice of Time" on the regular weekly network program using his true name, Westbrook Van Voorhis. When I became a full-time staff announcer in 1932, the chief announcer told me to change my name since no one would understand my true one, Henry von Ost, Jr. What about Harry Von Zell? I asked. Or, for that matter, Van Voorhis? The chief, resplendent in a name he had conjured up for himself (A. L. Alexander), was adamant.

An announcer spent his long days making up introductions for the "acts" that followed one another for sixteen hours a day. None of them was paid unless some advertiser picked up the program, and then it was a matter of five or ten dollars a show. Hungarian two-piano teams, Polish oompah bands, Madame Charme the beauty expert, Elmo Russ at the studio organ, the Lord himself knows what came through in the course of the day.

Over on the networks the serials had started, and those who played leads became the gentry of the business. Graham McNamee, an aspiring baritone, had been sent out to do a sports broadcast and, his enthusiasm overcoming his lack of knowledge, was the first announcer to become gentry in that field. David Ross read poetry in a rich, faky voice and won a "diction" award. Paul D. Fleisher dropped the Fleisher and, as Paul Douglas, would holler into the innards of an open grand piano, "Buck . . . Rogers . . . in the twenty-fifth . . . CEN . . . tury!" It had a nice hollow effect.

In the thirties I spent half my life in Harlem. All the great bands were up there, and we would broadcast them every night from ten until three in the morning. I was announcer for Don Redman, Fletcher Henderson, Teddy Wilson, Lucky Millinder, Claude Hopkins, Chick Webb, Father Hines, the Mills Blue Ribbon Band, Cab Calloway, Willie Stephens Bryant, Andy Kirk and His Clouds of Joy—are you *sure* they're not coming back?

Once, thirty announcers auditioned to replace Norman Brokenshire as the announcer on the Chesterfield program and I won. By the time I got upstairs Ted Husing had been assigned to the show. I listened in that night and was a bit surprised to hear Paul Douglas. It went that way more often than not.

I was too fresh for A. L. Alexander at WMCA and he fired me —possibly because I had laughed at him. He was the voice that introduced *Tom Noonan's Chinatown Mission* on Sundays, and Alex took it big. Each week his intro got flossier, until the day he said, "Here within the confines of the broadcast enclosure . . ." It was mean to fire the youngest full-time staff announcer in the country, and I rushed over to NBC to audition for Pat Kelly, *their* chief announcer. He said he'd send me to Cleveland, but I knew I was good enough for New York, so I rushed over to CBS, won an audition, and was sent to Philadelphia. It went that way too.

The head man at WCAU Philadelphia for announcer types was Stan Lee Broza. He fired me for laughing during the "Missing Persons" report and for getting stuck in the elevator while running it myself at night and for throwing burning wastebaskets in on my roommate while he was working and for knocking off in the afternoon to go have a drink with Paul Douglas. The fact that in a few years Douglas would be a big star in *Born Yesterday* didn't impress Broza a bit.

This sent me to WEBC Duluth. I told the boss I was twenty-six, and he made *me* chief announcer.

The following year I went to WNAC Boston to replace a staff man who was going to New York to seek his fortune. In twenty-five short years he went from Dan Seymour, announcer for *Aunt Jenny*, to the presidency of J. Walter Thompson.

By 1938 I was up to forty a week at WOR back home. One day the management came around and suggested that I kidded around too much on the air, would I mind taking fifteen minutes to get it out of my system? I wouldn't mind. About this time the station sold a program called *Superman*, which went on Mondays, Wednesdays, and Fridays at five-fifteen. Would I mind doing Tues., Thurs., and Sat.? No. I introduced myself as "Here's Morgan" but then would state that I was better known as "Super-Morg." They made me cut that out too.

Meanwhile, back at NBC's third floor . . .

The "gentry" of the early thirties was now an aristocracy. The American Federation of Radio Artists had been formed and salaries had gone up. John's Other Brother now had a house in Westchester and no longer suffered the indignity of having to audition for a job. There was a telephone-answering service that did nothing but keep track of radio actors and their jobs. There were direct telephone lines to the third floor, to CBS, even to a couple of the restaurants where the actors went for coffee. Some of them had left for other things; Frank Lovejoy, John Hodiak, Burgess Meredith, José Ferrer had gone. Rudy Vallee and Eddie Cantor had given impetus to some of the more talented. Major Bowes had created "units" that criss-crossed the country and made the Major richer and richer but, more important, kept a lot of actors eating.

Mr. Morgan, meanwhile, having announced his way in and out of a number of jobs, was hired to do the sell on *Lone Journey*. This was the first program to peddle a detergent (Dreft), and it took five minutes to explain what *that* meant. Another three minutes were used for the "lead in"—the business where the announcer explains what has happened to date.

The rest of the fourteen and a half minutes were devoted to the story.

A word about "kidding the sponsor." I started this in 1938 (Arthur Godfrey did it in a much different way a few years later in Washington, but neither of us knew of the other). But this was a canard, because I didn't kid the sponsor at all. I kidded bad advertising, including my own. If Old Man Adler, one of my clients, handed me a piece of copy that said his shoes were the greatest in the world, I would say that they hadn't been tested out quite that far but that perhaps they were the second greatest. Once he brought out a new spring line of some kind of hinky-dink canvas numbers in dreadful colors, puce, lemon and lime, stuff like that. I said that I wouldn't wear them to a dogfight but that perhaps some of the listeners would like them. Adler got mad and threatened to cancel his advertising. The following night I retracted. I said okay, I *would* wear them to a dogfight. It made him happy.

Television warmed up after World War II, and radio started its dive somewhere around 1951 or 1952. Radio actually died when *Stop the Music* got higher ratings than Fred Allen. Bert Parks went on from *Music* to become the celebrated singer on the Miss America pageants, which are still thrilling people who get thrilled by things like that, but all that's left of radio is in the pages that follow.

Foreword

Five years have elapsed since the publication of *Radio's Golden Age*, the first encyclopedia of old radio programs. In the intervening years our research has continued, aided by readers who had knowledge or evidence of additional information. The result of it all is this book: *The Big Broadcast 1920–1950*.

Compared with *Radio's Golden Age*, this new book is bigger and better in every respect. There are now special narrative sections on "Announcers," "Big Band Remotes," "Comedy and Comedians," "Comic Strips to Radio," "Commercials," "Cowboys," "FM," "Hollywood Reporters," "Interviewers," "Musicians," "Networks," "News and Newscasters," "Orchestra Leaders," "Quiz Shows," "Religion," "Singers," "Soap Operas," "Sound Effects Men," "Sports and Sportscasters," "Women's Programs," and a catch-all titled "Animal Imitators, Baby Criers, Doubles, Mimics, and Screamers."

Countless dates and network origination information have been verified and added to the program listings along with more actual script excerpts and the names of sponsors.

That's not all. We've unearthed forty-three more rare photographs to enrich the book. And the added feature of an index makes it easier to find quickly the particular information you are seeking.

Whether your question is:

Who played Pepper Young? (Mason Adams wasn't the only actor in that role)

How did they always get the audience to laugh at the beginning of *Truth or Consequences?*

What was the theme song of *Young Widder Brown?*

Did Bill Stern ever broadcast a World Series? (nope)

Did a man really play Beulah? (yep, for a while)

Who handled the sound effects on *Gangbusters?*

How did Walter Winchell open his show?

Who sponsored *Buck Rogers in the 25th Century?*

What was the history of *The Fitch Bandwagon?*

Who was the announcer for *The Lone Ranger?*

—you'll find the answer within these covers.

Many kind words have been written about *Radio's Golden Age*. However, we remember best a complaint from a reader who said our book deprived him of sleep; every time he looked up something, his attention was arrested by another item—and he invariably read on and on through the night.

So here it is. The result of a total of eight years' research and the cooperation of literally hundreds of people: your guide to radio as it was way back then!

1971

Frank Buxton
Bill Owen

Acknowledgments

We are indebted to the following for their assistance in the preparation of this book:

Sue Alenick, WABC-FM music librarian
Eve Baer, ZIV
Paul Balgley, Indiana University, *Vic and Sade* research
Cora Ballard, secretary to Fred Waring
Don Becker, writer
Ted Bell, director
Roswell Bigelow, lighting director
Ed Blainey, sound effects
May Bolhower, Young & Rubicam
Himan Brown, producer-writer-director
John Calabrese, ABC Records
Giff Campbell, WOR engineering department
Ray Campbell, director
Milton Caniff, comic-strip artist
Carroll Carroll, writer
Alice Clements, Clements Co., Inc.
Catherine Couture, English instructor
Jerry Devine, producer-director
Dan Enright, producer
Sheilah Fields, Easton Valley Press
Bess Flynn, writer
Elsie K. Frank, assistant to Elaine Carrington
Bud Gammon, Fuller, Smith & Ross
Bill Gately, director
Moses Gershuny, ABC engineering department
Bob Ginn, Wrather Corp., Beverly Hills, Calif.
Liliane Gonfrade, ABC music library
Helen Guy, ABC-TV sales
Mary Harris, director
Jeanne K. Harrison, producer-director
Ralph Hawkins, director
Joseph Hehn, children's radio serials research
Mimi Hoffmeier, NBC Program Information
Loomis Irish, BBDO
Adele Irving, ABC music library
James Jewell, producer
Jack Johnstone, writer
Stuart Kaminsky, Director of University of Chicago Public Information
Paul Kapp, General Music Publishing Company
Sibyl Lavengood, CBS Program Information
John T. Lyman, ABC announcing department supervisor
Kitty Lynch, ABC librarian
Kenneth W. MacGregor, director
Ellen MacKinnon, ABC Press Information
Len Magnus, director
Lloyd Marx, director
William McCaffrey, talent agent
James McMenemy, writer
Albert G. Miller, writer
Marjorie Morrow, talent agent
Kay Murphy, manager of ABC's Literary Rights Division
Harry Nelson, sound effects
Sylvia Olkin, CBS
Frank Olsen, ABC on-air promotion department
Dolph Opfinger, WOR
Dennis Oppenheim, director

Joseph Palmer, ABC engineering department
Frank Papp, director
Ted Patterson, sportscasting research
Pepsi Co., Inc.: Copyright 1940 by Pepsi Co., Inc. (formerly the Pepsi-Cola Company)
Bob Prescott, sound effects
Pete Prescott, sound effects
Herbert C. Rice, WILI Willimantic (Conn.)
Cantor William Robyn, former member of "Roxy's Gang"
Art Ronnie, 20th Century-Fox
Terry Ross, sound effects
Leo Russotto, pianist, arranger, and coach of "Roxy's Gang"
George Salerno, WABC news-writer
Jane Di Leo Sansone, assistant to Miss Hoffmeier at NBC Program Information
Carmine Santullo, assistant to Ed Sullivan
George Sax, ABC Radio
Walter P. Sheppard, WRVR-FM, research for *One Man's Family*
Ray Siller, director
Joan Sinclaire, director
Alexander Smallens, Jr., WABC-FM station manager
Warren Somerville, director
Gary Stevens, public relations
Bill Sweets, director
Robert Thorp, ABC engineering department
Chick Vincent, producer-writer-director
Frances A. Von Bernhardi, David Wolper Productions
Hal Wagner, MBS
Blair Walliser, writer-director
Bob Ward, ABC engineering department
Joseph Weill, WABC news-editor
George Wiest, director
Bob Wilbor, producer
Bill Williams, promotion manager, WSM Nashville (Tenn.)
Eddie N. Williams, University of Chicago Vice-President for Public Affairs
Frank Wilson, writer
David J. Wise, Radio Director of the Union of American Hebrew Congregations
Don Witty, writer
Wynn Wright, producer-director

And the following performers:

Goodman Ace
Bill Adams
Albert Aley
Hoyt Allen
Steve Allen
Jim Ameche
George Ansbro
Boris Aplon
Jack Arthur
Jon Arthur
Gene Autry
André Baruch
Jackson Beck
Ed Begley
Martin Begley
Joseph Bell
Ralph Bell
Bea Benaderet
Court Benson
Gertrude Berg
Rolly Bester
Mel Blanc
Martin Block
Lee Bowman
Frank Bresee
Ted Brown
Doug Browning
Warren Bryan
Louie Buck
Alan Bunce
Betty Caine
Phil Carlin
Fran Carlon
Cliff Carpenter
Ken Carpenter
Carl Caruso
John Causier
Helen Choate
Fred Collins
Bud Collyer
Hans Conried

Jack Costello
Staats Cotsworth
Thomas Cowan
Sam Cowling
Joel Crager
Milton Cross
Matt Crowley
Joseph Curtin
Stanley Davis
Ted de Corsia
Kenny Delmar
Don Dowd
Robert Dryden
Carl Eastman
Anne Elstner
Elspeth Eric
Ethel Everett
Roy Fant
Georgia Fifield
Laurette Fillbrandt
Michael Fitzmaurice
Cedric Foster
Fred Foy
Erwin Frankel
Florence Freeman
Don Gardiner
Chuck Goldstein
Peter Grant
Ben Grauer
Walter Greaza
Bill Griffis
Les Griffith
Jackie Grimes
Bob Hall
George Hayes
Ed Herlihy
Mary Jane Higby
Bob Hite
Al Hodge
Gilbert Hodges
Helen Holt
Arthur Hughes
Bill Idelson
John M. James
Leon Janney
Al Jarvis
Raymond Edward Johnson
Bill Johnstone
Dick Joy
Evelyn Juster
Kelvin Keech
Jack Kelk
Walter Kinsella
Adelaide Klein
Frank Knight
Richard Kollmar
Mandel Kramer
Chester Lauck
Abby Lewis
Bill Lipton
Ronald Liss
Don Lowe
Peg Lynch
Ted Mack
Albert Madru
Charlotte Manson
Peggy Marshall
Grace Matthews
Bob Maxwell
John K. M. McCaffery
Gordon McLendon
Harry McNaughton
Marvin Miller
Jim Monks
Claudia Morgan
Bret Morrison
Hon. George Murphy
Bill Myers
Hal Neal
Ozzie Nelson
Dan Ocko
Santos Ortega
Reynold Osborne
George Petrie
Howard Petrie
Roger Pryor
Mae Questel
Tony Randall
Elliott Reid
Bill Rice
Glenn Riggs
Rosa Rio
Jerry Roberts
Adele Ronson
David Ross
John Scott
Alexander Scourby
Dan Seymour
Alfred Shirley
Ethel Shutta

Vivian Smolen
Guy Sorel
Olan Soule
Jeff Sparks
Lionel Stander
Edgar Stehli
Bill Stern
Julie Stevens
Doug Storer
Maurice Tarplin
St. John Terrell
Ann Thomas
Phil Tonkin
Art Van Horn
Dickie Van Patten
Luis Van Rooten
Vicki Vola
Gene von Hallberg
Jimmy Wallington
C. Hames Ware
Gertrude Warner
Jack Webb
Bruno Wick
Ireene Wicker
Johnny Winters
Charles Woods
Lesley Woods
Ruth Yorke

Our thanks also to:

American Federation of Television and Radio Artists—New York, Chicago, and Hollywood offices, especially Ray Jones, Reggie Dowell, Burton Jacoby, Barbara Temple, Sonya Hall, and Carol Hanger
American Society of Composers, Authors and Publishers
Directors Guild of America, Inc., especially Ernest Ricca, executive secretary, and his assistant Fred Poller
Musicians Local 802—New York
Screen Actors Guild, Inc., especially Carol Ferres
Writers Guild of America East, especially James R. Wendland
Writers Guild of America West, especially Blanche W. Baker
Ashley-Famous Agency, Inc.
Comics Council, Inc.
Decca Records
Editor and Publisher magazine
Field & Stream magazine, especially Esther Foote
King Features Syndicate
Macfadden-Bartell Publications, publishers of *TV Radio Mirror*, especially Teresa Buxton
Mercury Records
New York Daily News Information Service
New York Herald Tribune Syndicate, especially Lillian Cutler
New York Public Library
New York Times Information Service
Walt Disney Productions
And our wives, Elizabeth Buxton and Rosemary Owen, for their help and patience

Photos courtesy of:

ABC
CBS
NBC
George Ansbro
Jack Arthur
Jackson Beck
Edgar Bergen
Alice Clements
Don Dowd
Anne-Marie Gayer
Mary Jane Higby
Arthur Hughes
Joseph Julian
Jack Kelk
Walter Kinsella
Roger Krupp
Gilbert Mack
Charlotte Manson
Anne Elstner Matthews
Tom McCray
Marvin Miller
Adele Ronson Nahm
Jeanette Nolan and John McIntire
Harold Peary
Alan Reed
Alice Reinheart
Olan Soule
Lotte Stavisky
Maurice Tarplin
John Thomas
Les Tremayne
Joan Uttal
Jimmy Wallington
Ned Wever

AUTHORS' NOTE

This listing is comprised of nationally known programs, most of which were on a major network. The scope of the book covers the period from the earliest days of radio through approximately 1950.

Programs are listed alphabetically by the title of the show (excluding A, An, and The). For example:

Backstage Wife	under "B"
A Date with Judy	under "D"
Jack Armstrong, The All-American Boy	under "J"
The Jack Benny Program	under "J"
The Stebbins Boys	under "S"
Tom Mix	under "T"
The Victor Borge Show	under "V"

Several performers worked under two different names. These have been noted. For example:

Alan Reed (Teddy Bergman)

All times listed in this book are Eastern Standard Time unless otherwise noted.

"He claims he hears the A. & P. Gypsies."

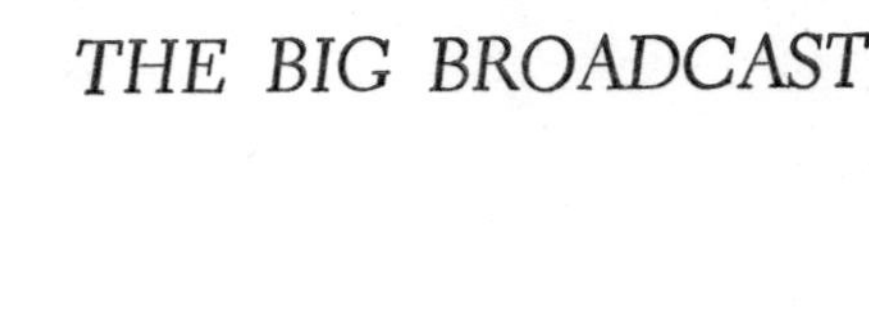
THE BIG BROADCAST

The A & P Gypsies

Music

Starring: Harry Horlick's Orchestra
With: Frank Parker, tenor
Announcers: Ed Thorgersen, Milton Cross, Phil Carlin
Theme: "Two Guitars"

This program, sponsored by the Great Atlantic & Pacific Tea Company, was first heard over WEAF New York in 1923.

The Abbott and Costello Program

Comedy

CAST:

Bud Abbott	Himself
Lou Costello	Himself

Also: Mel Blanc, Sid Fields, Iris Adrian
Vocalists: Marilyn Maxwell, Connie Haines
Orchestra: Will Osborne, Skinnay Ennis
Announcer: Ken Niles

Writers: Ed Forman, Ed Cherkose, Don Prindle, Len Stern, Paul Conlan, Pat Costello, Martin A. Ragaway
Sound Effects: Floyd Caton

Catch-phrases:
COSTELLO. I'm only thwee and a half years old.
COSTELLO. Hey, Abbott !!!
COSTELLO. I'm a b-a-a-a-d boy!
COSTELLO. Now I got it? I don't even know what I'm talking about!

This series was first heard over NBC in 1942. Abbott and Costello's "Who's on First?" routine, used frequently on the program, is a comedy classic.

WHO'S ON FIRST?

ABBOTT. All right, Lou. I'm the manager of a brand-new baseball team.
COSTELLO. Great. I would like to join your team.
ABBOTT. Oh, you would.
COSTELLO. I would like to know some of the guys' names on the team so if I play with them I'll know them . . . or if I meet them on the street or at home I can say "Hello" to them.
ABBOTT. Oh, sure. But you know baseball players have funny names . . . peculiar names . . . nowadays.
COSTELLO. Like what?
ABBOTT. Well, like Dizzy Dean . . . and Daffy Dean . . .
COSTELLO. Oh, yeah, a lot of funny names. I know all those guys.
ABBOTT. Well, let's see now. We have on our team, we have Who's on first . . . What's on second . . . I Don't Know's on third . . .
COSTELLO. That's what I want to find out, the guys' names.
ABBOTT. I'm telling you. Who's on first, What's on second, I Don't Know's on third . . .

COSTELLO. You're going to be the manager of the baseball team?
ABBOTT. Yes.
COSTELLO. You know the guys' names?
ABBOTT. Well, I should.
COSTELLO. Will you tell me the guys' names on the baseball team?
ABBOTT. I say Who's on first, What's on second, I Don't Know's on third . . .
COSTELLO. You ain't saying nothing to me yet. Go ahead, tell me.
ABBOTT. I'm telling you! Who's on first, What's on second and I Don't Know is on third.
COSTELLO. You know the guys' names on the baseball team?
ABBOTT. Yeah.
COSTELLO. Well, go ahead! Who's on first?
ABBOTT. Yeah.
COSTELLO. I mean the guy's name.
ABBOTT. Who.
COSTELLO. The guy playing first.
ABBOTT. Who.
COSTELLO. The guy playing first base.
ABBOTT. Who.
COSTELLO. The guy at first base.
ABBOTT. Who is on first.
COSTELLO. What are you asking me for? I don't know. I'm asking you who's on first.
ABBOTT. That's his name.
COSTELLO. Well, go ahead and tell me.
ABBOTT. Who.
COSTELLO. The guy on first.
ABBOTT. That's it. That's his name.
COSTELLO. You know the guy's name on first base?
ABBOTT. Sure.
COSTELLO. Well, tell me the guy's name on first base.
ABBOTT. Who.
COSTELLO. The guy playing first base.
ABBOTT. Who is on first, Lou.
COSTELLO. What are you asking me for?
ABBOTT. Now don't get excited. I'm saying Who . . .
COSTELLO. I'm asking a simple question. Who's on first?
ABBOTT. Yes.
COSTELLO. Go ahead and tell me.
ABBOTT. That's it.
COSTELLO. That's who?
ABBOTT. Yes.
COSTELLO. I'm asking you what's the guy's name on first base?
ABBOTT. Oh, no. What's on second. . . .

Abbott Mysteries

Drama

CAST:

Mr. Abbott — Charles Webster, Les Tremayne
Mrs. Abbott — Julie Stevens, Alice Reinheart
Also: Jean Ellyn, Luis Van Rooten, Sidney Slon
Announcer: Frank Gallop

These dramas were adapted from novels by Frances Crane.

Abie's Irish Rose

Situation Comedy

CAST:

Abie Levy — Richard Bond, Sydney Smith, Richard Coogan, Clayton "Bud" Collyer
Rosemary Levy — Betty Winkler, Mercedes McCambridge, Julie Stevens

Marion Shockley
Solomon Levy — Alfred White
Alan Reed (Teddy Bergman)
Patrick Joseph Murphy
Walter Kinsella
Mr. Cohen — Menasha Skulnik
Mrs. Cohen — Anna Appel
David Lerner — Carl Eastman
Father Whelan — Bill Adams
Casey, the secretary — Ann Thomas
Dr. Mueller — Fred Sullivan
Mrs. Mueller — Charme Allen
Mrs. Brown — Florence Freeman
Police Sergeant — Joe Boland
Maid — Amanda Randolph
The Twins — Dolores Gillen
Also: Paul Douglas
Announcer: Howard Petrie

Creator-Writer: Anne Nichols
Directors: Joe Rines, "Rip" Van Runkle
Writer: Morton Friedman
Theme: "My Wild Irish Rose"

Abie's Irish Rose was first heard over NBC in 1942, Saturday nights at 8:00.

Adelaide Hawley: see *Women's Programs.*

The Adventures of Captain Diamond

Drama

CAST:
Captain Diamond — Al Swenson
Mrs. Diamond — Florence Malone
Edmund "Tiny" Ruffner — Himself

Each week Tiny Ruffner visited Captain and Mrs. Diamond at their lighthouse and the Captain would spin a yarn. The series began over the Blue network in 1932.

The Adventures of Christopher Wells

Drama

CAST:
Christopher Wells — Les Damon
Stacy McGill, Wells' assistant
Vicki Vola

Creator-Director: Edward Byron
Writer: Robert J. Shaw

This was the story of a newspaper reporter with a penchant for getting himself badly beaten by gangsters. It made its debut over CBS in 1947.

The Adventures of Helen and Mary

Children

CAST:
Helen — Estelle Levy
Mary — Patricia Ryan

This program began over CBS in 1929. The title was changed in 1934 to *Let's Pretend* (which see).

The Adventures of Huckleberry Finn

Drama

CAST:
Huck Finn — Jack Grimes
Jim — Maurice Ellis

This program was based on the novel by Mark Twain.

The Adventures of M. Hercule Poirot

Detective-Adventure

CAST:

M. Hercule Poirot — Harold Huber

Director: Carl Eastman

This series was based on the character created by Agatha Christie.

The Adventures of Mister Meek

Situation Comedy

CAST:

Mortimer Meek — Wilbur Budd Hulick, Frank Readick
Agatha Meek — Adelaide Klein
Peggy — Doris Dudley
Louie, the brother-in-law — Jack Smart
Peggy's boy friend — John McIntire
The Meeks' first maid — Agnes Moorehead
Lily, the maid — Ann Thomas
Mr. Barker — Charlie Cantor
Mrs. Barker — Jeanette Nolan
Mr. Apple — Bill Adams

This program was first heard over CBS in 1940.

The Adventures of Nero Wolfe

Mystery-Adventure

CAST:

Nero Wolfe — Santos Ortega, Sydney Greenstreet
Archie — Louis Vittes

Based on the character created by Rex Stout, this program was first heard over ABC in 1943.

The Adventures of Ozzie and Harriet

Situation Comedy

CAST:

Ozzie Nelson — Himself
Harriet Hilliard Nelson — Herself
David Nelson — Tommy Bernard, Joel Davis, David Ozzie Nelson
Ricky Nelson — Henry Blair, Eric Hilliard (Ricky) Nelson
Thorny, the neighbor — John Brown
Harriet's mother — Lurene Tuttle
Emmy Lou — Janet Waldo
Gloria, the maid — Bea Benaderet
Mrs. Waddington — Bea Benaderet
Roger Waddington — Dink Trout

Orchestra: Billy May
Vocalists: The King Sisters, Ozzie Nelson, Harriet Hilliard
Announcer: Verne Smith

Producer-Director: Dave Elton
Director: Ted Bliss
Writers: Ozzie Nelson, Jack Douglas, John P. Medbury, Sherwood Schwartz, John L. Greene, Ben Gershman, Rupert Pray, Sol Saks, Bill Davenport, Frank Fox, Bill Manhoff, Paul West, Selma Diamond, Hal Kanter, Don Nelson, Dick Bensfield, Perry Grant

Opening:

MUSIC. *Up full and under . . .*

ANNOUNCER. The solid silver with beauty that lives forever is International Sterling. From Hollywood, International Silver Company, creators of International Sterling, presents *The Adventures of Ozzie and Harriet,* starring America's favorite young couple—Ozzie Nelson and Harriet Hilliard!

This series, which made its debut on October 8, 1944, over CBS became one of broadcasting's all-time long-running hits.

The Adventures of Philip Marlowe

Adventure

CAST:

Philip Marlowe — Gerald Mohr

Producer-Director: Norman Macdonnell
Writers: Robert Mitchell, Gene Levitt
Sound Effects: Cliff Thorsness, Clark Casey

This series, based on a character created by Raymond Chandler, began over CBS in 1949.

The Adventures of Topper

Comedy Fantasy

CAST:

Cosmo Topper — Roland Young
George Kerby, spirit — Paul Mann, Tony Barrett
Marion Kerby, spirit — Frances Chaney
Mr. Borris — Ed Latimer
Also: Hope Emerson

This series was based on the characters created by Thorne Smith.

The Affairs of Anthony

Drama

CAST:

Anthony Marleybone, Jr. — Henry Hunter (Arthur Jacobson)
Jane Daly — Lenore Kingston, Laurette Fillbrandt
Susan — Laurette Fillbrandt
Anthony Marleybone, Sr. — Marvin Miller

Director: Axel Gruenberg
Writer: Sandra Michael

The Affairs of Anthony was heard over the Blue network in 1939.

The Affairs of Peter Salem

Detective

CAST:

Peter Salem — Santos Ortega
Marty — Jack Grimes

Producer: Himan Brown
Director: Mende Brown
Writer: Louis Vittes
Sound Effects: Adrian Penner

The Affairs of Peter Salem was heard over Mutual in 1949.

The Affairs of Tom, Dick and Harry

Drama

CAST:

Tom — Bud Vandover
Dick — Marlin Hurt
Harry — Gordon Vandover
Also: Edna O'Dell

African Trek

Music

Host: Josef Marais
Also: Juano Hernandez
Burford Hampden

African Trek, which featured songs and stories of Africa, was first heard over the Blue network in 1939.

Against the Storm

Serial Drama

CAST:

Christy Allen Cameron — Gertrude Warner, Claudia Morgan
Philip Cameron — Arnold Moss, Alexander Scourby
Mr. Cameron — Alan Devitt
Prof. Jason McKinley Allen — Roger DeKoven
Mrs. Margaret Allen — May Davenport Seymour, Florence Malone
Siri Allen — Dolores Gillen, Joan Tompkins
Peter — Dolores Gillen
Mark Scott — Chester Stratton
Nicole Scott — Ruth Matteson, Joan Alexander
Mrs. Scott — Florence Malone
Dr. Reimer — Philip Clarke
Kathy Reimer — Charlotte Holland
Penny — Leslie Bingham
Lucretia Hale — Jane Erskine, Anne Seymour
Brook Lewis — Robert Shayne
Reid Wilson — James Meighan, Walter Vaughn
Mr. Fullerton — Rex Ingram
Nanny — Mona Hungerford
Kip Tyler — Mary Hunter
Pascal Tyler — Lawson Zerbe
Nurse Madeleine — Lotte Stavisky
Guy Aldis — William Quinn
Lisa de Beck — Sarah Burton
Torben Reimer — Edward Corben, James Monks, Sam Wanamaker
Manuel Sandoval — Michael Ingram
Nathan — Ian Martin
Ebba Fielding — Lenore Kingston
Announcers: Nelson Case, Richard Stark, Ralph Edwards

Director: Axel Gruenberg
Writer: Sandra Michael

Theme: "The Song of Bernadette"
Opening:
Against the storm keep thy head bowed,
For the greatest storm the world has ever known
Came to an end one sunny morning.

Against the Storm was first heard over NBC in 1939.

Aggie Horn: see *In Care of Aggie Horn.*

The Air Adventures of Jimmy Allen

Children's Drama

CAST:

Jimmy Allen — Murray McLean

Opening:

SOUND. *Hum of airplane*

ANNOUNCER. The Air Adventures of Jimmy Allen!

THEME. *Music up full*

A. L. Alexander's Good Will Court

Advice

Featuring: A. L. Alexander
Directors: Henry Souvaine, Carl Caruso

Albert L. Alexander started in radio as a cub announcer in 1925. During his early career he broadcast a man-in-the-street program, among others, by strapping a portable transmitter to his back and interviewing people on the sidewalk. In 1936 his *Good Will Court* was broadcast over New York station WMCA and sixty-six stations of NBC. The program dispensed legal and marital advice to anonymous couples who aired their domestic problems. Later that year the New York Supreme Court, on a recommendation of the New York County Lawyers Association, forbade lawyers to give legal advice "in connection with a publicity medium of any kind." That ended the *Good Will Court*. Alexander then began *Alexander's Mediation Board*, with a panel of educators, teachers, and social workers instead of lawyers, and this program continued in various forms for some twenty-five years. The motto of *Alexander's Mediation Board* was "There are two sides to every story," and one of Alexander's personal goals, as reflected in the spirit of his radio program, was to have national and international problems solved by the process of mediation rather than by warfare.

A program of similar nature was *The Goodwill Hour*, presided over by Mr. Anthony (which see).

The Al Jolson Show: see *Kraft Music Hall; Shell Chateau.*

Al Pearce and His Gang

Comedy

CAST:

Elmer Blurt — Al Pearce
The Human Chatterbox — Arlene Harris
Tizzie Lish — Bill Comstock
Yahbut — Jennison Parker
Cheerily — Bill Wright
Lord Bilgewater — Monroe Upton
Eb — Al Pearce
Zeb — Bill Wright
Mr. Kitzel — Artie Auerbach
The Laughing Lady — Kitty O'Neil
Yogi Yorgeson — Harry Stewart

Also: Mabel Todd ("The Little Ray of Sunshine"); Tony Romano; Harry Foster; Morey Amsterdam; Andy Andrews; Orville Andrews; Hazel Werner; Marie Green and Her Merry Men; Cal (Clarence)

Pearce, Al's brother; The Three Cheers—E. J. Derry, Travis Hale, Phil Hanna
Orchestra: Carl Hoff, Harry Sosnik, Larry Marsh
Announcer: Ken Roberts

Writers: Arthur Hargrove Krib, Don Prindle, Roz Rogers, Jennison Parker
Sound Effects: Ray Erlenborn

Al Pearce and His Gang came to radio in 1933 over NBC Blue. While sponsored by the Ford Motor Company, the show was called *Watch the Fords Go By.* It was also sponsored by Pepsodent.

Among the memorable characters were "Elmer Blurt," "Arlene Harris," and "Tizzie Lish." "Elmer" was a shy door-to-door salesman who rapped on the door in a distinctive pattern and then said, "Nobody home, I hope, I hope, I hope." "Arlene" carried on non-stop telephone conversations about domestic troubles with her friend "Mazie," who was never heard, and Tizzie Lish gave recipes that were ridiculous. She (or "he" because Tizzie Lish was impersonated by a man) would start out with a hearty "Hello, folksies!" and would always wait until you got a pencil so you could write down the recipe.

The Alan Young Show

Comedy

CAST:

Alan Young	Himself
Mrs. Johnson	Ruth Perrott
Papa Dittenfeffer	Ed Begley
Hubert Updike	Jim Backus
Betty	Doris Singleton
Zero	Charlie Cantor

Also: Ken Christy, Jean Gillespie
Smart Set Quintet—Patricia Corrigan, Mike Corrigan, Gerry Salathiel, Gloria Wood, Leo Dukehorn
Announcers: Jimmy Wallington, Larry Elliott, Michael Roy

Director: Eddie Pola
Writers: Jay Sommers, Norman Paul, Dave Schwartz, Sam Packard

"Hubert Updike" was an extremely rich character who once sold his "Cah-dillac" because it was headed in the wrong direction. He would use such an expression as "Heavens to Gimbels!"

This show was first heard over ABC in 1944.

Album of Familiar Music: see *The American Album of Familiar Music.*

The Aldrich Family

Situation Comedy

CAST:

Henry Aldrich — Ezra Stone, Norman Tokar, Raymond Ives, Dickie Jones, Bobby Ellis
Sam Aldrich, Henry's father — Clyde Fillmore, House Jameson, Tom Shirley
Alice Aldrich, Henry's mother — Lea Penman, Katharine Raht, Regina Wallace

Mary Aldrich, Henry's sister
Betty Field
Jone Allison
Mary Mason
Charita Bauer
Mary Shipp
Mary Rolfe
Ann Lincoln
Will Brown — Ed Begley
Howard Smith
Arthur Vinton
Homer Brown — Jackie Kelk
Kathleen Anderson, Henry's girl friend — Mary Shipp
Ann Lincoln
Ethel Blume
Jean Gillespie
Willie Marshall — Norman Tokar
Geraldine — Pat Ryan
Agnes Lawson — Judith Abbott
Stringbean Kittinger — Joan Jackson
Aunt Harriet — Ethel Wilson
Dizzy Stevens — Eddie Bracken
George Bigelow — Charles Powers
Mr. Bradley — Bernard Lenrow
Mr. De Haven — Ward Wilson
Mrs. Brown, Homer's mother
Agnes Moorehead
Leona Powers
Toby Smith — Dickie Van Patten
Mrs. Anderson — Alice Yourman

Also: Thelma Ritter
Orchestra: Jack Miller
Announcers: Dwight Weist, Dan Seymour, Ralph Paul, George Bryan, Harry Von Zell

---

Directors: Bob Welsh, Joseph Scibetta, Lester Vail, Edwin Duerr, Day Tuttle, Sam Fuller, George McGarrett
Writers: Norman Tokar, Ed Jurist, Frank Tarloff, Clifford Goldsmith, Phil Sharp, Sam Taylor, Pat and Ed Joudry
Sound Effects: Bill Brinkmeyer

Theme: "This Is It"
Opening:
MRS. ALDRICH. Henry! Henry Aldrich!
HENRY (*In his adolescent, cracked voice*). Coming, Mother!

The Aldrich Family was adapted from Clifford Goldsmith's Broadway play *What a Life!* It was also known to radio listeners as *Henry Aldrich* and was first heard on radio as a sketch on *The Rudy Vallee Show;* later it was a regular feature on *The Kate Smith Show.* The thirty-minute version was first heard over NBC Blue in 1939 for Jell-O.

Alexander's Mediation Board: see A. L. *Alexander's Good Will Court.*

Alias Jimmy Valentine

Adventure

CAST:
Jimmy Valentine — Bert Lytell
James Meighan

Producers: Frank and Anne Hummert

Alias Jimmy Valentine was based on the exploits of the notorious safecracker, a character originally created by O. Henry. The series was first heard on NBC Blue in 1937.

All the News

News

Directors: Ed Pettit, Ben Baldwin, John S. Fraser.

This fifteen-minute Mutual network newscast, heard Monday through Friday nights in the late 1940s, was unique in that it was an attempt to popularize a new format of news reportage. Instead of having one newscaster, the program used two Mutual announcers who introduced themselves and then promptly raced through the news, alternating the reading of items. By reading at top speed but still intelligibly, the two announcers succeeded in easily outdoing other news programs in the quantity of items covered, making the program a high-speed newspaper of the air.

Allen Prescott: see *Crossword Quiz; Women's Programs.*

Alma Kitchell: see *Women's Programs.*

Amanda of Honeymoon Hill

Serial Drama

CAST:

Charity Amanda Dyke — Joy Hathaway
Joseph Dyke — John MacBryde
Edward Leighton — Boyd Crawford, George Lambert, Staats Cotsworth
Colonel Leighton — John Connery
Sylvia Meadows — Helen Shields
Aunt Maizie — Florence Edney, Cecil Roy
Charlie Harris — Roger DeKoven
Jim Tolliver — Jackie Kelk
Job — Juano Hernandez
Roger Manning — John M. James
Mrs. Leighton — Elizabeth Love
Olive Courtleigh — Ruth Yorke
Walter Courtleigh — George Lambert
Bret Allen — Richard Rider
Dot — Linda Watkins
Nat — Edward Andrews
Mr. Lenord — John Brown
Mrs. Lenord — Ruth Gates
Mrs. Gilder — Florence Malone
Roy Calvert — John Raby
Marion Leighton — Jay Meredith
Susan Leighton — Irene Hubbard, Muriel Starr
Fraser Ames — Reese Taylor
Claire Treman — Patricia Wheel
Tom Ames — Chester Stratton
Irene Miller — Elizabeth Eustis
Bruce Douglas — Lamont Johnson
Martin Douglas — Rod Hendrickson
Ralph Daly — Paul Conrad
Jean Curtis — Evelyn Juster
Mr. Schultz — Sanford Bickart

Announcers: Frank Gallop, Hugh Conover, Howard Claney

Producers: Frank and Anne Hummert
Directors: Ernest Ricca, Arnold Michaelis
Writer: Elizabeth Todd

Opening:

ANNOUNCER. The story of love and marriage in America's romantic South. The story of Amanda and Edward Leighton. [And for a time:] *Amanda of Honeymoon Hill* . . . laid in a world few Americans know.

Amanda of Honeymoon Hill was heard over the Blue network in 1940.

The Amateur Hour: see *Major Bowes and His Original Amateur Hour.*

The Amazing Mr. Malone

Adventure

CAST:

Mr. Malone — Eugene Raymond
Frank Lovejoy
George Petrie

Producer: Bernard L. Schubert
Director: Bill Rousseau
Writer: Gene Wang
Sound Effects: Jack Robinson

This was first aired over ABC in 1948.

The Amazing Mr. Smith

Comedy-Mystery

CAST:

Gregory Smith — Keenan Wynn
His valet — Charlie Cantor
Also: Elizabeth Reller, John Brown, Santos Ortega, Ward Wilson, Allen Drake, Cliff Carpenter, Brad Barker
Announcer: Harry Von Zell

Director: George McGarrett
Writers: Martin Gosch, Howard Harris
Musical Director: Harry Salter

America in the Air

Drama

Producer-Director: Les Weinrot

This series was produced on CBS during World War II as a service to the Air Corps.

The American Album of Familiar Music

Music

Featuring: Frank Munn, Donald Dame, Evelyn MacGregor, Margaret Down, Jean Dickenson, Daniel Lieberfeld, Arden and Arden, Bertrand Hersch, Gustave Haenschen
Announcers: André Baruch, Roger Krupp, Howard Claney
Producers: Frank and Anne Hummert
Director: James Haupt

Opening:

ORCHESTRA. *Theme music up full and under*

ANNOUNCER. *The American Album of Familiar Music* . . . presenting America's widely discussed young singing star Donald Dame . . . Evelyn MacGregor, Margaret Down, Jean Dickenson, Daniel Lieberfeld, Arden and Arden, Bertrand Hersch, and Gustave Haenschen. Tonight, *The American Album of Familiar Music* offers for your enjoyment a program of supremely lovely songs and melodies that capture all hearts . . . beginning with Donald Dame singing "Your Eyes Have Told Me So."

This durable program began over NBC in 1931 and was sponsored by Bayer Aspirin.

American Forum of the Air

Discussion

Moderator: Theodore Granik
Producer-Director: Larry Dorn

This long-running Mutual Network program made its debut in 1934 and was known originally as *The Mutual Forum Hour*. In 1938 the title was changed to *American Forum of the Air*.

The American School of the Air

Education

Featuring: Dr. Lyman Bryson, Ray Collins, Parker Fennelly, Chester Stratton, Mitzi Gould
Announcer: Robert Trout
Directors: Earle McGill, Albert Ward, Marx Loeb, Brewster Morgan, Howard Barnes, John Dietz, Robert B. Hudson, Oliver Daniel, Richard Sanville, Leon Levine
Writers: Howard Rodman, Edward Mabley, Harry Granich
Musical Directors: Channon Collinge, Dorothy Gordon

This program was required listening in many American classrooms. It was first heard over CBS in 1930 and dramatized history, current events, and great literature. The original title of the show was *School of the Air of the Americas*.

A popular segment of the program was "The Hamilton Family," which was on for about three years in the mid-thirties. *The American School of the Air* was on every weekday afternoon, concentrating on a different subject. "The Hamilton Family" presented the geography lesson with the family touring the world. The cast included Gene Leonard as Father, Betty Garde as Mother, and John Monks, Ruth Russell, Walter Tetley, and Albert Aley as the children. These segments were first directed by Knowles Entriken, later by Kirby Hawkes.

American Woman's Jury

Courtroom Drama

CAST:
Judge Emily Williams — Deborah Springer
Jane Allen, defense lawyer — Evelyn Hackett
Robert Coulter, opposition lawyer — Bill Syran

Twelve housewives served as jurors and heard the cases which had been submitted by listeners.

American Women

Drama

Narrator: Eloise Kummer, Charlotte Manson
Producer-Directors: Bob Brown, Ted Robertson
Writers: Frank and Doris Hursley, David Harmon

This CBS series was broadcast during World War II in behalf of the recruitment of women for the war effort. It began in 1943.

America's Hour

Documentary

Featuring: Orson Welles, Joseph Cotten, Ray Collins, Frank Readick, Agnes Moorehead, Betty Garde, John Monks, *et al.*

Director: Knowles Entriken

America's Hour was a sixty-minute, Sunday-night documentary on CBS that presented stories of America—its farming, industry, aviation, shipping, history, etc.

America's Lost Plays

Drama

This 1939 series featured radio adaptations of such plays as *A Trip to Chinatown, Mistress Nell,* and *Metamora.*

America's Town Meeting

Discussion

Moderator: George V. Denny, Jr.
Announcers: Ed Herlihy, Gene Kirby, George Gunn
Directors: Wylie Adams, Richard Ritter, Leonard Blair

The discussions were on subjects of national significance, and the studio audience played an active part in them. The program, heard on NBC at 9:30 P.M. on Thursdays, originated in Town Hall, New York. It was first heard in 1935.

Amicus Curiae: see *Jonathan Kegg.*

Amos 'n' Andy

Comedy

CAST:

Amos Jones — Freeman Gosden
Andy (Andrew H. Brown) — Charles Correll
Kingfish (George Stevens) — Freeman Gosden
Lightnin' — Freeman Gosden
Henry Van Porter — Charles Correll
Ruby Taylor — Elinor Harriot
Madame Queen — Harriette Widmer
The Little Girl (Arbadella) — Terry Howard
Shorty, the barber — Lou Lubin
Sapphire Stevens — Ernestine Wade
Stonewall, the lawyer — Eddie Green
Miss Genevieve Blue — Madaline Lee
Orchestra and Chorus: Jeff Alexander
The Jubalaires singing group—George MacFadden, Theodore Brooks, John Jennings, Caleb Ginyard
Announcers: Bill Hay, Del Sharbutt, Olan Soule, Harlow Wilcox

---

Executive Producers: Bob Connolly and Bill Moser
Directors: Glenn Middleton, Andrew Love
Writers: Freeman Gosden, Charles Correll, Bob Connolly, Bill Moser, Octavus Roy Cohen, Bob Fischer, Robert J. Ross, Bob Moss, Arthur Slander, Paul Franklin, Harvey Helm, Shirley Illo
Sound Effects: Frank Pittman, Ed Ludes, Gus Bayz, Dave Light
Organist: Gaylord Carter
Themes: "The Perfect Song," "Angel's Serenade"

Catch-phrases:
Here they ah! (Bill Hay introducing Amos 'n' Andy)
I'se regusted!
Ow wah, ow wah, ow wah!
Buzz me, Miss Blue!
Check and double-check.
Now ain't that sumpin'?
Holy mackerel, Andy!

Gosden and Correll made their debut on radio on January 12, 1926, as the blackface characters *Sam 'n' Henry*. The program was carried over WGN Chicago. On March 19, 1928, over WMAQ Chicago, they introduced *Amos 'n' Andy*, which went on to become one of the most popular and longest-running programs in radio history. The series ran six nights a week for a while, then five nights, first at 11:00 P.M. and later at 7:00 P.M. The first network broadcast was over NBC on August 19, 1929. During the height of its popularity almost the entire country listened to *Amos 'n' Andy*. Department stores open in the evening piped in the broadcasts so shoppers wouldn't miss an episode; movie theaters scheduled their features to end just prior to 7:00 P.M. and to start again at 7:15, while they too piped in *Amos 'n' Andy;* and the program was frequently referred to in the *Congressional Record*.

"Amos," "Andy," and many of the other characters belonged to the "Mystic Knights of the Sea Lodge," of which "George Stevens" was "The Kingfish." "Amos" and "Andy" ran the "Fresh-Air Taxi Company," with the more stable, married "Amos" doing most of the work while "Andy" chased girls. One of the best-remembered sequences was the time "Andy" almost married "Madame Queen." Each year at Christmas time, "Amos" interpreted the Lord's Prayer for his little daughter Arbadella in a perennially popular sequence.

During the first years of its run *Amos 'n' Andy* was a fifteen-minute program. It was sponsored by Pepsodent from 1929 to 1937 and by Campbell's Soup from 1937 to 1943. Later the program ran once a week, was thirty minutes long, and was sponsored by Rinso and then Rexall. In the 1950s Amos and Andy performed in a weekly half-hour series called *The Amos 'n' Andy Music Hall*.

The Andrews Sisters Eight-to-the-Bar Ranch

Musical Variety

Starring: The Andrews Sisters (Patty, Maxene, and LaVerne)
Featuring: Gabby Hayes
Also: Judy Canova, Riders of the Purple Sage

Orchestra: Vic Schoen
Announcer: Marvin Miller

Producer: Lou Levy
Director: Manny Mannheim
Writers: Cottonseed Clark, Stanley Davis, Elon Packard, Joe Errens

This program was first heard over ABC in 1945. It was a half-hour weekly broadcast for Nash-Kelvinator. It normally originated from Hollywood although a few shows were done on the road.

Animal Imitators, Baby Criers, Doubles, Mimics, and Screamers

Most of the programs in early radio were "live"—not recorded or taped. Thus, since animals, babies, and often actors couldn't always be relied upon to bark, cry, or scream precisely on cue, a number of people were gainfully employed during radio's Golden Age to create the howls of wolves for *Renfrew of the Mounted*, to cry for baby Robespierre (Baby Snooks' brother), or to scream for other actresses in the horrific situations on *Lights Out*.

Among the better-known animal imitators were Brad Barker and Donald Bain, who could imitate with their voices anything from a single canary to a pride of lions. Like all actors, Barker and Bain "lived" their parts and often seemed to take on the appearance and manner of the animal they were impersonating. Mary Jane Higby, in her book *Tune in Tomorrow*, relates that once an actor jokingly told her that he had just seen Brad Barker running down Madison Avenue carrying Donald Bain in his mouth! Other animal imitators were David Dole, Earl Keen (*Lassie*), Clarence Straight (Animal News Club), Harry Swan, and Henry Boyd, whose clear bob-white whistle was used on the Rinso White commercials.

Several actresses spent a lifetime crying like babies. It was a strange sight indeed to see an otherwise well-dressed and distinguished-looking lady walk to the microphone and suddenly gurgle, whine, or bawl like an infant. Some of them used a pillow to cry into to help achieve the desired effect. Among the more familiar "babies" were Sarah Fussell, Madeleine Pierce, and Leone Ledoux.

Imitating other people's voices kept many radio mimics busy too. On such programs as *The March of Time* the voices of actual celebrities in the news were re-created by imitators. In addition, many variety programs featured the skills of such mimics as The Radio Rogues (Jimmy Hollywood, Ed Bartell, and Henry Taylor), Sheila Barrett, Arthur Boran, and Florence Desmond.

Many actors and actresses "doubled" for other performers in cases where the voices of the originals were either too heavily accented or where someone had deemed their speaking voices "not right for radio." While Dave Rubinoff, for instance, actually played the violin on *The Eddie Cantor Show*, his speaking voice was done by Lionel Stander or Teddy Bergman. On *Shell Chateau*, Mary Jane Higby was the speaking voice of singer Nadine Connor, who, someone decided, sounded just fine singing but not right talking. Allyn Joslyn did the same thing for Lanny Ross in the early days of *Show Boat*.

Finally, while most actresses were adept at reading their lines, when it came to screaming with fear they were often unable to do so or risked the possibility of straining their voices. "Screamers" were employed to fill the gap—actresses who made a specialty of screaming loud and clear—such as seventeen-year-old Nancy Kelly to whom fell the responsibility of screaming on *Gangbusters*, *Front Page Farrell*, and *The March of Time*.

Animal News Club: see *Animal Imitators, Baby Criers*, etc.

Anniversary Club

Audience Participation

M.C.: Ben Alexander

Announcers

The announcing profession has undergone a genuine metamorphosis since the days of radio's heyday. The announcers of that era were considered glamorous figures, often ranking on a level with the programs' stars. They were nationally known and were frequently integrated into the program content as characters who made specific contributions to the plot, not just disembodied voices who "announced" the shows. Good voices and stylish delivery were valued assets, especially in the very early days of relatively poor transmission and reception. Diction and pronunciation were also important, and announcers were expected not only to be authorities on the English language but to be able to pronounce correctly the names of obscure foreign composers and conductors. While the announcers of that era were not often required to depart from a prepared script, the ability to ad-lib was an asset too. The goal of every announcer was perfection. A fluff or mispronunciation would strike terror into the heart of the announcer who committed it and would be the subject of discussion by network executives and alert listeners for days.

An announcer had several functions. He usually introduced the program and its star, often read the commercials, and frequently was called upon to act as straight man for the comedian. In addition, a number of network announcers were used before the actual broadcast to "warm-up" the studio audience. They would walk onstage a few minutes before broadcast time, tell a few jokes, and give instructions on how and when to applaud. Their routine would usually call for them to introduce the cast. Some programs were constructed so that they began with applause or laughter, and it was the warm-up announcer's duty to time such audience reaction so that it would be up full just as the program took to the air. The announcer would go to any lengths to trigger audience laughter —a sure-fire way was to drop his trousers unexpectedly.

Some of the standard gags used during warm-ups included the announcer's instructions to the audience, "When we wave at you, it means to applaud. Don't wave back!"; "Okay, folks, we have thirty seconds to go . . . if anybody has to!"; "Now be sure to clap real loud so the folks back home in Des Moines can hear you!"; and, after telling people that they should get acquainted with each other, "Now, just turn around and shake hands with the fellow behind you." When they did turn around, of course, the fellow behind was also turned around. Another favorite gag was to tell everyone to hold hands and then ask a man on the end of the aisle to stick his finger in the electric socket.

One of the most elaborate warm-ups took place on *Truth or Consequences*. The warm-up actually started some thirty minutes before the program went on the air, and most of that time was taken up with picking the contestants for that night's consequences. At about three minutes before airtime two men from the audience—usually sailors or other servicemen—were brought onstage to participate in a contest. Each was given a suitcase and told that the first one who could get dressed using the contents of the suitcase would win a prize. The suitcases were filled with women's clothes—bras, girdles, slips, etc.—and the contestants' struggles with these garments never failed to bring the audience to peaks of laughter just as the program went on the air with the announcer saying, "Hello, there. We've been waiting for you. It's time to play *Truth or Consequences!*"

Few announcers of that era were able to escape reciting dreadful clichés, which somehow, despite constant repetition on hundreds of broadcasts, didn't seem as trite as they do today. A common line used as a transition in a narrative would be something akin to "Meanwhile, back at the ranch. . . ." In signing off a program the announcer might be required to say, "Well, the little clock on the studio wall tells us it's time to go . . ."; or, "Keep those cards and letters coming in, folks." Frequently the announcer (or the star of the show) would have to get the show off the air with, "We're a little late, folks, so good night!"

Some of the early announcers were identified only by letters since the station managements usually preferred their announcers to remain anonymous. Thomas Cowan, generally credited with being radio's first announcer, was known only as ACN ("A" for announcer, "C" for Cowan, and "N" for Newark) in the beginning.

Many of the top announcers were identified with a particular program for long periods of time such as Don Wilson (*Jack Benny*); Ken Carpenter (*Edgar Bergen, Kraft Music Hall*); Jimmy Wallington (*Eddie Cantor, Burns and Allen*); Milton Cross (*Metropolitan Opera Broadcasts*); Harry Von Zell (*Eddie Cantor, Burns and Allen*); Bill Hay (who introduced *Amos 'n' Andy* with "Here they ah"); Pierre André (*Little Orphan Annie*); Franklyn MacCormack (*Jack Armstrong*); George Ansbro (*Young Widder Brown*); Harlow Wilcox (*Fibber McGee and Molly*); Fred Foy (*The Lone Ranger*); Bill Goodwin (*Bob Hope, Burns and Allen*); André Baruch (*Your Hit Parade*); Ford Bond (*Manhattan Merry-Go-Round*); Verne Smith (*Kay Kyser's Kollege of Musical Knowledge*); Dan Seymour (*Aunt Jenny*); and Hugh James (*The Voice of Firestone*). Bill Hay was also famous for his Bible readings, and Franklyn MacCormack for his poetry readings.

Among the other outstanding announcers of radio's Golden Age were Mel Allen, who became one of radio's top sportscasters; Ken Banghart (also a noted newscaster); Martin Block (one of radio's first disc jockeys); Norman Brokenshire ("How *do* you do?"); Graham McNamee (who became the most prominent of the early sportscasters); Bert Parks, who became one of radio's youngest announcers after serving his apprenticeship as warm-up man and applause-cuer on Kate Smith's *A & P Bandwagon;* David Ross (an outstanding poetry reader); Ed Thorgersen (also a prominent sportscaster); Bill Slater (also a sportscaster); also George Bryan, Phillips Carlin, Fred Collins, Jack Costello, Bill Cullen, Don Dowd, George Fenneman, Michael Fitzmaurice, Frank Gallop, Art Gilmore, Ben Grauer, Les Griffith, Art Hannes, Alois Havrilla, Dick Joy, Leslie Joy, Kelvin Keech, Harry Kramer, Bob Lemond, Don Lowe, Stuart Metz, Marvin Miller, Tom Moore, brothers Ken and Wendell Niles, Charles O'Connor, Glenn Riggs, Ken Roberts, Basil Ruysdael, Charles Stark, Richard Stark, and Warren Sweeney. Still other announcers are listed in the various programs.

The Answer Man

Information

Starring: Albert Mitchell as The Answer Man
Writer: Bruce Chapman

This often-parodied program was an early evening, fifteen-minute show featuring the answers to questions on various subjects submitted by listeners.

Arabesque

Drama

CAST:
Achmed, the Arab Chieftain — Reynolds Evans
The Captain — Frank Knight
Narrator: David Ross
Also: Georgia Backus, Geneva Harrison
Orchestra: Emery Deutsch and His Gypsy Violins

Writer: Yolanda Langworthy
Theme: "Scheherazade" by Rimsky-Korsakov

Arabesque was a popular Sunday evening program set in the wilds of the Arabian Desert. David Ross opened the program with a reading of "Drifting Sands in the Caravan."

Archie Andrews

Situation Comedy

CAST:
Archie Andrews — Charles Mullen, Jack Grimes, Burt Boyer, Bob Hastings
Jughead Jones — Harlan Stone, Jr., Cameron Andrews
Betty Cooper — Doris Grundy, Joy Geffen, Rosemary Rice
Veronica Lodge — Gloria Mann, Vivian Smolen
Fred Andrews, Archie's father — Vinton Hayworth, Arthur Kohl, Reese Taylor
Mary Andrews, Archie's mother — Alice Yourman, Peggy Allenby
Reggie Mantle — Paul Gordon
Mr. Weatherbee, the principal — Arthur Maitland
Mr. Lodge — Bill Griffis
Also: Joe Latham, Grace Keddy, Maurice Franklin, Fred Barron
Announcers: Ken Banghart, Dick Dudley

Creator: John L. Goldwater
Directors: Herbert M. Moss, Floyd Holm, Kenneth W. MacGregor
Writers: Carl Jampel, Howard Merrill
Sound Effects: Agnew Horine
Organist: George Wright

This program was based on the comic strip by Bob Montana. It was first heard over Mutual in 1943.

Are You a Genius?

Quiz

M.C.: Ernest Chappell

This was a quiz for children. Among the regular features was a contest for "The Worst Joke."

Armchair Adventures

Dramatic Narration

Narrator: Marvin Miller
Directors: Ralph Rose, Gomer Cool
Writers: Jerry Schwartz, Everett Tomlinson, Rich Hall, John Boylan, Ralph Rose, Paul West

Armchair Adventures first appeared over CBS in 1952, but it is included in this book because of its uniqueness. It was a fifteen-minute adventure program done like a normal drama with sound effects. However, only the voice of Marvin Miller was heard. He did the narration and made full voice changes for the various characters. It ran for one season, utilizing, for the most part, original stories.

The Armour Hour: see *The Phil Baker Show.*

Armstrong of the SBI

Science Adventure

CAST:

Jack Armstrong	Charles Flynn
Vic Hardy	Ken Griffin
	Carlton KaDell
Betty Fairfield	Patricia Dunlap
Billy Fairfield	Dick York

Announcers: Ed Prentiss, Ken Nordine

Producer-Director: James Jewell
Chief Writer and Story Editor: James Jewell
Writers: Donald Gallagher, Kermit Slobb, Paul Fairman, Alan Fishburn, Jack Lawrence, Thomas Elvidge

---

Opening:

ORGAN. *Chord*

ANNOUNCER. (*Echo*) (Sponsor's name) makers of (sponsor's product) presents . . .

ORGAN. *Chord*

ANNOUNCER. *Armstrong of the SBI!*

ORGAN. *Theme*

ANNOUNCER. Tonight we shall hear a dramatic mystery of suspense and intrigue as Armstrong, Chief Investigator of the famous SBI, brings us . . . (title of episode).

ORGAN. *Descending run—dissonant*

Armstrong of the SBI (Scientific Bureau of Investigation) was a thirty-minute complete drama produced three times a week over ABC from

September 5, 1950, to June 28, 1951. It originated in Chicago. (See also *Jack Armstrong, the All-American Boy.*)

Armstrong Theater of Today

Drama

CAST:

The Armstrong Quaker Girl: Elizabeth Reller, Julie Conway

Announcers: Bob Sherry, George Bryan

Producer: Ira Avery
Directors: Ken Webb, Al Ward
Sound Effects: Jim Rinaldi

This durable half-hour Saturday daytime series started on CBS in 1941. It featured guest stars in half-hour programs.

The Army Hour

Variety

Announcer: Ed Herlihy
Producer-Director: Wyllis Cooper
Director: Edwin L. Dunham

This program spotlighted the activities of the United States Army. It began over the Blue network in 1940.

Arnold Grimm's Daughter

Serial Drama

CAST:

Constance, the daughter — Margarette Shanna, Betty Lou Gerson, Luise Barclay
Arnold Grimm — Don Merrifield
Dal Tremaine — Ed Prentiss, Robert Ellis
Jim Kent — Frank Dane
Madame Babette — Jeanne Juvelier
Gladys Grimm — Jean McDonald, Bonita Kay
Tom Grimm — James Andelin, Frank Behrens
Sonia Kirkoff — Genelle Gibbs
Stanley Westland — Bret Morrison
Bill Hartley — Verne Smith
Judy, the maid — Mento Everitt
Mr. Tremaine — Orson Brandon
Mrs. Tremaine — Gertrude Bondhill
Mr. Tweedy — Butler Manville
Mrs. Grimm — Jeanne Dixon, Judith Lowry, Edith Davis
Arthur Hall — Stanley Harris
Marie Martel — Mary Patton
Paul Martel — Nelson Olmsted
Lily — Mary Young
Mrs. Higsby-Smith — Ethel Wilson
Bernice Farraday — June Travis, Louise Fitch
Dr. David McKenzie — Clifford Soubier
Baby Dal — Patty Willis
Aunt Gladys — Hazel Dopheide
Mr. Duffy — Sidney Ellstrom
Pat Patterson — John Hodiak
Louie Sterling — Carl Kroenke
Dr. Milburn — Eugene Eubanks
Kirby Willoughby — Fred Sullivan
Stephanie Summers — Dorothy Francis
Bunny Shapiro — Josephine Gilbert
Anne Goodwin — Irene Purcell
Jeff Corbett — Bill Bouchey
Meredith Jones — Ruth Bailey
Marian Moore — Joan Kay
Thelma — Rosemary Lambright

Announcer: Roger Krupp

———

Arnold Grimm's Daughter was first heard over CBS in 1937. It originated in Chicago.

Arthur Godfrey Time

Variety

Host: Arthur Godfrey
Vocalists: Patti Clayton, Bill Lawrence, Janette Davis, Lu Ann Simms, Frank Parker; The Jubalaires, vocal quartet; The Mariners, vocal quartet—James Lewis, Martin Karl, Thomas Lockard, Nathaniel Dickerson; The Chordettes, vocal quartet—Jinny Osborn, Dottie Schwartz, Janet Erlet, Carol Hagedorn
Orchestra: Hank Sylvern, Archie Bleyer
Announcer: Tony Marvin
Producer-Director: Will Roland
Director: Frank Dodge
Writers: Bob Carman, Chuck Horner, Henry Miles, Andy Rodney, Charles Slocum, Tom Gorman
Themes: "Seems Like Old Times," "In the Blue Ridge Mountains of Virginia"

Arthur Godfrey, who was described by Fred Allen as "Peck's Bad Boy of Radio," started his professional radio career in Washington, D.C., on WTOP in the early thirties. Known as "Red" Godfrey, he would chat and sing and play the ukulele, and his casual, relaxed style soon caught on with listeners in the Washington area. One of his sponsors was a furrier, and Godfrey's description of the moth-eaten stuffed polar bear that stood on the sidewalk in front of the store became the subject for running comment—and business for the furrier.

Walter Winchell was partly responsible for bringing Godfrey to New York. He had heard Godfrey while in Washington and urged the executives in New York to bring him to the network headquarters. For many years Godfrey was "the morning man" at the CBS station in New York, then called WABC, and was as casual and unpredictable in that time-slot as he always was anywhere on the dial. Often he would show up late—the program started at 6:00 A.M. —and the on-duty announcer would simply say, "This is the *Arthur Godfrey Show*. Arthur's not here," and play records until Godfrey arrived. Even then, Godfrey's penchant for using humor that bordered on questionable taste was evident. One of his sponsors, for instance, was Bayer Aspirin and somehow when Godfrey said it we heard three words—bare ass prin. No matter—the audience loved it, and "Did you hear what Godfrey said this morning?" was the daily talk of businessmen, housewives, and even school kids. Godfrey was one of those fascinating personalities to whom you simply had to listen or be out of the mainstream of conversation in New York.

In later years Godfrey left the local morning show and appeared as the star of a daily morning variety hour whose format differed only in that the music was live and the chat was now passed around among the cast members. The latter program was on the CBS network and proved to be one of the longest-running programs in radio history.

Godfrey's immense appeal was based upon his intimate style of delivery. He was just like a friendly neighbor, or someone with whom you were personally acquainted, and his abilities to entertain and sell products were a prime asset of CBS for many years. His description of the funeral procession of President Franklin Roosevelt was moving and sincere and probably affected more people than any other commentator's remarks. The others were, as usual, dispassionate. Godfrey wept.

Many performers came to prominence on his program, including Julius La Rosa (who joined the cast in October 1951, outside the scope of our book), and The McGuire Sisters (Dorothy, Phyllis, and Christine). The on-the-air dismissal of La Rosa and others by Godfrey is well remembered by listeners of that time.

Arthur Godfrey's Talent Scouts

Talent Contest

Starring: Arthur Godfrey
Vocalists: Peggy Marshall and the Holidays
Orchestra: Archie Bleyer
Announcer: George Bryan
Producer-Director: Jack Carney
Producer: Irving Mansfield
Writer: Ken Lyons
Theme: (Sung by Peggy Marshall and the Holidays)
Here comes Arthur Godfrey
Your talent scout M.C.
Brought to you by Lipton's
Brisk Lipton Tea.
You know it's Lipton Tea
If it's B-R-I-S-K
Now here comes Arthur Godfrey
The talent's on its way!

Arthur Hopkins Presents

Drama

Producer: Arthur Melancthon Hopkins
Director: Herb Rice

This NBC series of the 1940s featured guest stars in dramatizations of top Broadway plays. Arthur Hopkins was a distinguished Broadway producer.

Arturo Toscanini: see *NBC Symphony*.

As the Twig Is Bent: see *We Love and Learn*.

The Ask-It Basket

Quiz

M.C.: Jim McWilliams, Ed East

This program was first heard over CBS in 1938.

At the Village Store: see *Village Store*.

Atlantic Spotlight

Variety

M.C.: Ben Grauer

Guest Stars: Eddie Cantor, Jimmy Durante, *et al.*

This pioneer variety broadcast was heard on NBC at 12:30 P.M. on Saturdays. Ben Grauer would chat across the Atlantic Ocean with a counterpart at the BBC in London.

Attorney-at-Law

Serial Drama

CAST:

Attorney Terry Regan Jim Ameche
Henry Hunter (Arthur Jacobson)
Sally Dunlap, Regan's secretary
Fran Carlon
Betty Winkler
Terry's mother Grace Lockwood
Terry's father Fred Sullivan
Terry's sister Lucy Gilman
Dorothy Wallace Webb
June Meredith

Attorney-at-Law was first heard over NBC Blue in 1937.

Atwater Kent Auditions

Talent Contest

Announcer: Graham McNamee

This program, sponsored by the makers of Atwater Kent Radios, gave amateur talent an opportunity to be heard. Graham McNamee also frequently sang on the program.

Auction Gallery

Audience Participation

Host: Dave Elman

Items were offered at auction to the audience.

Auctioneers

Many tobacco auctioneers appeared on the Lucky Strike commercials for the American Tobacco Company. T. Ray Oglesby became well known for his appearances, but the most famous of all were F. E. Boone (Forest E. Boone) of Lexington, Kentucky, and L. A. "Speed" Riggs (Lee Aubrey Riggs) of Goldsboro, North Carolina. For a time they appeared on every program sponsored by Luckies. They always ended their auction chant with "Sold . . . American!" (See also *Commercials.*)

Aunt Jemima

Music

Featuring: Harriette Widmer as "Aunt Jemima"
M.C.-Announcer: Marvin Miller
Vocalists: Mary Ann Mercer, Bill Miller
Vocal group: Old Plantation Sextet
Director: Palmer Clark
Writer: Mason Ancker
Musical Director: Harry Walsh

Aunt Jemima was broadcast over CBS from 1942 to 1944 as a once-a-week, five-minute program for Aunt Jemima pancake flour. Midway through the series the sponsor switched to pushing Muffets and renamed the program *The Mary Ann Mercer Show.* Later it was again called *Aunt Jemima.* Amanda Randolph played the character in an earlier radio series.

Aunt Jenny

Serial Drama

CAST:

Aunt Jenny — Edith Spencer, Agnes Young
Danny — Dan Seymour
Aunt Jenny's whistling canary — Henry Boyd

Also: Franc Hale, Ed Jerome, Ruth Yorke, Alfred Corn (later known as Alfred Ryder), Ed MacDonald, Ann Pitoniak, Peggy Allenby, Nancy Kelly, Eddie O'Brien, Maurice Franklin, Toni Darnay, Helen Shields, Virginia Dwyer

---

Directors: Thomas F. Vietor, Jr., Bill Steel, Robert S. Steele, Tony Wilson, Ralph Berkey, John Loveton
Writers: David Davidson, Douglas McLean, Elizabeth McLean, Edwin Halloran, Lawrence Klee, Doris Halman, Eleanor Abbey, Carl Alfred Buss, Elinor Lenz, Bill Sweets
Sound Effects: Jim Dwan, Harold Forry
Organist: Elsie Thompson
Theme: "Believe Me, If All Those Endearing Young Charms"

This program was first heard over CBS in 1936. It was also known as *Aunt Jenny's Real Life Stories*. Each day Aunt Jenny would introduce the story with the help of her announcer Danny. They both extolled the virtues of Spry, their perennial sponsor. The program was known to Canadian listeners as *Aunt Lucy*.

Aunt Mary

Serial Drama

CAST:

Aunt Mary — Jane Morgan
Jessie Ward Calvert — Irene Tedrow
Lefty Larkin — Fred Howard
Peggy Mead — Jane Webb
Ben Calvert — Pat McGeehan
Kit Calvert — Josephine Gilbert
Bill Mead — Jack Edwards
David Bowman — Jay Novello
Dr. Lew Bracey — C. Hames Ware

Also: Tom Collins, Cy Kendall, Betty Gerson, Ken Peters
Announcers: Vincent Pelletier, Marvin Miller (1946–1947)

Director: George Fogle
Writers: Gil Faust, Virginia Thacker, Lee and Virginia Crosby

The setting for *Aunt Mary* was "Willow Road Farm." The program originated on the West Coast.

Author Meets the Critics

Literary Discussion

Host: Barry Gray, John K. M. McCaffery
Producer: Martin Stone

During the first half of the program, one literary critic would argue for the guest-author's book while a second critic would argue against it. The second half of the program consisted of a general discussion among the author and the critics. It was first heard over Mutual in 1946.

Author's Playhouse

Drama

This was a dramatic program with scripts by various writers. It was first heard over Mutual in 1941. Wynn Wright created the show; Roy Shields and his orchestra furnished the music.

B

The Babe Ruth Show: see *Here's Babe Ruth.*

Baby Criers: see *Animal Imitators, Baby Criers, Doubles, Mimics, and Screamers.*

Baby Rose Marie

Variety

Starring: Baby Rose Marie

Baby Rose Marie, one of radio's first child stars, sang and acted in this series, which was first heard over NBC Blue in 1932. Her career was reborn years later when she became an adult television star.

The Baby Snooks Show

Comedy

CAST:

Baby Snooks	Fanny Brice
Daddy Higgins	Hanley Stafford
Mommy	Lalive Brownell
	Arlene Harris
Robespierre, Snooks' brother	Leone Ledoux
Roger	Georgia Ellis
Phoebe	Sara Berner

Orchestra: Carmen Dragon
Vocalist: Bob Graham
Announcers: Ken Roberts, Harlow Wilcox

Directors: Walter Bunker, Ted Bliss, Roy Rowlan
Writers: Everett Freeman, Jess Oppenheimer, Bill Danch, Jerry Seelen
Theme: "Rock-a-Bye Baby"

Opening:
ORCHESTRA. *Sleepy Strings*
ANNOUNCER. Sanka is the coffee that lets you sleep . . . but now . . .
ORCHESTRA. *Punctuate Crash*
ANNOUNCER. Wake up! It's time for . . .
ORCHESTRA. *Punctuate Crash*
ANNOUNCER. Baby Snooks!
[*Applause*]
ORCHESTRA. *Segue to Theme.*
ANNOUNCER. Yes, it's *The Baby Snooks Show* starring Fanny Brice as Baby Snooks, with Hanley Stafford as Daddy, Carmen Dragon and his orchestra, Bob Graham, vocalist, and yours truly Harlow Wilcox, and brought to you by Sanka Coffee . . . the coffee that is *one-hundred-per-cent flavor-rich* . . . so you'll always enjoy it! And ninety-seven-per-cent caffeine free . . . so it will never interfere with sleep.
ORCHESTRA. *Up to finish.*

"Baby Snooks" won her greatest fame as a comedy feature on *Maxwell House Coffee Time.* The character was first heard on radio as an act on *Ziegfeld Follies of the Air.*

Hanley Stafford's real name was Alfred John Austin. He took his stage name from his birthplace: Hanley, Staffordshire, England. (See also *John's Other Wife, Ziegfeld Follies of the Air.*)

Bachelor's Children

Serial Drama

CAST:
Dr. Bob Graham — Hugh Studebaker, Art Kohl*
Ruth Ann Graham — Marjorie Hannan, Laurette Fillbrandt
Janet Ryder — Patricia Dunlap
Sam Ryder — Olan Soule
Ellen Collins — Marie Nelson, Hellen Van Tuyl
Don Carpenter — David Gothard
Lawrence Mitchell — Frank Dane
Susan Grant — Muriel Bremner
Michael Kent — Charles Flynn
Marjory Carroll — Ginger Jones
Glenda — Mary Patton
Theresa Pech — Olga Rosenova
Davie Lane — John Hodiak
Kathleen Carney — Janice Gilbert
Margaret Gardner — Dorothy Denver
Mrs. Fred Hopkins — Marion Reed
Dr. Bruce Porter — Raymond Edward Johnson
Dr. Madelyn Keller — Alice Hill
Alison Radcliffe — Peg Hillias
Wilton Comstock — Arthur Peterson
Miss Bennett — Sunda Love
Marjorie — Ruth Bailey
Joe Houston — Nelson Olmsted
Elsie Jones — Kay Westfall
Norma Starr — Beryl Vaughn
Announcers: Don Gordon, Russ Young

---

* For three months during Studebaker's illness.

Directors: Burr Lee, Russ Young
Writer: Bess Flynn
Theme: "Ah, Sweet Mystery of Life"

Bachelor's Children was first heard over CBS in 1935 for Old Dutch Cleanser and ran until 1946. It received the Movie-Radio Guide Award of 1941 as "radio's best daytime serial program." It was also selected by the Co-ordinator of Inter-American Affairs as "the most representative script on the way of life of an average American family."

As a typical soap opera, *Bachelor's Children* was a fifteen-minute program broadcast five days a week. It originated in Chicago. Rehearsal was at 7:30 A.M., with the first show at 8:45. This broadcast was for the East and Midwest. Since there was no audio tape in those days, a "repeat for the West Coast" was broadcast at 2:30 P.M. Olan Soule, who played the part of "Sam Ryder," once suffered the embarrassment of missing a repeat performance when his watch stopped!

The Back Home Hour: see *Religion.*

The Back to God Hour: see *Religion.*

Backstage Wife

Serial Drama

CAST:

Mary Noble	Vivian Fridell
	Claire Niesen
Larry Noble	Ken Griffin
	James Meighan
	Guy Sorel
Lady Clara, Larry's mother	Ethel Owen
Marcia Mannering	Eloise Kummer
Betty Burns	Patricia Dunlap
Goldie	Eileen Palmer
Tess Morgan	Gail Henshaw
Alice Duffy	Gail Henshaw
Katharine Monroe	Betty Ruth Smith
Ward Elmond	Paul Luther
Sylvia King	Dorothy Francis
Tod Goodhue	George Niese
Dennis Conroy	Carlton KaDell
Katy Hamilton	Maxine Gardenas
Joe Binney	Sherman Marks
Jennifer Davis	Elmira Roessler
Doris Dee	Virginia Dwyer
Sago	Norman Gottschalk
Tom Bryson	Frank Dane
	Charles Webster
	Mandel Kramer
Arnold Carey, stage manager	John M. James
Taylor	Hoyt Allen
Pop, the stage doorman	Alan MacAteer
Kitty Marshall	Ginger Jones
	Vicki Vola
Peter Darnell	John Larkin
Uncle Ed Jackson	Leo Curley
Maida	Lesley Woods
Gerald Marshall	Malcolm Meecham
Sandra Carey	Luise Barclay
Judith Merritt	Donna Creade
Tom Blake	Dan Sutter
Susan Nelson	Louise Fitch
Christine	Bonita Kay
Callahan	Don Gallagher
Mrs. Dubois	Bess McCammon
Ada, the maid	Kay Renwick
Cliff Caldwell	Phil Truex
Virginia Lansing	Helen Claire
Irene	Andree Wallace
Maude Marlowe	Henrietta Tedro
	Ethel Wilson

Sandra Barclay	Eloise Kummer
Marcelle Betrand	Charlotte Manson
Cosmo	Rod Hendrickson
Mercy	Charme Allen
Rodney Brooks	Marvin Miller
Fritz Sterner	Marvin Miller
Edward de Manfield	Marvin Miller
Captain Amhurst, Coast Guardsman	Marvin Miller
Ocko	George Ansell
Vi Waters	Joyce Hayward
Marty Rufus	George Petrie
Regina Rawlings	Anne Burr
Margot	Dorothy Sands
Jean Baker	Susan Douglas
Larry, Jr.	Wilda Hinkel
Rupert	Bartlett Robinson
Julia	Anita Anton
Beatrice	Charlotte Keane
Ramsey	John McGovern
Victor	Ken Lynch

Announcers: Harry Clark, Ford Bond, Sandy Becker, Roger Krupp

Producers: Frank and Anne Hummert
Directors: Blair Walliser, Richard Leonard, Joe Mansfield, Fred Weihe, Lou Jacobson, Les Mitchel
Writers: Frank and Anne Hummert, Elizabeth Todd, Phil Thorne, Ned Calmer, Ruth Borden
Sound Effects: Chet Hill
Theme: "Rose of Tralee," played by Chet Kingsbury

Opening:

ANNOUNCER. *Backstage Wife,* the story of Mary Noble and what it means to be the wife of a famous Broadway star—dream sweetheart of a million other women.

Backstage Wife told of the trials and tribulations of an Iowa stenographer who fell in love with and married Larry Noble, a Broadway matinee idol. The program was aired on NBC Monday to Friday at 4:15 P.M. It was first heard over Mutual in 1935. It originated in Chicago.

The Bakers Broadcast: see *The Joe Penner Show.*

Band Remotes: see *Big Band Remotes.*

Barnacle Bill

Children

CAST:

Barnacle Bill, the Sailor	Cliff Soubier

Baron Münchhausen: see *The Jack Pearl Show.*

Barry Cameron

Serial Drama

CAST:

Barry Cameron	Spencer Bentley
Anna Cameron	Florence Williams
Maraine Clark	Dorothy Sands
Vinnie, the maid	Doris Rich
John Nelson	Scott McKay
Mrs. Mitchell	Helen Carewe
Josephine Whitfield	Elsie Hitz
Will Stevenson	King Calder
Martha Stevenson	Mary Hunter
Frances	Colleen Ward
Gloria Mulvaney	Rolly Bester

Announcer: Larry Elliott

Writers: Peggy Blake, Richard Leonard

Barry Cameron was first heard over NBC in 1945.

Barry Gray on Broadway

Discussion

Moderator: Barry Gray

This discussion program usually erupted in on-the-air controversy.

The Barton Family

Serial Drama

CAST:

Bud Barton	Dick Holland
Grandma Barton	Kathryn Card
Herman Branch	Cliff Soubier
Colonel Francis Welch	Ed Prentiss
Francis Welch, Jr.	Donald Kraatz
Judge Summerfield	Fred Sullivan
Bill Murray	Henry Hunter (Arthur Jacobson)
Pa	Bill Bouchey
Joy Wynn	Rosemary Garbell

Also: Hellen Van Tuyl, Karl Weber, Betty Jeffries, Jackie Harrison, Arthur Kohl, Hugh Muir, Bonita Kay, Ray Johannson, Arthur Peterson, Fern Persons, Ian Keith, Bob Jellison, Jane Webb

Director: Frank Papp
Writer: Harlan Ware

This program was heard over NBC Blue in 1939. It was also known as *The Story of Bud Barton* and *Those Bartons.*

Batman: see *Superman.*

Battle of the Sexes

Quiz

M.C.: Frank Crumit and Julia Sanderson, Walter O'Keefe, Jay C. Flippen
Announcer: Ben Grauer

Battle of the Sexes was heard over NBC in 1938.

B-Bar-B-Ranch: see *Bobby Benson's Adventures.*

Beat the Band

Musical Quiz

Hostess: "The Incomparable Hildegarde"
M.C.-Announcers: Marvin Miller, Tom Shirley
Vocalists: Marvel Maxwell, Marilyn Thorne
Musical Directors: Harry Sosnik, Ted Weems
Director: Jack Simpson
Writer: Hobart Donovan

Catch-phrase:
HILDEGARDE. Give me a little traveling music, Harry.

Listeners sent in musical questions and it was up to the band to identify songs from a few clues. Prizes of twenty-five dollars and a carton of the sponsor's cigarettes (Raleigh) went to contestants whose questions did *not* "beat the band." If the question did beat the band, the contestant received fifty dollars and two cartons of cigarettes and the boys in the band had to throw a pack of cigarettes "on the old bass drum for the men in service overseas." *Beat the Band* was heard over NBC in 1940. It originated in Chicago and moved to New York in 1944.

Hildegarde's full name was Hildegarde Loretta Sell. (See also *The Raleigh Room.*)

Behind the Mike

Drama

Host: Graham McNamee
Announcer: Harry Von Zell

Behind the Mike related stories of behind-the-scenes in broadcasting. It began over CBS in 1931.

Behind the Story

Documentary

Narrator: Marvin Miller
Directors: William Gordon, Lee Bolen, Larry Hays, J. C. Lewis, Bill Lutz, Norman Smith, Robert Turnbull, Don McCall
Writers: Richard Sharp, Robert Turnbull, Robert Hecker, Joyce Erickson, Marvin Miller, Elizabeth Dawson Miller, Sidney Omarr, Don Yerrill, Ruth Walliser

Behind the Story was a fifteen-minute, five-times-a-week, early evening program heard over Mutual from 1949 to 1957. For a time it was broadcast on the full Mutual network; later it ran on the Don Lee division of Mutual, which covered the Pacific and Mountain time zones. The series was originally written in the Schwimmer & Scott offices in Chicago. The subsequent West Coast shows gave many successful television and motion-picture writers their first commercial experience. All the stories were completely factual and well researched but concerned little-known incidents. The programs were presented as yarns, interspersed with dialogue scenes or direct quotes, with Marvin Miller doing all the characters, as many as thirteen in one show.

Believe It or Not

Unusual Facts

Host: Robert L. Ripley, Gregory Abbott (when Ripley was away)
Vocalist: Harriet Hilliard
Orchestra: B. A. Rolfe, Ozzie Nelson
Announcer: Bill Griffis
Creator-Producer: Doug Storer
Director: Ed King
Writers: Charles C. Speer, Claris A. Ross, Robert D. Maley, George Lefferts, Richard E. Davis, David Davidson

This program was based on Ripley's syndicated newspaper feature dealing with unusual facts. It was heard over NBC in 1930.

Ben Bernie

Music

Starring: Ben Bernie
Vocalists: Little Jackie Heller, Buddy

Clark, Mary Small, Jane Pickens, Pat Kennedy, Frank Prince, Bill Wilgus, Dick Stabile (also a saxophonist), Colonel Manny Prager (also a saxophonist)

With: Al Goering, pianist; Mickey Garlock, violinist; Ward Archer and Gilbert Grau on drums; "Whistlin'" Pullen, whistler

And: guest vocalists Gracie Barrie, Gale Robbins

Also: Billy Hillpot and Scrappy Lambert; Fuzzy Knight, comedy songs; Agnes Moorehead; Lew Lehr; *et al.*

Announcers: Harlow Wilcox, Bob Brown, Harry Von Zell

Writers: Albert G. Miller, Parke Levy, Gary Stevens, Alan Lipscott

---

Closing:

Bernie's closing theme was a familiar sound on radio. Since he couldn't sing well, he closed with this monologue spoken over the music:

And now the time has come to lend an ear to—
Au revoir. Pleasant dre-ams.
Think of us . . . when requesting your themes.
Until the next time when . . .
Possibly you may all tune in again.
Keep the Old Maestro always . . . in your schemes.
Yowsah, yowsah, yowsah.
Au Revoir . . .
This is Ben Bernie, ladies and gentlemen,
And all the lads
Wishing you a bit of pleasant dre-ams.
May good luck . . . and happiness,
Success, good health, attend your schemes.
And don't forget—
Should you ever send in your request-a
Why, we'll sho' try to do our best-a
Yowsah.
Au revoir, a fond cheerio,
a bit of a tweet-tweet,
God bless you . . . and
Pleasant dre-ams!

Ben Bernie, "The Old Maestro," conducted his orchestra's renditions of "sweet" music on various band remote broadcasts and on his own program during the 1930s. In addition, he's remembered for his "friendly feud" with Walter Winchell—the two of them exchanging humorous insults on their respective programs.

Dick Stabile later became a well-known orchestra leader. Colonel Henry Prager's greatest fame came from his singing of "The King's 'Orses."

Bess Johnson: see *The Story of Bess Johnson.*

Best Sellers

Drama

Host and narrator: Bret Morrison
Leading roles: Jim Boles

The Better Half

Quiz

On this program husbands and wives competed against each other. The loser paid a penalty. *The Better Half* first appeared on radio over Mutual in 1942.

Betty and Bob

Serial Drama

CAST:

Betty Drake	Elizabeth Reller
	Beatrice Churchill
	Alice Hill
	Arlene Francis
	Edith Davis
	Mercedes McCambridge
Bob Drake	Don Ameche
	Les Tremayne
	Spencer Bentley
	Carl Frank
	J. Anthony Hughes
	Van Heflin
Mae Drake, Bob's mother	Edith Davis
Jane Hartford	Dorothy Shideler
George	Frank Dane
Gardenia	Edith Davis
Carl Grainger	Herbert Nelson
Ethel Grainger	Eleanor Dowling
Peter Standish	Francis X. Bushman
Kathy Stone	Eloise Kummer
Mary Rose Spencer Vance	Marion B. Crutcher
Alan Bishop	Ned Wever
Madeline	Loretta Poynton
Marcia	Betty Winkler
Tony Harker	Don Briggs
Mrs. Cary	Grace Lockwood
Mrs. Hendrix	Grace Lockwood
Carlotta Van Every	Ethel Waite Owen
Pamela Talmadge	Ethel Kuhn
Jim Howard	Forrest Lewis
Blue Howard	Peggy Wall
William, the butler	Henry Saxe
Harvey Brew	Bill Bouchey
Bobbie Drake	Frankie Pacelli

Writers: Leonard Bercovici, Edwin Morse
Theme: "Salut d'Amour"

Betty and Bob first appeared on NBC Blue in 1932. It originated in Chicago.

Betty Boop Fables

Children

CAST:

Betty Boop	Mae Questel
Ferdie Frog	Red Pepper Sam
	William Costello

Orchestra: Victor Erwin

This program presented the adventures of the movie cartoon character created by Max Fleischer.

Betty Crocker: see *Women's Programs.*

Between the Bookends

Poetry and Conversation

Host: Ted Malone
Organist: Rosa Rio
Theme: "Auld Lang Syne"

Between the Bookends was heard over CBS in 1935.

Beulah

Comedy

CAST:

Beulah	Marlin Hurt
	Bob Corley
	Hattie McDaniel

Louise Beavers
Lillian Randolph

Bill Jackson, Beulah's boy friend
Marlin Hurt
Ernest Whitman

Harry Henderson — Hugh Studebaker
Jess Kirkpatrick

Alice Henderson — Mary Jane Croft
Lois Corbett

Donnie Henderson — Henry Blair

Oriole — Ruby Dandridge

Mr. Jenkins — John Brown

Also: Vivian Dandridge, Dorothy Dandridge (sister of Vivian), Butterfly McQueen, Nicodemus Stewart, Amanda Randolph, Jester Hairston, Roy Glenn, "Lasses" White, Marvin Miller

Vocalists: Carol Stewart, Penny Piper

Orchestra: Buzz Adlam, Albert Sack

Announcers: Hank Weaver, Ken Niles, Marvin Miller, Johnny Jacobs

---

Directors: Helen Mack, Tom McKnight, Jack Hurdle, Steve Hatos

Writers: Charles Stewart, Phil Leslie, Arthur Phillips, Hal Kanter, Sol Stewart, Seaman Jacobs, Sol Schwartz, Sol Saks

Sound Effects: Vic Livoti

Catch-phrases:

BEULAH. Love dat man!

BEULAH. Somebody bawl for Beulah?

BEULAH. On the con-positively-trairy!

Opening:

ANNOUNCER. Tums—famous for quick relief for acid indigestion—presents . . . *The Marlin Hurt and Beulah Show* . . .

ORCHESTRA. *Theme in and up* (*APPLAUSE*)

ANNOUNCER. (*Over*) with lovely Carol Stewart . . . the music of Albert Sack and His Orchestra . . . and starring . . . Marlin Hurt . . . and . . .

ORCHESTRA. *Music up full*

BEULAH (*sings*):

Got the world in a jug, Lawd
Got the stopper in my hand! . . .

(*Chuckles*)

ANNOUNCER. Yes, sir, it's . . . Beulah! (*Applause*)

The character of Beulah, a Negro maid, was first portrayed by Marlin Hurt, a white man, on *Fibber McGee and Molly*. One of the peculiarities of radio was that it was possible for such a situation to occur—a white man playing a Negro woman—with no one the wiser among the home audience. As a matter of fact, great use was made of the surprise element on *Fibber McGee and Molly* since Hurt stood quietly with his back to the mike as Beulah's entrance neared and then suddenly on cue whirled around and screamed out her opening line. The studio audience never failed to register surprise, laughter, and applause.

Later, as a "spin-off," Beulah became the central character on the *Beulah* show as a half-hour, once-a-week CBS program sponsored by Tums. As the above script excerpt indicates, it was also known as *The Marlin Hurt and Beulah Show*. Following Hurt's death in 1947, the program was revived on ABC, also in a half-hour, once-a-week format. Finally, it moved to CBS as a fifteen-minute, three-times-a-week, early evening broadcast with the startling innovation of letting an actual Negro woman play Beulah.

Bob Corley was twenty-two years old when he took over the Beulah role. He later became a television director in his hometown of Atlanta, Georgia. He claimed that "age and hormones" eventually prevented him from being able to do the Beulah voice.

Beyond These Valleys

Serial Drama

CAST:

Rebecca Lane — Gertrude Warner
David — Shirling Oliver

Director: Basil Loughrane
Writer: Don Becker, who also composed the original theme music.

The Bickersons

Comedy

CAST:

John Bickerson — Don Ameche
Blanche Bickerson — Frances Langford, Marsha Hunt
Amos, John's brother — Danny Thomas

Creator-Writer: Phil Rapp

These comedy skits featured a quarreling husband and wife and were first heard on Edgar Bergen's *Chase and Sanborn Hour.*

Big Band Remotes

During the era of the big bands—in the 1930s and 1940s—most bands spent a good portion of their year playing one-nighters in ballrooms from coast to coast. The networks had permanent broadcasting installations in the ballrooms of major cities and could easily set up temporary lines in small clubs in smaller cities. Since these originations were from outside the studios the broadcasts came to be known as "band remotes." It was not unusual, late on a Saturday night, to be able to tune in to half-a-dozen band remotes from as many locations. Typically, a local announcer would be sent out to introduce the program, the bandleader, and the musical numbers, and you might hear:

ANNOUNCER. From the beautiful Westwood Room of the fabulous Park Sheridan Hotel in downtown metropolitan Buffalo, New York, it's the danceable rhythms of Claude Hudson and His Twenty-one Gentlemen of Swing!

MUSIC. *Band theme up full, then under . . .*

ANNOUNCER. Yes, once again the Mutual Broadcasting System is proud to bring you a full half-hour of music for your listening and dancing pleasure. The happy crowd here is ready for your first number, Claude. What'll it be?

CLAUDE. Well, Bill, here's the lovely Ginny Parsons to ask the musical question, "Do You Remember Me?"

MUSIC. *"Do You Remember Me?"*

Not all the bands were as obscure as our mythical Claude Hudson. Glenn Miller, Benny Goodman ("The King of Swing"), Gene Krupa, Harry James, the Dorsey Brothers (Tommy and Jimmy)—all the major musical groups of the time were heard frequently from remote locations such as the Trianon and Aragon ballrooms in Chicago, the Glen Island Casino in New Rochelle, New York, and the Mocambo in Hollywood.

Among the other orchestras were Blue Barron (Harry Freedlin), Charlie Barnet, Nat Brandwynne, Henry Busse, Cab Calloway, Carmen Cavallaro ("The Poet of the Piano"), Russ Columbo, Bob Crosby ("Bob Crosby's Bobcats"), Xavier Cugat, D'Artega, Meyer Davis, Eddie Duchin, Duke Ellington, Shep Fields ("Rippling Rhythm"), Ted Fiorito, Larry Funk ("The Band of a Thousand Melodies"), Jan Garber ("The Idol of the Airlanes"), Glen Gray ("The Casa Loma Orchestra"), Johnny Green, Lennie Hayton, Richard Himber ("The Studebaker Champions"), Ina Ray Hutton (leader of an all-girl band), Isham Jones, Dick Jurgens, Hal Kemp, Wayne King ("The Waltz King"), Ted Lewis ("Is everybody happy?"), Guy Lombardo* ("The Royal Canadians—with the sweetest music this side of Heaven"), Vincent Lopez** ("Hello, everybody. Lopez speaking."), Jimmy Lunceford, Abe Lyman, Enric Madriguera, Chico Marx, Barry McKinley, Vaughn Monroe, Russ Morgan ("Music in the Morgan Manner"), Red Nichols, Will Osborne, Erno Rapee, Nat Shilkret, Jack Teagarden, The Three Suns (an instrumental trio comprised of Al Nevins on guitar, Morty Nevins, accordion, and Arty Dunn, electric organ), Ted Weems, and Paul Whiteman.

* Guy Lombardo's Royal Canadians became well known for their traditional radio appearances on New Year's Eve. Guy was the most famous member of the musical Lombardo family. Musicians Victor, Carmen, and Lebert often appeared with him, as did their sister, vocalist Rose Marie Lombardo.

** Vincent Lopez made his radio debut on November 27, 1921. He was usually heard from the Hotel Taft in New York. (See also *Musicians; Orchestra Leaders, Singers.*)

Big Brother: see *Uncle Don* and *Rainbow, House.*

Big Jon and Sparkie

Children's Adventure

CAST:

Big Jon	Jon Arthur
Sparkie	Jon Arthur
Mayor Plumpfront	Jon Arthur
Ukey Betcha	Jon Arthur
Gil Hooley (Gil Hooley and His Leprechaun Marching Band)	William J. Mahoney, Jr.

Producer: Jon Arthur
Technical Producer: William J. Mahoney, Jr.
Writer: Donald Kortekamp
Theme: "The Teddy Bear's Picnic"

Catch-phrase:
JON ARTHUR. Hi . . . hey . . . hello there!

Big Jon and Sparkie originated in Cincinnati in 1948 and ran on ABC from 1950 to 1958. It was on the network for an hour a day Monday through Friday. A similar show called *No School Today* was heard on Saturday mornings for two hours. Jon Arthur thereby had one of the largest blocks of radio network time ever assigned to one performer—seven hours per week. The daily program was eventually reduced to a fifteen-minute show entitled *The Further Adventures of Big Jon and Sparkie.*

The Big Show

Variety

Hostess: Tallulah Bankhead
Orchestra: Meredith Willson
Celebrity Guests: Fred Allen, Groucho Marx, *et al.*
Announcers: Ed Herlihy, Jimmy Wallington
Writer: Goodman Ace

Opening:

TALLULAH. You are about to be entertained by some of the biggest names in show business. For the next hour and thirty minutes, this program will present—in person—such bright stars as:

GUEST STARS. (*each reading his own name*): Louis Armstrong . . . Bob Hope . . . Deborah Kerr . . . Frankie Laine . . . Jerry Lewis . . . Dean Martin . . . Dorothy McGuire . . . Meredith Willson . . .

TALLULAH. And my name, dahlings, is Tallulah Bankhead.

MUSIC. *Theme in . . . up and under for . . .*

ANNOUNCER. The National Broadcasting Company presents . . . *The Big Show!*

MUSIC. *Theme in full with chorus and under for . . .*

ANNOUNCER. *The Big Show!* Ninety minutes with the most scintillating personalities in the entertainment world, brought to you this Sunday and every Sunday at this same time as the Sunday feature of NBC's All Star Festival . . . and here is your hostess, the glamorous, unpredictable Tallulah Bankhead!

MUSIC. *Out*

(*Applause*)

This was one of radio's last big variety programs. As evidenced by the above opening from the December 17, 1950, NBC broadcast from Hollywood, the guest list was always spectacular. Among the best-remembered portions of the show were Miss Bankhead's predilection for calling everyone "dahling," Meredith Willson's acknowledgment of her introduction with "Thank you, Miss Bankhead, sir," and Miss Bankhead's closing, when she sang in her husky voice "May the Good Lord Bless and Keep You."

Big Sister

Serial Drama

CAST:

Ruth Evans Wayne, the big sister — Alice Frost, Nancy Marshall, Marjorie Anderson, Mercedes McCambridge, Grace Matthews
Sue Evans Miller, Ruth's sister — Haila Stoddard, Dorothy McGuire, Peggy Conklin, Fran Carden
Nurse Burton — Vera Allen
Little Ned Evans (Neddie) — Michael O'Day
Samson — Chester Stratton
Cornelius Porter — Harold Vermilyea
Vera Wayne — Helene Dumas

Rodger Allen	Carl Benton Reid
Paul Gerond	Guy de Vestel
Horace	Oscar Polk
Asa Griffin	Teddy Bergman
Jerry Miller	Ned Wever
Diane Carvell Ramsey	Elspeth Eric
Mrs. Carvell	Evelyn Varden
Dr. Duncan Carvell	Santos Ortega
Elsa Banning	Erin O'Brien-Moore
Ernest Banning	Horace Braham
Frank Wayne	Eric Dressler
Dr. John Wayne	Martin Gabel
	Paul McGrath
	Staats Cotsworth
Pete Stone	Ed Begley
Addie Price	Charlotte Holland
Ginny Price	Patsy Campbell
Hope Melton Evans	Ann Shepherd (Scheindel Kalish)
	Teri Keane
Waldo Briggs	Ed Begley
	Horace Braham
Dr. Reed Bannister	Berry Kroeger
	Ian Martin
	Arnold Moss
	David Gothard
Mary Tyler	Ann Shepherd (Scheindel Kalish)
Eunice	Susan Douglas
Richard Wayne	Jim Ameche, Jr.
	Ruth Schafer
Pete Kirkwood	Joe Julian
Margo Kirkwood	Louise Fitch
Charles Daniels	Ed Begley
Ricki Lenya	Ann Shepherd (Scheindel Kalish)
Mrs. Warren	Adelaide Klein
Michael West	Richard Kollmar
	Joe Julian
David Brewster	Alexander Kirkland
Harriet Durant	Elizabeth Love
Wellington Durant	Charles Webster
Lola Mitchell	Arlene Francis
Eric Ramsey	Richard Widmark
Doris Monet	Joan Tompkins
Dr. Marlowe	Mason Adams
Dr. Seabrook	Everett Sloane

Also: Ralph Bell, Anne Burr

Announcers: Jim Ameche, Hugh Conover

Creator: Lillian Laufferty

Directors: Mitchell Grayson, Theodore T. Huston, Thomas F. Vietor, Jr.

Writers: Julian Funt, Carl Bixby, Robert Newman, Bill Sweets

Musical Director: William Meeder

Sound Effects: Bill Brown

Organist: Richard Leibert

Theme: "Valse Bluette"

Opening:

ANNOUNCER. Rinso presents . . . *Big Sister.*

SOUND. *Tower clock striking*

ANNOUNCER. Yes, there's the clock in Glens Falls Town Hall telling us it's time for Rinso's story of *Big Sister.*

This program was first heard over CBS in 1936. (See also *Bright Horizon.*)

The Big Story

Drama

Narrator: Robert Sloane

Announcer: Ernest Chappell

Directors: Harry Ingram, Thomas F. Vietor, Jr.

Writers: Robert Sloane, Gail Ingram, Max Ehrlich, Arnold Perl

Sound Effects: Al Scott

Theme: "*Ein Heldenleben*" by Richard Strauss (section titled "Prowess in Battle")

The program dramatized stories of newspaper reporters. At the conclusion of the broadcast, the actual reporter was introduced on the air and congratulated for his story. The series was first heard over NBC in 1947 and was sponsored by Pall Mall cigarettes.

Big Town

Adventure

CAST:

Steve Wilson, Editor of the *Illustrated Press*, a crusading newspaper — Edward G. Robinson, Edward Pawley, Walter Greaza
Lorelei Kilbourne, society editor — Claire Trevor, Ona Munson, Fran Carlon
Tommy Hughes — Ed MacDonald
Miss Foster — Helen Brown
District Attorney Miller — Gale Gordon
Eddie, the cabdriver — Ted de Corsia
Inspector Callahan — Dwight Weist
Dusty Miller, the photographer — Lawson Zerbe, Casey Allen
Fletcher — Bill Adams
Barky — Robert Dryden
Danny — Michael O'Day
Harry the Hack — Mason Adams
Willie the Weep — Donald MacDonald
Mozart — Larry Haines
Newsboy at the opening who shouted, "Get your *Illustrated Press*" — Bobbie Winkler, Michael O'Day
Narrator — Dwight Weist
Also: Jerry Hausner, Cy Kendall, Paula Winslowe, Jack Smart, George Petrie, Thelma Ritter
Announcer: Ken Niles

Producer-Writer-Director: Jerry McGill
Producer: Phil Cohen
Directors: Richard Uhl, Joseph Bell, Crane Wilbur, William N. Robson
Musical Director: Leith Stevens
Sound Effects: John Powers
Organist: John Gart
Theme: "Tell the Story"

This program was heard over CBS beginning in 1937.

Bill Stern Sports Newsreel: see *The Colgate Sports Newsreel Starring Bill Stern.*

The Billie Burke Show

Comedy

CAST:

Billie Burke — Herself
Billie's brother — Earle Ross
Billie's maid — Lillian Randolph
Colonel Fitts, a suitor for Billie's hand — Marvin Miller
Banker Guthrie, another suitor — Marvin Miller
Also: Hattie McDaniel, Arthur Q. Bryan
Announcers: Tom Dickson, Marvin Miller

Directors: Axel Gruenberg, Dave Titus
Writers: Ruth F. Brooks, Paul West

The Billie Burke Show was first heard over CBS in 1944 and ran until 1946.

Billy and Betty

Children's Adventure

CAST:

Billy White — Jimmy McCallion
Betty White — Audrey Egan
Melvin Castlebury — Elliott Reid
Announcer: Kelvin Keech

Theme:

Here comes the milkman
Hooray! Hooray!
He's bringing milk from Sheffield Farms
That's sealed, select Grade A.

Here comes the milkman
He's ringing at your door
(*sound of doorbell ringing and door opening*)
Here's the milk you always drink
It's select Grade A.

Billy and Betty was first heard over NBC in 1935.

Billy Graham: see *Religion*.

Billy Sunday: see *Religion*.

The Bing Crosby Show

Music

Starring: Bing Crosby
Vocal group: Jud Conlon's Rhythmaires
Orchestra: John Scott Trotter
Also: Skitch Henderson
Announcers: Ken Carpenter (when show was in Hollywood); Glenn Riggs (when show was in New York)
Producer-Writer: Bill Morrow
Director: Murdo McKenzie
Theme (sung by Crosby):

Where the blue of the night
Meets the gold of the day
Someone waits for me.

The Bing Crosby Show went on the air after Crosby left the *Kraft Music Hall* in the spring of 1946, when Kraft refused to let him record his shows. From the fall of 1946 until December 1956, *The Bing Crosby Show* was sponsored by Philco, Chesterfield, and General Electric. While under Philco sponsorship, the program was known as *Philco Radio Time*. (See also *Kraft Music Hall*.)

The Bishop and the Gargoyle

Adventure

CAST:

The Bishop — Richard Gordon
The Gargoyle — Milton Herman
Ken Lynch

Director: Joseph Bell
Writer: Frank Wilson

"The Bishop," who had a dilettante's interest in crime, had served on the parole board of Sing Sing prison, where he met the man he called "The Gargoyle"—a convict who was never known by any other name on the program. When "The Gargoyle" became an ex-convict, he served as an aide to "The Bishop," and the two men solved crimes together. "The Bishop," of course, avoided violence while "The Gargoyle" supplied the physical force necessary in certain situations. The program was first heard over the Blue network in 1936.

The Black Castle

Mystery-Drama

Opening:

ANNOUNCER. Now . . . up these steps to the iron-studded oaken door which yawns wide on rusted hinges . . . bidding us enter.

MUSIC. *Mysterious organ music under . . .*

ANNOUNCER. Music—do you hear it? Wait . . . it is well to stop. For here is the Wizard of the Black Castle.

SOUND. *Weird animal cries followed by cackling laughter and more animal cries . . .*

WIZARD. There you are. Back again, I see. Well, welcome. Come in, come in.

SOUND. *Animal cries . . .*

WIZARD. You'll be overjoyed at the tale I have for you tonight!

This fifteen-minute thriller first appeared on Mutual in 1943.

The Black Hood

Adventure

CAST:

The Cop	Scott Douglas
Girl reporter	Marjorie Cramer

Writer: Walt Framer

Opening:

SOUND. *Gong*

ANNOUNCER. The Black Hood!

SOUND. *Gong*

VOICE. Criminals, beware . . . The Black Hood is everywhere!

SOUND. *Eerie, howling noise up full and under . . .*

VOICE. I, The Black Hood, do solemnly swear that neither threats nor bribes nor bullets nor death itself shall keep me from fulfilling my vow—to erase crime from the face of the earth!

This was the story of a rookie cop who acquired magical powers when he donned a black hood.

The Black Museum

Mystery

Host: Orson Welles

Blackstone, the Magic Detective

Adventure

CAST:

Blackstone	Ed Jerome

Also: Fran Carlon, Ted Osborne
Announcer: Alan Kent
Director: Carlo de Angelo
Writers: Joan and Nancy Webb
Musical Director: Bill Meader

Blackstone Plantation

Variety

Featuring: Frank Crumit and Julia Sanderson

Also: Don Rodrigo and Don Felipe Escondido, Santos Ortega, Ted de Corsia

Blackstone Plantation was first heard over CBS in 1929.

Blind Date

Audience Participation

Hostess: Arlene Francis
Director: Tom Wallace
Writers: Arlene Francis, Kenneth Rouight

On this program, which was first heard over ABC in 1943, hostess Arlene Francis helped arrange dates.

Blondie

Situation Comedy

CAST:

Blondie	Penny Singleton
	Alice White
	Patricia Van Cleve
	Ann Rutherford
Dagwood Bumstead	Arthur Lake
J. C. Dithers, Dagwood's boss	Hanley Stafford
Fuddle, the neighbor	Arthur Q. Bryan
	Harry Lang
Alexander (Baby Dumpling)	Leone Ledoux
	Larry Sims
	Jeffrey Silver
	Tommy Cook
Cookie	Marlene Ames
	Joan Rae
	Norma Jean Nilsson
Cora Dithers	Elvia Allman
Herb Woodley, the neighbor	Hal Peary
	Frank Nelson
Alvin Fuddle	Dix Davis
Harriet	Mary Jane Croft
McGonnigle	Howard Petrie
Dimples Wilson	Veola Vonn
	Lurene Tuttle

Orchestra: Harry Lubin
Announcers: Bill Goodwin, Howard Petrie

Producer-Director: Don Bernard
Director: Eddie Pola
Writer: Johnny Greene
Sound Effects: Parker Cornell

Catch-phrase:
DITHERS. Bumstead! I'll run your little finger through the pencil sharpener!
Opening:
ANNOUNCER. Uh-uh-uh . . . don't touch that dial! Listen to . . .
DAGWOOD. (*shouting*). B-l-o-o-o-o-n-d-i-e!!!

Blondie came to radio over CBS in 1939. It featured all the elements familiar to readers of the comic strip created by Chic Young and to viewers of the long-run motion-picture series. One oft-repeated sequence on the radio program had "Mr. Dithers" yelling for "Dagwood" to "come into my office" counterpointed by a muted trumpet obbligato.

Blue Playhouse

Drama

Featuring: Frank Lovejoy, Joan Banks, Santos Ortega

Blue Ribbon Town

Comedy-Variety

Featuring: Groucho Marx, Virginia O'Brien, Donald Dickson, Kenny Baker
Orchestra: Robert Armbruster
Producer-Writer-Director: Dick Mack

Virginia O'Brien was famous for her deadpan expression while singing up-tempo songs. *Blue Ribbon Town* took its name from the sponsor's beer, Pabst Blue Ribbon. The program made its debut March 27, 1943.

Bob and Ray

Comedy

CAST:

Bob	Bob Elliott
Ray	Ray Goulding
Wally Ballou	Bob Elliott
Mary McGoon	Ray Goulding
Webley Webster	Ray Goulding
Tex Blaisdell	Bob Elliott
Biff Burns	Ray Goulding
Steve Bosco	Bob Elliott

Bob and Ray started doing comedy together when they were both staff announcers on local radio in Boston. Their program, *Matinee with Bob and Ray*, preceded the Red Sox baseball games, and whenever the game was rained out Bob and Ray stayed on the air all afternoon. Eventually they were brought to network radio with a Saturday-night program on NBC, and subsequently they appeared from time to time on all the networks at various hours. Bob and Ray played all the parts of the regular cast characters as well as all the characters in their dramas. Among the fairly regular features were:

"Wally Ballou" on remote location interviewing various people. Wally always started his reports with his mike turned off so that he was first heard in the middle of a word. He announced himself as "Wally Ballou, winner of over seven international diction awards," or, "Radio's highly regarded Wally Ballou." His microphone was usually turned off before he was quite through. Occasionally "Wally" would refer to his family, his wife "Hulla Ballou" and his son "Little Boy Ballou." He denied being related to either the "Beale Street Ballous" or the "Wang Wang Ballous."

"Mary McGoon's" recipes. At Thanksgiving, "Mary" had a recipe for "Mock Turkey" which was made of mashed potatoes shaped into the form of a turkey with hot dogs for legs and wings.

"Steve Bosco," sportscaster, calling in with what was supposed to be a sports story. He always seemed to be a little bit drunk and was perpetually worried about getting the connection cut off. He usually asked for some money to get himself out of some financial scrape and then signed off with, "This is Steve Bosco rounding third and being thrown out at home."

"Biff Burns," the other sportscaster. He usually displayed an egotistical ignorance of his subject and signed off with, "This is Biff Burns saying, until next time, this is Biff Burns saying good-by."

"Mary Backstayge, Noble Wife"—a take-off on soap operas. It opened with announcer "Word Carr" saying, "And now, for the many fans who wait for her on the radio, we present the interesting story 'Mary Backstayge, Noble Wife,' the story of a girl from a deserted mining town out West who came to New York to become the wife of handsome Harry Backstayge, Broadway star, and what it means to be the wife of the idol of a million other women."

"Tex Blaisdell," Bob and Ray's cowboy country and Western entertainer, who traveled and performed with the "Smokey Valley Boys." "Romeo" was the comic rustic with the "Smokey Valley Boys." Tex did rope tricks on the radio and perpetually plugged his upcoming appearances at county fairs and supermarket openings.

"One Feller's Family"—a take-off on "One Man's Family." Bob played "Father Butcher" and mumbled a lot to himself, ending with "Fanny, Fanny, Fanny." Ray played "Mother Butcher" and usually wound up exasperatedly telling Father Butcher to "shut up and stop mumbling, you senile old man." It always ended with the announcer saying, " 'One Feller's Family' is written and directed by T. Wilson Messy. This has been a Messy Production."

"Lawrence Fechtenberger, Interstellar Officer Candidate"—a take-off on adventure serials—which was brought to you "by chocolate cookies with white stuff in between." Ray played "Lawrence," and Bob was his side-kick, "Mugg Mellish," always sneering.

"Widen Your Horizons"—a program of self-help in which experts would explain how to put salt in salt shakers, how to look up names in the telephone directory, etc.—brought to you by the "Croftweiler Industrial Cartel, makers of all kinds of things out of all kinds of stuff."

"Dean Archer Armstead," Bob and Ray's agricultural expert from the "Lackawanna, New York, Field Station." His theme was a scratchy record of a piano version of "Old MacDonald."

"Natalie Attired," Bob and Ray's "Song Sayer." Played by Ray in his "Mary McGoon" voice, "Natalie" would "say" songs. She was accompanied by her drummer, "Eddie" (Bob), and would merely speak the words of popular songs to Eddie's drum accompaniment.

"The Bob and Ray Gourmet Club." Here "Claude" and "Clyde" would describe the colorful ceremony attending the presentation and unwrapping of some celebrity's sandwich, which would subsequently be placed on a velvet cushion in a place of honor where the guests of "The Gourmet Club" could dance by and look at it.

Bob and Ray signed off each broadcast with:

RAY. Write if you get work . . .

BOB. . . . And hang by your thumbs.

(In their very early days, Ray spoke both lines and Bob added, "And remember, it's milder . . . much milder.")

The Bob Becker Program

Pets

Featuring: Bob Becker

In this series Bob Becker discussed

problems encountered in the training of pets, primarily dogs.

The Bob Burns Show

Comedy

CAST:

The Arkansas Traveler — Bob Burns
Sharon O'Shaughnessey — Ann Thomas

Directors: Joe Thompson, Andrew Love
Writers: R. E. "Duke" Atterberry, Victor McLeod, Glen Wheaton
Theme: "The Arkansas Traveler"

Bob Burns made his radio debut on *The Fleischmann Hour* with Rudy Vallee and subsequently made several guest appearances. In 1936 he joined Bing Crosby on *Kraft Music Hall,* where he played second banana to Bing for five years. Later he got his own show, which was heard over CBS in 1941. Burns had a musical instrument made of a funnel and two gas pipes that he called a bazooka. During World War II a United States Army weapon was named after Burns' bazooka.

The Bob Crosby Show

Variety

M.C.: Bob Crosby
Orchestra: Bob Crosby's Bobcats
Announcers: Les Tremayne, John Lund
Director: Bob Brewster
Writers: Carroll Carroll, David Gregory

Each week a different up-and-coming female vocalist was featured on the show; among them were Peggy Lee, Kay Starr, and Jo Stafford when they were still relatively unknown.

Bob Elson Aboard the Century

Interviews

Host: Bob Elson

Bob Elson interviewed people riding the Twentieth-Century Limited train between Chicago and New York.

The Bob Hawk Show

Quiz

Quizmaster: Bob Hawk

Bob Hawk interspersed gags with the questions on this program, which was heard over CBS in 1945. A studio contestant could become a "Lemac" by answering questions correctly. "Lemac" was simply Camel, the sponsor, spelled backward. A winning contestant was, of course, rewarded financially and serenaded with a chorus of "You're a Lemac now."

The Bob Hope Show

Comedy

CAST:

Starring: — Bob Hope
Professor — Jerry Colonna
Vera Vague — Barbara Jo Allen
Brenda — Blanche Stewart
Cobina — Elvia Allman

John L. C. Sivoney Frank Fontaine
Miriam of the Pepsodent commercials ("Dear Miriam, poor Miriam, neglected using Irium") Trudy Erwin
Santa Claus Jack Kirkwood
Honey Chile Patricia Wilder
Claire Hazel

Also: Irene Ryan

Vocalists: Judy Garland, Gloria Jean, Doris Day, Frances Langford

Hits and a Miss (vocal group that varied from Three Hits and a Miss to Six Hits and a Miss)—Pauline Byrnes, Bill Seckler, Vincent Degen, Marvin Bailey, Jerry Preshaw, Howard Hudson, Mack McLean

Orchestra: Al Goodman, Red Nichols, Skinnay Ennis, Les Brown

Announcers: Wendell Niles, Art Baker, Larry Keating, Bill Goodwin, Hy Averback

---

Producer: Bill Lawrence

Directors: Bob Stephenson, Tom Sawyer, Norman Morrell, Al Capstaff

Writers: Ted McKay, Albert Schwartz, Mel Shavelson, Norman Sullivan, Jack Douglas, Paul Laven, Dr. Samuel Kurtzman, Fred S. Fox, Hal Block, Larry Marks, Al Josefsberg

Sound Effects: Parker Cornell, Walter Snow

Theme: "Thanks for the Memory"

Catch-phrases:

HOPE. Who's Yehoodi?

COLONNA. Greetings, Gate!

Bob Hope entered radio, after a successful career in vaudeville and on Broadway, as a guest on *The Rudy Vallee Show,* followed by brief appearances on such short-lived programs as *The Bromo-Seltzer Intimate Hour, The Atlantic Oil Program,* and *The Woodbury Soap Hour.* Then came the long-running, extremely popular program sponsored by Pepsodent, which was first heard over NBC Blue in 1934. Many well-remembered sequences developed on this Tuesday night show on NBC, among them Colonna's phone calls to Hope:

COLONNA. Hello, Hope? This is Colonna.

HOPE. Professor! Where are you?

COLONNA. I'm here in England building a bridge across the Atlantic.

HOPE. Nonsense, Professor. You can't build a bridge across the Atlantic.

COLONNA. I can't??? [*Pause*] Okay, boys. Tear it down!

"Vera Vague" was a man-chasing character, as were "Brenda" and "Cobina," vague parodies of the then prominent real-life society girls Brenda Frazier and Cobina Wright, Jr.

In one sketch Jack Kirkwood appeared as a street-corner Santa Claus with a little kettle and admonished Hope to "Put something in the pot, boy," which became an oft-repeated catch-phrase.

Judy Garland was virtually a permanent cast member for over a year although she was usually accorded "guest-star" billing. In addition, Hope had as frequent guests many Hollywood stars, including Madeleine Carroll, Mickey Rooney, William Powell, Paulette Goddard, Pat O'Brien, Olivia de Havilland, Dorothy Lamour, Constance Bennett, and his "feuding partner" Bing

Crosby. At one point Basil Rathbone and Nigel Bruce appeared as "Sherlock Holmes" and "Doctor Watson" to help Hope find his mythical Yehoodi. They finally concluded that Yehoodi was the little man who pushes up the next piece of Kleenex!

Frequently there were rumors that Hope had been cut off the air for allegedly using racy material. While he often skirted the bounds of what was then acceptable, the stories of his being censored on the air are apocryphal.

During the years of World War II, Hope began what was to turn out to be a life-long career of entertaining servicemen at various United States and overseas bases. His tireless efforts were a major factor in boosting American morale, and the laughs, whistles, and applause were not only indicative of the appreciation of the servicemen but also provided a lift for the home front. Hope usually started each of these broadcasts with something like "This is Bob, Camp Pendleton, Hope saying that if you want to help out our boys in blue, send them some socks . . . and some kisses, too!" (*Whistles, cheers, and applause.*) He also made frequent use of the local names and customs wherever he was, again to much appreciation by the audience. (See also *The Woodbury Soap Hour.*)

Bobby Benson's Adventures

Children

CAST:

Bobby Benson — Richard Wanamaker; Ivan Cury; Billy Halop

Polly Armstead — Florence Halop

Windy Wales, the handyman (Wild Tales by Windy Wales) — Don Knotts

Harka, the Indian — Craig McDonnell

Irish — Craig McDonnell

Tex Mason (originally Buck Mason) — Herb Rice; Neil O'Malley; Charles Irving; Al Hodge; Tex Ritter

Chinese cook — Herb Rice

Black Bart — Eddie Wragge

Aunt Lilly — Lorraine Pankow

Announcers: Bob Emerick, "Two-gun" André Baruch, "Cactus" Carl Warren, Carl Caruso

---

Creator: Herbert C. Rice
Director: Bob Novak
Writer: Jim Sheehan and others

Bobby Benson's Adventures was first heard over CBS in 1932 and was set originally on the "H-Bar-O Ranch" because it was sponsored by H-O Oats; later it was set on the "B-Bar-B Ranch." (See also *Songs of the B-Bar-B.*)

Boston Blackie

Detective

CAST:

Boston Blackie — Chester Morris; Richard Kollmar

Mary — Lesley Woods; Jan Miner

Inspector Faraday — Maurice Tarplin; Richard Lane; Frank Orth

Shorty — Tony Barrett
Announcer: Larry Elliott

Producer-Director: Jeanne K. Harrison
Writers: Kenny Lyons, Ralph Rosenberg

Opening:
ANNOUNCER. Boston Blackie! Enemy to those who make him an enemy; friend to those who have no friends!

Radio fans have frequently debated the question of whether or not Chester Morris played "Boston Blackie" on radio in addition to his role in the movies. As the cast list indicates, Morris actually did originate the radio character, playing the part while the show was a summer replacement for *Amos 'n' Andy*.

Box 13

Adventure

CAST:
Dan Holiday — Alan Ladd
Suzy — Sylvia Picker

Brave Tomorrow

Serial Drama

CAST:
Louise Lambert — Jeannette Dowling
Hal Lambert — Raymond Edward Johnson
Roger DeKoven
Jean Lambert — Nancy Douglass
Flora Campbell
Marty Lambert — Jone Allison
Andree Wallace
Phil Barnes — Carl Eastman
Brad Forbes — Frank Lovejoy
Whit Davis — House Jameson

Writer: Ruth A. Knight

Break the Bank

Quiz

M.C.: John Reed King
Johnny Olson
Bert Parks
Clayton "Bud" Collyer
Orchestra: Peter Van Steeden
Director: Jack Rubin
Writers: Joseph Kane, Walt Framer, Jack Rubin

Break the Bank was first heard over Mutual in 1945.

Breakfast at Sardi's

Audience Participation

M.C.: Tom Breneman
Assistant: Bobby, a Filipino busboy
Announcer: Carl Webster Pierce

Prizes were awarded for the tallest, fattest, etc., in the audience. Tom Breneman often tried on hats of female guests for a gag.

The Breakfast Club

Variety

CAST:
M.C.: — Don McNeill
Sam (Fiction and Fact from Sam's Almanac) — Sam Cowling
Aunt Fanny, a country character who

dispensed gossip and stories; her theme, "She's Only a Bird in a Gilded Cage" Fran Allison
Fibber McGee and Molly
Jim and Marian Jordan
Mr. Wimple Bill Thompson
Also: Russell Pratt, Gale Page
The Three Romeos—Sam Cowling, Gil Jones, Louie Perkins, Boyce Smith (replacement); The Vagabonds—Ray "Pappy" Grant, Robert O'Neil, John Jordan, Norval Taborn; The Cadets—Al Stracke, Carl Scheibe, Jack Halloran, Homer Snodgrass, Bob Childe, Reo Fletcher, Arnold Isolany, Sam Thompson; The Merry Macs—Cheri McKay and the McMichaels (Joe, Judd, and Ted); The Morin Sisters and The Ranch Boys—Marge Morin, Pauline Morin, Evelyn Morin, Jack Ross, Hubert "Shorty" Carson, and Joe "Curley" Bradley
Vocalists: Jack Owens (the Cruising Crooner, sang as he wandered through the audience), Janette Davis, Jack Baker (the Louisiana Lark), Johnny Johnston, Johnny Desmond, Clark Dennis, Dick Teela, Johnny Thompson, Edna O'Dell, Annette King, Eugenie Baird, Patsy Lee, Nancy Martin, Helen Jane Behlke, Evelyn Lynne, Mildred Stanley, Ilene Woods, Marion Mann; The Escorts and Betty—Betty Olson, Ted Claire, Cliff Petersen, Floyd Holm, Douglas Craig (accompanist and arranger)
Orchestra: Walter Blaufuss, Harry Kogen, Rex Maupin, Joe Gallichio, Eddie Ballantine
Announcers: Charles Irving, Don Dowd, Bob Brown, Durward Kirby, Bob McKee, Fred Kasper, Bob Murphy, Franklyn Ferguson, Louis Roen, Ken Nordine

---

Director: Cliff Petersen

Opening Theme:
Good morning, breakfast clubbers,
Good morning to yah.
We got up bright and early,
Just to how-dy-do yah.

Catch-phrase:
MCNEILL. Be good to yourself!
Daily Features:
The march around the breakfast table.
The morning prayer:
Each in his own words,
Each in his own way
For a world united in peace
Bow your heads, and let us pray.

The show was originally called *The Pepper Pot.* McNeill became the M.C. on June 23, 1933, and changed the title to *The Breakfast Club.*

Breakfast in Hollywood

Audience Participation

M.C.: Tom Breneman
Garry Moore
Jack McElroy
Announcers: John Nelson, Carl Webster Pierce
Producers: Charles Harrell, Ralph Hunter
Directors: Jessie Butcher, John Masterson, John Nelson, Claire Weidenaar, Carl Webster Pierce
Writers: Vance Colvig, Jack Turner

Tom Breneman of *Breakfast in Hollywood* carried on one of radio's familiar "friendly feuds" with Don

McNeill of *The Breakfast Club*. *Breakfast in Hollywood* was first heard over ABC in 1943.

Breen and DeRose

Music and Talk

Featuring: Peter DeRose, and May Singhi Breen (his wife)
Announcer: Don Lowe

This program was first heard over the Blue network in 1927, Tuesday nights at 10:30. In later years one of the features of the program was Peter's presentation of a fresh orchid to his wife. DeRose was the composer of "Deep Purple."

Brenda Curtis

Serial Drama

CAST:

Brenda Curtis	Vicki Vola
Jim Curtis	Hugh Marlowe
The mother-in-law	Agnes Moorehead

Also: Helen Choate, Michael Fitzmaurice

Brenda Curtis was first heard over CBS in 1939.

Brenthouse

Serial Drama

CAST:

Portia Brent	Georgia Backus
	Kathleen Fitz
Jane	Florence Baker
Nancy	Lurene Tuttle
Peter	Ernest Carlson
	Larry Nunn
Martha Young Dudley	Margaret Brayton
Lance Dudley	Wally Maher
Nora Mawson	Jane Morgan
Gabrielle Faure	Anne Stone
Daphne Royce	Naomi Stevens
Michael	Frederic MacKaye
Steve Dirk	Al Cameron
Dr. Norfolk	Gavin Gordon
Philip West	Ben Alexander
Joe Edwards	Edward Archer
Driz Gump	Grant Bayliss
Jay	Jack Zoller

Brenthouse was first heard over the Blue network in 1938.

Brewster Boy: see *That Brewster Boy*.

Bride and Groom

Audience Participation

M.C.: John Nelson
Announcer: Jack McElroy
Directors: John Nelson, John Reddy, Edward Feldman, John Masterson
Writer: John Reddy

Weddings were actually performed on *Bride and Groom*, which was first heard over ABC in 1945. The couples taking part in the ceremonies were showered with gifts.

Bright Horizon

Serial Drama

CAST:

Michael West	Joe Julian

	Richard Kollmar
Carol West	Sammie Hill
	Joan Alexander
Ruth Wayne	Alice Frost
Bobby	Ronald Liss
Barbara	Renee Terry
Keith Richards	Lon Clark
Margaret Anderson McCarey	Lesley Woods
Charles McCarey	Dick Keith
Ted	Jackie Grimes
Cezar Benedict	Stefan Schnabel
Lily	Alice Goodkin
Mrs. Anderson	Irene Hubbard
Bonnie	Audrey Totter
Larry Halliday	Frank Lovejoy
Penny	Will Geer

Also: Santos Ortega, Sid Slon, Chester Stratton

Announcer: Marjorie Anderson

Directors: Henry Hull, Jr., Day Tuttle

Writers: John M. Young, Stuart Hawkins, Kathleen Norris

Organist: John Gart

Bright Horizon evolved from the Michael West character on *Big Sister.* The character of "Ruth Wayne," played by Alice Frost, was heard only on the initial broadcasts to help establish the story. *Bright Horizon* was first heard over CBS in August 1941.

The Brighter Day

Serial Drama

CAST:

Liz Dennis	Margaret Draper
	Grace Matthews
Richard Dennis (Poppa)	Bill Smith
Althea Dennis	Jay Meredith
Barbara (Bobby) Dennis	Lorna Lynn
Grayling Dennis	Billy Redfield
Patsy	Pat Hosley
Jerry	John Raby
Cliff Sebastian	John Larkin
French girl	Charlotte Manson
Sandra Talbot	Ann Hilary

Also: Bob Pollock, Paul McGrath, Joan Alexander, Dick Seff, Judith Lockser, Inge Adams, Joe Di Santis

Announcer: Bill Rogers

Producer: David Lesan

Directors: Ted Corday, Ed Wolfe, Arthur Hanna

Writers: Irna Phillips, Orin Tovrov

Musical Director: Bill Meeder

Sound Effects: Bill Brown, Jack Anderson

Opening:

ANNOUNCER. *The Brighter Day.* Our years are as the falling leaves . . . we live, we love, we dream . . . and then we go. But somehow we keep hoping, don't we, that our dreams come true on that Brighter Day.

This program was first heard over NBC in 1948. It took place in the town of "Three Rivers."

Bring 'Em Back Alive

Adventure

Starring: Frank Buck

Buck, of course, was the well-known animal handler and jungle adventurer.

Bringing Up Father

Situation Comedy

CAST:

Jiggs — Neil O'Malley, Mark Smith
Maggie — Agnes Moorehead
Nora, their daughter — Helen Shields, Joan Banks
Dinty Moore — Craig McDonnell

Bringing Up Father was based on the comic-strip characters created by George McManus.

Brownstone Theater

Drama

Leading roles: Jackson Beck, Gertrude Warner
Narrator: Clayton Hamilton

Director: Jock MacGregor
Musical Director: Sylvan Levin

Buck Rogers in the 25th Century

Science-Fiction Adventure

CAST:

Buck Rogers — Matt Crowley, Curtis Arnall, Carl Frank, John Larkin
Wilma Deering — Adele Ronson
Ardala Valmar, the villainess — Elaine Melchior
Dr. Huer — Edgar Stehli
Buddy — Ronald Liss
Black Barney — Jack Roseleigh, Joe Granby
Killer Kane — Bill Shelley, Dan Ocko, Arthur Vinton
Willie, Barney's child protégé — Junius Matthews, Walter Tetley

Also: Everett Sloane, Paul Stewart, Henry Gurvey, Dwight Weist, Walter Greaza, Fred Uttal, Walter Vaughn, Alice Frost, Vicki Vola, John Monks, Frank Readick, Eustace Wyatt
Announcers: Fred Uttal, Paul Douglas, Jack Johnstone

Producer-Writer-Director: Jack Johnstone
Writers: Joe A. Cross, Albert G. Miller, Dick Calkins

Opening:

SOUND. *Thunder roll on drum*

ANNOUNCER. (*With echo effect*). Buck Rogers in the Twenty-fifth Century!

This program was based on the popular comic strip created in 1929. The idea for the strip was conceived by syndicator John F. Dille, who selected Dick Calkins as the first artist and Phil Nowlan as the first author. Much that occurred on the show from 1931 to 1939 seemed fanciful at the time but eventually became plausible and even commonplace. "Dr. Huer" invented such things as the psychic restriction ray, the teleradioscope, the atomic disintegrator, the molecular expansor and contractor beams, radio transmission of power, force rays, ultrasonic death rays, robot rocket ships with "radio-vision" transmitters, the mechanical mole for burrowing deep into the earth, etc., etc.

Listeners could become "Solar Scouts" by responding to premium offers, and they could receive such items as "planetary maps" and sketches of the principal characters by sending in "two inches of the strip of tin that comes off a can of Cocomalt when you open it."

Bud Barton: see *The Barton Family*.

Buddy Rogers: see *Mary Pickford and Buddy Rogers*.

Bulldog Drummond

Mystery-Adventure

CAST:

Captain Hugh "Bulldog" Drummond
George Coulouris
Santos Ortega
Ned Wever

Denny, Drummond's assistant
Everett Sloane
Luis Van Rooten
Rod Hendrickson

Also: Agnes Moorehead, Paul Stewart, Ray Collins

Producer-Director: Himan Brown

Writers: Edward J. Adamson, Leonard Leslie, Jay Bennett, Allan E. Sloane

---

Opening:

SOUND. *Foghorn blasts . . . slow footsteps . . . gunshot . . . police whistle*

MUSIC. *Organ music up full and under . . .*

ANNOUNCER. Out of the fog . . . out of the night . . . and into his American adventures . . . comes . . . Bulldog Drummond!

Bulldog Drummond was first heard over Mutual in 1941.

Burbig's Syncopated History

Comedy

Host: Henry Burbig

Burns and Allen

Comedy

CAST:

Starring: George Burns and Gracie Allen, husband-and-wife comedy team

The Happy Postman — Mel Blanc
Tootsie Stagwell — Elvia Allman
Mrs. Billingsley — Margaret Brayton
Muriel — Sara Berner
Waldo — Dick Crenna
Herman, the duck — Clarence Nash

Also: Gale Gordon, Hans Conried, Henry Blair

Vocalists: Milton Watson, Tony Martin, Jimmy Cash, Dick Foran

Orchestra. Jacques Renard, Ray Noble, Paul Whiteman, Meredith Willson

Announcers: Ted Husing, Harry Von Zell, Jimmy Wallington, Bill Goodwin, Toby Reed

---

Directors: Ralph Levy, Al Kaye, Ed Gardner

Writers: Paul Henning, Keith Fowler, Harmon J. Alexander, Henry Garson, Aaron J. Ruben, Helen Gould Harvey, Hal Block, John P. Medbury
Theme: "Love Nest"

George Burns and Gracie Allen were among the many vaudevillians who attained great success in radio. George was essentially the straight man for Gracie's addled responses. Often, when their time was up or his patience exhausted, George would end their comedy routines with "Say good night, Gracie," which Gracie would cheerfully do. (See also *The Robert Burns Panatela Program.*)

One of the best-remembered characters on the program was "The Happy Postman," played by Mel Blanc, who was the antithesis of his description. Speaking in a voice just on the verge of tears, he spoke of cheerful things in a most depressing tone.

The Buster Brown Gang

Children

CAST:

Smilin' Ed	Ed McConnell
Buster Brown	Jerry Marin
Sounds of dog Tige	Bud Tollefson
Froggie	Ed McConnell

Also: June Foray, John Dehner, Lou Krugman, Marvin Miller, Bobby Ellis, Tommy Cook, Tommy Bernard, Billy Roy, Jimmy Ogg, Peter Rankin
Announcer: Arch Presby

Producer: Frank Ferrin
Writer-Director: Hobart Donovan

Catch-phrases:
BUSTER BROWN. I'm Buster Brown and I live in a shoe
This is my dog Tige, and he lives there too.
SMILIN' ED. Plunk your magic twanger, Froggie!

The Buster Brown Gang was also known as *The Buster Brown Show* and *The Smilin' Ed McConnell Show.* It was a revival of an earlier show called simply *Buster Brown* that had first appeared on radio over CBS in 1929. The sponsor of both programs was Buster Brown Shoes, which had acquired the use of the Buster Brown character from the comic strip by R. F. Outcault.

The Buster Brown Gang, featuring singer Ed McConnell, turned up on NBC in 1943 and was broadcast from Hollywood on Saturdays from 11:30 A.M. to 12:00 noon before an audience of hundreds of youngsters. McConnell played the piano, sang simple songs, and offered comedy sketches featuring such characters as "Froggie the Gremlin" and "Squeakie the Mouse." He then narrated a story that usually dealt with one of four heroes: "Baba"—an Arabian boy with a horse; "Ghangi"—a Hindu lad with an elephant named Teelah; "Little Fox"—an American Indian boy; and "Kulah," who had a "Jug-Genie." The four young heroes were played variously by Bobby Ellis, Tommy Cook, Tommy Bernard, Billy Roy, Jimmy Ogg, and Peter Rankin. Lou Merrill was the "Jug-Genie."

By Kathleen Norris

Serial Drama

CAST:

Kathleen Norris, narrator — Ethel Everett

Also: Helen Shields, Anne Teeman, Joan Banks, James Meighan, Irene Hubbard, House Jameson, Chester Stratton, Teresa Dale, Eleanor Audley, Nancy Sheridan, Ed Jerome, Jay Meredith

Announcer: Dwight Weist

Producers: Phillips H. Lord, May Bolhower

Director: Jay Hanna

This program was first heard over CBS in 1939 with adapted stories of Kathleen Norris. Among the best-remembered was "Mother," featuring Irene Hubbard in the title role.

C

Call the Police

Adventure

CAST:

Bill, the Police Captain — George Petrie

The girl assistant — Amzie Strickland

Police Sergeant — Robert Dryden

Producer-Director: John Cole

The Callahans

Music

Featuring: Ethel Owen, Jack Arthur

Orchestra: Van Alexander

Calling All Cars

Police Adventure

Opening:

ORCHESTRA. *Theme "A"*

FIRST VOICE. *Calling All Cars* . . . a copyrighted program . . . created by Rio Grande!

SOUND. *Motor running*

SECOND VOICE. Los Angeles Police calling all cars; attention all cars to broadcast two-five-four regarding a fire. Assist Fire Department arson squad in investigation. That is all. Rosenquist.

SOUND. *Motor and siren . . . build siren to peak . . . segue*

ORCHESTRA. *Theme "B"*

Calling All Detectives

Mystery

CAST:

Robin, the narrator	Vincent Pelletier
Neil Fowler	Frank Lovejoy
Toby	Owen Jordan

Listeners were awarded prizes for solving mysteries on *Calling All Detectives*.

Camel Caravan

Variety

This title was given to a number of programs sponsored by Camel cigarettes. Some were quiz shows (*The Bob Hawk Show*) and others were variety programs. *The Camel Comedy Caravan* in 1943, for instance, featured Freddie Rich's Orchestra, Connie Haines, Herb Shriner, and M.C. Jack Carson.

Probably the best remembered was a Camel Comedy Caravan series that was on the air in 1943. With the unlikely teaming of Jimmy Durante ("the Nose") and Garry Moore ("the Haircut"), a very successful comedy-variety program was born. This series featured many of the performers who appeared on *The Jimmy Durante Show*—announcer Howard Petrie, vocalist Georgia Gibbs, and Roy Bargy's Orchestra—but was really popular because of the chemistry between Durante and Moore, the former a knock-about word-mangling comedian and the latter a crew-cut literate humorist. Durante didn't understand Moore and nobody understood Durante!

One of the funniest weekly segments was Moore describing to Durante one of his various previous occupations, and Durante repeating the material in his garbled version. For instance, Moore would zip through, at top speed and without a mistake, "I used to work in Wauwatosa, Wisconsin, in the Water Works, as a reasonably reliable referee for the refrigerator repair wreckers, recluses, and renegade rum runners, Jimmy."

And, after a long breath, Durante would proceed to plow straight through to a strangled finish—hitting about every third word vaguely correctly. Moore's ability was all the more remarkable since as a youth he had had to overcome a rather bad case of stuttering.

Other features of the Durante-Moore *Camel Caravan* were the standard opening in which Jimmy called in to Moore from some remote location from which he couldn't seem to extricate himself; a Garry Moore "song"—Garry would start singing a quiet ballad, stop to tell a story of a tragic love affair that ended in violence, then pick up softly the last few bars of the ballad; and Durante's standards, such as "Inka-Dinka-Doo" and "You Gotta Start Off Each Day with a Song."

Durante and Moore were also sponsored for a time by Rexall. (See also *The Jimmy Durante Show; Take It or Leave It; Club Matinee; The Bob Hawk Show.*)

Campbell Playhouse

Drama

This drama series featured radio adaptations of famous books. Orson Welles supervised the adaptations, which included: *A Farewell to Arms* by Ernest Hemingway, starring Katharine Hepburn; *The Glass Key* by Dashiell Hammett; *Arrowsmith* by Sinclair Lewis; *State Fair* by Philip Duffield Stong, starring "Amos 'n' Andy" (played by Freeman Gosden and Charles Correll) and Burgess Meredith.

This program was sponsored by Campbell's Soup and was first heard over CBS in 1939.

Can You Top This?

Comedy Panel

Joke-teller: Peter Donald
Host: Ward Wilson
Panel: "Senator" Ed Ford, Harry Hershfield, Joe Laurie, Jr.
Announcer: Charles Stark
Directors: Alan Dingwall, Jay Clark, Roger Bower

Opening:

SOUND. *Audience laughter up full and under . . .*

STARK. *Can You Top This?!* Welcome to another laugh-hour, half-hour with *Can You Top This?* . . . starring . . . Senator Ford . . .

FORD. Good evening!

STARK. Harry Hershfield . . .

HERSHFIELD. Howdy!

STARK. Joe Laurie, Jr. . . .

LAURIE. Hel-lo!

STARK. And now, here's your master of ceremonies for *Can You Top This?*, Ward Wilson.

WILSON. Thank you, Charles Stark. *Can You Top This?* is unrehearsed and spontaneous, and our top rule is "keep 'em laughing." Anyone can send in a joke, and if your joke is told by our storytelling genius, Peter Donald, you get ten dollars. Each of the three wits tries to top it with another joke on the same subject. Each time they fail to top you, you get five dollars . . . so you have a chance to win as much as twenty-five dollars. But regardless of whether you win ten or twenty-five dollars, you will receive a recording of Peter Donald telling your story on the air. Laughs are registered on the *Can You Top This?* Laugh-Meter in full view of our studio audience, and, in all cases, the decision of our judges is final.

Closing:

WILSON. And thus ends another laugh session of *Can You Top This?*, originated by Senator Ford. Join us again next week . . . same time, same gang, other jokes, some new, some old. Until then, we remain yours for bigger and better laughs . . .

FORD. Senator Ford . . .

HERSHFIELD. Harry Hershfield . . .

LAURIE. Joe Laurie, Jr. . . .

DONALD. Peter Donald . . .

WILSON. Ward Wilson . . .

STARK. And Charles Stark. This is the Mutual Broadcasting System.

Can You Top This? was first heard over Mutual in 1940. The "Laugh-Meter" (also known as "the Colgate Laugh-Meter") was simply a volume-measuring meter connected to the audience microphone.

Senator Ford used "Ditsy Bomwortle" and "Mrs. Fafoofnick" as the central characters of his stories. Ford's actual name was Edward M. Ford. He became "Senator" in his early twenties when he was mistakenly introduced as "Senator Ford" at a club dinner.

Candid Microphone

Audience Participation

M.C.: Allen Funt, Raymond Edward Johnson
Director: Joseph Graham

Candid Microphone was first heard over ABC in 1947. People's conversations were recorded with hidden microphones. The subjects were not aware that they were being recorded for broadcast.

The Canovas

Music

Featuring: The Canovas

The Canovas—Judy, her sister Annie, and their brother Zeke—presented programs of hillbilly music. Later Judy became a major radio star on her own. (See also *The Judy Canova Show.*)

The Capitol Family Hour: see *The Family Hour.*

Captain Diamond: see *The Adventures of Captain Diamond.*

Captain Flagg and Sergeant Quirt

Situation Comedy

CAST:

Captain Flagg	Victor McLaglen
	William Gargan
Sergeant Quirt	Edmund Lowe

This program was based on Maxwell Anderson's play *What Price Glory?*. It was first heard over the Blue network in 1941.

Captain Midnight

Adventure Serial

CAST:

Captain Midnight	Ed Prentiss
	Bill Bouchey
	Paul Barnes
Joyce Ryan	Angeline Orr
	Marilou Neumayer
Chuck Ramsey	Bill Rose
	Jack Bivens
	Johnny Coons
Ichabod (Ichy) Mudd	Hugh Studebaker
	Art Hern
	Sherman Marks
Ivan Shark	Boris Aplon
Fury Shark (Ivan's daughter)	Rene Rodier
	Sharon Grainger

Gardo — Earl George
Rogart — Marvin Miller
Dr. Glazer — Maurice Copeland
SS-11 — Olan Soule
Captain Einman (Nazi) — Marvin Miller

Announcers: Pierre André, Don Gordon

Directors: Kirby Hawkes, Russell Young, Alan Wallace

Opening:

SOUND. *Gong tolling midnight . . . airplane . . . swooping down*

ANNOUNCER. Cap . . . tain . . . Mid . . . night!

"Captain Midnight's" cohorts were members of "The Secret Squadron." The series was first heard over Mutual in 1940 from Chicago.

Captain Tim Healy's Stamp Club

Children's Program

Featuring: Tim Healy

This fifteen-minute program was first heard over NBC in 1938. It featured news of stamps for young collectors and was heard at 5:15 p.m. on Tuesday, Thursday, and Saturday. It was sponsored by Ivory Soap.

Carl Carmer

Folklore

Featuring: Carl Carmer

Carl Carmer, a collector of folklore, related fascinating stories on this series.

Carlton Fredericks: see *Living Should Be Fun.*

The Carnation Contented Hour

Music

Featuring: Percy Faith's Orchestra
With: Buddy Clark, vocalist; Reinhold Schmidt, bass; Josephine Antoine, soprano
Announcer: Vincent Pelletier
Producers: Harry K. Gilman, C. H. Cottington
Theme: "Contented"

This long-running music program was sponsored by the Carnation Milk Company. It first appeared over NBC in 1931.

Carol Kennedy's Romance

Serial Drama

CAST:

Carol Kennedy — Gretchen Davidson
Kathy Prentice — Mitzi Gould
Gary Crandall — Gene Morgan
Peter Clarke — Edwin Jerome
Randy — Elliott Reid
Dr. Owen Craig — Carleton Young

Carol Kennedy's Romance was first heard over CBS in 1937.

The Carters of Elm Street

Serial Drama

CAST:

Mr. Carter — Vic Smith

Mrs. Carter — Virginia Payne
Mildred Carter Randolph — Ginger Jones
Jess Carter — Billy Rose
Bernice Carter — Ann Russell
Sid Randolph — Herb Nelson
Mattie Belle — Harriette Widmer

Writer: Mona Kent

The Carters of Elm Street made its debut over NBC in 1939, originating in Chicago.

The Case Book of Gregory Hood

Mystery

CAST:

Gregory Hood — Gale Gordon
Elliott Lewis
Jackson Beck
Paul McGrath
Martin Gabel
George Petrie
Sandy — Bill Johnstone
Also: John McGovern, Art Carney, Kathleen Cordell

Producer: Frank Cooper
Directors: Martin Andrews, Ray Buffum, Lee Bolen
Writers: Anthony Boucher, Dennis Green, Ray Buffum
Sound Effects: Art Sorrance

Casey, Crime Photographer

Adventure

CAST:

Casey — Staats Cotsworth
Ann Williams — Alice Reinheart
Betty Furness
Jone Allison
Lesley Woods
Jan Miner
Ethelbert, the bartender — John Gibson
Police Captain Logan — Jackson Beck
Bernard Lenrow
Also: Jack Hartley, John Griggs, Bryna Raeburn, Art Carney, Robert Dryden
Orchestra: Archie Bleyer
Announcer: Bob Hite

Director: John Dietz
Writers: Alonzo Deen Cole, Harry and Gail Ingram, Milton J. Kramer
Sound Effects: Art Strand, Jerry McCarthy
Pianists: Herman Chittison, Teddy Wilson

Opening:
SOUND. *Double click of camera shutter.*
CASEY. Got it! Look for it in "The Morning Express"!

Casey, Crime Photographer was first heard over CBS in 1946.

The Cass Daley Show: see *The Fitch Bandwagon.*

The Catholic Hour: see *Religion.*

Cavalcade of America

Drama

Featuring: Jack Smart, Edwin Jerome, Agnes Moorehead, John McIntire, Jeanette Nolan, Bill Johnstone, Bill

Adams, Frank Readick, Raymond Edward Johnson, Paul Stewart, Orson Welles, Staats Cotsworth, Joseph Cotten, Ray Collins, Ted de Corsia, Ted Jewett, Everett Sloane, Luis Van Rooten
Orchestra: Donald Voorhees
Announcer: Clayton "Bud" Collyer
Producer: Roger Pryor
Directors: John Zoller, Paul Stewart, Homer Fickett, Bill Sweets
Historical Consultant: Dr. Frank Monaghan
Writers: Virginia Radcliffe, Stuart Hawkins, Ben Kagan, Peter Lyon, Arthur Miller, Paul Peters, Norman Rosten, Edith R. Sommer, Robert Tallman, Milton Wayne, Russ Hughes
Sound Effects: Bill Verdier, Jerry McGee, Al Scott
Organist: Rosa Rio

Cavalcade of America, sponsored by DuPont, presented dramatizations of American history. The program started over CBS in 1935.

The CBS Church of the Air: see *Religion.*

CBS Is There: see *You Are There.*

Central City

Drama

CAST:
Emily Olson — Elspeth Eric
Robert Shallenberger — Myron McCormick

Central City was first heard over NBC in 1938.

Challenge of the Yukon

Adventure

CAST:
Sergeant Preston — Jay Michael, Paul Sutton, Brace Beemer
Inspector — John Todd

Announcers: Bob Hite, Fred Foy
Creator: Fran Striker
Director: Al Hodge
Theme: "Donna Diana Overture" by von Reznicek.

These stories featured "Sergeant Preston" and his dog "Yukon King." The series began its run over ABC in 1947.

The Chamber Music Society of Lower Basin Street

Music and Satirical Commentary

Commentator: Milton Cross
Gene Hamilton ("Dr. Gino")
Featuring: Jack McCarthy as "Dr. Giacomo"
Vocalists: Diane Courtney, Dinah Shore, Jane Pickens, Lena Horne
Orchestras: Paul LaValle, Henry Levine
Also: Ernest Chappell, Jimmy Blair
Creator-Writer: Welbourn Kelley
Director: Tom Bennett
Writers: Jay Sommers, Jack McCarthy

The Chamber Music Society of Lower Basin Street, which made its debut over NBC Blue on February 11, 1940, featured swing music with a tongue-in-cheek commentary in the long-hair style. It was dedicated to "The Three B's—Barrelhouse, Boogie-Woogie, and the Blues." There were some fourteen musicians who doubled between such groups as Henry "Hot-Lips" Levine's Dixieland Octet ("the Barefoot Philharmonic") and Paul LaValle's Double Woodwind Quintet ("The Woodwindy Ten"). Henry Levine was also known as "The Gabriel of the Gowanus."

Among the guests who appeared on the program were the duo-piano team of Henry Brant and Richard Baldwin, who played the first swing treatment of Haydn's "Surprise Symphony"; and harpsichordist Sylvia Marlowe, who played Mozart's "Turkish March," retitled "Old Man Mozart on the Mooch."

Chance of a Lifetime

Quiz

M.C.: John Reed King
Director: Charles T. Harrell

This was first heard over ABC in 1949.

Chandu the Magician

Adventure

CAST:

Chandu	Jason Robards, Sr. Gayne Whitman Howard Hoffman Tom Collins

Also: Olan Soule, Margaret MacDonald, Cornelia Osgood, Audrey McGrath, Leon Janney, Ian Martin, Bryna Raeburn

Producer: Cyril Armbrister
Director: Blair Walliser
Writers: Sam Dann, Vera Oldham

Opening:

ANNOUNCER (*mysteriously*). Chandu . . . the Magician!

MUSIC. *Oriental music up full*

This series was based on material created by Harry A. Earnshaw. In the story, "Chandu" was actually an American secret agent, Frank Chandler, who picked up the ancient arts of the occult from a Hindu yogi and used the supernatural powers to combat evildoers. The series was first heard over ABC in 1949.

Chaplain Jim

Drama

CAST:

Chaplain Jim	John Lund Don MacLaughlin

Announcers: George Ansbro, Vinton Hayworth
Producers: Frank and Anne Hummert
Directors: Richard Leonard, Martha Atwell
Writer: Lawrence Klee

This World War II series was based on actual battle experiences. It began over ABC in 1942.

Charlie and Jessie

Comedy

CAST:

Charlie — Donald Cook
Jessie — Diane Bourbon
Florence Lake

Announcer: Nelson Case
Writer: Red Cooper

Charlie Chan

Mystery

CAST:

Charlie Chan — Walter Connolly
Ed Begley
Santos Ortega
Number One Son — Leon Janney
Announcer: Dorian St. George

Producer-Directors: Alfred Bester, Chick Vincent
Writers: Alfred Bester, John Cole, Judith Bublick, James Erthein

This mystery series featuring the Chinese detective was based on characters created by E. D. Biggers. Although many people associate only Ed Begley and Santos Ortega with the title role, it was Walter Connolly who played "Charlie Chan" when the series first came to radio over the Blue network in 1932.

Charlie McCarthy: see *The Edgar Bergen and Charlie McCarthy Show.*

Charlie Wild, Private Eye

Detective

CAST:

Charlie Wild — George Petrie
McCoy, Charlie's assistant — Peter Hobbs

Director: Carlo De Angelo

This series was the successor to *Sam Spade.*

The Charlotte Greenwood Show

Comedy-Variety

Starring: Charlotte Greenwood
Also: John Brown, Harry Bartell, Will Wright

The Chase and Sanborn Hour

Comedy-Variety

This program started as an all-music show in 1928. Chase and Sanborn hired Maurice Chevalier at the unheard-of price of $5000 a week to star on the show. Later Eddie Cantor took over the broadcast, and it became the top-rated radio program in the country for several years. Abbott K. Spencer was the director. The head writer was David Freedman with help from Bob Colwell, Phil Rapp, Everett Freeman, Carroll Carroll, Sam Moore, and many others. It was produced by the J. Walter Thompson

Company. When Cantor took time off in the summer, the show went on with other comedy stars, such as Jimmy Durante and Bert Lahr. It was finally taken over by Edgar Bergen. (See also *The Eddie Cantor Show; The Edgar Bergen and Charlie McCarthy Show.*)

Cheerio

Talk

Featuring: "Cheerio"

Talk shows were extremely popular in the early days of radio. Among the most listened-to personalities of the late 1920s and early 1930s was a talk-show host who identified himself only as "Cheerio." His name was actually Charles K. Field. The program was first heard over NBC in 1927, originally six times a week at 8:30 a.m.

The Chesterfield Supper Club

Music

Vocalists: Perry Como, Mary Ashworth, Don Cornell, Dick Edwards, Laura Leslie, Bill Lawrence, Kay Starr, Jo Stafford, Peggy Lee, Frankie Laine, The Fontane Sisters (Geri, Marge, and Bea), The Satisfiers (Art Lambert, Helen Carroll, Bob Lange, Kevin Gavin), The Pied Pipers, Fred Waring and His Pennsylvanians

Orchestras: Ted Steele, Sammy Kaye, Mitchell Ayres, Glenn Miller, Lloyd Schaefer, Paul Weston, Dave Barbour

Announcers: Paul Douglas, Martin Block, Tom Reddy

Producers: Bob Moss, Eldridge Packham

Directors: Ward Byron, Eldridge Packham

Writers: Frank Moore, Dave Harmon, Mike Dutton, Bob Weiskopf

Sound Effects: Sam Hubbard

Themes: "A Cigarette, Sweet Music and You," "Smoke Dreams"

One of the non-music segments of the program was the reading of the baseball scores. A high note was sounded by the orchestra following the score of the winning team, and a low, dismal note was played after the loser's score. If the victorious team scored an exceptional number of runs, the note was played with extra enthusiasm.

The Chicago Theatre of the Air

Variety

Featuring: Marion Claire (Mrs. Henry Weber), soprano
Colonel Robert McCormick

Resident Tenor: Attilio Baggiore

Resident Baritones: Bruce Foote, Earl Willkie

Resident Contralto: Ruth Slater

Guest Artists: James Melton, Thomas L. Thomas, Igor Gorin, Jan Peerce, Felix Knight, Allan Jones, John Brownlee, John Carter, Frederick Jagel, Richard Tucker, Robert Merrill

Dramatic Cast: Marvin Miller, Olan Soule, Betty Winkler, Laurette Fillbrandt, Willard Waterman, Norman Gottschalk, Luise Barclay, Alice Hill, Barbara Luddy, Betty Lou Gerson, Donna Reade, Fran Carlon, Patricia Dunlap, Muriel Bremner, Kay Westfall, Bret Morrison, Bob Bailey, Everett Clarke, Ken Griffin, Les Tremayne, Bob Jellison, John Larkin, Phil Lord, John Barclay, John Goldsworthy, Charles Penman, Hazel Dopheide, Rosemary Garbell, Marilou Neumayer, Rita Ascot

Announcers: John Weigle, Marvin Miller

Creator: William A. Bacher

Directors: Fritz Blocki, Joe Ainley, Kenneth W. MacGregor, Jack La-Frandre

Choral Director: Bob Trendler

Assistant Choral Director: Ray Charles

This long-running program was first heard over Mutual in 1940 and originated in the studios of WGN Chicago, which was owned and operated by the Chicago *Tribune*. In fact, the *Tribune's* slogan, "World's Greatest Newspaper," provided the call letters For WGN. *The Chicago Theatre of the Air* was a tremendously popular "live" program, and every Saturday night Chicagoans and tourists lined up for blocks to get in. It was eventually broadcast from the huge Shrine Auditorium in Chicago.

As the feature attraction, a musical comedy or "familiar" opera (*Carmen, Faust*) was performed with Marion Claire as the leading lady supported by Robert Merrill, Richard Tucker, Igor Gorin, etc. A dramatic cast doubled for the singers in the speaking parts.

One of the highlights of the weekly program was a talk by the publisher of the *Tribune*, Colonel Robert McCormick, who considered himself one of the world's leading authorities on the Civil War. Between the acts he gave a five-minute (or longer) lecture, frequently based on a celebrated military incident.

Chick Carter, Boy Detective

Detective

CAST:

Chick Carter (adopted son of detective Nick Carter) — Billy Lipton, Leon Janney

Sue — Jean McCoy, Joanne McCoy (Jean's sister)

Tex — Gilbert Mack

The Rattler — Stefan Schnabel

Rufus Lash — Bill Griffis

Director: Fritz Blocki

Writers: Fritz Blocki, Nancy Webb

Chicken Every Sunday

Situation Comedy

Featuring: Billie Burke, Harry Von Zell

The Children's Hour

Talent

Host: Milton Cross

Featuring: Rise Stevens, Ann Blyth, Peter Donald, Billy Halop, Florence Halop, Jimmy McCallion, The Mauch Twins (Bobby and Billy), Walter Tetley

This program featured many child actors who later became adult stars. It later became *Coast-to-Coast on a Bus* (which see, and also *The Horn and Hardart Children's Hour*).

A Christmas Carol

Christmas Special

Charles Dickens' *A Christmas Carol* was performed annually with Lionel Barrymore playing the role of "Ebenezer Scrooge." The distinguished actor was a member of a brilliant family of the theater. His brother John and his sister Ethel also appeared on many radio broadcasts.

Christopher Wells: see *The Adventures of Christopher Wells.*

Cimarron Tavern

Drama

CAST:

Joe Barton — Chester Stratton
Star Travis — Paul Conrad
Announcer: Bob Hite

Director: John Dietz
Writer: Felix Holt

Cimarron Tavern was first heard over CBS in 1945.

The Circle

Variety-Discussion

M.C.: Ronald Colman
Madeleine Carroll
Cary Grant
Carole Lombard
Groucho Marx
Basil Rathbone
Chico Marx
Director: Cal Kuhl
Writers: George Faulkner, Dick Mack, Carroll Carroll

Although *The Circle* ran only a few months, it became the most talked about failure in all radio. The concept was the forerunner of the discussion-panel-entertainment shows which many years later became popular on late-night television. The M.C. duties rotated among the all-star cast. They talked about current events, literature, drama; they acted, played music, told jokes. In short, it was way ahead of its day.

Circus Days

Drama

CAST:

Shoestring Charlie (circus owner) — Jack Roseleigh
General manager of circus — Walter Kinsella
Equestrienne — Betty Council
Trapeze artist — Bruce Evans
Lion-tamer — Henry Gurvey
Roustabouts — Frank Wilson, Ernest Whitman
Animal sounds — Brad Barker
Also: Griffin Grafts, Milton Herman, Wally Maher
Announcer: Ben Grauer

Director: Carlo De Angelo
Writer: Courtney Riley Cooper

Circus Days made its debut over NBC in 1933 and was sponsored by Scott's Emulsion.

Circus Night

Variety

Featuring: Joe Cook, comedian; Tim and Irene, comedy team
Singers: Lucy Monroe, Peg La Centra

Tim and Irene were Tim Ryan and Irene Noblette, a husband-and-wife team.

The Cisco Kid

Adventure

CAST:

The Cisco Kid	Jackson Beck
	Jack Mather
Pan Pancho	Louis Sorin
	Harry Lang
	Mel Blanc

Also: Marvin Miller
Announcers: Marvin Miller, Michael Rye (Rye Billsbury)
Directors: Jock MacGregor, Jeanne K. Harrison, Fred Levings
Writers: John Sinn, Ralph Rosenberg, Kenny Lyons
Sound Effects: Jack Dick

Opening:

THE CISCO KID. Of all the señoritas I have known . . . you are the most beautiful.
GIRL. Oh, Cisco!
MUSIC. *Up full*
[The opening was, at one time:]
PANCHO. Cisco, the sheriff and hees posse . . . they are comeeng closer.
THE CISCO KID. This way, Pancho. *Vamonos!*

The Cisco Kid was first heard over Mutual in 1943.

The Cities Service Concert

Music

Featuring: Jessica Dragonette, Lucille Manners, Ross Graham, Frank Banta and Milton Rettenberg (piano team), The Cavaliers Quartet, Rosario Bordon's Orchestra, Paul Lavalle's Band
Announcer: Ford Bond

The Cities Service Concert was one of network radio's earliest music programs, first heard over NBC in 1927. Many guests appeared on the program. For a time Grantland Rice turned up on the broadcasts during the football season.

City Desk

Drama

CAST:

Jack Winters	James Meighan
	Donald Briggs
	Chester Stratton
Linda Webster	Gertrude Warner
Caruso	Jimmy McCallion
Mrs. Cameron	Ethel Owen
Dan Tobin	Geoffrey Bryant

Directors: Kenneth W. MacGregor, Himan Brown
Writers: Frank Dahm, Frank Gould, Stuart Hawkins

City Desk was first heard over CBS in 1940.

Clara, Lu and Em

Serial Drama

CAST:

Clara — Louise Starkey
Lu (Lulu Casey) — Isabel Carothers
Em (Emma Krueger) — Helen King

Clara, Lu and Em was first heard over the Blue network in 1931 and originated in Chicago. It was one of radio's first serial dramas—the story of three gossips. The parts were later played by Fran Harris, Dorothy Day, and Harriet Allyn.

Claudia

Drama

CAST:

Claudia Naughton — Patricia Ryan, Katherine Bard
David Naughton — Richard Kollmar, Paul Crabtree
Mother — Jane Seymour
Mrs. Brown — Frances Starr

This program was also known as *Claudia and David.*

Cliché Club

Panel Quiz

Panel: Walter Kiernan, Edward Hill, Alice Rogers, Carol Lynn Gillmer, Frederick Lewis Allen
Announcer: Les Griffith

Clicquot Club Eskimos

Music

This program featured the music of Harry Reser, banjoist-orchestra leader. The theme, composed by Reser, was "The Clicquot March." Phil Carlin was the announcer. The program was first heard over NBC in 1926.

Cloak and Dagger

Drama

CAST:

The Hungarian Giant — Raymond Edward Johnson
Impy the Midget — Gilbert Mack

Director: Sherman Marks

Club Fifteen

Music

Host: Bob Crosby
Vocalists: Jo Stafford, Margaret Whiting, Patti Clayton, Evelyn Knight, Dick Haymes
Orchestras: Bob Crosby's Bobcats, Jerry Gray
Vocal groups: The Andrews Sisters (Patty, Maxene, and LaVerne), The Modernaires.
Announcer: Del Sharbutt
Directors: Cal Kuhl, Ace Ochs
Writers: Carroll Carroll, David Gregory

Club Matinee

Variety

Featuring: Garry Moore
Also: Ransom Sherman (who was also radio's "Hap Hazard"), Durward Kirby, Bill Short (bass player who spoke pure Brooklynese), The Three Romeos—Louie Perkins, Sam Cowling, Gil Jones
Vocalists: Johnny Johnston, Evelyn Lynne, Phil Shukin
Orchestra: Rex Maupin
Writer: Ransom Sherman

Club Matinee was first heard over the Blue network in 1937. One of the best-remembered features of this afternoon program was the famous out-of-tune orchestra that played such familiar selections as the "William Tell Overture" in an off-beat, off-key arrangement.

The Clyde Beatty Show

Drama

This program dramatized incidents in the life of animal-trainer Clyde Beatty.

Coast-to-Coast on a Bus

Children

CAST:

Conductor	Milton Cross
The Lady Next Door	Madge Tucker
Mumsy Pig	Audrey Egan

Also: Gwen Davies (Estelle Levy), Jackie Kelk, Susan Robinson, Niels Robinson, Lawrence Robinson, Carmina Cansino, Jean Harris, Diana Jean Donnenwirth, Edwin Bruce, Bill Lipton, Billy Redfield, Ronald Liss, Pam Prescott, Jeanne Elkins, Billy and Bobby Mauch, Ann Blyth, Michael O'Day, Renee and Joy Terry, Jimmy McCallion, Tommy Hughes, Donald Kelly, John Bates, Peter Fernandez, Bob Hastings, Laddie Seaman, Eddie Wragge, Joan Tetzel, Helen Holt

Producer-Director-Writer: Madge Tucker
Assistants to Miss Tucker: Ethel Hart, Hilda Norton
Director: Tom DeHuff
Musical Director: Walter Fleischer

This program was the successor to *The Children's Hour.* It opened with the sounding of a bus horn, then the opening voice (usually Michael O'Day, Ronald Liss, or Jackie Kelk) said, "The White Rabbit Line . . . Jumps Anywhere, Anytime." Then the children all sang the theme song, "On the Sunny Side of the Street." (See also *The Children's Hour.*)

Cobina Wright: see *Interviews.*

The Coke Club

Music

Featuring: Morton Downey, tenor
Hostess: Leah Ray
Orchestra: Jimmy Lytell
Vocalists: The Coke Club Quartet

Announcer: David Ross

Opening:

DOWNEY. *Whistles theme-opening bars*

ANNOUNCER. Yes, friends. It's time for another transcribed session of *The Coke Club* . . . which brings you the romantic voice of Morton Downey.

The Colgate Sports Newsreel Starring Bill Stern

Sports

Starring: Bill Stern
Announcer: Arthur Gary
Directors: Chuck Kebbe, Maurice Robinson, Joseph Mansfield
Writer: Mac Davis
Sound Effects: Chet Hill
Original Music: Murray Ross
Theme:

Bill Stern the Colgate shave-cream man is on the air
Bill Stern the Colgate shave-cream man with stories rare.
Take his advice and you'll look nice
Your face will feel as cool as ice
With Colgate Rapid shaving cream.

[or]

Bill Stern the Colgate shave-cream man is on the air
Bill Stern the Colgate shave-cream man with stories rare.
Take his advice and you'll look keen
You'll get a shave that's smooth and clean
You'll be a Colgate brushless fan.

Opening:

BILL STERN. Good evening, ladies and gentlemen. This is Bill Stern bringing you the 225th edition of the Colgate shave-cream Sports Newsreel . . . featuring strange and fantastic stories . . . some legend, some hearsay . . . but all so interesting we'd like to pass them along to you!

Closing:

BILL STERN. And that's our three-o mark for tonight!

This was one of the most successful and most listened to shows in radio history. Sportscaster Bill Stern dramatized events in the lives of sports heroes and also of people who were somehow related to sports. The stories were often capped by Stern's comments—"Portrait of an athlete!" or "Portrait of a man!"

The Sports Newsreel was on the air from September 1939 to June 1951 once a week and earned consistently high ratings. Stern was also famous for his coverage of countless sports events, including football bowl games, National Football League championships, tennis, golf, basketball, horse-racing, crew racing, hockey, track and field (including the 1936 Berlin Olympics and the 1948 London Olympics), fishing, bowling, skiing, rodeo, and boxing (including most of Joe Louis's title fights). He covered baseball, of course, though he never broadcast a World Series. (See also *Sportscasters.*)

College of Musical Knowledge: see *Kay Kyser's Kollege of Musical Knowledge.*

The Collier Hour

Variety

Editor: Jack Arthur
Arthur Hughes
Phil Barrison
Orchestra: Ernest LaPrade
Also: Bill Adams, John B. Kennedy, Joseph Bell
Producer: Malcolm LaPrade
Director: Colonel Davis

The Collier Hour, sponsored by *Collier's* magazine, was one of radio's earliest variety programs. It was first heard over the Blue network in 1927. One of the most popular segments was a serialization of *Fu Manchu*, based on the character created by Sax Rohmer. Arthur Hughes played the title role.

Columbia Presents Corwin

Drama

This drama series broadcast in 1944 presented various radio plays written, produced, and directed by Norman Corwin. Casts for some of the plays:

UNTITLED

Hank Peters — Fredric March
Mrs. Peters — Charme Allen
Music teacher — Hester Sondergaard
Editor — Kermit Murdock
Nazi — Michael Ingram
Also: Robert Dryden

EL CAPITAN AND THE CORPORAL

The Corporal, Cal — Joseph Julian
Betty — Katherine Locke
Fat Man — Kermit Murdock
Traveling Minnesinger — Burl Ives
Miriam Maizlish — Minerva Pious
Also: Robert Dryden

SAVAGE ENCOUNTER

Pilot — Carl Frank
Ara — Joan Alexander
Native — Arnold Moss
Prosecutor — Norman Corwin

YOU CAN DREAM, INC.

V.P. in Charge of Sales — John Griggs
Esthete — Ralph Bell
Minnie — Minerva Pious
Dad — Samuel Raskyn
Steve — Joseph Julian
Blonde — Ruth Gilbert
Robert Trout — Himself
Harry Marble — Himself

MOAT FARM MURDER

Dougal — Charles Laughton
Cecile — Elsa Lanchester

NEW YORK: A TAPESTRY FOR RADIO

Narrator — Martin Gabel
Orson Welles

THERE WILL BE TIME LATER

Soliloquist — House Jameson
Teacher — Hester Sondergaard

The Columbia Workshop

Drama

The Columbia Workshop, as its name implies, was a workshop for unknowns and for newcomers to radio. Many prominent actors were involved, as well as up-and-coming young performers, writers, directors, and producers. Among the writers whose works were featured were William Saroyan, Archibald MacLeish ("Fall of the City"), Lord Dunsany ("The Use of Man"), Irving Reis ("Meridian 7–1212"—Reis was also a founder of the Workshop), Wilbur Daniel Steele ("A Drink of Water"), Ambrose Bierce, Dorothy Parker ("Apartment to Let"), and Norman Corwin. Among the production personnel were Orson Welles, William N. Robson, Max Wylie, Douglas Coulter, and Davidson Taylor. The series made its debut over CBS in 1936.

Comedy and Comedians

Radio developed a unique form of comedy. In other entertainment forms the basis for most of the comedy effects were visual—a funny face, a physical move, a humorous setting. Radio comedy, however, was totally reliant upon words and mental pictures supplied by the listener's imagination. The listener, then, was not just a passive receptor but actually took an active role in developing the comedy.

Take, for instance, Fibber McGee's closet. In reality the sound-effects men simply dropped and rattled a lot of hardware and tin pans and then topped this off with a little tinkly bell. In the mind of the listener, however, Fibber actually opened the door of the hall closet at 79 Wistful Vista, and a ton of personal items—tennis rackets, golf clubs, cardboard cartons, raccoon coats, bicycles, etc.—cascaded out of the closet.

Consider, too, the fact that the character of Beulah, a Negro maid, was played originally by a white man. And how odd that ventriloquism, which depends upon a visual illusion for its basic effect, became a mainstay of several successful programs. The audience not only accepted these unconventional circumstances but through the use of "the theater of the mind" actually contributed to the final comedic result.

There were several types of comedians who became popular—ventriloquists, comedy actors, dialecticians, monologuists—and a majority of these came to radio from vaudeville. They developed lasting characters and styles, and even though many of them were already top vaudeville stars they found their greatest fame in radio. Among these were Jack Benny, Fred Allen, Burns and Allen, and Phil Baker. Benny, in particular, developed the "Jack Benny character" to such a degree that today, many years after radio, it is still instantly identifiable even to people who never heard him on radio.

Because of the necessity of entertaining an audience week after week, many comedy stars surrounded themselves with a stock company of superb supporting players, most of whom got the good comedy lines, which used the star as the butt of the jokes. This was a variation of the "stooge" technique common in vaudeville. Phil Baker had Beetle and Bottle; Phil Harris had Frankie Remley; Judy Canova had Pedro; Eddie Cantor had The Mad Russian; and Jack Benny had Rochester, Don Wilson, Mary, Dennis, and all the rest. In this way the star could go on forever while the stooges came and went.

Radio would not, on the surface, seem to be a particularly satisfactory medium for ventriloquists. After all, anyone who could alter his voice could simply do a program in a studio without using dummies and bill himself as a ventriloquist. Who would know whether he could actually throw his voice? Still, a number of ventriloquists achieved popularity on radio, with home audiences apparently trusting that the performers actually were skilled at their craft.

The most successful, however, was not necessarily the most skilled. Edgar Bergen was clearly the top-ranked ventriloquist of radio's Golden Age, but his dummy, "Charlie McCarthy," often kidded him about the fact that Bergen's lips moved perceptibly. Bergen's secret was in the excellence of the character development of his dummies—"Charlie McCarthy," "Mortimer Snerd," and "Effie Klinker"—and in the high quality of the scripts. Ranking just behind Bergen was Tommy Riggs, whose alter ego, "Betty Lou," was a major attraction. Other ventriloquists who appeared frequently on radio were Kay Carrol, with her dummy "Tommy"; Shirley Dinsdale with "Judy Splinters"; and Paul Winchell with "Jerry Mahoney."

Sometimes grouped with comedians, but really quite different, were the unique entertainers properly classified as humorists. Fred Allen certainly falls into this class although he is generally referred to as a comedian. Among other humorists who appeared from time to time were Robert Benchley, Irvin S. Cobb, Will Rogers, Herb Shriner, and Cal Tinney.

A number of outstanding comedians turned up as guests on different programs or were featured on programs that had brief runs—such performers as Morey Amsterdam; Joe E. Brown; Joe Cook; Stuart Erwin; Joe Frisco, the stuttering comedian; Harry Gibson, known as "Harry The Hipster"; George Givot, "the Greek Ambassador of Good Will"; Rube Goldberg, a newspaper cartoonist known for his amusing inventions; Jack Haley; Sir Harry Lauder, a Scottish entertainer; dialectician Lou Holtz; Tony Labriola, playing a character named Oswald whose catch-phrase was "Ooooh, yeah!"; Bert Lahr; Pinky Lee, known for his lisping speech; Lew Lehr ("Monkeys is duh cwaziest peepul!"), known as "Dribblepuss"; Jerry Lester; Robert Q. Lewis, who was a frequent substitute host on such programs as *Arthur Godfrey Time*; Jack Oakie; Georgie Price; Slapsie Maxey Rosenbloom, a former boxer; Phil Silvers; Ned Sparks, who played a sourpuss character; and dialectician Georgie Stone.

Among the top comediennes were Belle Baker, Gracie Fields, Beatrice Lillie, and Martha Raye, all of whom were singers as well.

Then, too, there were the comedy teams—Fishface and Figgsbottle (Elmore Vincent played Senator Frankenstein Fishface while Don Johnson was Professor Figgsbottle); Gaxton and Moore (Billy Gaxton and Victor Moore); blackface comics Honey Boy and Sassafras (Honey Boy was George Fields and Sassafras was Johnnie Welsh); Howard and Shelton (Tom Howard and George Shelton); Olsen and Johnson (Ole Olsen and Chick Johnson); Pick and Pat (Pick Malone and Pat Padgett); Potash and Perlmutter (Joe Greenwald played Abe Potash and Lew Welch played "Mawruss" Perlmutter); Sam 'n' Henry (played by Freeman Gosden and Charles Correll in the days before Amos 'n' Andy); Tony and Gus (Tony, the Italian, was played by Mario Chamlee and George Frame Brown played the part of Gus the Swede); The Two Black Crows (blackface comics played by the team of Moran and Mack—George Moran and Charlie Mack); Van and Schenck (Gus Van and Joe Schenck); Weber and Fields (Joe Weber and Lew Fields); Wheeler and Ladd (Bert Wheeler and Hank Ladd); and Wheeler and Woolsey (the same Bert Wheeler and Robert Woolsey).

In addition, there were the man-and-woman teams of Block and Sully (Jesse Block and Eve Sully); Carol Dee and Marty Kay; and the female duo of Nan and Maude (Nan Rae and Maude Davis, who were actually sisters Nan and Maude Clark).

Finally, there were three people in particular who we feel made a major contribution to comedy Americana during the heyday of radio. One was Fred Allen, whose wit and erudition crossed all lines to appeal equally to truck drivers and college professors. Another was writer Don Quinn, the genius behind *Fibber McGee and Molly*, who brought to all America a lasting friendship with a dozen or so characters in comic conflict who reflected the way we, too, would act in similar situations. The third was writer Paul Rhymer, whose bizarre and hilarious *Vic and Sade* ambled through many years of Midwestern life surrounded by "just folks," who complicated one another's lives by tracking mud through the living-room, going to washrag sales, and sending one another postcards from "exotic places" a few miles away. One way of judging the depth of an artist's work is to see if it stands the test of time. Any Fred Allen, *Fibber McGee*, or *Vic and Sade* broadcast preserved on tape is as hilarious today as it was then.

This is not to say that all of radio comedy was great. Many of the situation comedies, such as *Blondie* and *The Adventures of Ozzie and Harriet*, were as bland and time-filling as their counterparts on television. Nor was all radio comedy timeless. Most of Bob Hope's monologues were topical and therefore relatively meaningless today.

Much of the credit for the success of the comedians has to go to the writers who devised the characters, developed them, and sustained them through years of exposure. No matter how brilliant the performer, he could not have been so successful without a good script. We've already mentioned Paul Rhymer and Don Quinn as outstanding in their field, but probably the best comedy came, as now, from the combination writer-performer—Goodman Ace, Fred Allen, Ed "Archie" Gardner, Bob and Ray, Henry Morgan, and the like.

Comic Strips to Radio

Many popular comic strips served as the basis for successful radio programs with the leading characters transferred directly to the air. Often the same continuity was employed for the radio program's plot lines. Among them were *Blondie; Bringing Up Father; Buck Rogers in the 25th Century; Buster Brown; Dick Tracy; Don Winslow of the Navy; Flash Gordon; Gasoline Alley; The Gumps; Harold Teen; Joe Palooka; Jungle Jim; Li'l Abner; Little Orphan Annie; Major Hoople; Mandrake the Magician; Mark Trail; Mr. and Mrs.; The Nebbs; Popeye the Sailor; Red Ryder; Reg'lar Fellers; The Sad Sack; Skippy; Smilin' Jack; Superman; Terry and the Pirates; Tillie the Toiler;* and *The Timid Soul.*

Commercials

In the very early days of radio there were no commercials since most programs were presented as "a public service." But then the people who were supplying broadcast material—music publishers, artists, etc.—began to ease in low-key references to their companies or product. In bits and pieces advertising came to radio in such diverse forms as a lecture on the history of beards that ended with a few sentences about the joys of shaving with a safety razor (curiously enough invented by a man named Gillette), and with the introduction of orchestras like the A & P Gypsies and the Clicquot Club Eskimos. Probably the first fully sponsored program was *The Eveready Hour,* which made its debut in 1923.

As radio advertising grew and grew, sponsors became more interested in moving goods.

Much early advertising was "institutional"—designed to sell a company name rather than a specific product. This practice carried over through the Golden Age with such sponsors as Bell Telephone, United States Steel, Hallmark, Texaco, and Firestone.

The point of a commercial was to sell a specific product:

"Rush right down to your neighborhood drugstore and ask for . . ."

"Get some . . . TODAY!"

"Don't forget to put it on your shopping list."

Through constant repetition—"L.S./M.F.T., L.S./M.F.T.,* L.S./M.F.T."—or the use of celebrity testimonials or any one of a number of advertising gimmicks, radio proved to be a tremendous sales tool for the advertiser.

Sponsor identification, of course, was extremely important. The best way to achieve the highest percentage of sponsor identification was to integrate the commercials into the show's content, to involve the star in the commercial, to work the sponsor's name into the show's title, or for a sponsor to remain associated with one particular program or time-slot for a

* "L.S./M.F.T., L.S./M.F.T. Lucky Strike Means Fine Tobacco." This famous line was delivered over the click of a telegraph key. The announcer described the tobacco further: "So round, so firm, so fully packed. So free and easy on the draw."

long run. Among the sponsors who achieved the best sponsor identification over the years were Oxydol ("Oxydol's own Ma Perkins"); Wheaties (*Jack Armstrong*); Jell-O ("Jell-O again, this is Jack Benny"); Chase and Sanborn (Edgar Bergen and Charlie McCarthy); Lucky Strike (again Jack Benny); Campbell's Soup (*Amos 'n' Andy*); Rinso (again *Amos 'n' Andy*); Ipana ("For the smile of beauty") and Sal Hepatica ("For the smile of health"–Eddie Cantor); Ovaltine (*Little Orphan Annie*); Ralston ("Tom Mix and the Ralston Straight Shooters are on the air"); Pepsodent ("This is Bob 'Pepsodent' Hope, saying that if you brush your teeth with Pepsodent you'll have a smile so fair that even Crosby will tip his hair!"); Eversharp (*Take It or Leave It*); Kellogg's (*The Singing Lady*); Johnson Wax ("It's the Johnson Wax program, starring Fibber McGee and Molly"); Kraft ("Hi, this is Bing Crosby here in the old Kraft Music Hall"); Fitch Shampoo ("Laugh a while, let a song be your style, use Fitch Shampoo" on *The Fitch Bandwagon*); Mars candy (Doctor I.Q.); Campana Italian Balm (*The First Nighter*); H-O Oats (*Bobby Benson's Adventures*); Pall Mall (*The Big Story*); Colgate ("Bill Stern the Colgate shave-cream man is on the air . . ."); Coca-Cola (Morton Downey); Helbros watches (*Quick as a Flash*); Dr. Lyon's Tooth Powder (*Manhattan Merry-Go-Round*).

Sponsors who maneuvered their names into program titles included *The A & P Bandwagon, Maxwell House Showboat, The Fitch Bandwagon*, etc. Many newspapers balked at listing the programs by these titles since this constituted free advertising, so they simply put "Bandwagon" or "Showboat" or the name of the star.

A few curiosities of radio advertising included "Little Miss Bab-O," who was only known as such on-the-air but was in reality child star Mary Small; and the early singing duo, Ernie Hare and Billy Jones, who were known practically simultaneously as "The Tastyeast Jesters," "The Best Foods Boys," and "The Interwoven Pair" for various sponsors. There was a well-publicized law suit involving Tallulah Bankhead–when Prell Shampoo introduced their unbreakable plastic tube, they attempted to establish a commercial character, "I'm Tallulah, the tube of Prell." Miss Bankhead got a "cease and desist" order, claiming that she was the one and only Tallulah–and the courts agreed.

Probably the most famous "living trademark" was the shrill-voiced bellboy named "Johnny" who worked for Philip Morris cigarettes. To the tune of "On The Trail" from Ferde Grofé's "Grand Canyon Suite," Johnny would shout, "Call for Philip Mor-rees!" The part of Johnny was usually played by Johnny Roventini, occasionally by Freddy (Buddy) Douglas, both midgets. Pictures and life-size blow-ups of Johnny were prominently featured in cigar stores; on the radio Johnny was described as "stepping out of thousands of store windows across the country." It's alleged that one night in a restaurant when a waiter dropped a tray of glasses, Groucho Marx filled the silence by shouting, "That was Johnny you heard . . . stepping out of thousands of store windows across the country."

Listing all the catch-phrases and jingles identified with particular products over the years would be impossible, but here are some of the landmarks, highlights, and best-remembered ones:

THE PEPSI-COLA JINGLE

Pepsi-Cola hits the spot,
Twelve full ounces, that's a lot.
Twice as much for a nickel, too.
Pepsi-Cola is the drink for you.
Nickel, nickel, nickel, nickel,
Trickle, trickle, trickle, trickle. . . .

Composed by Austin Herbert Croom Croom-Johnson from an old English hunting song "D'ye Ken John Peel?" with lyrics written by Alan Bradley Kent (later just Alan Kent when he became an announcer). This was one of the earliest "singing commercials" on a national basis. It was written in 1939 for the now defunct Newell-Emmett advertising agency and was originally performed by a vocal trio called The Tune Twisters, comprised of Andy Love, Gene Lanham, and Bob Walker. Even though it has often been referred to as the first singing commercial, there had been several others prior to 1939, such as the one for Barbasol and the tunes sung by The Happiness Boys for their various sponsors.

SUPER SUDS

Super Suds, Super Suds,
Lots more suds with Super Suds.
Richer, longer lasting, too,
They're the suds with super-doo-oo-oo.

ADAM HATS

GIRL SINGER (Ginger Grey). I go for a man who wears an Adam Hat!
WHISTLE (Lanny Grey). Whee-whew!

RINSO

SOUND EFFECT. *Bird call . . . bob-white whistle twice* (whistled by Henry Boyd)
GIRL SINGER (*imitating*).
Rinso white!
Rinso bright!
Happy little washday song!

TIDE

Tide's in, dirt's out.
Tide's in, dirt's out.
Tide gets clothes cleaner than any soap.
T-I-D-E, Tide!

LUSTRE CREME SHAMPOO

(to the tune of "Toyland" by Victor Herbert)
(Sung by Ken Carson)
Dream girl, dream girl,
Beautiful Lustre Creme girl.
You owe your crowning glory to . . .
A Lustre Creme Shampoo.

HALO SHAMPOO

Halo, everybody, Halo.
Halo is the shampoo that glorifies your hair.
Halo, everybody, Halo.
So Halo shampoo, Halo!

LIFEBUOY SOAP

ANNOUNCER. Lifebuoy really stops . . .
FOGHORN EFFECT. *Beeeeeeee . . . ohhhhhhhhhhh!*

BROMO-SELTZER

SOLOVOX. (*Steam Locomotive Effect*). Bromo-Seltzer, Bromo-Seltzer, Bromo-Seltzer

. . .

DUZ SOAP

Duz . . . does everything!

PALL MALL CIGARETTES

FIRST ANNOUNCER (Ernest Chappell). Outstanding!

SECOND ANNOUNCER (Cy Harrice). And . . . they are mild.

IVORY SOAP

ANNOUNCER (often Nelson Case). Ivory soap . . . ninety-nine and forty-four one-hundredths per-cent pure. It floats.

ANACIN

ANNOUNCER. Anacin is like a doctor's prescription . . . that is, not just one but a combination of medically proven active ingredients. Perhaps your doctor or dentist has given you a few Anacin tablets to relieve headaches, neuritis, or neuralgia. That's Anacin . . . A-N-A-C-I-N . . . Anacin.

EVERSHARP

ANNOUNCER. The pen that's guaranteed not for years, not for life, but guaranteed *forever!*

DOAN'S PILLS

These commercials featured a dramatization of some homely situation involving a case of "nagging backache" such as Grandma's participation in a Virginia reel. Someone always recommended that she try Doan's Pills, at which point the announcer screamed: "Good advice!!!"

SCHICK INJECTOR RAZORS

ANNOUNCER.
Push, pull; click, click.
Change blades that quick.

WHIZ CANDY

ANNOUNCER. Wh-i-i-i-i-z-z-z-z! The best nickel candy there i-z-z-z-z-z-z!

VOICE. You can say that again!

ANNOUNCER. All right, I will! Wh-i-i-i-i-z-z-z-z! The best nickel candy there i-z-z-z-z-z!

BULOVA WATCHES

ANNOUNCER. The time is — o'clock, B-U-L-O-V-A, Bulova watch time.

ROYAL PUDDING

MALE SINGER.
Royal . . . Pudding.
Rich, rich, rich with flavor,
Smooth, smooth, smooth as silk
More food energy than sweet, fresh milk!

PABST BLUE RIBBON BEER

(The melody was freely adapted from the children's song "Ten Little Indians")

BARTENDER. What'll you *have?*

FIRST VOICE. Pabst Blue Ribbon!

BARTENDER. What'll *you* have?

SECOND VOICE. Pabst Blue Ribbon!

BARTENDER. *What'll* you have?

THIRD VOICE. Pabst Blue Ribbon!
CHORUS. Pabst Blue Ribbon Beer!

GEM RAZOR BLADES

SOUND. *Metronome up full then under and hold in BG . . .*
SOUND. *Tolling Clock*
DEEP, OMINOUS VOICE. Avoid . . .
SOUND. *Tolling Clock*
DEEP, OMINOUS VOICE. Five . . .
SOUND. *Tolling Clock*
DEEP, OMINOUS VOICE. O'clock . . .
SOUND. *Tolling Clock*
DEEP, OMINOUS VOICE. Shadow!
SOUND. *Tolling Clock*
ANNOUNCER. Use Gem Blades! Use Gem Blades! Use Gem Blades!

GILLETTE RAZOR BLADES

ANNOUNCER. Look sharp!
SOUND. *Prizefight bell*
ANNOUNCER. Feel sharp!
SOUND. *Prizefight bell*
ANNOUNCER. *Be* sharp!
SOUND. *Prizefight bell*
ANNOUNCER. Use Gillette Blue Blades . . . with the sharpest edges ever honed.

CAMEL CIGARETTES

CHORUS. C-am-el-s! [or] C-am-el-yes!

LAVA SOAP

BASS VOICE (to drum accompaniment). L-a-v-a.

CRISCO

ANNOUNCER.
Keep cookin' with Crisco.
It's all vegetable.
It's digestible.

LONGINES

ANNOUNCER (Frank Knight). Longines . . . the world's most honored watch.

See also *The Colgate Sports Newsreel Starring Bill Stern; The Fitch Bandwagon; Jack Armstrong, the All-American Boy; Little Orphan Annie; The Moylan Sisters; Olivio Santoro; Singin' Sam, the Barbasol Man.*

Community Sing

Music

Featuring: Billy Jones and Ernie Hare
Tommy Cecil Mack ("Who's excited??!!")
Milton Berle
Wendell Hall
Announcer: Paul Douglas

As the title implies, this was a program in which the studio audience was directed in community singing. Heard for a time from 9:00 to 9:45 p.m. on CBS on Sundays, the program often originated from two locations at once—Milton Berle and Wendell Hall directing a studio audience in New York, while Jones and Hare directed another one in Philadelphia.

Concert in Rhythm

Music

Featuring: Raymond Scott and His Orchestra

The Contented Hour: see *The Carnation Contented Hour.*

Corliss Archer: see *Meet Corliss Archer.*

Coronet Storyteller

Drama

Narrator and all voices: Marvin Miller
Announcer: Vic Perrin
Directors: Alan Fishburn (Chicago), Ted MacMurray (Hollywood)

Coronet Storyteller was a five-minute broadcast heard five nights a week on ABC from 1944 to 1947. It featured stories adapted from *Coronet* magazine, its original sponsor. Later it became a portion of an early-morning news program sponsored by Kellogg's. The stories were generally factual, but if a piece of fiction appeared in *Coronet,* it too might be adapted.

Correction, Please

Quiz

M.C.: Jim McWilliams

The Count of Monte Cristo

Adventure

CAST:
The Count of Monte Cristo — Carleton Young
René — Parley Baer

Director: Jaime Del Valle

Theme: "The Sylvia Ballet" by Delibes.

This program was based on the character created by Alexandre Dumas. It came to radio via Mutual in 1946.

Counterspy

Adventure

CAST:
David Harding, Counterspy — Don MacLaughlin
Peters, Harding's assistant — Mandel Kramer
Announcers: Bob Shepherd, Roger Krupp

Producer: Phillips H. Lord
Directors: Bill Sweets, Robert Steen, Victor Seydel, Marx Loeb, Leonard Bass
Writers: Phillips H. Lord, John Roeburt, Emile C. Tepperman, Jacqueline W. Trey, Arva Everitt, Peggy Lou Mayer, John Mole, Palmer Thompson, Stanley Niss, Edward J. Adamson, Milton J. Kramer, Morton Friedman

Counterspy was first heard over ABC in 1942.

The Country Doctor

Serial Drama

CAST:
The Country Doctor — Phillips H. Lord

This was first heard over NBC Blue in 1932.

County Fair

Audience Participation

M.C.: Win Elliot, Jack Bailey
Announcer: Lee Vines
Producer: Bill Gannett
Directors: William Gernannt, John Hines, Lenie Harper, Leonard Carlton, Carl Young
Writers: Martin Ragaway, Norman W. Hay, Ray Harvey, Peter Donald
Sound Effects: Al De Caprio

County Fair was first heard over CBS in 1945. It featured stunts and prizes, often with a "country" theme. One contest, for instance, had a young farm boy lifting a bull calf each week until he could no longer pick it up.

County Seat

Serial Drama

CAST:

Doc Hackett, the country druggist — Ray Collins
Jerry Whipple — Cliff Carpenter
Billy Moorehead — Jackie Jordan
Sarah Whipple — Charme Allen
Laura Paige — Lucille Meredith
Dr. Abernathy — Guy Repp
Dr. George Priestley — Luis Van Rooten

Director: Norman Corwin
Writer: Milton Geiger

This was first heard over CBS in 1938.

The Couple Next Door

Drama

Featuring: Olan Soule, Elinor Harriot, Jack Brinkley, Harold Vermilyea, Lillian Gish
Director: Kirby Hawkes

This Mutual program presented Olan Soule, Elinor Harriot, and Jack Brinkley when it originated in Chicago. Harold Vermilyea and Lillian Gish were in the New York cast.

The Court of Human Relations

Human Interest

CAST:

Judge — Percy Hemus
Court Clerk — Porter Hall
Allyn Joslyn
Brian Donlevy

Writer-Director: Bill Sweets

The Court of Human Relations was first heard over NBC in 1933 and was sponsored by *True Story* magazine. Many of radio's top performers appeared on the program at one time or another; Van Heflin made his radio debut on one of the broadcasts.

The Court of Missing Heirs

Human Interest

M.C.: Jim Waters
Also: Everett Sloane, Kenneth Del-

mar, Edwin Jerome, Jeanette Nolan, Carl Frank
Director: John Loveton
Organist: Rosa Rio

This program attempted to find the missing heirs to large and small fortunes. It was first heard over CBS in 1939.

Cowboys

Programs featuring cowboy entertainers were an important part of radio's Golden Age. Gene Autry and Roy Rogers (their horses were Champion and Trigger, respectively) both starred on popular radio shows. Another Western hero, Tom Mix, was the subject of a popular radio program but Mix did not appear himself. His part was taken by various actors. Other cowboy stars of the era were not so successful on radio but did appear on various broadcasts from time to time, among them Buck Jones and Johnny Mack Brown. (See also *Gene Autry's Melody Ranch; Roy Rogers; Tom Mix.*)

Crime Clues: see *Eno Crime Club.*

Crime Doctor

Drama

CAST:

Dr. Benjamin Ordway — Ray Collins
House Jameson
Everett Sloane
John McIntire
District Attorney Miller — Edgar Stehli
Harold Sayers — Walter Vaughn
Inspector Ross — Walter Greaza
Frieda and female "heavies" — Edith Arnold

Director: Paul Monroe
Writer: Max Marcin

Crime Doctor was first heard over CBS in 1940. Toward the end of each program the announcer would say: "Doctor Ordway will be back in exactly forty-seven seconds with the solution to tonight's case." Somehow the commercial always ran longer.

Crime Fighters

Adventure

Producer-Director: Wynn Wright
Writer: Paul Milton

Crime Fighters was first heard over Mutual in 1949.

Crime Photographer: see *Casey, Crime Photographer.*

Crossroads

Serial Drama

CAST:

Ann — Doris Kenyon

Crossword Quiz

Quiz

Host: Allen Prescott

Crumit and Sanderson: see *Frank Crumit and Julia Sanderson.*

The Cuckoo Hour

Comedy

CAST:

Ambrose J. Weems — Raymond Knight
Mrs. George T. Pennyfeather — Adelina Thomason
Also: Jack Arthur (singer), Mary McCoy (singer), Mary Hopple, Ward Wilson, Carl Matthews, Sallie Belle Cox
Orchestra: Robert Armbruster

Writer: Raymond Knight

Opening:

ANNOUNCER. Good evening, friends—and what of it? The next fifteen minutes are to be devoted to a broadcast of *The Cuckoo Hour,* radio's oldest network comedy program, and if you don't think that's something—well, maybe you're right. The Cuckoos feature Raymond Knight, the radio humorist, as station KUKU's Master of Ceremonies, and Ambrose J. Weems, and a lot of other disreputable characters. We now turn you over to station KUKU.

KNIGHT. Good evening, fellow pixies, this is Raymond Knight, the Voice of the Diaphragm e-nun-ciating.

Feature:

KNIGHT. There will be a brief pause, ladies and gentlemen, while we throw at you Mrs. Pennyfeather's Personal Service for Perturbed People, in which Mrs. George T. Pennyfeather brings to you her weekly talks on "The Home and What to Do with It."

The Cuckoo Hour was one of radio's first comedy programs. Raymond Knight wrote, produced, directed, and played in it from its inception on January 1, 1930, until 1938, when he "retired" to write plays. The program was originally broadcast on Wednesday nights at 9:30.

The Curt Massey and Martha Tilton Show

Music

Vocalists: Curt Massey and Martha Tilton
Announcer: Charles Lyon

This show was a fifteen-minute program of light songs broadcast over CBS and sponsored by Alka-Seltzer. Curt Massey played the violin occasionally in addition to vocalizing. Martha Tilton was often referred to as "Liltin' Martha Tilton."

Curtain Time

Drama

Starring: Harry Elders, Beryl Vaughn, Betty Winkler, Raymond Edward Johnson
Director: Norman Felton
Musical Director: Joseph Gallichio

Curtain Time was first heard over Mutual in 1938 on Fridays at 10 p.m. Later it turned up on NBC on Wednesday nights at 10:30.

D

Daddy and Rollo

Dialogue

CAST:

Daddy — Craig McDonnell
Rollo, the son — Georgie Ward
Donald Hughes

Dale Carnegie

Talk

Featuring: Dale Carnegie

In this series Dale Carnegie, the author of the best-selling book *How to Win Friends and Influence People,* served as an adviser on human relations.

Dan Harding's Wife

Serial Drama

CAST:

Mrs. Rhoda Harding (Dan's wife) — Isabel Randolph
Donna Harding — Loretta Poynton
Dean Harding — Merrill Fugit
Mrs. Graham — Judith Lowry
Arnie Topper — Carl Hanson
Eula Sherman — Margarette Shanna
Mr. Tiller — Cliff Soubier
Mr. Gorham — Cliff Soubier
Margot Gorham — Templeton Fox
Mabel Klooner — Templeton Fox
Fowler — Robert Griffin
Penny Latham — Alice Goodkin
Jack Garland — Willard Farnum
Stooge Lowe — Hugh Rowlands
Ralph Fraser — Herbert Nelson
Eva Foster — Tommye Birch
Rex Kramer — Herb Butterfield

Announcer: Les Griffith

Writer: Ken Robinson

This serial drama began over NBC in 1936 and originated in Chicago. "Dan Harding's wife" was a widow; therefore the character of "Dan Harding" was not in the story.

Dangerous Assignment

Adventure

CAST:

Steve Mitchell — Brian Donlevy

This half-hour adventure series was first heard over NBC in 1950, Saturday nights at 8:00.

Dangerous Paradise

Serial Drama

CAST:

Gail Brewster — Elsie Hitz
Dan Gentry — Nick Dawson

This was first heard over NBC Blue in 1933.

The Danny Kaye Show

Comedy-Variety

Starring: Danny Kaye
Featuring: Everett Sloane, Jim Backus, Butterfly McQueen, Goodman Ace, Everett Clark, Jane Cowl, Lionel Stander, Eve Arden, Joan Edwards, Rush Hughes
Mr. Average Radio Listener: Kenny Delmar
Orchestra: David Terry, Harry James and His Musicmakers, Lyn Murray, Harry Sosnik
Vocalists: Four Clubmen
Announcers: Dick Joy, Ken Niles
Director: Goodman Ace
Writers: Goodman Ace, Sylvia Fine

A Running Gag:
ACTOR. My brother-in-law is Irish.
KAYE. Oh, really?
ACTOR. No, O'Reilly.

The Danny Kaye Show was first heard over CBS in 1944.

A Date with Judy

Situation Comedy

CAST:

Judy Foster — Dellie Ellis, Louise Erickson, Ann Gillis
Mitzi — Louise Erickson
Randolph Foster, Judy's brother — Dix Davis
Oogie Pringle — Harry Harvey, Richard Crenna
Mr. Foster (Melvyn) — Stanley Farrar, John Brown
Mrs. Foster (Dora) — Myra Marsh, Lois Corbett
Edgar — Barry Mineah

Announcer: Marvin Miller (1949–50)
Director: Helen Mack
Writers: Aleen Leslie, Sidney H. Fields, David Victor
Sound Effects: Bob Holmes

A *Date with Judy* was first heard over NBC in 1943.

Dave Garroway: see *Reserved for Garroway*.

Davey Adams, Son of the Sea

Drama

Starring: Franklin Adams
Announcer: Olan Soule
Organist: Eddie House
Director: Courtenay Savage

David Harding, Counterspy: see *Counterspy*.

David Harum

Serial Drama

CAST:

David Harum — Wilmer Walter, Craig McDonnell, Cameron Prud'Homme
Susan Price Wells — Peggy Allenby, Gertrude Warner, Joan Tompkins
Aunt Polly — Charme Allen, Eva Condon

Charlie Cullom — Paul Stewart
James Benson — Bennett Kilpack
Zeke Swinney — Arthur Maitland
Brian Wells — Philip Reed
Donald Briggs
Ken Williams
Tess Terwilliger — Florence Lake
Lish Harum — William Shelley
John Lennox — Joe Curtin
Willy — Billy Redfield
Clarissa Oakley — Marjorie Davies
Claudia Morgan
Elsie Anderson — Ethel Everett
Grandpa — Junius Matthews
Mr. Finke — Ray Bramley
Henry Longacre — Richard McKay
Mark Carter — Paul Ford
Deacon Perkins — Roy Fant
Announcer: Ford Bond

Producers: Frank and Anne Hummert
Directors: Ed King, John Buckwalter, Martha Atwell, Arthur Hanna, Lester Vail
Writers: Noel B. Gerson, Johanna Johnston, John DeWitt, Charles J. Gussman, Mary W. Reeves, Peggy Blake
Theme: "Sunbonnet Sue" (hummed by Stanley Davis to his own guitar accompaniment)

"David Harum" was a banker in a small town. The series was first heard over NBC in 1936.

A Day in the Life of Dennis Day

Situation Comedy

CAST:
Dennis Day — Himself
Mildred Anderson — Betty Miles
Barbara Eiler
Mr. Anderson — Francis "Dink" Trout
Mrs. Anderson — Bea Benaderet
Mr. Willoughby — John Brown
Lustre Creme Shampoo Singer: Ken Carson

Producer-Director: Bill Harding
Director: Frank O'Connor
Writer: Frank Galen

A Day in the Life of Dennis Day, starring the talented tenor, comedian, and mimic, was first heard over NBC in 1946.

Deadline Drama

Drama

Featuring: Ireene Wicker, Joan Banks, Frank Lovejoy, Bob White
Director: Charles Martin
Organist: Rosa Rio

Listeners submitted twenty-word situations for which they were awarded United States Savings Bonds. The cast was given two minutes in which to improvise a story built around the situation; the dialogue was then adlibbed. The "Mystery Theme" was composed by Rosa Rio.

Dear John

Serial Drama

CAST:
Faith Chandler — Irene Rich
Noel Chandler — Ray Montgomery
Carol Chandler — Betty Moran

Violet Shane	Elaine Barrie
Josh Chandler	Norman Field
Michael Murry	Mel Ruick
Pamela	Dellie Ellis
Lynn Reed	Howard Duff
Poindexter Brice	Janet Beecher
Judge	J. Arthur Young
Jules Carlshorn	Gerald Mohr
Miles Novak	Tom Collins

Director: Bill Sweets

This program made its debut in 1933, sponsored by Welch's Grape Juice.

Dear Mom

Situation Comedy

CAST:

Private Homer Stubbs John Walsh
Corporal Red Foster Dolph Nelson
Sergeant Mike Monihan Marvin Miller
Private Ulysses Hink Lou Krugman
Also: Eloise Kummer, Leo Curley
Announcer: Tom Moore

Directors: Bob Brown, Phil Bowman

Dear Mom made its debut over CBS in 1941 and ran for one year as a twenty-five-minute, Sunday show sponsored by Wrigley. It related humorous incidents in a boot camp during the days of pre-World War II mobilization. "Stubbs" was a classic not-too-bright buck private who wrote of his experiences in his weekly letter home to his mother (hence the title). "Foster" was a perfect soldier. "Monihan" was a tough, roaring topkick. The program was dropped abruptly on December 7, 1941, and replaced two weeks later by a series called *The First Line.*

Death Valley Days

Western Adventure

CAST:

The Old Ranger Tim Daniel Frawley, George Rand, Harry Humphrey, John MacBryde
The Old Prospector Harvey Hays
The Lonesome Cowboy John White
Bobby Keen Edwin Bruce
Sheriff Mark Chase Robert Haag
Cassandra Drinkwater (Cousin Cassie) Olyn Landick (a man)
Also: Frank Butler, Milton Herman, Rosemarie Broncato, Helen Claire, Jack Arthur, Jean King, Geoffrey Bryant
Announcer: George Hicks
Orchestra: Joseph Bonime

Creator: Ruth Woodman
Producer: Dorothy McCann
Writers: Ruth Woodman, Ruth Adams Knight
Sound Effects: Bob Prescott, Keene Crockett
Original Music for Trumpet Call: Joseph Bonime

These Western adventures were first heard over the Blue network in September 1930. In 1944 the program's title was changed to *Death Valley Sheriff* and in 1945 to *The Sheriff* (which see).

Deems Taylor

Music Commentary

Featuring: Deems Taylor

Deems Taylor, a distinguished music commentator, critic, and composer, discussed music on this program.

The Dennis Day Show: see *A Day in the Life of Dennis Day.*

Detect and Collect

Quiz

M.C.: Fred Uttal and Wendy Barrie, Lew Lehr
Director: Walter Tibbals
Writer: Mildred Fenton

Detect and Collect was first heard over ABC in 1945.

Dial Dave Garroway: see *Reserved for Garroway.*

Dick Daring's Adventures

Adventure

CAST:

Dick Daring	Merrill Fugit
Coach Greatguy	Donald Briggs

The Dick Haymes Show

Music

Starring: Dick Haymes
Featuring: Cliff Arquette as "Mrs. Wilson"
Vocalists: Six Hits and a Miss (see *The Bob Hope Show*), Helen Forrest, Martha Tilton
Orchestra: Gordon Jenkins

Dick Steele, Boy Reporter

Adventure

CAST:

Dick Steele	Merrill Fugit

Dick Tracy

Adventure Serial

CAST:

Dick Tracy	Ned Wever (1940–45)
	Matt Crowley
	Barry Thomson
Junior Tracy	Andy Donnelly
	Jackie Kelk
Pat Patton	Walter Kinsella
Chief Brandon	Howard Smith
Tess Trueheart	Helen Lewis
Tania	Beatrice Pons

Also: John Griggs, Mercedes McCambridge, Craig McDonnell, Gil Mack, James Van Dyk, Ralph Bell
Announcers: Don Gardiner, George Gunn, Dan Seymour, Ed Herlihy

---

Directors: Mitchell Grayson, Charles Powers
Writers: Sidney Slon, John Wray

Opening:
ANNOUNCER. And now . . . Dick Tracy!
SOUND. *Radio code signals up full and under . . .*

TRACY. This is Dick Tracy on the case of ______. Stand by for action!

SOUND. *Departing car followed by siren wail*

TRACY. Let's go, men!

ANNOUNCER. Yes, it's Dick Tracy. Protector of law and order!

This adventure serial was based on the comic strip created by Chester Gould. It was first heard over Mutual in 1935.

Dimension X

Science Fiction

Featuring: Art Carney, Jack Grimes, Jack Lemmon, Santos Ortega, Norman Rose, Jackson Beck, Mandel Kramer, Peter Lazer, Joan Lazer, Larry Haines, Everett Sloane, Joan Alexander, Jan Miner, Claudia Morgan, Ralph Bell, Raymond Edward Johnson, Bryna Raeburn, Patricia Wheel, Joyce Gordon, Ronald Liss

Announcers: Bob Warren, Fred Collins

Directors: Danny Sutter, Ed King, Fred Weihe

Writers: Ray Bradbury, Earl Hamner, Jr.

Sound Effects: Sam Monroe, Agnew Horine

Dimension X, later known as *X Minus One*, was one of the first radio shows to be recorded on tape. Indeed, the technique was so primitive that one of the programs in the series, "Mars Is Heaven," had to be rerecorded three times because an NBC engineer, in the process of editing the show, erased the tape clean three times. As a result, the performers were all paid the original fee for each rerecording.

The Do Re Mi Program

Music

CAST:

Do	Ann Balthy
Re	Mabel Ross
Mi	Evelyn Ross

This singing trio, later known as The Bluebirds, was comprised of a blonde, a brunette, and a redhead.

Doc Barclay's Daughters

Serial Drama

CAST:

Doc Barclay	Bennett Kilpack
Connie Barclay	Elizabeth Reller
Mimi Barclay	Mildred Robin
Marge Barclay	Vivian Smolen
Clarabelle Higgins	Janice Gilbert
Tom Clark	Albert Hayes

Doc Barclay's Daughters was first heard over CBS in 1938.

Dodsworth

Serial Drama

CAST:

Sam Dodsworth	McKay Morris
Fran Dodsworth	Rosaline Greene

This program was based on the novel by Sinclair Lewis.

The Don Ameche Show

Variety

Starring: Don Ameche
Announcer: Marvin Miller
Directors: Carlton Alsop, Howard Wiley

The Don Ameche Show replaced *The Rudy Vallee Show* for Drene Shampoo on NBC in the summer of 1946. It went off the air in 1947. The program was built around dramatic sketches starring Don Ameche.

Don Winslow of the Navy

Adventure

CAST:

Don Winslow	Bob Guilbert
	Raymond Edward Johnson
Red Pennington	Edward Davison
	John Gibson
Mercedes Colby	Betty Lou Gerson
	Lenore Kingston
Lotus	Betty Ito
Misty	Ruth Barth

Director: Ray Kremer
Writers: Al Barker, Albert Aley
Theme: "Columbia, the Gem of the Ocean"
Sound Effects: Ray Kremer

This series was based on the comic strip by Frank Martinek and was first heard over the Blue network in 1937. It originated in Chicago.

Dorothy Dix on the Air

Advice

Featuring: Barbara Winthrop as "Dorothy Dix"
Director: Perry Lafferty

Dorothy Gordon

Dorothy Gordon had one of the most distinguished careers of any woman in radio. She was in charge of the first radio program for children, which was carried over WEAF New York in 1924. She also directed music programs for *The American School of the Air,* served as hostess of *Yesterday's Children,* and moderated *The New York Times Youth Forum.* The Youth Forum, which had its première in April 1943, was a weekly broadcast over WQXR New York. Children from various schools chose their own representatives as panel members. Originally the panelists were nine to eleven years of age; later, older children and college students served as panelists. The programs were recorded, and study outlines were supplied to schools. Many outstanding adults appeared on the programs—among them, Fannie Hurst, Dwight D. Eisenhower, Norman Thomas, William O. Douglas, Dr. Ralph Bunche, and Robert M. Hutchins. (See also *Yesterday's Children.*)

The Dorothy Lamour Program

Variety

Starring: Dorothy Lamour

This series featured the glamorous Hollywood star, who became famous for her roles in the series of "Road" pictures with Bob Hope and Bing Crosby (*Road to Singapore, Road to Zanzibar, Road to Morocco,* etc.). Through her film appearances she helped popularize the sarong.

Dot and Will

Serial Drama

CAST:

Dot Horton	Florence Freeman
Will Horton	James Meighan
Dulcy	Helene Dumas
Roger	Allyn Joslyn
Mother Horton	Irene Hubbard
Prof. Knapp	Ralph Locke
Marietta	Nora Stirling
Pete Sloan	Sidney Smith
Mother Aldridge	Effie Lawrence Palmer
Madge	Rosemary De Camp
Julia	Peggy Allenby
Corinne	Nora Stirling
Rosie	Agnes Moorehead

Double or Nothing

Quiz

M.C.: Walter Compton
Todd Russell
Walter O'Keefe
John Reed King
Announcer: Fred Cole
Producer: Diana Bourbon
Directors: Harry Spears, John Wellington, Thomas F. Vietor, Jr.
Writers: Gerald Rice, Harry Bailey, Carroll Carroll
Theme: "Three Little Words"

Contestants could stop and take the money they had already won or take a chance and try to double it. But contestants could lose the money they had already earned. The program began over Mutual in 1940 and was sponsored by Feen-a-mint.

Doubles: see *Animal Imitators, Baby Criers, Doubles, Mimics, and Screamers.*

Dr. Christian

Drama

CAST:

Dr. Paul Christian	Jean Hersholt
Judy Price, nurse	Lurene Tuttle
	Helen Claire
	Rosemary De Camp
	Kathleen Fitz (occasional substitute for Rosemary De Camp)

Announcer: Art Gilmore

Directors: Neil Reagan, Florence Ortman
Writer: Ruth Adams Knight
Sound Effects: Clark Casey
Theme: "Rainbow on the River"

Opening:
SOUND. *Telephone ring*
JUDY (*answering*). Dr. Christian's office.

This program made its debut over CBS in 1937. In later years listeners were invited to write scripts for the series. The announcer called the program "the only show in radio where the audience writes the scripts." As much as $2000 could be won in this competition for "The Dr. Christian Award."

The series was also known as *The Vaseline Program* after its long-time sponsor—Vaseline.

Dr. Dolittle

Drama for Children

Dr. Dolittle was a fifteen-minute children's program that started on the Blue network in 1932. It was heard at 5:15 p.m. twice a week. The series was based on the stories of Hugh Lofting.

Dr. I. Q.

Quiz

CAST:
Dr. I. Q., the Mental Banker:
Lew Valentine
Jimmy McClain
Stanley Vainrib
Announcer: Allan C. Anthony

Creator: Lee Segall
Directors: Harry Holcomb, Paul Dumont
Writer: Bob Schultz

Opening:

ANNOUNCER. Presenting Dr. I. Q.!

AUDIENCE. *Applause.*

ANNOUNCER. Mars Incorporated, makers of America's most enjoyable candy bars, bring you another half-hour of fun with your genial master of wit and information—Dr. I. Q., the Mental Banker! And now here is that wise man with the friendly smile and the cash for your correct answers . . . Dr. I. Q.!

AUDIENCE. *Applause.*

DR. I. Q. Thank you, thank you, Mr. Anthony. And good evening, ladies and gentlemen. My assistants are stationed throughout the audience with portable microphones which will enable members of the theater audience to remain in their seats while answering questions which I ask from the stage.

This quiz show, sponsored by Mars Incorporated, makers of Snickers, Milky Way, Three Musketeers, Forever Yours, and Mars bars, was broadcast from different cities where it played in a local theater. At the start of the program, Dr. I. Q. would introduce several announcers who were stationed in various parts of the theater with hand-held microphones. The announcers would select contestants in the audience, and frequently you would hear, "I have a lady in the balcony, Doctor." Then Dr. I. Q. would say, "I have ten silver dollars for that lady if she can tell me . . ." (The amount of money varied with the difficulty of the question.) Winning contestants were paid in silver dollars, and losers received a box of the sponsor's candy bars and "two tickets to next week's production here at Loew's Victoria!" Dr. I. Q. frequently told losing contestants, "Oh, I'm so sorry but I think you'll find the answer is . . ."

One of the regular features was "The Biographical Sketch," which was worth seventy-five silver dollars if the subject of the biography was identified correctly on the first clue. The prize diminished with each succeeding clue, but the amount not earned was added to the $250 awarded to the listener who submitted the clues. Thus a home listener could earn as much as $325. Another feature was "The Monument to Memory: the Thought Twister." A typical Thought Twister (which the good doctor cautioned he could say "one time and one time only") went like this:

"Jim is slim," said Tim to Kim.

"Jim *is* slim, Tim," to him said Kim.

The program was first heard over NBC in 1939 on Monday nights. Announcer Allan C. Anthony became well known for his ability to make the sponsor's candy bars sound so appetizing as he drooled over such words in the commercials as "nougat," "creamy," "chocolate" and "delicious."

Dr. I. Q. Jr.

Quiz

Quizmaster: Lew Valentine
Announcer: Allan C. Anthony
Director: Lew Valentine
Writer: E. Elam

This was the children's version of *Dr. I. Q.*

Dr. Kate

Serial Drama

CAST:

Dr. Kate Allen	Cornelia Burdick
Jack Halsey	Charles MacAllister
Sarah Tuttle	Helen Kleeb
Dr. Fred Crowley	Mont Maher

Writer: Hal Burdick

Dr. Kenrad's Unsolved Mysteries

Mystery

CAST:

Dr. Kenrad	Stanley Peyton

Dr. Susan: see *The Life and Love of Dr. Susan.*

Dragnet

Police Drama

CAST:

Joe Friday	Jack Webb
Sergeant Ben Romero	Barton Yarborough

Announcers: George Fenneman and Hal Gibney

Writers: James E. Moser, John Robinson, Frank Burt
Sound Effects: Bud Tollefson, Wayne Kenworthy
Theme: "Dragnet" by Walter Schumann

Catch-phrases:
FRIDAY. My name's Friday. I'm a cop. (*This was part of opening narration.*)
FRIDAY. Just the facts, ma'am.

Dragnet featured dramatized cases taken from the files of the Los Angeles Police Department. Police Chief William Parker was always acknowledged at the close. The announcers reminded listeners, "The story you have just heard is true. Only the names have been changed to protect the innocent." Then, following a commercial break, the results of a trial or a hearing in the case were given. The dramas were made all the more authentic by Friday's frequent references to the time—"Twelve-twenty-eight. We were working the day watch out of homicide"—and by the attention paid to the mundane details of police work in tracking down criminals. The program was also noted for its "natural" writing and acting and its frequent use of "punch-lines" at the end of each segment.

The program was first heard over NBC in 1949. The theme became known for its first four notes—dum-de-dum-dum—and was thoroughly parodied, a sure sign of success.

Dreft Star Playhouse

Serial Drama

Guest Stars: Gale Page, Rosemary De Camp, Les Tremayne, *et al.*
Announcers: Terry O'Sullivan, Marvin Miller
Directors: Les Mitchel, Axel Gruenberg

Dreft Star Playhouse was heard on NBC from 1944 to 1945. Using famous movie scripts, it attempted to accomplish in a five-times-a-week soap-opera format what *Lux Radio Theatre* had done in the night-time format. Each story ran from one to five weeks on *Dreft Star Playhouse.*

Duffy's Tavern

Comedy

CAST:

Archie, the manager — Ed Gardner
Miss Duffy — Shirley Booth, Florence Halop, Gloria Erlanger, Florence Robinson, Sandra Gould, Hazel Shermet
Clifton Finnegan — Charlie Cantor
Eddie, the waiter — Eddie Green
Clancy the cop — Alan Reed (Teddy Bergman)
Wilfred, Finnegan's kid brother — Dickie Van Patten
Dolly Snaffle — Lurene Tuttle
Vocalists: Benay Venuta, Tito Guizar, Bob Graham, Helen Ward
Orchestras: Joe Venuti, Reet Veet Reeves, Matty Malneck
Announcers: Jimmy Wallington, Marvin Miller, Jack Bailey, Perry Ward, Alan Reed (Teddy Bergman), Rod O'Connor
Also: Weekly Guest Stars

Directors: Tony Sanford, Rupert Lucas, Jack Roche, Mitchell Benson
Writers: Ed Gardner, Abe Burrows, Larry Marks, Lew Meltzer, Bill Manhoff, Raymond Ellis, Alan Kent, Ed Reynolds, Manny Sachs,

Norman Paul, Dick Martin, Vincent Bogert

Theme: "When Irish Eyes Are Smiling"
Opening:
MUSIC. *Theme up full, under . . .*
SOUND. *Telephone ringing, receiver pick-up*
ARCHIE. Hello. Duffy's Tavern, where the elite meet to eat. Archie, the manager, speaking. Duffy ain't here. Oh, hello, Duffy. . . .

The program, which made its debut in April 1941, was sponsored by Bristol-Myers (Trushay, Sal Hepatica, and Minit-Rub) and was heard for a time on Tuesday nights at 8:30 on NBC. It also appeared on NBC on Wednesday nights. The character of "Archie" was created by Ed Gardner and George Faulkner for a CBS show called *So This Is New York*, which lasted for a brief period on the air—just long enough for Gardner to develop "Archie" and decide after extensive auditions that he himself should play the role. In 1949 Gardner moved to Puerto Rico and transcribed *Duffy's Tavern* there to take advantage of a twelve-year tax holiday declared by the government to attract new industry to the island. Incidentally, "Duffy" never appeared on the program.

The Dunninger Show

Variety

Starring: Joseph Dunninger, The Master Mentalist
Featuring: Bill Slater, Marilyn Day, Andy Love's vocal group
Orchestra: Mitchell Ayres
Announcers: Don Lowe, Roger Krupp
Producer: George Wiest
Writer: Marjorie D. Sloane

Dunninger performed amazing stunts of "mind-reading" although he preferred to be called a "mentalist" and never claimed to be able to read minds. Dunninger said, "My feats could be done by a child of three—provided he knew how and had thirty years' experience!"

He made his radio debut over ABC on September 12, 1943, as *Dunninger, The Master Mind.* He was heard later over NBC for Lever Brothers.

E

East of Cairo

Adventure

Featuring: John McGovern, Tim Frawley, Bill Shelley, Harry Neville, Arthur Hughes
Director: Joseph Bell
Writer: Ray Scudder
Original music: Sven and Gene von Hallberg

Easy Aces

Comedy

CAST:

Goodman Ace	Himself
Jane Ace	Herself
Marge	Mary Hunter
Miss Thomas	Ann Thomas
Johnny	Paul Stewart
Cokey	Ken Roberts
Betty	Ethel Blume
Laura, the maid	Helene Dumas

Announcers: Ford Bond, Ken Roberts

Writer: Goodman Ace
Theme: "Manhattan Serenade"

Easy Aces, first on the air from Kansas City, Missouri, in 1930, moved to network in Chicago in 1931 and to New York in 1933, where it continued through 1945 as a fifteen-minute program. All the scripts were written by Goodman Ace.

It was a witty, urbane "domestic comedy," with Goodman Ace as the long-suffering husband of the slightly addled Jane. Jane's malapropisms were legendary—"You've got to take the bitter with the batter," "I'm really in a quarry," "This hang-nail expression," and "Up at the crank of dawn." To these and similar misuses of the English language Goody often replied, "Isn't that awful?" Jane often referred to her brother Paul who hadn't worked in twelve years "because he's waiting for the dollar to settle down."

The show was revived in 1948 in a weekly thirty-minute format under the title of *Mr. Ace and Jane.* The scripts were all based on the original fifteen-minute story lines but with revisions and added gags to accommodate a live audience's reaction.

Easy Does It

Music

M.C.: Ted Steele
Vocalists: Betty Randall, Kenny Gardner

Echoes of the Orient

Music

Echoes of the Orient began on WEAF New York on Sunday, June 30, 1929. The von Hallberg brothers, Sven and Gene, were featured performers as well as composers for the program. The show at first presented standard Greek, Turkish, and other Near East tunes; but in a few weeks most of the available material had been used up so the von Hallberg brothers contributed their own numbers, giving them fanciful Near East titles. The tunes had such an authentic flavor that requests poured in from people of Near East ancestry for information as to where they could purchase the music. However, the material was never published.

The Ed Sullivan Show

Variety

Host: Ed Sullivan, newspaper columnist

The Ed Sullivan Show began over CBS in 1931. Sullivan was then a columnist for the *New York Graphic*, which ceased publication in July 1932. Comedian Jack Benny made his professional radio debut on this show on May 2, 1931. The program has also been credited with marking the first radio appearances of Irving Berlin, Jack Pearl, George M. Cohan, and Flo Ziegfeld.

The Ed Wynn Show: see *The Fire Chief*; *The Texaco Star Theater*.

The Eddie Bracken Show

Situation Comedy

CAST:

Eddie Bracken	Himself
Mrs. Pringle	Ruth Perrott
Betty Mahoney	Shirley Booth

Also: William Demarest, Ann Rutherford, Janet Waldo

Announcer: John Wald

Producer: Mann Holiner

Director: Nat Wolff

Writer: Robert Riley Crutcher

Musical Director: Lee Harlin

The Eddie Bracken Show was first heard over CBS in 1946.

The Eddie Cantor Show

Comedy-Variety

Starring: Eddie Cantor

CAST:

The Mad Russian	Bert Gordon
Parkyakarkas	Harry Einstein
Rubinoff	Dave Rubinoff
	Lionel Stander
	Teddy Bergman
Mr. Guffy	Sidney Fields
Mademoiselle Fifi	Veola Vonn

With: Shirley Dinsdale, ventriloquist, and her dummy Judy Splinters; Nan Rae and Maude Davis, comedy duo; John Brown; Frank Nelson; The Sportsmen Quartet

Vocalists: Dinah Shore, Bobby Breen, Deanna Durbin, Margaret Whiting, Nora Martin

Orchestra: Cookie Fairchild, Louis Gress, George Stoll, Jacques Renard

Announcers: Jimmy Wallington, Harry Von Zell

Directors: Abbott K. Spencer, Vick Knight, Manning Ostroff

Writers: David Freedman, Bob Colwell, Phil Rapp, Carroll Carroll,

Barbara Hotchkiss, Matt Brooks, Eddie Davis, Ed Beloin, Izzy Elinson, Bobbie O'Brien, John Quillen, Everett Freeman, Sam Moore
Sound Effects: Cliff Thorsness

Theme: "One Hour with You"
I love to spend one hour with you,
As friend to friend, I'm sorry it's through.

Catch-phrases:
THE MAD RUSSIAN. How do you do?
THE MAD RUSSIAN. You min it?

Eddie Cantor was already an established vaudeville and Broadway star when he made his debut on radio on Rudy Vallee's program in February 1931. He started his own program in September of that year and continued for many years, under many sponsors, with one of the most popular comedy-variety programs on radio. He introduced many "protégés," such as Deanna Durbin, Dinah Shore, and Bobby Breen. He often joked about his wife Ida and their five daughters: Marjorie, Natalie, Edna, Marilyn, and Janet. He acquired the nickname "Banjo-Eyes" during his career on the musical stage and often made comedy references to his enormous eyes. Some of the songs he was famous for singing were "If You Knew Susie," "Makin' Whoopee," and "Now's the Time to Fall in Love."

Dave Rubinoff actually played the violin but his lines were spoken by Lionel Stander and later Teddy Bergman (who worked under the name Alan Reed after 1939).

The Eddie Cantor Show was also known as *The Chase and Sanborn Hour* and later *Time to Smile.*

The Edgar Bergen and Charlie McCarthy Show

Comedy-Variety

Starring: Edgar Bergen ventriloquist, and dummies Charlie McCarthy, Mortimer Snerd, and Effie Klinker
M.C.: Don Ameche

CAST:

Pasquale	Don Ameche
Ersel Twing	Pat Patrick
Charlie's principal	Norman Field
Vera Vague	Barbara Jo Allen
Professor Lemuel Carp	Richard Haydn
The Bickersons (John and Blanche)	Don Ameche and Frances Langford

Also: Eddie Mayehoff, Jim Backus, The Stroud Twins, Marsha Hunt
Guest Stars: George Raft, John Barrymore, Basil Rathbone, W. C. Fields, Nelson Eddy, Dorothy Lamour, Rosalind Russell, Barbara Stanwyck, Bob Burns, Rudy Vallee, Ethel Barrymore, Orson Welles, Jane Powell, *et al.*
Vocalists: Donald Dixon (baritone), Anita Ellis, Dale Evans, Anita Gordon
Orchestra: Robert Armbruster, Ray Noble

Announcers: Ken Carpenter, Ben Alexander, Bill Goodwin, Bill Baldwin
Director: Earl Ebi
Writers: Alan Smith, Robert Mosher, Zeno Klinker, Roland MacLane, Royal Foster, Joe Connelly, Dick Mack, Stanley Quinn, Joe Bigelow, Carroll Carroll

---

Catch-phrases:

CHARLIE. I'll clip ya! So help me, I'll mow ya down!

EDGAR. Mortimer, how can you be so stupid?

ERSEL TWING. Friends, and you are my friends. Friends . . .

This popular Sunday-evening program was also known as *The Chase and Sanborn Hour,* a reference to the show's long-standing sponsor, Chase and Sanborn. ("What Mr. Chase didn't know about coffee, Mr. Sanborn did!") Bergen and McCarthy joined *The Chase and Sanborn Hour* on NBC in 1936. "Charlie" was Bergen's principal dummy. He wore a monocle over his right eye and generally appeared in formal dress, including a top hat. He never seemed to run out of quips about pretty girls, his troubles in school, and his friend "Skinny Dugan." "Charlie" also persistently needled Bergen about the ventriloquist's lips moving during their act. "Mortimer" was a stupid, good-natured, buck-toothed character from the country. "Effie" was an unattractive old maid whose chief interest was in catching a man. "Charlie" and "Mortimer" appeared regularly on the program while "Effie" turned up occasionally. Coca-Cola took over sponsorship of the broadcast toward the end of its long run. (See also *Comedy and Comedians.*)

Editor's Daughter

Serial Drama

CAST:

Henry Foster	Parker Fennelly
Mary Foster	Joan Banks
Mrs. Foster	Effie Palmer

Directors: Martha Atwell, Jeanne K. Harrison

Edna Wallace Hopper: see *Women's Programs.*

Elder Michaux: see *Religion.*

Eleanor Howe's Homemaker's Exchange: see *Women's Programs.*

The Electric Hour

Music

Featuring: Nelson Eddy, baritone
Orchestra: Robert Armbruster
Announcer: Frank Graham

The Electric Hour, sponsored by the Electric Companies of America, was first heard over CBS in 1943.

Ellen Randolph

Serial Drama

CAST:

Ellen Randolph	Elsie Hitz
	Gertrude Warner
George Randolph	John McGovern
	Ted Jewett
Robert Randolph	Jackie Jordan
Ted Clayton	Macdonald Carey
Claire Clayton	Helene Dumas
Andy Barrett	Robert Regent
Mrs. Barrett	Fanny May Baldridge
Mr. Barrett	Milo Boulton
Rena Fletcher	Jay Meredith

Kathleen Conway	Colleen Ward
La Ling	Inge Adams
Amy Brown	Florida Friebus
Mark Hilton	Ken Daigneau
Skipper	Parker Fennelly
Dr. Lewis	Bernard Lenrow
Carl Richmond	Edward Trevor
Dakim	John McIntire
Peter Chang	George Wallach
Agnes Foy	Kathryn Bishop
Jerome Brooks	Bart Robinson
Dr. Keith	Maurice Franklin
Mrs. Matthews	Effie Palmer
Nadine	Eloise Ellis
Vince Kennedy	Walter Burke

Director: Carlo De Angelo
Writer: Margaret Sangster

Ellen Randolph came to radio over NBC in 1939.

Ellery Queen

Detective

CAST:

Ellery Queen — Hugh Marlowe, Larry Dobkin, Carleton Young, Sidney Smith
Inspector Queen, his father — Bill Smith, Santos Ortega
Nikki, Ellery's assistant — Marion Shockley, Barbara Terrell, Virginia Gregg, Charlotte Keane, Gertrude Warner
Sergeant Velie — Howard Smith, Ted de Corsia, Ed Latimer

Announcer: Roger Krupp

Directors: Phil Cohan, William P. Rousseau, Robert S. Steele, George Zachary

This program was based on characters created by Frederic Dannay and Manfred Bennington Lee. One of the program's features was "The Armchair Detective." A guest celebrity would serve as an armchair detective and try to guess the solution of the mystery just before Ellery Queen revealed the actual answer. The series made its debut over CBS in 1939.

Elsie Beebe: see *Life Can Be Beautiful*.

Emily Post: see *Women's Programs*.

Eno Crime Club

Mystery-Adventure

CAST:

Spencer Dean, manhunter — Edward Reese, Clyde North
Dan Cassidy — Jack MacBryde
Jane Elliott — Helen Choate
Also: Adele Ronson, Gloria Holden, Ralph Sumpter, Georgia Backus, Elaine Melchior, Helene Dumas, Ray Collins, Ruth Yorke, Brian Donlevy

Writers: Stewart Sterling, Albert G. Miller

Eno Crime Club was first heard over CBS in 1931. It was later known as *Crime Clues*.

Escape

Drama

Narrator: William Conrad
Paul Frees
Producer-Director: William N. Robson, Norman Macdonnell
Director: Richard Sanville
Sound Effects: Bill Gould, Cliff Thorsness

Theme: "Night on Bald Mountain" by Moussorgsky
Opening:
NARRATOR. Tired of the everyday routine? Ever dream of romantic adventure in a far-off land? Want to get away from it all? We offer you . . . *Escape!*
MUSIC. *Theme up full*

[or]

NARRATOR. Tired of the everyday grind? Ever dream of a life of romantic adventure? Want to get away from it all? We offer you . . .
MUSIC. *Dramatic chord*
NARRATOR. *Escape!*
MUSIC. *Dramatic chords*
ANNOUNCER. *Escape!* . . . designed to free you from the four walls of today for a half-hour of high adventure.
MUSIC. *Theme up full*

Escape was one of the last of the great half-hour horror-adventure series. Among the best-remembered programs was "Three Skeleton Key," a story of three men trapped on a lonely lighthouse island as rats take over the island. "Three Skeleton Key" had been heard previously on *Suspense* with Vincent Price as star.

The Eternal Light

Drama

Featuring: Alexander Scourby, Adelaide Klein, Roger DeKoven, Bernard Lenrow, Edgar Stehli, Norman Rose, *et al.*
Directors: Frank Papp, Anton M. Leader
Writers: Morton Wishengrad, Virginia Mazer, Joe Mindel, many others
Sound Effects: Arthur Cooper

This series dealt with the humanities and featured dramatizations of literature, the Bible, history, biography and other sources. Guest speakers were also presented on the program.

Ethel and Albert

Comedy

CAST:
Ethel Arbuckle — Peg Lynch
Albert Arbuckle — Richard Widmark (first six months), Alan Bunce
Baby Susy — Madeleine Pierce
Announcers: George Ansbro, Fred Cole, Don Lowe, Cy Harrice, Glenn Riggs, Herb Sheldon

---

Directors: Bob Cotton (1944–49), William D. Hamilton (1949–50)
Writer: Peg Lynch
Organists: Rosa Rio, Dolph Gobel, Lew White
Theme: "Love Nest"

The setting for *Ethel and Albert* was

the town of "Sandy Harbor." Rarely was anyone other than "Ethel" and "Albert" heard, as the program was primarily a duologue between these two, with other characters talked about. "Baby Susy," "born" March 15, 1946, was the first voice heard on the show other than "Ethel" and "Albert." The first other adult character was Paul Whiteman, who played the part of a door-to-door salesman. Also appearing on occasion were Ed Begley, Raymond Edward Johnson, Leon Janney, Julie Stevens, and Don MacLaughlin.

The program was also known as *The Private Lives of Ethel and Albert*. There was a fifteen-minute and then a thirty-minute version of this durable comedy series, which was first heard over ABC in 1944.

The Ethel Merman Show

Musical Variety

Starring: Ethel Merman

Evelyn Winters

Serial Drama

CAST:

Evelyn Winters	Toni Darnay
Gary Bennett	Karl Weber
	Martin Blaine
Maggie	Kate McComb
Ted Blades	Stacy Harris
Janice King	Flora Campbell
Miss Bean	Linda Carlon-Reid
Charlie Gleason	Ralph Bell
Jinny Roberts	Mary Mason
Robbie DeHaven	James Lipton
Cleve Harrington	Vinton Hayworth
Edith Winters Elkins	Helen Claire
Tracey Endicott	John Moore

Announcer: Larry Elliott

Producers: Frank and Anne Hummert
Director: Ernest Ricca
Writers: Peggy Blake, H. L. Algyir

This series, which was first heard over CBS in 1944, was also known as *The Strange Romance of Evelyn Winters.*

The Eveready Hour

Variety

Featuring: Julia Marlowe, John Drew, George Gershwin, Moran and Mack (George Moran and Charlie Mack), Weber and Fields (Joe Weber and Lew Fields), The Flonzaley String Quartet, Irvin S. Cobb, Eddie Cantor, Walter C. Kelly ("The Virginia Judge"), Van and Schenck (Gus Van and Joe Schenck), Will Rogers, Elsie Janis, D. W. Griffith, *et al.*
Supervisors: Douglas Coulter and George Furness

This was the first big variety show on radio. It made its debut on December 4, 1923, over WEAF in New York. The premiere program had a concert orchestra, a jazz band, and a one-act play—"The Bungalow," with Gene Lockhart, Eva Taylor, and Lawrence Grattan.

The Eveready Hour was sponsored by the National Carbon Company, makers of Eveready batteries. It was a truly spectacular program, even by today's standards. Among its most popular features, besides the appearances by major Broadway stars, was a true story adventure by Red Christianson, a New York taxi-driver who had been marooned in the Galápagos Islands. Another favorite was Edgar White Burrill's reading of Ida Tarbell's "I Knew Lincoln," which was repeated each year for Lincoln's Birthday.

Radio adaptations of historical events and plays, such as "Joan of Arc" (starring Rosaline Greene as the Maid) were presented. In 1924 Wendell Hall, The Red-Headed Music-Maker, was first presented. His most remembered song was "It Ain't Gonna Rain No Mo'." He became such a big star that his wedding was solemnized on the program.

Everyman's Theater

Drama

Guest Stars: Joan Crawford, Bette Davis, Katharine Hepburn, Raymond Massey, Boris Karloff, Alla Nazimova
Featuring: Raymond Edward Johnson, Betty Caine, Gilbert Mack, Luis Van Rooten, Ann Shepherd (Scheindel Kalish), Bill Lipton
Writer: Arch Oboler

Among the plays presented were:

NONE BUT THE LONELY HEART

Peter Tschaikovsky — Raymond Edward Johnson
Mrs. Tschaikovsky (Antonina, his wife) — Betty Caine
Madame Von Meck — Alla Nazimova

IVORY TOWER

Starring — Alla Nazimova
Also — Raymond Edward Johnson

BABY

Starring — Bette Davis
Also — Raymond Edward Johnson

TWO

Starring — Joan Crawford
Also — Raymond Edward Johnson

"Two" was the story of two people left in the world after an atomic holocaust.

THE LAUGHING MAN

"The Laughing Man" was the story of a wise man many centuries in the future who laughed hysterically at people who had annihilated themselves with a peculiar bomb.

THE UGLIEST MAN IN THE WORLD

The Ugliest Man — Raymond Edward Johnson
The Prostitute — Betty Caine

This broadcast was repeated five times by popular request.

LUST FOR LIFE

Vincent Van Gogh — Raymond Edward Johnson
Van Gogh's brother — Martin Gabel

Exploring the Unknown

Science Drama

Featuring: Guest Stars
Producer-Director: Sherman Dryer

Many well-known performers appeared in these dramatizations. Walter Huston performed in "A Drink of Water." Orson Welles starred in "The Battle Never Ends"—the story of man's fight against insect plagues. The series was first heard over Mutual in 1945.

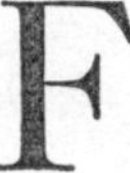

The Falcon

Mystery-Adventure

CAST:

Mike Waring, The Falcon — James Meighan, Les Damon, Berry Kroeger, Les Tremayne, George Petrie

Nancy — Joan Banks

Renee — Ethel Everett

Also: Joan Alexander, Mandel Kramer, Robert Dryden

Announcer: Ed Herlihy

Producer: Bernard Schubert, Jr.

Directors: Carlo De Angelo, Stuart Buchanan, Richard Lewis

Writers: Palmer Thompson, Eugene Wang, Stanley Niss, Jay Bennett, Bernard Dougall

Sound Effects: Adrian Penner

The Falcon made its debut over Mutual in 1945.

Falstaff Fables

Comedy

Featuring: Alan Reed (Teddy Bergman), Alan Reed, Jr.

Writers: Don Johnson, Alan Reed

Falstaff Fables was broadcast over ABC for Mars candy bars in 1949. Alan Reed and his son performed rhymed versions of children's classics.

The Family Hour

Variety

M.C.: Major Edward Bowes
Ted Mack
Vocalist: Belle "Bubbles" Silverman
Directors: Lloyd Marx, J. Robert Blum
Theme: "Clair de Lune" by Debussy

This program was also known as *The Capitol Family Hour, The Major Bowes Family Hour,* and *The Ted Mack Family Hour.* It was sponsored by General Mills and Swanson's Foods. (See also *The Prudential Family Hour; Major Bowes and His Original Amateur Hour.*)

Belle Silverman later became famous as Beverly Sills.

The Family Theater

Drama

Host: Father Patrick Peyton
Guest Stars: Bing Crosby, Bob Hope, Gary Cooper, Perry Como, Macdonald Carey, Ann Blyth, Marvin Miller, Fred Allen, Irene Dunne, Loretta Young, Spencer Tracy, Maureen O'Sullivan, Ethel Barrymore, Ray Milland, *et al.*
Announcer: Tony La Frano
Directors: Dave Young, Mel Williamson, John Kelley, Robert O'Sullivan
Writers: John Kelley, Robert O'Sullivan

The Family Theater was first heard over Mutual in 1947 and ran until 1957.

Famous Fireside Plays

Drama

This 1942 drama series featured radio adaptations of such plays as *Holiday* by Philip Barry, *The Front Page* by Ben Hecht and Charles MacArthur, and *Officer 666* by Augustin MacHugh.

Famous Fortunes

Drama

Narrator: Mark Hawley

Famous Jury Trials

Drama

CAST:

The Judge	Maurice Franklin
Narrator	Roger DeKoven
	DeWitt McBride

Also: True Boardman, Byron Kane, Jean Paul King, Raymond Edward Johnson, Frank Readick, Mandel Kramer, *et al.*
Announcers: Peter Grant, Hugh James, Roger Krupp

Directors: Wylie Adams, Robert H. Nolan, Clark Andrews, Carl Eastman, Charles Powers
Writers: Milton J. Kramer, Bill Rafael, Ameel Fisher, Len Finger, Martin H. Young, Jerry McGill, Daisy Amoury, Stedman Coles,

Joseph L. Greene, Lawrence Menkin, Paul Monash

The program began with crowd noises and the sound of a gavel. After each witness testified, the bailiff would state in a deep voice, "Step down." The series began over Mutual in 1936.

Fanny Brice: see *The Baby Snooks Show; Maxwell House Coffee Time; Ziegfeld Follies of the Air.*

The Farm and Home Hour: see *The National Farm and Home Hour.*

The Fat Man

Mystery-Adventure

CAST:

Brad Runyon, The Fat Man — J. Scott Smart
Sergeant O'Hara — Ed Begley
Lila North — Mary Patton
Also: Dan Ocko, Rolly Bester, Robert Dryden

Directors: Clark Andrews, Charles Powers
Writers: Robert Sloane, Dan Shuffman
Musical Director: Bernard Green
Sound Effects: Ed Blainey

Opening:

WOMAN. There he goes . . . into that drugstore. He's stepping on the scales.
SOUND. *Clink of a coin*
WOMAN. Weight . . . two hundred and thirty-seven pounds.
SOUND. *Card dropping*
WOMAN. Fortune . . . danger!
MUSIC. *Sting*
WOMAN. Whoooo is it?
MAN. The Fat Man!

This series was created for radio by Dashiell Hammett. It was first heard over ABC in 1945.

Father Coughlin

Commentary

Father Charles Edward Coughlin, a Roman Catholic priest who broadcast from the Shrine of The Little Flower in Royal Oak, Michigan, was one of the more controversial figures of early radio broadcasting. His first broadcast was on October 17, 1926, over WJR Detroit. He was later heard over CBS, usually at 4:00 p.m. on Sundays, until they refused to carry his broadcasts in the mid-thirties. He then formed his own network of forty-seven stations. Originally a booster of Franklin D. Roosevelt, he later called FDR a "great liar and betrayer." He aligned himself with Huey Long of Louisiana and eventually chose his own presidential candidate, William Lemke of North Dakota. Father Coughlin guaranteed that he would never broadcast again if Lemke did not get nine million votes in 1936 as the Union Party candidate. Lemke polled 891,858 votes. Father Coughlin did leave the air for a few months but returned to present his plans for a "Corporate State," which proposed the scrapping of Congress.

He once had millions of listeners, and in 1934 a poll showed that he was considered the most important public figure in the United States except for the President. Twice attempts were made on his life. By the early 1940s his audience had dwindled, and he left the air after a censorship board was set up by the Church to examine his scripts prior to broadcast.

Father Knows Best

Situation Comedy

CAST:

Jim Anderson, father — Robert Young
Margaret Anderson, mother — June Whitley
Betty Anderson, daughter — Rhoda Williams
Bud Anderson, son — Ted Donaldson
Kathy Anderson, daughter — Norma Jean Nilsson
Elizabeth Smith — Eleanor Audley
Hector Smith — Herb Vigran
Billy Smith — Sam Edwards
Announcers: Marvin Miller, Bill Forman

Creator-Writer: Ed James
Directors: Ken Burton, Fran Van Hartesfeldt, Murray Bolen

Father Knows Best was first heard in 1949 over NBC at 8:30 p.m. on Thursdays. It was sponsored by Maxwell House.

Favorite Story

Drama

Featuring: Guest Stars

Opening:

ANNOUNCER. Here's an invitation to radio's most dramatic half-hour . . . *Favorite Story!*

MUSIC. *Tymp Roll into theme . . . fade for . . .*

ANNOUNCER. Bullock's in downtown Los Angeles—one of America's great stores—proudly originates this radio program for the nation . . . *Favorite Story!*

MUSIC. *Theme to tag*

ANNOUNCER. And here to introduce tonight's *Favorite Story* is our star . . .

Favorite Story originated from KFI Los Angeles. Each week a star was asked to select a story to be used on the program. For example, Jane Cowl chose *Brigadoon* for the program of February 17, 1948.

The FBI in Peace and War

Adventure

CAST:

FBI Field Agent Sheppard — Martin Blaine
Also: Jackson Beck, Edith Arnold, Walter Greaza, Frank Readick, Ralph Bell, John M. James, Robert Dryden
Announcers: Warren Sweeney, Len Sterling

Directors: Betty Mandeville, Max Marcin
Writers: Louis Pelletier, Jacques Finke, Fred Collins
Musical Director: Vladimir Selinsky
Sound Effects: Al Hogan, Byron Winget, Ed Blainey

Theme: "March" from "Love for Three Oranges" by Prokofiev

The program concluded with this disclaimer: "All names and characters used on this program are fictitious. Any similarity to persons living or dead is purely coincidental. This program is based upon Frederick L. Collins' copyrighted book *The FBI in Peace and War*, and the broadcast does not imply endorsement, authorization, or approval of the Federal Bureau of Investigation." The series was first heard over CBS in 1944.

The Feg Murray Show

Hollywood Gossip

Starring: Feg Murray
Orchestra: Ozzie Nelson
Vocalist: Harriet Hilliard

Murray was the cartoonist of the newspaper feature "Seein' Stars."

Fibber McGee and Molly

Comedy

CAST:

Fibber McGee	Jim Jordan
Molly McGee	Marian Jordan
Throckmorton P. Gildersleeve	Hal Peary
Doc Gamble	Arthur Q. Bryan
Mayor La Trivia	Gale Gordon
The Old Timer	Cliff Arquette Bill Thompson
Wallace Wimple	Bill Thompson
Beulah, the maid	Marlin Hurt
Lena, the maid	Gene Carroll
Silly Watson	Hugh Studebaker
Mrs. Uppington	Isabel Randolph
Alice Darling	Shirley Mitchell
Mort Toops	Jim Jordan
Sis	Marian Jordan
Teeny	Marian Jordan
Geraldine	Marian Jordan
Old Lady Wheedledeck	Marian Jordan
Mrs. Wearybottom	Marian Jordan
Lady Vere-de-Vere	Marian Jordan
Horatio K. Boomer	Bill Thompson
Vodka	Bill Thompson
Nick Depopolous	Bill Thompson
Uncle Dennis	Bill Thompson Ransom Sherman
Mrs. Carstairs	Bea Benaderet

Also: Jess Kirkpatrick
The King's Men, vocal quartet—Ken Darby, Jon Dodson, Bud Linn, Rad Robinson
Musical Conductors: Rico Marchielli, Ted Weems, Billy Mills
Announcer: Harlow Wilcox

Director: Frank Pittman
Writers: Don Quinn, Phil Leslie
Sound Effects: Frank Pittman

Catch-phrases:

FIBBER (To mythical telephone operator). Oh, is that you, Myrt?

FIBBER (*swearing*). Dad-rat the dad-ratted . . .

MOLLY (*responding to Fibber's explanation of a joke*). Tain't funny, McGee.

MOLLY. How do you do, I'm sure.

MOLLY. Heavenly days![1]

BEULAH. Somebody bawl for Beulah?

BEULAH (*laughs*). Love that man!

OLD TIMER. That's purty good, Johnny, but that ain't the way I

[1] This became the title of one of their movies.

heerd it. Way I heerd it, one fella sez t'other fella, s-a-a-a-a-y, he sez.

GILDERSLEEVE. You're a hard man, McGee.

SIS. Why, mister, why, mister, why, mister, why?

Fibber McGee and Molly had its early beginnings as a program called *The Smackouts*, which Don Quinn wrote and the Jordans played as a five-times-a-week serial over NBC. Jordan played a garrulous grocery-store proprietor who was always just "smack out" of everything. He spent most of his time spinning yarns. *The Smackouts* lasted for four years, from 1931 to 1935. "Fibber" and "Molly" were created in 1935 for Johnson Wax, which was looking for a new program to sponsor. The show, for a time, was known as *The Johnson Wax Program with Fibber McGee and Molly*. The company became the long-time sponsor, and its commercials were among the first to be integrated into the show itself with the announcer playing a character in the story. "Fibber" often addressed announcer Harlow Wilcox as "Waxy." Wilcox, to Fibber's consternation, invariably steered his casual conversations with Fibber into a commercial for Johnson Wax.

Fibber McGee and Molly stayed on the air until 1952, for the most part at 9:30 p.m. each Tuesday (which was promoted, quite properly, as "comedy night on NBC").

Actually there was no "story" to the programs. Usually a situation was established and then various characters would enter the McGee home at 79 Wistful Vista and help or hinder the action. The program introduced two characters who moved on to their own programs—"Gildersleeve" and "Beulah." (See also *The Great Gildersleeve; Beulah.*)

Many of the characters, situations, and catch-phrases became familiar nationwide. A weekly occurrence was Fibber's opening of the hall closet door, much to the horror of Molly. As soon as the door opened, everything in the closet fell out, ending up with a small tinkly bell. This sequence of sound effects became one of the most familiar sounds in radio. The crash would be observed by Fibber, who then would declare, "Gotta straighten out that closet one of these days."

Each character was a distinct individual. "Doc Gamble" and McGee argued all the time and the Doc was usually the victor. "Mrs. Wearybottom" spoke with a monotone without pausing for punctuation. "Sis" was a little girl from next door who harassed McGee. "Mrs. Uppington" was always one-up on McGee in repartee. "Wallace Wimple" was a henpecked husband who referred to his wife as "Sweety-Face, my big fat wife." There were several characters who never appeared but were referred to frequently such as "Myrt, the telephone operator," and "Fred Nintny of Starved Rock, Illinois." (See also *Comedy and Comedians.*)

Final Edition

Drama

Newspaper Reporter: Dick Powell

Fiorello: see *Mayor LaGuardia Reads the Funnies.*

The Fire Chief

Variety

The Fire Chief: Ed Wynn
Announcer: Graham McNamee
Writers: Ed Wynn, Eddie Preble

Catch-phrases:
WYNN: Sooooo-o-o-o-o.
WYNN: The program's going to be different tonight, Graham.

Ed Wynn, as Texaco's "Fire Chief," pioneered many innovations in broadcasting. One of the first performers to insist on a live studio audience to react to his comedy antics, he also wore costumes and make-up and created a "theater atmosphere" for his broadcasts.

The Fire Chief made its debut April 26, 1932. Wynn had previously broadcast an entire Broadway stage show—*The Perfect Fool*—on June 12, 1922. Subsequently he appeared on radio on *Gulliver* (1935–36), *The Perfect Fool* (1937), and *Happy Island* (1944). At one time he attempted to form his own radio network with WNEW in New York as the key station. In fact, the E and W in WNEW stand for Ed Wynn.

Fireside Chats

Talks

During his four terms in office, President Franklin Delano Roosevelt frequently used radio as the medium to reach as many Americans as he could in as intimate a manner as possible. These talks were called *Fireside Chats* because his style and manner of presentation gave the impression that he was seated by a roaring fire in his den, talking to an individual listening at home. So natural was FDR's style that during his fourth *Fireside Chat* (July 24, 1933) he stopped and asked for a glass of water, which he sipped while on the air.

At one point the President was voted the most popular personality on radio, with Jack Benny and other top stars finishing behind him. The announcer who introduced the President was usually Robert Trout, who has generally been credited with creating the title.

The First Line

Drama

Producer-Directors: Bob Brown, Ted Robertson
Writers: Ed Gardner, Ken Robinson

The First Line was a CBS series presented during World War II in behalf of the United States Navy.

First Nighter

Drama

The Genial First Nighter:
Charles P. Hughes
Bret Morrison
Marvin Miller
Don Briggs
Michael Rye
(Rye Billsbury)
Co-starring: Don Ameche and June Meredith (1929–36)

Don Ameche and Betty Lou Gerson (1936)
Les Tremayne and Barbara Luddy (1936–42)
Olan Soule and Barbara Luddy (1943–53)
Also: Macdonald Carey, Cliff Soubier, Raymond Edward Johnson, Jack Doty
Musical Directors: Eric Sagerquist, Caesar Petrillo, Frank Worth
Announcer: Vincent Pelletier
Producer-Director: Joe Ainley
Writers: Edwin Halloran, George Vandel, Virginia Safford Lynne, Arch Oboler, Dan Shuffman
Original Music: Frank Smith
Theme: "Neapolitan Nights"

This program, which was first heard over NBC Blue in 1929, simulated a theater atmosphere. The dramas were billed as being broadcast from "The Little Theater off Times Square," although it originated only in Chicago and Hollywood, never in New York. "Mr. First Nighter" was always shown to his seat by an "usher" just before curtain time. At intermission, between the acts, an usher would call out, "Smoking in the downstairs and outer lobby only, please!" After the commercial a buzzer would sound and the usher would call out, "Curtain going up!" *First Nighter* left the air in 1953.

The First Piano Quartet

Music

Pianists: Adam Garner (Adam Gelbtrunk), Hans Horwitz, Vee Padwa (Vladimir Padva), George Robert, Frank Mittler, Edward Edson
Announcer: Gene Hamilton
Producer-Writer: Edwin Fadiman
Directors: James E. Kovach, Paul Knight, Arthur Austin
Theme: "Variations" by Paganini

The First Piano Quartet played classical music especially arranged for four pianos. The quartet was heard on NBC starting in 1941.

The Fish and Hunt Club

Outdoors

Commentator: Sanford Bickart
Also: Jim Boles

The Fishing and Hunting Club of the Air

Outdoors

Panelists: Jim Hurley, Dave Newell, Roland Winters, Martin Begley
Announcers: Don Lowe, Bill Slater
Producer-Writer-Director: R. C. Woodruff
Director: Victor Seydel

Hurley, who was Fishing and Hunting Editor of the *New York Mirror*, and Newell, who served in the same capacity on *Field & Stream* magazine, were the experts, while Winters and Begley contributed the "amateur" viewpoint to the discussions.

The Fitch Bandwagon

Variety

The title *The Fitch Bandwagon* was given to several programs sponsored by Fitch Shampoo. Originally guest orchestras appeared on the show.

Later Phil Harris and Alice Faye were starred.

CAST:

Phil Harris — Himself
Alice Faye Harris — Herself
Little Alice — Jeanine Roos
Phyllis — Anne Whitfield
Frankie Remley, the guitar player — Elliott Lewis
Wamond Wadcliffe — Arthur Q. Bryan
Julius Abbruzio, the wisecracking grocery boy — Walter Tetley
Grogan — Sheldon Leonard
Alice's mother — Jane Morgan
Emily Williams — June Foray

Also: Robert North
Orchestra: Phil Harris, Walter Sharp
Announcers: Jack Costello, Bill Forman, Toby Reed
Producer-Writer: Ward Byron
Director: Paul Phillips
Writers: George D. Faber, Martin A. Ragaway, Milton Josefsberg, Ray Singer, Dick Chevillat
Sound Effects: Bob Grapperhouse

Theme: (To the tune of "Smile for Me")

Laugh a while
Let a song be your style
Use Fitch Shampoo.
Don't despair
Use your head, save your hair
Use Fitch Shampoo.

The Fitch Bandwagon had its beginnings in 1932 when F. W. Fitch decided that after many years of sales exclusively to barber shops he would market his shampoo to the public through drugstores. An advertising and marketing test was made, primarily in Iowa, using Wendell Hall (The Red-Headed Music-Maker), who was then on tour and was heard on WOC Davenport. The first program was also carried by WHO Des Moines. It was a fifteen-minute show with a talent cost of sixty dollars.

The test proved successful, and in the fall of 1933 the show was expanded to the basic NBC network, which at that time consisted of twenty-three stations. The talent cost for this fifteen-minute program soared to $2,046.71. Various talents appeared on this version of *The Fitch Bandwagon,* including Irene Beasley, The Morin Sisters, and The Ranch Boys. Jerry Belcher did an interview segment called "Interesting Neighbors."

In 1937 the program became a half-hour on Sunday night. It was then that the "bandwagon" idea came to be as a format, featuring the name bands of the day. During this time it was written and produced mostly by Ward Byron and was aired from New York, Chicago, and later Hollywood.

One of the most popular features of the program was the yearly opening of the Ringling Brothers and Barnum & Bailey Circus at Madison Square Garden in New York. For this program the circus band, on its own bandwagon, opened the show with a parade around the circus ring before an audience of hundreds of New York area orphans. The Ringling Band was directed by Merle Evans, and every year F. W. Fitch donned a musician's uniform, climbed aboard the bandwagon, and faked trombone.

Even though many people thought that *The Fitch Bandwagon* was lucky to be sandwiched in between *Jack Benny* at 7:00 p.m. and *Edgar Bergen* at 8:00 on NBC, the *Bandwagon* program actually occupied its Sunday-night-at-7:30 time-slot long before the other two programs were added to the Sunday line-up. *The Bandwagon,* in fact, pioneered in Sunday-evening entertainment programing because prior to its appearance most broadcasters felt that Sunday programing should be of a more religious or serious nature . . . even in the evening.

Some of the program's summer replacements included *Richard Diamond, Vic and Sade,* and *The Cass Daley Show,* which featured Cass Daley (a comedienne), Larry Keating, Henry Russell, Francis "Dink" Trout, and Freddy Martin's Orchestra.

The Fitzgeralds

Conversation

This talk program featured the husband-and-wife team of Ed and Pegeen Fitzgerald.

Five Star Jones

Serial Drama

CAST:

Tom Jones (Five Star Jones) — John Kane
Sally Jones — Elizabeth Day
City Editor of "The Register" — Bill Johnstone
Ma Moran — Effie Palmer

Five Star Jones was first heard over CBS in 1935.

The Fix-It Shop: see *The Mel Blanc Show.*

Flash Gordon

Science-Fiction Adventure

CAST:

Flash Gordon — Gale Gordon, James Meighan
Dr. Zarkoff — Maurice Franklin
Ming — Bruno Wick
Also: Teddy Bergman, Everett Sloane, Charlie Cantor, Ray Collins

Producer: Himan Brown

Flash Gordon was based on the comic strip by Alex Raymond. The series was first heard over Mutual in 1935.

The Fleischmann Hour: see *The Rudy Vallee Show.*

Flying Patrol

Drama

Featuring: Hugh Rowlands, Sharon Grainger

This series dramatized stories about Coast Guard fliers. It was first heard over the Blue network in 1941.

The Flying Red Horse Tavern

Variety

M.C.: Walter King

This program, sponsored by Mobil, was first heard in 1935 at 8:00 p.m. on Fridays. The title was derived from the Mobil Oil symbol—"the flying red horse."

Flying Time

Drama

CAST:

Hal Falvey	Sidney Ellstrom
Halvorsen	Sidney Ellstrom
Sprague	Phil Lord
Sue	Betty Lou Gerson
Beasley	Billy Lee
Harry Blake	Willard Farnum
Major Fellowes	Hal Peary
Tony	Hal Peary
Captain Russ	Ted Maxwell
Ruth Morrow	Loretta Poynton

FM

FM radio was developed in the 1930s by Edwin Armstrong, a professor at Columbia University. FM is the abbreviation for Frequency Modulation and involves the transmission of radio by varying the radio signal. FM is also used for the sound portion of television. There are a number of advantages over the older method of transmission, called AM (for Amplitude Modulation). Among them are a higher quality sound through greater freedom from static, interference, hum, fading, and signal drift; the ability to transmit a wider range of frequencies, which is better for stereo transmission; and the further capability of a single band being able to transmit two or more different signals simultaneously. However, the FM signal is greatly limited in range compared with AM.

In 1941 the Federal Communications Commission authorized FM experimentation. The nation's first licensed FM station was WSM-FM Nashville. But FM was of virtually no significance in radio's Golden Age, not only because it was on an uncertain course in terms of its eventual role in broadcasting, but for the added reason that few radios were then equipped with FM bands.

Folies Bergère of the Air

Variety

Featuring: Willie and Eugene Howard, comedians

Follow the Moon

Serial Drama

CAST:

Clay Bannister	Nick Dawson
Jean Page (Mrs. Clay Bannister)	Elsie Hitz
Tetlow	Richard Gordon

Follow the Moon was first heard over NBC in 1936.

The Ford Sunday Evening Hour

Music

This CBS Sunday-night program (9:00 p.m.) featured stars of "good music," such as violinist Efrem Zimbalist. It was first heard over CBS in

1934 and was sponsored by the Ford Motor Company.

Ford Theater

Drama

Featuring: Guest Stars
Announcer: Nelson Case
Producer-Director: Fletcher Markle
Director: George Zachary
Musical Director: Cy Feuer

Dozens of top-flight Hollywood actors and actresses performed on this program, which was sponsored by the Ford Motor Company. The series made its debut over NBC in 1947.

Foreign Assignment

Adventure

CAST:
The Foreign Correspondent — Jay Jostyn
His assistant — Vicki Vola

Director: Chick Vincent

Forever Ernest

Situation Comedy

Featuring: Jackie Coogan, Lurene Tuttle, Arthur Q. Bryan
Orchestra: Billy May
Announcer: Dick Joy

Forever Ernest was heard over CBS.

Forever Young: see *Pepper Young's Family.*

Forty-Five Minutes from Hollywood

Drama

This was a popular night-time show of the mid-thirties that presented condensed versions of still-unreleased Hollywood movies with various radio actors and actresses playing the roles of the film stars. Frank Readick, for example, took a Jimmy Cagney role, and Bert Parks, then a CBS staff announcer, got a big break by singing and acting a Dick Powell part. The program was directed by Tom Harrington.

Four Corners, U.S.A.

Drama

CAST:
Jonah Crowell — Arthur Allen
Eben Crowell — Parker Fennelly
Mary Crowell — Jean McCoy

(See also *Snow Village.*)

Foxes of Flatbush

Serial Drama

CAST:
Jennie Fox — Mignon Schreiber
Benny, the son — Murray Forbes

Frances Scott: see *Women's Programs.*

Frank and Anne Hummert: see *Soap Operas.*

The Frank Buck Show: see *Bring 'Em Back Alive.*

Frank Crumit and Julia Sanderson

Music

Starring: Frank Crumit and Julia Sanderson
Announcer: Alan Kent
Theme: "Sweet Lady"

This program presented the husband-and-wife singing team of Frank Crumit and Julia Sanderson. In addition to singing, Crumit played the ukulele. (See also *Battle of the Sexes; Blackstone Plantation; Universal Rhythm.*)

The Frank Fay Show

Variety

This program was on the air less than thirteen weeks but was somewhat unique in that the star, comedian Frank Fay, served as M.C., announcer, director, and writer, and even furnished the music.

Frank Merriwell

Adventure

CAST:

Frank Merriwell	Lawson Zerbe
Inza Burrage	Elaine Rost
Bart Hodge	Hal Studer
Elsie Bellwood	Patricia Hosley

Announcer: Harlow Wilcox

Directors: Ed King, Fred Weihe
Writers: Bill Welch, Ruth and Gilbert Brann
Musical Director: Paul Taubman
Sound Effects: Max Russell

Opening:

MUSIC. *Organ up and under . . .*

SOUND. *Trotting horse up and under . . .*

ANNOUNCER. There it is . . . an echo of the past . . . an exciting past . . . a romantic past. The era of the horse and carriage . . . gas-lit streets . . . and free-for-all football games. The era of one of the most beloved heroes in American fiction, Frank Merriwell . . . the famous character created by Burt L. Standish. Merriwell is loved as much today as ever he was. And so the National Broadcasting Company brings him to radio in a brand-new series of stories.

Frank Merriwell was first heard over NBC in 1946.

The Frank Morgan Show

Variety

Starring: Frank Morgan
M.C.: Robert Young
Also: Cass Daley, Eric Blore
Vocalist: Carlos Ramirez
Orchestra: Albert Sack
Announcer: Harlow Wilcox

(See also *Maxwell House Coffee Time.*)

The Frank Sinatra Show

Variety

M.C.: Frank Sinatra
With: Guest Stars
Orchestra: Axel Stordahl
Director: Bob Brewster
Writer: Carroll Carroll

This show, starring the popular singer, was first heard over CBS in 1943. (See also *Songs by Sinatra; Songs for Sinatra; Your Hit Parade.*)

Frank Watanabe and Honorable Archie

Comedy

CAST:

Frank Watanabe	Eddie Holden
Archie	Reggie Sheffield
Cynthia	Georgia Fifield
Mrs. Hipplewater	Georgia Fifield
Sarah Hathaway	Georgia Fifield

This program originated over KNX Los Angeles.

Franklin Delano Roosevelt: see *Fireside Chats.*

The Fred Allen Show

Comedy-Variety

CAST:

Fred Allen	Himself
Portland Hoffa	Portland Hoffa Allen
Titus Moody	Parker Fennelly
Mrs. Pansy Nussbaum	Minerva Pious
Senator Beauregard Claghorn	Kenny Delmar
Ajax Cassidy	Peter Donald
Falstaff Openshaw	Alan Reed (Teddy Bergman)
Senator Bloat	Jack Smart
John Doe	John Brown
Socrates Mulligan	Charles Cantor
Mr. Pinkbaum	Irwin Delmore
Dottie Mahoney	Shirley Booth

The Town Hall Quartet–Scrappy Lambert, Bob Moody, Tubby Weyant, Leonard Stokes

Also: the De Marco Sisters (Lily, Mary, and Ann), Eileen Douglas, Sam Levene, Walter Tetley, Roy Atwell, Phil Duey, Kenny Baker, "Uncle Jim" Harkins

Musical Conductors: Lou Katzman, Peter Van Steeden, Lennie Hayton, Al Goodman, Ferde Grofé

Guest Stars: Orson Welles, Lauritz Melchior, Maurice Evans, Beatrice Lillie, Leo Durocher, Charles Laughton, Tallulah Bankhead, James and Pamela Mason, Helen Traubel, Alfred Hitchcock, Richard Rodgers and Oscar Hammerstein II (composers), Bing Crosby, George Jessel, Jack Haley, Henry Morgan, Bert Lahr, Bob Hope, Edgar Bergen, Doc Rockwell, Jack Benny, *et al.*

Announcers: Jimmy Wallington, Harry Von Zell, Kenny Delmar

Directors: Victor Knight, Howard Reilly

Writers: Fred Allen, Larry Marks, Aaron Ruben, Nat Hiken, Herb Lewis, Harry Tugend, Arnold

Auerbach, Herman Wouk, Albert G. Miller
Sound Effects: Agnew Horine
Theme: "Smile, Darn Ya, Smile"

This program made its debut over CBS on October 23, 1932, as *The Linit Show,* which was also known as *The Linit Bath Club.* It was subsequently known as *The Salad Bowl Revue* (for Hellmann's Mayonnaise), *The Sal Hepatica Revue* (*The Hour of Smiles*), *Town Hall Tonight, The Texaco Star Theater,* and, finally, *The Fred Allen Show.* It ran as an hour show thirty-nine weeks a year for eight years and was the last full-hour comedy program on radio before it changed to a half-hour format after the program of June 28, 1942. It ran as a half-hour show for another seven years.

Among the many features were "The News Reel"—later "Town Hall News" and still later "The March of Trivia"; "People You Don't Expect to Meet"; "The Workshop Players" (a take-off on the popular *The Columbia Workshop*), which was later called "The Mighty Allen Art Players"; Portland's comedy spot; and "The Average Man's Round Table." Various comedy sketches were performed using the visiting guest stars; among the best remembered are the parody on *Oklahoma!* with Allen and Bea Lillie, and the early-morning "Mr. and Mrs. Show" parody with Allen and Tallulah Bankhead. Allen frequently portrayed an Oriental detective, "One Long Pan," who warned everyone that "He has a lewolewer!" as he solved various crimes in comedy skits.

Beginning performers appeared, and many later became famous, such as Frank Sinatra, Connie Haines, Bob Eberly, Beatrice Kaye, Jerry Colonna, and Garry Moore.

During the early days somebody connected with the program liked organ music, so Ann Leaf played the organ at the Paramount Theater some two miles away from the rest of the broadcast, and the "startling" fact that the music was being played from two miles away was dutifully announced.

One of the most famous continuing sequences was the "feud" with Jack Benny, which began on December 30, 1936, when Allen had as a guest ten-year-old violinist Stuart Canin, who played Franz Schubert's "The Bee." Allen ad-libbed that "a certain alleged violinist" should hide his head in shame for his poor fiddling. Benny picked this up on his next broadcast, and the needling jokes flew fast and furious until the comedy feud culminated in the broadcast of a fight between the two from the Hotel Pierre in New York on March 14, 1937. The fight, of course, never came off, but the "feud" continued over the years.

The most popular feature was "Allen's Alley" which made its debut on December 13, 1942. For the first three years various characters came and went in the Alley. Among these were "Socrates Mulligan" (played by Charles Cantor), who eventually migrated to *Duffy's Tavern,* where he became "Clifton Finnegan"; and "Falstaff Openshaw" (played by Alan Reed), who recited such poems as "Back the patrol wagon to the sidewalk, Sergeant. That step's too high for my mother." In 1945 the Alley settled down to the characters best remembered—"Senator Claghorn," "Mrs. Nussbaum," "Titus Moody," and "Ajax Cassidy."

"Senator Claghorn" was a politician from the South who responded to a knock on his door with, "Somebody, Ah say somebody's knockin' on mah door!" He constantly made puns on well-known names. For example: "Senator Glass is all broken up about it!" and "They're goin' to bring Senator Aiken back—achin' back. . . ." He would wind up with his most famous catch-phrase, "That's a joke, son!" He referred to the Nashville Philharmonic as being conducted by Arturo Tuscaloosa, playing "The Poet and the Sharecropper."

"Mrs. Nussbaum" was a Jewish housewife who would answer her door with, "You were expecting maybe the Fink Spots?" or "You were expecting maybe the King Cohen Trio?" She referred frequently to "mine husband, Pierre."

"Titus Moody" was a taciturn New England character who always answered his door with, "Howdy, bub." His allusions were usually bucolic, and when he laughed it was an obvious effort.

"Ajax Cassidy" was a garrulous Irishman who greeted Allen each week with, "W-e-e-e-l-l-l, how do ye do?"

Interestingly enough, these four stereotype characters were never criticized as being anti-Southern, anti-Semitic, anti-New England, or anti-Irish. The warmth and good humor with which they were presented made them acceptable even to the most sensitive listeners.

Fred Allen, who wrote ninety per cent of what was heard on his program, was one of the all-time great American writers. Among his best-remembered lines were his two definitions of Hollywood:—"Hollywood is a nice place—if you're an orange" and "You can take all the sincerity in Hollywood, put it in a flea's navel, and have room left over for three caraway seeds and an agent's heart." He also wrote that the Holland Tunnel was built "so commuters can go to New Jersey without being seen." Many of his most famous ripostes were with network and agency brass. He described an agency vice-president as "a man who comes into his office at nine o'clock in the morning and finds a molehill on his desk. It's his job to make a mountain out of it by five o'clock." After Captain Ramshaw, a pet eagle, had gotten away from his trainer during a 1940 broadcast and deposited a rather obvious bird trademark in NBC's studio 8H, Allen referred to "l'affaire eagle" as having resulted in Mr. Rockefeller's carpet receiving a "ghost's beret." Allen's wit was not confined to the typewriter though. He often ad-libbed so brilliantly while on the air that frantic cuts had to be made in the program. It would seem likely that Fred Allen used the expression "We're a little late, folks, so good night," more than any other performer.

In the later years of *The Fred Allen Show* some unexpected competition arrived on another network (ABC) in the form of *Stop the Music*, a big-money quiz show with home participation. There was much scrambling to woo back his audience, including Allen's guarantee to award $5,000 to anyone who was called by *Stop the*

Music while listening to Allen, but to no avail. The last Fred Allen broadcast took place on June 26, 1949. Appropriately enough, Jack Benny was the guest. (See also *Comedy and Comedians.*)

The Fred Astaire Show

Variety

Starring: Fred Astaire
Featuring: Charlie Butterworth, Conrad Thibault, Francia White, Trudy Wood, *et al.*
Orchestra: Johnny Green

This short-lived program made its debut on NBC on Tuesday, September 8, 1936, at 8:30 p.m. Curiously, Astaire was not on his inaugural broadcast. He was in Europe at the time and didn't appear until the second week. Jack Benny and Mary Livingstone pinch-hit with guests Ginger Rogers, Francia White, and Allan Jones. The sponsor was Packard automobiles.

The Fred Waring Show

Music

Starring: Fred Waring and His Pennsylvanians
Featuring: Honey and The Bees (Diane Courtney, later Daisy Bernier, as Honey; Hal Kanner and Murray Kane as The Bees); Stella and The Fellas (Stella Friend, Paul Gibbons, Craig Leitch, and Roy Ringwald); The Lane Sisters (Priscilla and Rosemary); The Three Girl Friends (Stella Friend, Ida Pierce, and June Taylor); Babs and Her Brothers (Babs Ryan, Charlie Ryan, and Little Ryan); Stuart Churchill, tenor; Gordon Goodman, tenor; Jane Wilson, soprano; Joanne Wheatley, vocalist; Donna Dae, vocalist; Gordon Berger, vocalist; Robert Shaw, vocalist; Mac Perron, vocalist; Ruth Cottingham, vocalist; Ferne Buckner, solo violinist; Virginia Morley and Livingston Gearhart, piano team; Les Paul, guitarist; Kay Thompson, comic vocals; Lumpy Brannum, bass viol and comic vocals; Johnny "Scat" Davis, horn player and comic; Tom Waring, pianist; The MacFarland Twins (George and Arthur); Poley McClintock, drummer and "froggy voices"
Announcers: David Ross, Bob Considine, Paul Douglas, Bill Bivens
Producer-Director: Tom Bennett
Writers: Jack Dolph, Jay Johnson

Opening Theme: "I Hear Music"
I hear music, I hear melodies,
Sparkling songs of love, tingle from your touch

Closing Theme: "Sleep"
Catch-phrase:
DAVID ROSS. Mellow. Mellow as a cello. [A reference to both Waring's music and Old Gold cigarettes, Waring's first sponsor.]

The Fred Waring Show appeared at various time periods in different formats. Waring's first broadcast was carried by WWJ Detroit in the early 1920s. For five years he was the star of *The Chesterfield Supper Club.* In the early thirties his sponsor was Old Gold cigarettes on a Wednesday-night CBS show.

Friend in Deed

Variety

Featuring: Richard Maxwell

Friend in Deed was first heard over CBS in 1940. Richard Maxwell served as both tenor and philosopher.

Front Page Farrell

Serial Drama

CAST:

David Farrell	Richard Widmark
	Carleton Young
	Staats Cotsworth
Sally Farrell	Florence Williams
	Virginia Dwyer
Kay Barnett	Betty Garde
Sammy Warner	George Sturgeon
Mrs. Howard	Evelyn Varden
Lucy Beggs	Katherine Emmet
Tim O'Donovan	William Shelley
Carol Peters	Vivian Smolen
Luther Warren	James Monks
Ella	Elspeth Eric
Sherry	Athena Lorde
Nick	Peter Capell
Lizette	Eleanor Sherman
Rory Applegate	Sylvia Leigh
George Walker	Frank Chase
Lieutenant Carpenter	Robert Donley
Grover Courtney	James Van Dyk

Producers: Frank and Anne Hummert
Directors: Bill Sweets, Frank Hummert, Arthur Hanna, John Buckwalter, Richard Leonard, Ed Slattery, Blair Walliser
Writers: Harold Gast, Bob Saxon, Alvin Boretz, Robert J. Shaw
Sound Effects: Ross Martindale, Manny Segal
Organist: Rosa Rio
Theme: "You and I Know"

Front Page Farrell was first heard over Mutual in 1941.

Fu Manchu

Mystery-Adventure

CAST:

Fu Manchu	John C. Daly
	Harold Huber
Karameneh, the slave girl	Sunda Love
	Charlotte Manson
Malik, the French detective	Stanley Andrews
Nayland Smith	Charles Warburton
Dr. Petrie	Bob White

Fu Manchu became a CBS series in 1932. It was based on the Chinese villain and mad scientist character created by Sax Rohmer. The John C. Daly who portrayed "Fu Manchu" was *not* the well-known newscaster (and later host of television's *What's My Line?*) named John Charles Daly. The actor John C. Daly died in 1936. (See also *The Collier Hour.*)

Fun Fair: see *Jay Stewart's Fun Fair.*

Fun for All

Variety

Starring: Arlene Francis, Bill Cullen

This program of comedy and music was heard on Saturday afternoons.

Fun in Swing Time

Variety

Featuring: Tim and Irene, comedy team
Orchestra: Bunny Berrigan
Writer: Hal Kanter

Tim Ryan and Irene Noblette's program was broadcast from the New Amsterdam Roof in New York City.

The Further Adventures of Big Jon and Sparkie: see *Big Jon and Sparkie.*

G

Galen Drake

Talk

Featuring: Galen Drake

Galen Drake directed his informal, rambling chats on everyday topics primarily to housewives.

Game Parade

Children's Quiz

M.C.: Arthur Elmer

Gangbusters

Drama

CAST:
Narrator — Phillips H. Lord
Colonel H. Norman Schwarzkopf
John C. Hilley
Dean Carlton
Chief Investigator — Lewis J. Valentine
Also: Art Carney, Richard Widmark, Ethel Owen, Santos Ortega, Bryna Raeburn, Elspeth Eric, Adelaide Klein, Joan Banks, Don MacLaughlin, James McCallion, Helene Dumas, Alice Reinheart,

Linda Watkins, Leon Janney, Frank Lovejoy, Grant Richards, Larry Haines, Roger DeKoven, Robert Dryden, Bill Lipton, Raymond Edward Johnson, Anne-Marie Gayer, *et al.*

Announcers: Charles Stark, Frank Gallop, H. Gilbert Martin, Don Gardiner, Roger Forster

---

Producer-Director: Phillips H. Lord

Directors: Paul Munroe, Harry Frazee, Jay Hanna, Bill Sweets, Leonard Bass, George Zachary

Writers: Phillips H. Lord, Stanley Niss, Brice Disque, Jr., John Mole

Sound Effects: Ray Kremer, Jim Rogan, Bob Prescott, Ed Blainey, Byron Winget, Jerry McCarthy

---

Opening:

SOUND EFFECTS. *Marching feet, machine-gun fire, siren wail*

VOICE. Calling the police! Calling the G-men! Calling all Americans to war on the underworld!

ANNOUNCER. Gangbusters! With the cooperation of leading law-enforcement officials of the United States, Gangbusters presents *facts* in the relentless war of the police on the underworld . . . *authentic case histories* that show the never-ending activity of the police in their work of protecting our citizens.

The exceptionally loud opening sound effects of guns and sirens gave rise to the expression "coming on like gangbusters"—which means anything that has a strong beginning. The programs were based on true stories, and the police were able to report many arrests because of the closing, which was a description of wanted criminals. In 1936, under the sponsorship of Palmolive Brushless Shaving Cream, *Gangbusters* was heard at 10:00 p.m., Wednesday, over CBS.

Garry Moore: see *Camel Caravan; Take It or Leave It; Club Matinee.*

Gasoline Alley

Drama

CAST:

Skeezix	Jimmy McCallion Billy Idelson Bill Lipton
Nina Clock	Janice Gilbert Jean Gillespie
Auntie Blossom	Irna Phillips
Wumple, Skeezix' boss	Clifford Soubier
Idaho Ida	Hazel Dopheide
Ling Wee, Chinese waiter	Junius Matthews

Also: Mason Adams

Directors: Charles Schenck, John Cole

Writers: Kay Chase, Kane Campbell

This program was based on the comic strip by Frank King.

The Gay Mrs. Featherstone

Situation Comedy

CAST:

Mrs. Featherstone	Billie Burke

Announcer: Marvin Miller

Director: Robert Hafter

The Gay Mrs. Featherstone appeared

on NBC in 1945, replacing *The Red Skelton Show* for Raleigh cigarettes for one season after Skelton went into the service.

Gay Nineties Revue

Musical Variety

CAST:

Featuring: Beatrice Kay, Joe Howard, Billy M. Greene

Broadway Harry	Frank Lovejoy
Danny Donovan	Jack Arthur

Also: Elm City Four—Philip Reed, first tenor; Claude Reese, second tenor; Hubie Hendry, baritone; Darrel Woodyard, bass; Four Clubmen, Floradora Girls
Orchestra: Ray Bloch

Gay Nineties Revue was first heard over CBS in 1940.

Gayelord Hauser

Diet Talk

Featuring: Gayelord Hauser

In this series of broadcasts Gayelord Hauser, the author of *Look Younger, Live Longer* and *The Gayelord Hauser Cook Book*, discussed food and diet problems.

Gene and Glenn with Jake and Lena

Music and Comedy

CAST:

Gene	Gene Carroll
Glenn	Glenn Rowell
Jake	Gene Carroll
Lena	Gene Carroll

Glenn was the straight man for this music-and-comedy duo. Gene played the piano and did the voices for "Lena," who ran a boarding house where Gene and Glenn were boarders, and "Jake," who was the handyman. Later "Lena" turned up on *Fibber McGee and Molly*.

Gene Autry's Melody Ranch

Western Variety

Starring: Gene Autry
Featuring: Pat Buttram, Jim Boles, Tyler McVey
With: The Cass County Boys, trio (Carl Cotner, leader and arranger)
The King Sisters, vocal quartet
Mary Ford
Announcer: Lou Crosby
Producer: Bill Burch
Writers: Ed James, Irwin Ashkenazy, Doris Gilbert, Carroll Carroll, George Anderson
Sound Effects: Dave Light, Gus Bayz, Gene Twombly

Autry's Theme: "Back in the Saddle Again"
I'm back in the saddle again
Out where a friend is a friend.

Gene Autry's Melody Ranch was first heard in January 1940 as a Sunday-afternoon CBS program and then later as a Saturday-evening (8:00) half-hour program. Featured on the Saturday-night program were Pat Buttram and The Cass County Boys. The long-time sponsor was Wrigley's Doublemint chewing gum; "Its easy chewing makes those little jobs go a little easier. I like it!" The program consisted of Western adventure interspersed with interludes of music.

General Motors Concerts

Music

This Sunday-night NBC program of classical music featured Erno Rapee conducting a seventy-piece symphony orchestra. Such famous guest artists as Albert Spalding, Lauritz Melchior, Gladys Swarthout, Lotte Lehmann, and Arturo Toscanini appeared. The series began in 1934.

George Burns and Gracie Allen: see *Burns and Allen.*

George Fisher: see *Hollywood Reporters.*

The George Jessel Show

Comedy-Variety

Starring: George Jessel

George Jessel was a former vaudeville star famous for his "Hello, Momma" routine. A brilliant after-dinner speaker, Jessel became known as the nation's "Toastmaster General."

Gibbs and Finney, General Delivery

Drama

CAST:

Gibbs	Parker Fennelly
Finney	Arthur Allen

(See also *Snow Village.*)

The Gibson Family

Drama

CAST:

Dot Gibson	Loretta Clemens
Bobby Gibson	Jack Clemens
	Al Dary
Sally Gibson	Adele Ronson
Mother	Anne Elstner
Father	Bill Adams
Awful, the butler	Ernest Whitman
Boy	Warren Hull

Also: John McGovern
Singers: Conrad Thibault, Lois Bennett
Orchestra: Donald Voorhees
Announcer: Jimmy Wallington

This was one of the first dramatic programs to have music written especially for it. (See also *Show Boat.*)

Gildersleeve: see *The Great Gildersleeve.*

The Gillette Cavalcade of Sports: see *Sports and Sportscasters.*

Girl Alone

Serial Drama

CAST:

Patricia Rogers, the girl alone	Betty Winkler
Ty DeYoe	Raymond Edward Johnson
Scoop Curtis	Don Briggs
	Pat Murphy
	Arthur Jacobson
Alice Ames Warner	Joan Winters

Leo Warner	Willard Waterman
	Ted Maxwell
Dick Conover	Herbert Nelson
Mike Barlow	Sidney Ellstrom
John Knight	Karl Weber
	Les Damon
	Syd Simons
Virginia Hardesty	Laurette Fillbrandt
Emmett Dayton	Ian Keith
Henry Senrich	Willard Waterman
Lieutenant Custer	Arthur Peterson
Muggsy Modoc	Bob Jellison
Lewis	Bob Jellison
Ruth Lardner	Fran Carlon
Joe Markham	Arthur Kohl
Arthur Cook	Charles Penman
W. C. Green	Stanley Gordon
Chuprin	Don Gallagher
Dr. John Richman	Michael Romano
Jack Rogers	Frank Pacelli
Aunt Kate	Kathryn Card
Hazel Bird	Jane Green
Scotson Webb	Henry Hunter (Arthur Jacobson)
Dr. Warren Douglas	Henry Hunter (Arthur Jacobson)
Stormy Wilson Curtis	June Travis
Jack	Jack Chalbeck
Ziehm	Herbert Butterfield
Dick Sheridan	Dan Sutter
Louise Stulir	Fern Persons
Jerry Stulir	John Hodiak
Clara Schend	Hope Summers
Ray	Earl George
Tessie Monroe	Betty Caine
Stella Moore	Janet Logan
Helen Adams	Betty Lou Gerson

Directors: Axel Gruenberg, Gordon Hughes
Writer: Fayette Krum
Theme: "Cecile Waltz" by McKee

Girl Alone was first heard over NBC in 1935. It originated in Chicago.

The Girl Next Door

Serial Drama

Featuring: Mary Smith, J. Anthony Hughes

Give and Take

Quiz

M.C.: John Reed King
Director: Jack Carney
Sound Effects: Art Strand

On this audience participation program, contestants first selected what they wanted from the prize table and then answered questions to win that prize. It was first heard over CBS in 1945. (See also *Quiz Shows*.)

Glamour Manor

Variety

M.C.: Kenny Baker, tenor

CAST:

Barbara	Barbara Eiler
Schlepperman	Sam Hearn
Mrs. Biddle	Elvia Allman
Mrs. Wilson	Cliff Arquette
Captain Billy	Cliff Arquette
Wanda Werewulf	Bea Benaderet

Also: Lurene Tuttle, Tyler McVey, Terry O'Sullivan, Jack Bailey, Hal Stevens, Charles Hale

---

Director: Ken Burton
Writers: Carl Jampel, Walt Framer, Sid Goodwin, Wright Esser, Charles Rinker, Frank Moore

Glamour Manor made its debut over ABC in 1944.

The Gloom Chasers: see *Stoopnagle and Budd*

Glorious One

Serial Drama

CAST:

Judith Bradley	Irene Rich
Jake Bradley	John Lake
Susan Bradley	Florence Baker
Don Bradley	Larry Nunn
Madge Harrington	Anne Stone
Lillian, the maid	Jane Morgan
Dr. Ralph Stevens	Gale Gordon
Mrs. Gordon	Gladys Gwynne

The Goldbergs

Serial Comedy-Drama

CAST:

Molly Goldberg	Gertrude Berg
Jake Goldberg	James R. Waters
Rosalie Goldberg	Roslyn Siber
Sammy Goldberg	Alfred Ryder (Alfred Corn) Everett Sloane
Uncle David	Menasha Skulnik
Solly	Sidney Slon
Jane Brown	Joan Tetzel
Sylvia Allison	Zina Provendie
Seymour Fingerhood	Arnold Stang Eddie Firestone, Jr.
Esther Miller	Joan Vitez
Christopher Keator	Raymond Edward Johnson
Mr. Mendall	George Herman
Joyce	Anne Teeman
Libby	Jeannette Chinley
Mickey Bloom	Howard Merrill
Mrs. Melenka	Bertha Waldon
Mr. Schneider	Artie Auerbach
Martha Wilberforce	Carrie Weller
Michael's grandmother	Mimi Aguglia
Uncle Carlo	Tito Vuolo
Debbie Banner	Cecile Evans
Walter Jerome	Edward Trevor
Malcolm	Garson Kanin
Eli Edwards	Garson Kanin
Mr. Fowler, the handyman	Bruno Wick

Creator-Writer: Gertrude Berg
Director: Wes McKee
Sound Effects: Jim Lynch
Theme: Toselli's "Serenade"

Catch-phrase:
MOLLY. Yoo-hoo! Is anybody?

The Goldbergs was originally called *The Rise of the Goldbergs* and made its first appearance on the Blue network on November 20, 1929. It remained an extremely popular "soap opera" for many years. It differed from most of the other "soaps" in that its leading characters lived through relatively normal situations. Even though it was the story of a poor Jewish family in New York, it had identification for a wide segment of its listeners.

The famous singer Mme. Ernestine Schumann-Heink asked Miss Berg if she could appear on the show, so she was written into the script and made three appearances. Metropolitan Opera star Jan Peerce appeared on the show to sing on Yom Kippur and Passover. Among others who performed on *The Goldbergs* were Marjorie Main, Joseph Cotten, Keenan Wynn, Minerva Pious, Van Heflin, Philip Loeb, and George Tobias.

Good News: see *Hollywood Good News.*

The Good Will Court: see *A. L. Alexander's Good Will Court*

The Goodrich Silvertown Cord Orchestra

Music

Conductor: Milton Rettenberg
Jack Shilkret
Vocalists: The Silver Masked Tenor (Joseph M. White)
Announcer: Phil Carlin

This program, first broadcast in the late 1920s, was sponsored by the B. F. Goodrich Company.

The Goodwill Hour

Advice

Starring: John J. Anthony
Announcer: Roland Winters
Director: Thomas F. Vietor, Jr.

Opening:

ANNOUNCER. You have a friend and adviser in John J. Anthony. And thousands are happier and more successful today *because* of John J. Anthony.

Mr. Anthony (whose real name was Lester Kroll) dispensed advice on personal problems to people who would come before his microphone and bare their troubles and woes. He was continually admonishing them not to touch the microphone and to use "no names, please." The broadcasts began over Mutual on April 10, 1936, and remained on the air for some twenty-five years.

Gordon: see *Dorothy Gordon.*

The Gospel Hour: see *Religion.*

Grand Central Station

Drama

Narrator: Jack Arthur
Guest Actors: Hume Cronyn, Nancy Coleman, Beverly Bayne, Mary Mason, Arnold Moss, McKay Morris, Jim Ameche, *et al.*
Announcers: Tom Shirley, Ken Roberts
Producers: Martin Horrell, Himan Brown
Directors: William Rousseau, Ray H. Kremer, Ira Ashley
Writers: Martin Horrell, Jay Bennett, Ethel Abby, Elinor Lenz, Dena Reed
Sound Effects: Jim Rogan

Opening:

SOUND. *Train effects up full and under*

ANNOUNCER. As a bullet seeks its target, shining rails in every part of our great country are aimed at Grand Central Station, heart of the nation's greatest city. Drawn by the magnetic force of the fantastic metropolis, day and night great trains rush toward the Hudson River, sweep down its eastern bank for 140 miles, flash briefly by the long red row of tenement houses south of 125th Street, dive with a roar into the two-and-one-half-mile tunnel which burrows beneath the glitter and swank of Park Avenue and then . . .

SOUND. *Escaping steam from locomotive . . .*

ANNOUNCER. Grand Central Station . . . crossroads of a million private lives . . . gigantic stage on which are played a thousand dramas daily!

(The opening featured the sound of chugging steam engines although all trains to Grand Central Station were, in fact, electric.)

Grand Central Station was heard in various time-slots over the years. It was first heard over NBC Blue in 1937 as a Friday-night-at-8:00 series.

Grand Hotel

Drama

Featuring: Don Ameche, Anne Seymour, Betty Winkler, Phil Lord, Don Briggs, Jim Ameche, Barbara Luddy, Olan Soule, Raymond Edward Johnson
Telephone operator: Betty Winkler
Producer: Joe Ainley
Writer: George Vandel

Grand Hotel was first heard over the Blue network in 1933.

Grand Marquee

Drama

Starring: Olan Soule, Beryl Vaughn
Director: Norman Felton
Writer: Virginia Safford Lynne

The Grand Ole Opry

Variety

CAST:
The Solemn Old Judge — George D. Hay
Cousin Minnie Pearl — Sarah Ophelia Colley Cannon
The Duke of Paducah — Whitey Ford
Featuring: Rod Brasfield; Uncle Jimmy Thompson, fiddler and Civil War veteran; Sarie and Sally (first female stars of the Opry; actually sisters, Mrs. Edna Wilson and Mrs. Margaret Waters); Roy Acuff; Hank Williams; Ruth Douglas; Bill Monroe; Red Foley; Ernest Tubb; Gene Autry; Lasses White; Jamup and Honey (Jim Sanders and Lee Davis "Honey" Wilds); Grandpa Jones; Robert Lunn ("The Talkin' Blues Man"); Asher Sizemore and Little Jimmie (father and son); Pee Wee King; Rachel Veach, guitarist; The Cumberland Valley Boys; Paul Warmack and His Gully Jumpers; George Wilkerson and His Fruit Jar Drinkers; Dr. Humphrey Bate and His Possum Hunters; The Delmore Brothers (singing team of Alton and Rayburn Delmore); De Ford

Bailey, harmonica player; Uncle Dave Macon ("The Dixie Dewdrop") and his son Dorris; Eddy Arnold ("The Tennessee Plowboy"); many others

Announcer: Louie Buck

Originators: George D. Hay and Jimmy Thompson

Directors: Kenneth W. MacGregor, Jack Stapp, Ott Devine

Writers: Dave Murray, Cliff Thomas, Noel Digby

Catch-phrases:

COUSIN MINNIE PEARL. Howdy! I'm just so proud to be here!

DUKE OF PADUCAH. I'm goin' back to the wagon, boys. These shoes are killin' me.

The Grand Ole Opry, which made its debut on November 28, 1925, was broadcast over the facilities of WSM Nashville (Tennessee). It featured country music and comedy. Every big-name performer in the country music field appeared, as well as other entertainers such as Marguerite Piazza and Helen Traubel.

The *Opry* originally emanated from a small studio at WSM with no audience except a few friends and relatives of the performers. Then the program was moved into a larger room called Studio B, where the walls were knocked out to accommodate an audience of 200. Later, when a new wing was added to the building and Studio C was built, the program was broadcast before a studio audience of 500. Soon the program moved again—this time to the Little Theater on Belcourt Avenue, which had a seating capacity of 750. The show eventually outgrew this facility and went to the Dixie Tabernacle on Fatherland Street, which could accommodate an audience of 3500. Later the program was broadcast from the War Memorial Auditorium. In 1942 it moved to the Ryman Auditorium, which had a capacity of 3300. In 1961 the Ryman Corporation sold the auditorium to WSM, Inc., and the structure became known as the Grand Ole Opry House. In 1970 plans were formulated to erect a new 4340-seat auditorium, using the planks from the stage of the Ryman Auditorium along with some of the old bricks and a few of the pews.

The program originally lasted one hour and five minutes and was first known as *The WSM Barn Dance.* George D. Hay changed it to *The Grand Ole Opry* in February 1926 after he heard Dr. Walter Damrosch allude to "Grand Opry." Within two years it was a three-hour program and its time was steadily increased over the years until it reached a Saturday-night broadcast of five full hours. It was always broadcast in its entirety and never was pre-empted, never had a summer replacement, never had an intermission. In October 1939 NBC began to carry thirty minutes of the show on the network. Prince Albert tobacco sponsored this network portion. Only the network broadcast used writers—the rest of the broadcast was never scripted. There were many sponsors of the non-network portion —among them, Schick, Kellogg's, Coca-Cola, Lava, and Pet Milk.

Grand Slam

Musical Quiz

Starring: Irene Beasley
With: Dwight Weist
Directors: Kirby Ayers, Victor Sack
Writers: Irene Beasley, Lillian Schoen

This was a musical quiz operated on the principles of a bridge game. If a studio contestant missed a trick (fluffed an answer), the prize went to the listener who had submitted the question. Five tricks taken in a row was a "Grand Slam" for which the winner was awarded a $100 United States Savings Bond. The program was first heard over CBS in 1943.

Grandma Travels

Serial Drama

CAST:
Grandma — Hazel Dopheide
Announcer: Les Griffith

Grandma Travels was a syndicated program recorded in Chicago and sponsored by Sears, Roebuck and Company.

Grandpa Burton

Drama

Grandpa Burton and all other characters: Bill Baar

This program was first heard over NBC in 1935.

Grandstand Thrills

Sports

Narrator: Olan Soule
Producer: Dick Wells
Director: Les Weinrot

This was an episodic sports program in the style of *The March of Time.*

The Great Gildersleeve

Situation Comedy

CAST:
Throckmorton P. Gildersleeve — Hal Peary, Willard Waterman
Leroy Forrester, his nephew — Walter Tetley
Marjorie Forrester, his niece — Lurene Tuttle, Marylee Robb
Judge Hooker — Earle Ross
Birdie Lee Coggins, the maid — Lillian Randolph
Peavey, the druggist — Richard Legrand, Forrest Lewis
Oliver Honeywell — Hans Conried
Floyd, the barber — Arthur Q. Bryan
Adeline Fairchild — Una Merkel
Leila Ransom — Shirley Mitchell
Craig Bullard — Tommy Bernard
Bronco Thompson — Dick Crenna
Eve Goodwin — Bea Benaderet
Orchestra: Jack Meakin
Announcer: John Wald

Directors: Fran Van Hartesfeldt, Karl Gruener, Cecil Underwood
Writers: John Whedon, Sam Moore,

Virginia Safford Lynne, Andy White

Catch-phrases:

GILDERSLEEVE (*exasperated*). L-eeeee-roy!

PEAVEY. Well, now, Mr. Gildersleeve. I wouldn't say that.

"Gildersleeve" originated as a character on *Fibber McGee and Molly*. On his own program, which began on NBC, August 31, 1941, Gildersleeve was the bachelor uncle of two children—"Leroy," a pestiferous boy who called Gildersleeve "Unk," and "Marjorie," a teenager. They lived in the town of "Summerfield," where Gildy was the Water Commissioner. Many attempts were made to marry him off, particularly to the Southern belle, "Leila Ransom."

Great Gunns

Situation Comedy

CAST:

Veronica Gunn — Barbara Luddy
Chris Gunn — Bret Morrison
Pop Gunn — Phil Lord
Buster Gunn — Bob Jellison
Moe Hoffman, their agent — Marvin Miller
Gloomy, the butler — Marvin Miller
Myra — Donna Reade
Lorson Snells, actor-producer — Marvin Miller
Orchestra: Harold Stokes

Producer-Director: William A. Bacher
Writer: Forrest Barnes

Great Gunns was heard over Mutual in 1941 and ran for one season. It was a spoof of a modern stage family and got by with many uncensored bits far in advance of its time. "Lorson Snells" was, of course, a parody of Orson Welles.

Great Plays

Drama

Director: Charles Warburton

This series featured radio adaptations of such plays as *Biography* by S. N. Behrman, *The Truth* by Clyde Fitch, and *The American Way* by Kaufman and Hart. *Great Plays* was first heard over NBC Blue in 1938.

The Greatest Story Ever Told

Religious Drama

CAST:

Jesus — Warren Parker
Announcer: Norman Rose

Directors: Marx Loeb, Henry Denker
Writer: Henry Denker
Sound Effects: Terry Ross
Musical Director: Jacques Belasco

This series of dramatizations of the life of Christ was based on the famous book by Fulton Oursler, which was, in turn, based on the Bible. It was first heard in 1947 on Sunday at 6:30 p.m., sponsored by the Goodyear Tire and Rubber Company. The only announcement of its sponsorship, however, came at the end of the program when the announcer said simply, "*The Greatest Story Ever*

Told has been brought to you by the Goodyear Tire and Rubber Company." No other commercial or sponsor identification was given.

During its tenure on the air this program featured most of the regular New York dramatic radio actors; the only continuing role was that of Jesus. The sound effects were particularly unique. Instead of modern footsteps, for instance, the sound of sandals had to be employed; and unusual door effects had to be devised since there were no doors with modern latches and hinges in Biblical times.

The Green Hornet

Mystery-Adventure

CAST:

Britt Reid (The Green Hornet)
Al Hodge (1936–43)
Donovan Faust (1943)
Bob Hall (1943–46)
Jack McCarthy (1946–52)

Kato, Reid's faithful valet
Raymond Hayashi
Rollon Parker
Mickey Tolan

Lenore Case ("Casey"), Reid's secretary — Lee Allman

Michael Axford, reporter — Jim Irwin, Gil Shea

Ed Lowry, ace reporter — Jack Petruzzi

Newsboy — Rollon Parker

Announcers: Charles Woods, Mike Wallace, Fielden Farrington, Bob Hite, Hal Neal

---

Creators: Fran Striker, George W. Trendle

Producer-Writer-Director: James Jewell

Director: Charles Livingstone

Writer: Fran Striker

Theme: "Flight of the Bumblebee" by Rimsky-Korsakov

Opening:

ANNOUNCER. *The Green Hornet!*

SOUND. *Hornet buzz up full*

ANNOUNCER. He hunts the biggest of all game! Public enemies who try to destroy our America!

MUSIC. *Theme up full and under . . .*

ANNOUNCER. With his faithful valet, Kato, Britt Reid, daring young publisher, matches wits with the underworld, risking his life that criminals and racketeers, within the law, may feel its weight by the sting of The Green Hornet!

SOUND. *"Black Beauty" car pulls out . . . up full*

ANNOUNCER. Ride with Britt Reid in the thrilling adventure "Death Stalks the City." The Green Hornet strikes again!

SOUND. *Hornet buzz up full*

Green Hornet Appearance Segment:

ANNOUNCER. Stepping through a secret panel in the rear of the closet in his bedroom, Britt Reid and Kato went along a narrow passageway built within the walls of the apartment itself. This passage led to an adjoining building, which fronted on a dark sidestreet . . .

SOUND. *Footsteps cross garage floor . . . fade in and continue through . . .*

ANNOUNCER. Though supposedly abandoned, this building served as the hiding place for the sleek superpowered Black Beauty, streamlined car of The Green Hornet.

SOUND. *Footsteps to car . . . door open . . . car door slam*

ANNOUNCER. Britt Reid pressed a button . . .

SOUND. *Car start*

ANNOUNCER. The great car roared into life . . .

SOUND. *Car idle up . . . sound of wall section opening*

ANNOUNCER. A section of the wall in front raised automatically, then closed, as the Black Beauty sped into the darkness.

SOUND. *Car pull-out up full . . . two gear changes . . . cross fade music*

Closing:

MUSIC. *Theme up full and under . . .*

NEWSBOY. Special extry! Murderers in jail! City saved from deadly ray gun! Read all about it! Green Hornet still at large! Special extry! Paper!!!

MUSIC. *Theme up full*

Although the Green Hornet helped to bring criminals to justice, the police were constantly trying to capture him. They never did, though. The Hornet used a gas gun to subdue his enemies, but they were only temporarily immobilized—just long enough for him to leave his Green Hornet seal and escape before the police arrived.

"Axford," the reporter, was an Irishman with a thick brogue who was always kidding "Miss Case," the secretary, and using the expression, "Holy crow!" They worked at the newspaper that "Britt Reid" published, "The Daily Sentinel." One of the good stories of radio's Golden Age is that the faithful valet "Kato" was Japanese until December 7, 1941, when he suddenly was referred to as "Reid's faithful *Filipino* valet, Kato." Our research, however, uncovered no evidence of such an abrupt change.

Both *The Green Hornet* and *The Lone Ranger* were created by Fran Striker and George W. Trendle and were broadcast from Detroit, where a stock company of solid actors appeared on both programs. There were some interesting parallels between the two programs. The Green Hornet's name was Britt Reid, and The Lone Ranger's name was John Reid. Britt Reid was referred to as "The Lone Ranger's grand-nephew." Each had his "faithful side-kick"—Kato and Tonto, respectively. Each had a superior means of transportation, the Black Beauty and Silver. And each one fought crime, but not as part of a formal law-enforcement agency. Rather, they carried out their adventures as semi-fugitives from the law, always disappearing just before the law took over.

The Green Hornet was broadcast over Mutual beginning in 1938.

Green Valley, USA

Drama

Narrator: Santos Ortega
Producer-Director: Himan Brown
Writer: Millard Lampell

This program featured patriotic dramas.

Grits and Gravy

Serial Drama

Featuring: George Gaul, Peggy Paige
Also: Wilbur Lytell, Marjorie Main, Sarah Hayden
Writer: Louise Marion

The Groucho Marx Show: see *Blue Ribbon Town; You Bet Your Life.*

The Grummits

Situation Comedy

Featuring: Ed Ford, Eunice Howard, Peter Donald
Director: Roger Bower
Writer: Ed Ford

The Grummits was first heard over Mutual in 1935. The Ed Ford was "Senator" Ford, best remembered for *Can You Top This?*

The Guiding Light

Serial Drama

CAST:

Ned Holden — Ed Prentiss
Mary Ruthledge — Sarajane Wells, Mercedes McCambridge
Dr. John Ruthledge — Arthur Peterson
Ruth Craig — Beverly Ruby
Rose Kransky — Ruth Bailey, Charlotte Manson
Spike Wilson — Frank Dane
Ellis Smith ("Mr. Nobody from Nowhere") — Sam Wanamaker, Phil Dakin, Marvin Miller, Raymond Edward Johnson
Iris Marsh — Betty Arnold
Norma Greenman — Eloise Kummer
Dr. McNeill — Sidney Breese
Edward Greenman — Ken Griffin
Nancy Stewart — Laurette Fillbrandt
Peggy Gaylord — Jane Webb
Sister Ada — Alma Samuels
Sister Lillian — Annette Harper
Laura Martin — Gail Henshaw
Jacob Kransky — Seymour Young
Gordon Ellis — Raymond Edward Johnson
Rev. Tom Bannion — Frank Behrens
"The Past"[1] — Marvin Miller
Mrs. Kransky — Mignon Schreiber
Torchy Reynolds Holden — Gladys Heen
Fredericka Lang — Margaret Fuller, Muriel Bremner
Trudy Bauer — Laurette Fillbrandt
Ellen — Henrietta Tedro
Roy Fencher — Willard Waterman
Clifford Foster — Bret Morrison
Charles Cunningham — Bill Bouchey
Mrs. Cunningham — Lesley Woods
Martin Kane — Michael Romano
Dr. Charles Matthews — Hugh Studebaker
Julie Collins — Mary Lansing
Roger Collins — Sam Edwards, Leonard Waterman
Charlotte Brandon — Betty Lou Gerson
Ted White — Arnold Moss
Meta Bauer — Jone Allison
Celeste Cunningham — Carolyn McKay
Grandpa Ellis — Phil Lord
Phyllis Gordon — Sharon Grainger
Peter Manno — Michael Romano
Ethel Foster — Sunda Love

[1] See *The Right to Happiness*, p. 256, for explanation.

Bill Bauer — Lyle Sudrow
Announcer: Clayton "Bud" Collyer

Producer-Director: Joe Ainley
Producers: Carl Wester, David Lesan
Directors: Charles Urquhart, Gordon Hughes, Harry Bubeck, Howard Keegan, Gil Gibbons, Ted MacMurray
Writer: Irna Phillips
Sound Effects: Ralph Cummings, Hamilton O'Hara

Theme: "Aphrodite"
Opening:
ANNOUNCER. *The Guiding Light,* created by Irna Phillips.

The Guiding Light first appeared on NBC in 1938 and originated in Chicago. It told the story of "the Reverend Ruthledge," a kindly cleric who showed people how to live a good life through patience and understanding.

Irna Phillips was known as "the queen of the soap operas." She had dozens of writers in her stable. Her shows were produced by Carl Wester & Company, and the advertising agencies, sponsors, and networks had little control over them. Wester took it upon himself to be responsible for casting and announcers.

Gulliver: see *The Fire Chief.*

The Gumps

Comedy-Drama

CAST:

Andy Gump	Wilmer Walter
Min Gump	Agnes Moorehead
Chester Gump	Jackie Kelk

Announcer: Ralph Edwards

Writers: Himan Brown, Irwin Shaw

Catch-phrase:
ANDY. Oh, Min!

The Gumps was based on the comic strip by Sidney Smith. It became a network show via CBS in 1934. An earlier version was broadcast locally over WGN Chicago with the following cast:

Andy Gump	Jack Boyle
Min Gump	Dorothy Denver
Chester Gump	Charles Flynn, Jr.
Tilda, the maid	Bess Flynn

Gunsmoke

Western Adventure

CAST:
Matt Dillon, U.S. Marshal — William Conrad
Chester Goode, his deputy — Parley Baer
Kitty Russell — Georgia Ellis
Doc Adams — Howard McNear
Also: Joseph Kearns, Barney Phillips, Harry Bartell, Sam Edwards, Lawrence Dobkin, Vic Perrin

Sound Effects: Tom Hanley, Ray Kemper

Although this program first appeared on CBS in 1955, placing it outside the scope of this book, it is one of the best-remembered Western adventures series because of its excellent writing and acting and the remarkable realism of its sound effects, right down to the clink of spurs and the creak of floorboards whenever anyone walked across the saloon floor.

H

The Hal Peary Show

Situation Comedy

CAST:

Honest Harold, a radio commentator — Hal Peary
Gloria, Harold's girl friend — Gloria Holliday

This show was first heard over CBS in 1950.

The Hallmark Playhouse

Drama

Host-Narrator: James Hilton[1]
Producer-Director: Dee Engelbach
Writer: Jean Holloway
Sound Effects: Harry Essman, Gene Twombly
Musical Conductor: Lyn Murray
Theme: "Dream of Olwen" by Charles Williams

This program, sponsored by Hallmark greeting cards, was first heard over CBS in 1948 and featured dramatizations of outstanding stories from contemporary literature. In 1955 the program became known as *The Hallmark Radio Hall of Fame.*

[1] Author of *Random Harvest, Lost Horizon, Goodbye, Mr. Chips,* etc.

The Halls of Ivy

Drama

CAST:

Dr. William Todhunter Hall, college president — Ronald Colman
Victoria Cromwell Hall (Vicky), his wife — Benita Hume Colman
Mr. Merriweather — Willard Waterman
Clarence Wellman — Herbert Butterfield
Penny, the maid — Gloria Gordon

Creator-Writer: Don Quinn
Director: Nat Wolff
Theme: "The Halls of Ivy"

This series was first heard in 1949 over NBC at 8:00 p.m. on Fridays. It was set on a small college campus.

The Hamilton Family: see *The American School of the Air.*

Hannibal Cobb

Detective

CAST:

Hannibal Cobb, detective — Santos Ortega
Announcer: Les Griffith

Directors: William D. Hamilton, Charles Powers, Roy La Plante
Writers: Bernard Dougall, Ira Marion, Lillian Schoen
Organist: Rosa Rio

Opening:

MUSIC. *Organ march music up full, then under for . . .*

ANNOUNCER. Each weekday at this time the American Broadcasting Company presents . . . Hannibal Cobb . . . as you will find him in the Photocrime pages of *Look* magazine. Here is a dramatic story of human conflict vividly told from the point of view of someone closely involved.

Closing:

MUSIC. *Organ march music up full, then under for . . .*

ANNOUNCER. Be with us each weekday Monday through Friday at this time when Hannibal Cobb will bring you an exciting story of human conflict, presented by the American Broadcasting Company.

Hannibal Cobb was first heard over ABC in 1949. Cobb lived at 17 South Jackson.

The Happiness Boys

Music

Starring: Billy Jones and Ernie Hare

Theme:

(If your memory is long enough you'll remember it.) "How-do-you-do, everybody, how-do-you-do;
Don't forget your Friday date,
Seven-thirty until eight;
How-do-you-do, everybody, how-do-you-do!"

Jones and Hare are closely associated with the development of early radio as they were two of the medium's first big stars. On October 18, 1921, they sang and told jokes for ninety minutes over WJZ New York. This launched them on an eighteen-year radio career, which ended on March 9, 1939, when Ernie Hare died. His daughter Marilyn continued for a while as the Hare of Jones and Hare until November 23, 1940, when Jones died.

Jones and Hare sang their vocal duets of comic songs and sentimental ballads for various sponsors and, depending upon *which* sponsor, they were variously known as "The Happiness Boys," "The Interwoven Pair," "The Best Foods Boys," and "The Taystee Loafers."

Happy Hollow

Drama

Producer-Writer: Everett Kemp

This dramatic series was first heard over CBS in 1935. Set in a small American town, the stories featured such characters as "Uncle Ezra Butternut," "Aunt Lucinda Skinflint," "Little Douglas Butternut," "Aaron and Sarah Peppertag," "Charity Grubb," "Jennie Oaksberry," "Grandpa Beasley," etc.

Happy Island

Comedy

CAST:

King Bubbles	Ed Wynn

(See also *The Fire Chief*.)

The Hardy Family

Comedy-Drama

CAST:

Andy Hardy — Mickey Rooney
Judge Hardy, Andy's father — Lewis Stone
Mrs. Hardy — Jean Parker
Beasey — Dick Crenna
Also: Judy Garland, Fay Holden

Opening:

MUSIC. *Up and under . . .*

ANNOUNCER. We're proud to present *The Hardy Family,* based on the famous Metro-Goldwyn-Mayer motion-picture series which brought to life to millions and reflected the common joys and tribulations of the average American family.

Harold Teen

Situation Comedy

CAST:

Harold Teen — Charles Flynn, Willard Farnum, Eddie Firestone, Jr.
Shadow — Bob Jellison
Lillums — Loretta Poynton, Eunice Yankee
Harold's father — Willard Waterman
Cynthia — Beryl Vaughn
Josie — Rosemary Garbell
Beezie Jenks — Marvin Miller, Jack Spencer
Pop Jenks — Marvin Miller, Jack Spencer

Director: Blair Walliser
Writers: Blair Walliser, Fred Kress

Harold Teen was based on the comic strip by Carl Ed (pronounced "Eed"). The program originated in Chicago and had its debut August 5, 1941. It contributed to the airwaves such bits of dialogue as "Where were you bred, you crumb?"

Harv and Esther

Comedy

CAST:

Harv — Teddy Bergman
Esther — Audrey Marsh
Singers: Jack Arthur, The Rhythm Girls
Orchestra: Vic Arden

This series was first presented over NBC in 1935. It was sponsored by International Harvester. The names "Harv" and "Esther" were, of course, derived from the word "Harvester."

Harvest of Stars

Music

Starring: James Melton
Orchestra: Howard Barlow, Frank Black
Announcer: Don Hancock
Producer-Director: Glen Heisch

This NBC program, sponsored by International Harvester, began in 1941.

Hawaii Calls

Music

Featuring: Webb Edwards

This program of music from Hawaii, first heard over Mutual in 1945, naturally abounded with "Aloha," references to leis, the hula rhythm, and "as the sun sinks slowly in the west. . . ." It originated in the Hawaiian Islands, and listeners became inured to periodic fading of the transmission, which seemed to make the broadcast all the more charming and exciting.

Hawthorne House

Serial Drama

CAST:

Mother Sherwood	Pearl King Tanner
Mel Sherwood	Monty Mohn Jack Moyles
Marietta Sherwood	Bobbie Dean Florida Edwards
Billy Sherwood	Eddie Firestone, Jr. Sam Edwards
Chic Morgan	Ted Maxwell
Lois Liston	Natalie Park
Jerry Tremaine	Donald Dudley John Pickard
Miriam	Billie Byers
Linda Carroll	Ruth Sprague
Uncle Jim	Jack Kirkwood
Duke Calloway	Bert Horton
Martha	Dixie Marsh
Alice James	Ruth Sprague
Hilary Hobson	Don Holloway
Judge Carter	Earl Lee
Curley Brooks	Charles Gerard
Frenchy Hammond	Lou Tobin

Writers: David Drummond, Ray Buffum, Cameron Prud'Homme

Hawthorne House told the story of a wealthy family left penniless. The widow, "Mother Sherwood," had to provide for her children. She turned her mansion into a guest house and also found time to adopt a boy whom she raised as her own. The program originated in San Francisco on NBC.

Headline Hunters

News

Hosts: Floyd Gibbons, Lowell Thomas

Headline Hunters was one of radio's earliest news programs. It was first heard over NBC in 1929.

Hear It Now

Commentary

Featuring: Edward R. Murrow, news commentator

Hear It Now did replays of famous events heard on the air.

Hearthstone of the Death Squad: see *Mystery Theater*.

Heart's Desire

Audience Participation

M.C.: Ben Alexander
Director: Dave Grant

This was first heard over Mutual in 1946.

Hearts in Harmony

Drama

CAST:
Penny — Jone Allison
Mrs. Gibbs — Alice Yourman
Inspector Hale — King Calder
Penny's aunt — Ellen Maher
Penny's GI friends — Bill Lipton, Bill Redfield, Bob Walker, George Matthews

Vocalists: Bob Hanna, Anne Marlowe
Pianist: Vic Arden
Announcer: Ed Herlihy

Director: Martha Atwell

Hearts in Harmony, sponsored by Kroger, told the story of a volunteer entertainer in a USO club. Her adventures were bound up in patriotic efforts. When the script called for her to sing, Anne Marlowe took over.

Hedda Hopper: see *Hollywood Reporters.*

Helen and Mary: see *The Adventures of Helen and Mary.*

The Helen Hayes Theatre

Drama

Hostess: Helen Hayes
Announcer: George Bryan
Director: Lester O'Keefe

This prestige drama series featuring "The First Lady of the Theatre" was first heard on the NBC Blue network in 1935. A typical dramatization was "The Ghost and Mrs. Muir," starring Maurice Evans as Captain Daniel Gregg, and Helen Hayes as Mrs. Muir.

Helen Trent: see *The Romance of Helen Trent.*

Hello, Peggy

Serial Drama

CAST:
Peggy Hopkins — Eunice Howard
Ted Hopkins — Alan Bunce
Bellboys — Jackie Kelk, Andy Donnelly

Hello, Peggy was first heard over NBC in 1937.

Helpmate

Serial Drama

CAST:
Linda Emerson Harper — Arlene Francis, Fern Persons
Steve Harper — Myron McCormick, John Larkin
Grace Marshall — Judith Evelyn, Ruth Perrott
Irene Emerson — Kathryn Card
Clyde Marshall — Karl Weber
George Emerson — Sidney Ellstrom
Holly Emerson — Beryl Vaughn

Writer: Margaret Lerwerth

Helpmate made its debut over NBC in 1941 and originated in Chicago.

Henry Adams and His Book: see *Soap Operas.*

Henry Aldrich: see *The Aldrich Family.*

The Henry Morgan Show

Comedy

Starring: Henry Morgan

CAST:

Gerard	Arnold Stang
Hortense	Florence Halop
The Athlete	Art Carney
Mrs. Beethoven	Madeleine Lee
Gertrude	Madeleine Lee
Daphne	Alice Pearce

Also: Durward Kirby, Betty Garde, Minerva Pious, Maurice Gosfield

Orchestra: Bernie Green

Vocal group: Billy Williams

Announcers: Charles Irving, Ben Grauer, Art Ballinger (when the show was in California), David Ross, Dan Seymour, Ed Herlihy

---

Director: Charles Powers

Writers: Henry Morgan, Aaron Ruben, Joe Stein, Carroll Moore, Jr.

Theme: "For He's a Jolly Good Fellow"

Catch-phrases:

ATHLETE. Yessir, Mr. *Morgan!*

GERARD. Ich!

GERARD. What's to worry?

Opening:

MUSIC. *Theme . . . up full and under . . .*

MORGAN. Hello, anybody. Here's Morgan.

Closing:

MORGAN. Morgan'll be on this same corner in front of the cigar store next week at this same time.

Henry Morgan was one of radio's "angry young men." His acerbic satires left very little untouched. His first shows were on for fifteen minutes in the early evening on WOR New York, and he would play crazy records from his own collection and give his sponsors the needle. His penchant for satirizing even his own sponsors often cost him their patronage. Among the earlier sponsors were Adler Elevator Shoes, which was ripe for Morgan's kidding, and Life Savers, which Morgan claimed were "mulcting the public" because of the hole in the center. A later sponsor was Schick Injector Razors, whose slogan was "Push, pull, click, click—change blades that quick." At one point Morgan referred to the slogan as "Push, pull, nick, nick." He once started the program by announcing that Schick had called him on the carpet because sales were dropping, implying that his show was the reason. Morgan announced, "Frankly, I don't think it's my show. I think it's their razor!"

Her Honor, Nancy James

Serial Drama

CAST:

Nancy James	Barbara Weeks
Mayor Richard Wharton	Joseph Curtin
Anthony Hale, the D.A.	Ned Wever

Mrs. Evelyn Wharton	Kay Strozzi
Carrie Dean	Alice Reinheart
Madge Keller	Janice Gilbert
Stan Adamic	Chester Stratton
George Novack	Maurice Franklin
Ellen Clark	Joan Banks
Laura	Claire Niesen
Trixie	Janice Gilbert
Dr. Baxter	Michael Fitzmaurice
Closing voice	Basil Loughrane

This program was first heard over CBS in 1938.

Here's Babe Ruth

Sports

Starring: Babe Ruth
M.C.: Ben Grauer

This program featured baseball star Babe Ruth answering youngsters' questions.

The Hermit's Cave

Horror Drama

Opening:

SOUND. *Wind . . . dogs howling . . . cackling laughter for . . .*

THE HERMIT. Ghost stories, weird stories and murders too. The Hermit knows of them all. Turn out your lights. TURN THEM OUT!!! Ahhhhh. Have you heard the story—? Then listen while The Hermit tells you the story.

SOUND. *Effects up full and under . . .*

ANNOUNCER. The Mummers in the Little Theater of The Air present *The Hermit's Cave.*

Closing:

SOUND. *Wind . . . dogs howling*

THE HERMIT. The Hermit has more stories for you. Listen again next week for our hounds howling when I'll tell you the story of— Heh, heh, heh, heh!

High Places

Drama

Featuring: Clayton "Bud" Collyer

Highway Patrol

Adventure

CAST:

State Trooper Cpl. Steve Taylor	Michael Fitzmaurice
Taylor's side-kick	John McGovern

Director: Allen DuCovny

Highways in Melody

Music

This long-running musical program featured many performers. It made its debut on NBC on February 18, 1925.

Hilda Hope, M.D.

Drama

Hilda Hope	Selena Royle

Writer: Himan Brown

Hilltop House

Serial Drama

CAST:

Bess Johnson — Bess Johnson
Julie Erickson — Grace Matthews, Jan Miner
Jerry Adair — Jimmy Donnelly
Jean Adair — Janice Gilbert
Grace Doblen, superintendent — Vera Allen
Jeffrey Barton — John Moore
David Jeffers — John Moore
Dr. Robby Clark — Carleton Young, Spencer Bentley
Paul Hutchinson — Alfred Swenson, Jack Roseleigh
Thelma Gidley — Irene Hubbard
Steve Cortland — Joe Curtin
Stella Rudnick — Estelle Levy
Tulip Valentine Elson — Gee Gee James
Pokey — Maurice Ellis
Tiny Tim — Ronald Liss
Frank Klabber — Jay Jostyn
Gilda Boros — Ethel Everett
Dr. Boros — Richard Gordon
Capt. John Barry — David Gothard
Bill Grey — Wallace Warner
Pixie Osborne — Jeanne Elkins
Hannah — Lilli Darvas
Kevin Burke — Alvin Sullum
Clement Arnaud — Jimmy Tansey
Mrs. Jessup — Ethel Everett
David Burke — Dickie Wigginton
Linda Clark — Dorothy Lowell
Marny — Jackie Kelk
Lana — Helen Coulé
Gwen Barry — Evelyn Streich
Roy Barry — Jerry Tucker
Hazel — Margaret Curtis
Shirley — Nancy Peterson
Duke — Ray Walker
Clementine Arnaud — Iris Mann, Norma Jane Marlowe
Michael Paterno — Lamont Johnson
Ed Crowley — James Van Dyk
Daniel Findlay — Edwin Bruce

Also: Donald Briggs, Susan Thorne

Producer: Ed Wolfe
Directors: Carlo De Angelo, Jack Rubin
Writers: Adelaide Marston (pen name for Addy Richton and Lynn Stone)
Musical Director: Chester Kingsbury
Sound Effects: Hamilton O'Hara, John McCloskey
Theme: Brahms' "Lullaby"

Hilltop House was "dedicated to the women of America. The story of a woman who must choose between love and the career of raising other women's children." The program was carried by both Mutual and CBS in its first year on the air—1937. In March 1941, *Hilltop House* became *The Story of Bess Johnson* (which see). The Bess Johnson character and the actress moved from the orphanage, where she was a matron, to become the superintendent of a boarding school.

His Honor, the Barber

Drama

CAST:

Judge Fitz — Barry Fitzgerald

Also: Barbara Fuller, Leo Cleary, William Greene, Dawn Bender
Announcer: Frank Martin

Writer: Carlton E. Morse

The show was first heard over NBC in 1945.

The Hit Parade: see *Your Hit Parade.*

Hit the Jackpot

Quiz

M.C.: Bill Cullen
Orchestra: Al Goodman
Vocal group: Ray Charles Singers
Announcers: George Bryan, Richard Stark
Producers: Mark Goodson, Bill Todman
Director: Bill Todman
Sound Effects: Jim Rogan

This quiz show made its debut on CBS in 1948.

Hobby Lobby

Human Interest

M.C.: Dave Elman
Orchestra: Harry Salter, Harry Sosnik
Announcer: Alan Kent
Directors: Addison Smith, Edward Pola, Joe Hill
Writers: Ed Ettinger, Roy Maypole, Jr.

This program featured people with interesting and unusual hobbies. Each week a different celebrity was on hand to "lobby his hobby." *Hobby Lobby* was first heard over the Blue network in 1937.

Holly Sloan

Serial Drama

CAST:

Holly Sloan	Gale Page
Lauralee McWilliams	Marlene Ames
Henry Sloan	Charles Seel
Keturah	Georgia Backus
Johnny Starr	Bob Bailey
Millicent Starr	B. J. Thompson
Adele Kingman	Helene Burke
Wilbur Ramage	Bob Griffin
Prentiss Jeffries	Joe Forte
Clay Brown	Vic Perrin
Sally	Louise Arthur

Holly Sloan was first heard over NBC in 1947.

Hollywood Calling

Quiz

Host: George Murphy
Producer: Victor Knight

Hollywood Calling was a 1949 summer replacement for *The Jack Benny Program* on NBC. Contestants were tested on their knowledge of motion pictures while being given clues. Correct answers could lead to a jackpot of prizes valued at about $30,000.

Hollywood Good News

Variety

Host: Robert Young
James Stewart
Director: Ed Gardner

Hollywood Good News was the successor to *Show Boat* (which see).

Hollywood Hotel

Drama

Hosts: Dick Powell, Fred MacMurray, Herbert Marshall, William Powell
Hostess: Louella O. Parsons, gossip columnist

CAST:
Telephone operator — Duane Thompson (a woman)
Jinny, the soprano — Anne Jamison
Orchestra: Raymond Paige
Ted Fio Rito
Guests: Frank Parker, Jean Sablon, Igor Gorin, Frances Langford, Jerry Cooper, Jone Williams, Leo Carrillo
Announcer: Ken Niles

Producer: Bill Bacher
Director: George MacGarrett
Writers: Victor Chevigny, Ed James

Theme: "Blue Moon"
Opening:
TELEPHONE OPERATOR: Hollywood Hotel . . . Hollywood Hotel . . . good evening.

Hollywood Hotel, first heard over CBS in 1934, featured Hollywood stars in radio dramas. Its success, at a time when New York and Chicago were the major production centers, helped to make Hollywood an origination point for major radio programs.

Hollywood Jackpot

Variety

M.C.: Kenny Delmar
Announcer: Bill Cullen
Producer: Louis Cowan
Director: Gordon Auchincloss

Hollywood Jackpot was first heard over CBS in 1946. One of the most popular segments was the "Hollywood Screen Test." Members of the studio audience would be invited to take a screen test. They were asked to perform absurd stunts, such as to fly to the balcony or to read a part for Lassie, the famous dog. Guest stars appeared to plug personal appearances or new movies. Kenny Delmar played a character named "Rasputin X. Delmaroff."

Hollywood Playhouse

Drama

M.C.: Charles Boyer
Jim Ameche
Gale Page
Tyrone Power
Herbert Marshall
Musical Director: Harry Sosnik

Hollywood Playhouse was first heard over the Blue network in 1937.

Hollywood Reporters

Over the years, the gossip of Hollywood held a great fascination for listeners, and a number of people made entire radio careers by simply gathering rumors and bits of information and relating them on the air. Hedda Hopper, Jimmy Fidler ("Your Hollywood Reporter"), George Fisher, Sheilah Graham, and Louella O. Parsons ("My first exclusive . . .") were the most popular. Miss Parsons was the best known through her Sunday-night broadcasts on which she often had a guest star for an interview. Her distinctive voice and speech pattern were freely imitated by various radio comedians. Impersonators often drawled, "Now, Mar . . . vin," which she said frequently to Marvin Miller, who was her announcer during the entire run of her fifteen-minute, Sunday program from 1945 to 1951. She occupied the second half of a half-hour for Jergens. Walter Winchell was on from New York during the first fifteen minutes for Jergens Lotion, and Louella Parsons followed from Hollywood for Woodbury Soap. Her constant fear was that Winchell would scoop her on a hot Hollywood item—which he often did.

Hollywood Screen Test: see *Hollywood Jackpot*.

Home of the Brave

Serial Drama

CAST:

Joe	Tom Tully
	Ed Latimer
Casino	Sammie Hill (a woman)
Spencer Howard	Alan Bunce
Doc Gordon	Ed Latimer
Patrick Mulvaney	Ted de Corsia
Lois Farmer	Joan Banks
Lois Davisson	Jone Allison
Neil Davisson	Richard Widmark
	Vincent Donehue

Home of the Brave made its debut over CBS in 1940.

Home Sweet Home

Serial Drama

CAST:

Fred Kent	Cecil Secrest
Lucy Kent	Harriet MacGibbon
Dick	Billy Halop
Uncle Will	Joe Latham

Announcers: John Monks, George Ansbro

This series related "The dramatic struggle of Fred and Lucy Kent and their son for a home sweet home of their own."

Honest Harold: see *The Hal Peary Show*.

Honeymoon in New York

Audience Participation

M.C.: Durward Kirby
Joy Hodges
Orchestra: Jerry Jerome
Announcer: Herb Sheldon
Producer: George Voutsas
Writer: Arthur Henley

Honeymoon in New York was first heard over NBC in 1946.

The Honeymooners

Drama

Featuring: Grace and Eddie Albert

Hook 'n' Ladder Follies

Variety

CAST:

Captain Walt — Ralph Dumke
Stringbean Crachet — Wilbur Budd Hulick

Song-Spinners: Johnnie Neher, Margaret Johnson, Travis Johnson, Bella Allen, and Len Stokes

Also: John Cali, banjo-guitarist; King Ross, trombonist; Harry Breuer, xylophonist and vibra-harpist

Hookey Hall

Children's Variety

Starring: Bobby Hookey and His Rocking Horse Rhythm

Bobby, at the age of six, was billed as "America's Youngest National Network Radio Comedian."

Hop Harrigan

Adventure Serial

CAST:

Hop Harrigan — Chester Stratton, Albert Aley
Gail Nolan — Mitzi Gould
Tank Tinker — Kenny Lynch, Jackson Beck

Announcer: Glenn Riggs

Directors: Jessica Maxwell, Allen DuCovny, Jay Clark
Writer: Albert Aley
Sound Effects: Ed Blainey

Opening:

ANNOUNCER. Presenting Hop Harrigan! America's ace of the airwaves!

SOUND. *Airplane in flight*

HOP. CX-4 calling control tower. CX-4 calling control tower. Standing by! Okay, this is Hop Harrigan . . . coming in!

Hop Harrigan first appeared on the airwaves over ABC in 1942.

Hopalong Cassidy

Western Adventure

CAST:

Hopalong Cassidy — William Boyd
California, Hoppy's side-kick — Andy Clyde

Hopalong Cassidy came to radio via Mutual in 1949.

Horace Heidt: see *A Night with Horace Heidt.*

The Horn and Hardart Children's Hour

Children's Variety

Hosts: Paul Douglas (eight years), Ralph Edwards (two years), Ed Herlihy (seventeen years)
Uncle Morty: Mortimer Howard

Featuring: Bobby Hookey, "Termite" Daniels, Billy Daniels, Marion Loveridge, Connie Francis, Carol Bruce, Arthur Q. Lewis, Arnold Stang, The Nicholas Brothers, The Blackstone Twins, Eddie Fisher, Roy Langer, Bea Wain, Joey Heatherton
Producer-Writer-Director: Alice Clements

Theme: (Original music)
Less work for Mother,
Let's give her a hand.
Less work for Mother
And she'll understand.
She's your greatest treasure,
Just make her life a pleasure,
Less work for Mother dear.

Accompanist: W. M. "Billie" James

Although this was never a major network program, it was on the air continuously for twenty-nine years, sponsored by Horn and Hardart restaurants. It was the springboard for many child stars of the 1930s and 1940s. Alice Clements produced, wrote, and directed the program for all twenty-nine years; Paul Douglas, Ralph Edwards, and Ed Herlihy served as hosts for a total of twenty-seven of those twenty-nine years. (See also *Hookey Hall; The Little Betsy Ross Girl Variety Program.*)

Hotel for Pets

Drama

CAST:
Doc — Charlotte Manson
Also: Frank McHugh, Lloyd Richards, Abby Lewis

The Hour of Charm

Music

Starring: Phil Spitalny and His All-Girl Orchestra
Mistress of Ceremonies: Arlene Francis
Featuring: Evelyn and Her Magic Violin (Evelyn Kaye Klein); Vivien (Hollace Shaw); Maxine, vocalist; Jeannie, vocalist; Katharine Smith, cornetist; Viola Schmidt, percussionist
Announcers: Ron Rawson, Richard Stark
Director: Joseph Ripley
Writer: Alton Alexander
Theme: "American Patrol"

This program went on the air in 1929.

The Hour of Decision: see *Religion.*

The Hour of Faith: see *Religion.*

The Hour of Smiles: see *The Fred Allen Show.*

House in the Country

Serial Drama

CAST:
Husband — John Raby
Wife — Joan Banks
Shopkeeper — Raymond Knight
Plumber — Ed Latimer
Telephone operator — Abby Lewis
Also: Lyle Sudrow, Patsy Campbell
Writer: Raymond Knight

This was the story of a city couple's amusing problems when they moved to the country. Knight drew on his own experiences for the characters and situations. The program was first heard over the Blue network in 1941.

The House of Glass

Serial Drama

CAST:

Bessie Glass	Gertrude Berg
Ellen Mudge	Helene Dumas

Writer: Gertrude Berg

The House of Mystery

Mystery

CAST:

Roger Elliott, The Mystery Man — John Griggs

Director: Olga Druce
Writer: Johanna Johnston
Sound Effects: Jack Keane

In this series, children would ask The Mystery Man to tell them a story. They would make appropriate comments from time to time during the storytelling. The program made its debut over Mutual in 1944.

House Party

Audience Participation

M.C.: Art Linkletter
Announcer: Jack Slattery
Producer-Director: John Guedel
Director: Mary Harris
Writers: Jack Stanley, Martin Hill
Sound Effects: Ralph Cummings

House Party was first heard over CBS in 1944.

Houseboat Hannah

Serial Drama

CAST:

Hannah O'Leary	Henrietta Tedro
	Doris Rich
Dan O'Leary	Norman Gottschalk
Clem	Jim Andelin
Shamus	William Rose
Abe Finkelstein	Henry Saxe
Becky Finkelstein	Margaret Shallett
Barbara Hughes	Nancy Douglass
Boss Hughey	William Amsdell
Ellen Smith	Virginia Dwyer
Jim Nichols	Lester Damon
	John Larkin
P. Wallace Carver	Donald Gallagher
Alec Ferguson	Carl Kroenke
Kevin	Frank Derby
Margery Davis	Bonnie Kay

Announcers: Olan Soule, Gene Baker

Houseboat Hannah made its debut over Mutual in 1937. It originated in Chicago.

Howard Thurston, the Magician: see *Thurston, the Magician.*

Howie Wing

Aviation Adventure

CAST:

Howie Wing	William Janney

Donna Cavendish	Mary Parker
Captain Harvey	Neil O'Malley
Burton York	Raymond Bramley
Zero Smith	John Griggs
Typhoon	Robert Strauss
The Chief	Richard Bishop

Howie Wing was first heard over CBS in 1938.

Huckleberry Finn: see *The Adventures of Huckleberry Finn.*

The Hummerts: see *Soap Operas.*

Husbands and Wives

Interviews

Featuring: Allie Lowe Miles, Sedley Brown

I

I Deal in Crime

Mystery

CAST:

Ross Dolan	William Gargan

Director: Leonard Reeg

I Deal in Crime was first heard over ABC in 1945.

I Love a Mystery

Mystery-Adventure

CAST:

Jack Packard	Michael Raffetto
	Russell Thorson
	Jay Novello
	John McIntire
Doc Long	Barton Yarborough
	Jim Boles
Reggie Yorke	Walter Paterson
	Tony Randall
Gerry Booker, secretary	Gloria Blondell

Also: Luis Van Rooten, Mercedes McCambridge, Cathy Lewis, Elliott Lewis, Barbara Jean Wong

Creator-Writer: Carlton E. Morse
Director: Mel Bailey
Writer: Michael Raffetto

Theme: "Valse Triste" by Sibelius

Catch-phrase:
DOC. Honest to my grandma, son!

I Love a Mystery related the adventures of three men who met in an Oriental prison. Even though they were reported dead after a bombing in Shanghai, they survived and continued to roam the world solving crimes. Each had a specialty—"Jack" had an analytical brain, "Doc" could extricate himself from tight spots by picking complicated locks, and "Reggie" was exceptionally strong. "Gerry Booker" was a beautiful secretary who combined sleuthing with shorthand. The motto of the A-1 Detective Agency was: "No job too tough, no mystery too baffling."

Carlton E. Morse produced *One Man's Family* in addition to *I Love a Mystery*. In fact, the actors who originally played "Paul," "Cliff," and "Nicky" in the former series (Michael Raffetto, Barton Yarborough, and Walter Paterson) played "Jack," "Doc," and "Reggie" in the latter. The series was heard at various times on three networks—NBC Red, NBC Blue, and CBS. It was first heard over NBC Red in 1939 as a five-times-a-week program at 7:15 p.m. but moved to NBC Blue the following year as a half-hour, once-a-week series.

I Love Linda Dale

Serial Drama

CAST:
Linda Dale — Helen Shields
Eric Dale — Raymond Edward Johnson, James Meighan
Penny — Claire Howard
Dr. Bruce Porter — Raymond Edward Johnson
The Judge — Arthur Hughes
Sheila Blade — Kay Strozzi

Ida Bailey Allen: see *Women's Programs*.

I'll Never Forget

Drama

These stories featured songs by Frank Luther.

In Care of Aggie Horn

Serial Drama

CAST:
Aggie Horn — Harriet Allyn
Monica Lee — Muriel Bremner
Edgar Lee — Nelson Olmsted
Williams — John Goldworthy
Martin Lee — Danny Lupton
Gwyn Jennings — Marilou Neumayer
Beanie — Eugene Geisler
Baldy — Clarence Hartzell
Gertrude Stone — Ilka Diehl
Announcer: Don Dowd

In Care of Aggie Horn was first heard over the Blue network in 1941.

Information, Please!

Panel Quiz

Moderator: Clifton Fadiman

Panel: Oscar Levant, John Kieran, Franklin P. Adams (FPA), Guests
Announcers: Ed Herlihy, Milton Cross, Ben Grauer
Producer-Director: Dan Golenpaul
Pianist: Joe Kahn

Opening:
SOUND. *Rooster crowing*
ANNOUNCER. Wake up, America! It's time to stump the experts!

Information, Please! made its debut over NBC Blue on May 17, 1938, and was on the air for fourteen years. The original panel was comprised of Fadiman, Adams, and Kieran. Levant was added when Fadiman became moderator. Such guests as John Erskine, Hendrik Willem Van Loon, Warden Lewis E. Lawes, and Stuart Chase appeared to help the panel answer rather difficult and specialized questions submitted by listeners. A listener who stumped the experts received a set of the *Encyclopaedia Britannica.* When cash awards were given, the sound of a cash register could be heard.

Among the program's sponsors were Canada Dry and Mobil Oil.

Inner Sanctum

Mystery

Hosts: Raymond Edward Johnson
Paul McGrath
House Jameson
Announcer: Ed Herlihy
Producer-Director: Himan Brown
Writers: John Roeburt, Robert Sloane, Harry and Gail Ingram, Robert Newman, Milton Lewis, Sigmund Miller
Sound Effects: Jack Amerine

Opening:
ANNOUNCER. Palmolive Brushless and Palmolive Lather Shaving Cream present . . .
HOST. *Inner Sanctum Mysteries.*
MUSIC. *Organ mysterioso*
SOUND. *Door squeaks open*
HOST. Good evening, friends. This is Raymond, your host, welcoming you in to the Inner Sanctum. . . .

Closing:
HOST. Now it's time to close the door of the Inner Sanctum until next week when Palmolive Brushless and Palmolive Lather Shaving Cream bring you another Inner Sanctum mystery. Until then, good night . . . pleasant dreams.
SOUND. *Door squeaks shut*

Inner Sanctum, originally called *The Squeaking Door,* made its debut over the Blue network on January 7, 1941. The show was also referred to as *Inner Sanctum Mysteries.* The only regular cast member was the host. Many guest stars appeared on the program, including Richard Widmark, Boris Karloff, and Arthur Vinton.

Inspector Burke: see *Scotland Yard's Inspector Burke.*

Interviewers

Although every announcer and sportscaster found himself with the task of interviewing a guest occasionally, a number of performers refined the art and virtually made a career of interviewing people on radio. Jack Eigen developed a massive following with his nighttime interviews from Chicago. For many years he broadcast from the Chez Paree. The husband-and-wife teams of Tex and Jinx (Tex McCrary and Jinx Falkenburg) and Peter Lind Hayes and Mary Healy conducted countless interviews on their respective programs. Cobina Wright conducted an interview program called *Your Hostess.* Other prominent interviewers were Mary Margaret McBride, Maggi McNellis, and Bob Elson, one of baseball's top play-by-play broadcasters. (See also *Bob Elson Aboard the Century.*)

Invitation to Learning

Literary Discussion

Host: Dr. Lyman Bryson
Critics: Quincy Howe, Mark Van Doren, Mason Gross
Director: Stan Davis

Invitation to Learning was billed as "a discussion of books that the world thus far has not been willing or able to let die." It was first heard over CBS in 1940. Originally it was on the air Tuesday evenings at 10:30 but later it moved to a Sunday-morning slot.

Irene Rich Dramas

Drama

Starring: Irene Rich
Announcers: Ed Herlihy, Frank Goss, Marvin Miller

This program with Hollywood actress Irene Rich was first broadcast on the NBC Blue network in 1933. Miss Rich, who was famous for her figure preservation, was sponsored at one time by Ry-Krisp. Many top radio actors of the day appeared in the dramas. (See also *Woman from Nowhere.*)

Irna Phillips: see *The Guiding Light.*

It Can Be Done

Drama

Host: Edgar A. Guest
Director: Henry Kline
Assistant Director: James Cominos

This CBS program, hosted by the famous poet Edgar A. Guest, featured guest stars whose exploits and experiences were dramatized.

It Pays to Be Ignorant

Comedy Panel

Quizmaster: Tom Howard
Panelists: George Shelton, Lulu McConnell, Harry McNaughton
Vocalist: Al Madru
Vocal group: The Esquires
Announcers: Ken Roberts, Dick Stark
Creators: Robert and Ruth Howell
Producer: Tom Howard
Director: Herbert S. Polesie
Writers: Tom Howard, Ruth Howell

Catch-phrases:
SHELTON (*following the mention of a city*). I used to work in that town!
SHELTON or
MCNAUGHTON (*after mention of a particularly unpleasant item*). Now we're back to Miss McConnell.

MCNAUGHTON (*after a bad joke*). Hoo, ha, ha, ha. Hoo, ha, ha, ha. Hoo, ha, ha, ha. I don't get it.

MCNAUGHTON. I have written a poem.

MCCONNELL (*to male guests on the show*). What's your name, honey? Are you married, honey?

Theme: (Sung by Al Madru)

It pays to be ignorant
To be dumb, to be dense, to be ignorant.
It pays to be ignorant
Just like me!
When I was just a school kid
I wasn't very bright.
I had a pretty teacher
Who made me stay each night.
So you see
It pays to be ignorant
Just like me!

It pays to be ignorant
To be dumb, to be dense, to be ignorant.
It pays to be ignorant
Just like me!
I took my girl to dinner
We had a wonderful time.
I let her pay the check
Because I didn't have a dime.
So you see
It pays to be ignorant
Just like me!

It pays to be ignorant
To be dumb, to be dense, to be ignorant.
It pays to be ignorant
Just like me.
They say that I am stupid
And dumb in every way.
But ever since I joined this show
There's one thing I can say:
Ho, ho, ho!
It pays to ignorant
Have no brain, be inane, just ignorant.
It pays to be ignorant
Just like me!

This was a carefully written show in which the panel members failed to answer such questions as "What color is a white horse?" and "Which player on a baseball team wears a catcher's mask?" The three panelists exasperated Tom Howard with their lack of intelligence. Howard attempted to help them answer the simple questions, but Harry McNaughton, a stuffy Englishman, and his colleagues George Shelton and Lulu McConnell were beyond help and interrupted frequently with inane questions of their own. After groping unsuccessfully for the answer to an extremely easy question, one of the panelists would often respond with, "Would you repeat the question, please?" Tom Howard frequently signed off with, "Good night . . . and good nonsense!"

The program idea, a take-off on radio panel quizzes such as *Information, Please!*, was conceived by Tom Howard's daughter Ruth and her husband Robert Howell while they were working for WELI New Haven (Connecticut). They named the show *Crazy I.Q.'s* and submitted it to Howard. He liked it, wrote a sample script, and sent it to several people in radio as *It Pays to Be Ignorant*. However, nobody seemed willing to risk doing a program with such a name. Finally WOR New York agreed to put it on the air. It was first heard in June 1942. From WOR the show moved to WABC New York and later to the

CBS network, where the show remained for most of its run. Eventually it switched to NBC, where it remained until it left the air. Its best-remembered sponsor was Philip Morris cigarettes. In England the show was known as *Ignorance Is Bliss.*

It Takes a Woman: see *Women's Programs.*

J

Jack Armstrong, the All-American Boy

Adventure Serial

CAST:

Jack Armstrong
St. John Terrell (1933)
Jim Ameche (1933–38)
Stanley Harris (1938–39)
Charles Flynn (1939–43 and 1944–51)
Michael Rye (Rye Billsbury) (1943)

Billy Fairfield	Murray McLean
	John Gannon
	Roland Butterfield
	Milton Guion
	Dick York
Betty Fairfield	Scheindel Kalish
	Sarajane Wells
	Loretta Poynton
	Patricia Dunlap
Uncle Jim Fairfield	James Goss
Gwendolyn Devol	Sarajane Wells
	Naomi May
Coach Hardy	Arthur Van Slyke
	Olan Soule
Captain Hughes	Don Ameche
	Jack Doty
	Frank Dane
Babu	Frank Behrens
Blackbeard Flint	Robert Barron
Sullivan Lodge	Kenneth Christie

Pete	Art McConnell
Dickie	Dick York
Michael	Frank Behrens
Weissoul, the spy	Herb Butterfield

Also: William Rath, William Green, Marvin Miller, Butler Manville

Announcers: David Owen, Tom Shirley, Truman Bradley, Paul Douglas, Franklyn MacCormack, Bob McKee

---

Creator-Writer: Robert Hardy Andrews

Directors: Pat Murphy, James Jewell, Ted MacMurray, Ed Morse, David Owen

Writers: Colonel Paschal Strong, Talbot Mundy, Irving J. Crump, James Jewell, Lee Knopf

---

Theme: (Sung by The Norsemen: Kenneth Schon, Al Revere, Ed Lindstrom, Ted Kline, and James Peterson, pianist and arranger)

Wave the flag for Hudson High, boys,
Show them how we stand!
Ever shall our team be champion,[1]
Known throughout the land!
Rah Rah Boola Boola Boola Boola
Boola Boola Boola Rah Rah Rah.
Have you tried Wheaties?
They're whole wheat with all of the bran.
Won't you try Wheaties?
For wheat is the best food of man!
They're crispy and crunchy the whole year through.
Jack Armstrong never tires of them
And neither will you.
So just buy Wheaties
The best breakfast food in the land!

Opening:

VOICES (*echoing and reverberating*). Jack Armstrong, Jack Armstrong, Jack Armstrong . . .

ANNOUNCER. The All-American Boy!!!!!

The long-time sponsor of *Jack Armstrong, the All-American Boy* was Wheaties, Breakfast of Champions. For the appropriate box-tops—and money—you could receive such premiums as Jack Armstrong whistling rings, Jack Armstrong hike-o-meters (a simple sturdy pedometer), Jack Armstrong secret decoders, and Jack Armstrong Norden bombsights. "Uncle Jim Fairfield," the "father image" of the series, was an adventurer, explorer, and pilot of his own amphibian, "The Silver Albatross." Originating in Chicago, the program made its debut over CBS in 1933 and left the air in 1951. In 1946 "Uncle Jim" and "Betty Fairfield" were replaced by "Vic Hardy," a scientific crime investigator, and "Jim Butterfield," a teen-age "junior announcer" who assisted regular announcer Bob McKee. (See also *Armstrong of the SBI*.)

The Jack Benny Program

Comedy-Variety

CAST:

Jack	Jack Benny
Mary	Mary Livingstone

[1] There were several versions of the theme, and there is great difference of opinion about this line in particular. Some claim it should be "Every fellow should be a champion"; others remember it as "Ever fight to be a champion"; or, "Ever challenging we champions." The line was apparently sung differently from time to time.

(Mrs. Jack Benny)
Dennis — Dennis Day
Rochester, Jack's valet — Eddie Anderson
Phil — Phil Harris
Don — Don Wilson
Schlepperman — Sam Hearn
Mr. Kitzel — Artie Auerbach
Mabel Flapsaddle, telephone operator — Sara Berner
Gertrude Gearshift, telephone operator — Bea Benaderet
Dennis Day's mother — Verna Felton
Belly-laugh Barton — Dix Davis
Professor LeBlanc, the violin teacher — Mel Blanc
Sound of Jack's Maxwell automobile — Mel Blanc
Train announcer — Mel Blanc
John L. C. Sivoney — Frank Fontaine
Gladys Zabisco — Sara Berner
Ruby Wagner — Sara Berner
Martha and Emily, the old ladies who had a crush on Jack — Jane Morgan and Gloria Gordon
The New Year — Joel Davis

Also: Frank Nelson, Sheldon Leonard, Andy Devine, Blanche Stewart, Ronald and Benita Colman, Ethel Shutta (actress-singer)

Featuring: tenors Frank Parker, Michael Bartlett, James Melton, Kenny Baker, Larry Stevens, Dennis Day

With: The Sportsmen Quartet–Bill Days, Thurl Ravenscroft, Max Smith, John Rarig, Marty Sperzel, at various times

Orchestra: George Olsen, Ted Weems, Frank Black, Don Bestor, Johnny Green, Bob Crosby, Phil Harris

Announcers: George Hicks, Paul Douglas, Alois Havrilla, Don Wilson

---

Producers: Irving Fein, Hilliard Marks

Directors: Robert Ballin, Hilliard Marks

Writers: Sam Perrin, Milt Josefsberg, George Balzer, John Tackaberry, Bill Morrow, Jack Douglas, Ed Beloin

Sound Effects: Jimmy Murphy, Virgil Reime, Gene Twombly

Catch-phrases:

JACK BENNY. Now cut that out!

JACK BENNY. Wait a minute. Wait a minute! Wait a minute!!! (*trying to quiet someone, usually The Sportsmen*)

PHIL HARRIS (*to Benny*). How are you, Jackson?

PHIL HARRIS (*singing*).

Won't you come with me to Alabammy,
Back to see my dear old mammy?
She's fryin' eggs and cookin' hammy,
And that's what I like about the South.

ROCHESTER. Oh! Ohhh!! Oooooohhhhh!!! (*expressing gradual understanding*)

DENNIS DAY (*to Benny*). Yes, please.

TRAIN ANNOUNCER. Anaheim, Azusa, and Cuc-a-monga.

ANDY DEVINE (*to Benny*). Hiya, buck!

FRANK NELSON. Yeeeees?

SHELDON LEONARD (*to Benny*). Psst! Hey, buddy.

MR. KITZEL (*sings in Jewish accent*).
Pee-kle in the mee-dle and the mustard on top!
Just the way you like them and they're always hot!

Jack Benny became virtually an institution in broadcasting. He made his radio debut on *The Ed Sullivan Show* on May 2, 1931; in 1932 he appeared on his own program for Canada Dry over CBS, and then was sponsored by Chevrolet. After that came his long associations with Jell-O and Lucky Strike. Among the many running gags on his show were his "feud" with Fred Allen; Benny's perpetual age of thirty-nine; his stinginess; his ancient Maxwell automobile; the vault in his basement where he kept his money and where the guard hadn't seen the light of day since the Civil War; the polar bear named Carmichael that lived in Benny's basement and allegedly ate the gas man; Jack's blue eyes; his attempts to play the violin; etc., etc. The development of Benny's character was so complete that it was only necessary for a hold-up man to accost Benny with, "Your money or your life!" for the audience to react by laughing longer than any other studio audience in radio history. Their reaction, of course, was brought about by Jack's apparent inability to decide between parting with his money or his life. When the prolonged laughter finally subsided, the hold-up man repeated his demand, and Benny brought down the house again with the annoyed reply, "I'm thinking it over!"

The Jack Carson Show

Comedy

CAST:

Jack Carson — Himself
Mrs. Foster — Jane Morgan
Hubert Peabody — Mel Blanc
The Butler — Arthur Treacher
Jack's press agent — Eddie Marr
Aunt Sally — Elizabeth Patterson
Jack's nephew Tugwell — Dave Willock
"Little girl next door" — Norma Jean Nilsson

Also: Irene Ryan
Orchestra: Freddy Martin, Bud Dant
Announcers: Del Sharbutt, Howard Petrie

Producers: Victor Knight, Sam Fuller
Directors: Larry Berns, Sam Fuller
Writers: Henry Taylor, Jack Rose, Marvin Fisher, Jack Douglas, Leonard L. Levinson, Fred S. Fox, Larry Marks, Lou Fulton

The Jack Carson Show was first heard over CBS in 1943.

Jack Eigen: see *Interviewers*.

The Jack Kirkwood Show

Comedy

Starring: Jack Kirkwood
Featuring: Lillian Lee, Jeannie McKean, Gene Lavalle
Orchestra: Irving Miller
Announcer: Jimmy Wallington

The Jack Kirkwood Show made its

debut over CBS in 1944. (See also *Mirth and Madness.*)

The Jack Paar Show

Variety

After his discharge from the Army, Jack Paar was a summer replacement for *The Jack Benny Program.* He also hosted *Take It or Leave It* (which see).

The Jack Pearl Show

Comedy

CAST:

Baron Munchhausen	Jack Pearl
Sharlie	Cliff Hall

In this comedy show, which made its debut over NBC in 1933, Baron Munchhausen related tall tales. When Sharlie expressed doubt, the Baron would respond, "Vas you dere, Sharlie?"

Jane Arden

Serial Drama

CAST:

Jane Arden	Ruth Yorke
Betty Harrison	Florence Freeman
Bob Brandon	Frank Provo
Louise West	Helene Dumas
Jack Galloway	Howard Smith
Mr. Arden	Richard Gordon
Mrs. Arden	Betty Garde
Dr. Steve	Spencer Bentley
Jack Fraser	Bill Baar
Alabama Randall	Henry Wadsworth
E. J. Walker	Maurice Franklin

Jane Arden was first heard over the Blue network in 1938.

Jane Cowl

Talk

Hostess: Jane Cowl

Actress Jane Cowl conducted this fifteen-minute talk program over Mutual. It began in 1944.

Jay Stewart's Fun Fair

Audience Participation

M.C.: Jay Stewart

This was an audience participation show built around people and their pets.

Jeff Regan

Mystery-Adventure

CAST:

Jeff Regan	Jack Webb

Also: Marvin Miller

Director: Sterling Tracy

Jeff Regan was broadcast as a thirty-minute weekly series on CBS.

Jergens Journal: see *Walter Winchell.*

Jiggs: see *Bringing Up Father.*

Jimmy Allen: see *The Air Adventures of Jimmy Allen.*

The Jimmy Durante Show

Comedy

Starring: Jimmy Durante

CAST:

Hotbreath Houlihan — Florence Halop
Vera Vague — Barbara Jo Allen

Also: Don Ameche, Sara Berner, Candy Candido, Elvia Allman, Joseph Kearns, Arthur Treacher, Tommy Halloran
Vocalist: Georgia Gibbs
Orchestra: Xavier Cugat, Roy Bargy
Announcer: Howard Petrie
Director: Phil Cohan
Writers: Sid Zelinka, Leo Solomon, Sid Reznick, Jack Robinson, Jay Sommers, Stanley Davis
Themes: "Ink-a-Dink-a-Doo," "You Gotta Start Off Each Day with a Song"

Jimmy Durante was nicknamed "the Schnozz" for his more than ample nose, or "schnozzola." He was well known for several catch-phrases, such as "Everybody wants ta get inta da act!" and "It's da condishuns dat prevail!" He also created several characters who never appeared but were referred to with affection, such as "Umbriago" and "Mrs. Calabash." Durante usually signed off with "Good night, Mrs. Calabash, wherever you are!" Candy Candido contributed the catch-phrase, "I'm feelin' mighty low," done in a deep, guttural voice after using a high-pitched voice to lead up to the catch-phrase. "Hotbreath Houlihan" always spoke in a low, sexy voice, saying such provocative things as "C'mere, . . . Big Boy!" (See also *Camel Caravan; Jumbo.*)

Jimmy Fidler: see *Hollywood Reporters.*

The Jo Stafford Show

Musical Variety

Featuring: Jo Stafford
Orchestra: Paul Weston
Also: Clark Dennis, tenor
Vocal group: The Starlighters
Announcer: Marvin Miller

The Jo Stafford Show, sponsored by Revere cameras, was on the air over ABC from 1948 to 1949. In addition to the music, dramatic sketches were presented. The program was replaced by *Name the Movie* and eventually *A Date with Judy.*

Joan and Kermit

Drama

Featuring: Olan Soule, Fran Carlon
Writer: Milton Geiger

The Joan Davis Show: see *Leave It to Joan.*

Joe and Ethel Turp

Situation Comedy

CAST:

Joe Turp — Jackson Beck
Ethel Turp — Patsy Campbell
Uncle Ben — Jack Smart
Billy Oldham — Art Carney
Producer-Director: Larry Berns

Joe and Mabel

Situation Comedy

CAST:

Joe — Ted de Corsia
Mabel — Ann Thomas
Mike — Walter Kinsella
"Shoiman" Stooler, Mabel's brother — Jackie Grimes
Mrs. Stooler, Mabel's mother — Betty Garde
Dolly — Jean Ellyn
M.C. at the local beer joint — Arthur Elmer
Announcer: George C. Putnam

Writer: Irving Gaynor Neiman

The original title of this show was *Women and Children First.*

Joe and Vi: see *Mr. and Mrs.*

The Joe DiMaggio Show

Sports

M.C.: Jack Barry
Featuring: Joe DiMaggio
Also: Charlotte Manson
Director: Dan Ehrenreich (later known as Dan Enright)
Sound Effects: Jim Lynch

This program presented sketches from the lives of famous athletes, such as Lou Gehrig, Sonja Henie, and Florence Chadwick. It made its debut over CBS in 1949.

Joe Palooka

Comedy-Drama

CAST:

Joe Palooka — Teddy Bergman, Norman Gottschalk, Karl Swenson
Ann Howe — Elsie Hitz, Mary Jane Higby
Knobby — Frank Readick

This story of a boxing champion was based on the comic strip by Ham Fisher. The program was broadcast from Chicago.

The Joe Penner Show

Comedy

Starring: Joe Penner

CAST:

Susabelle — Gay Seabrook
Gertrude — Margaret Brayton
Joe's mother — Martha Wentworth
Stooge — Stephanie Diamond
Also: Dick Ryan, Monk Monsel
Vocalists: Gene Austin, Ozzie Nelson, Harriet Hilliard, Joy Hodges
Orchestra: Ozzie Nelson, Jimmy Grier

Director: Gordon Thompson

Writers: Carroll Carroll, George Wells, Hal Fimberg, Matt Brooks, Bob Phillips, Arnold G. Maguire, Parke Levy, Eddie Davis, Don Prindle

Catch-phrases:
JOE PENNER. Wanna buy a duck?
JOE PENNER. You nasty man!
JOE PENNER. Don't ever do that!

The Joe Penner Show was originally known as *The Bakers Broadcast*. After a two-year run starring Joe Penner, Robert Ripley became the host of *The Bakers Broadcast*, with Ed Gardner as the producer and Ozzie Nelson conducting the orchestra. Vocalists were Ozzie Nelson, Harriet Hilliard, Shirley Lloyd, and Martha Mears.

John J. Anthony: see *The Goodwill Hour*.

Johnny: see *Commercials*.

Johnny Dollar: see *Yours Truly, Johnny Dollar*.

Johnny Modero, Pier 23

Adventure

CAST:

Johnny Modero — Jack Webb
Also: Francis X. Bushman

Creator: Richard Breen
Writers: Herb Margolis, Louis Markeim

Johnny Modero was a San Francisco waterfront character who took on odd detective jobs. This program was the successor to Webb's *Pat Novak for Hire* and was heard on Wednesdays at 8:30 p.m. on NBC.

John's Other Wife

Serial Drama

CAST:

Role	Actor
John Perry	Hanley Stafford
	Matt Crowley
	Luis Van Rooten
	Richard Kollmar
	William Post, Jr.
	Joseph Curtin
Elizabeth Perry	Adele Ronson
	Erin O'Brien-Moore
Martha Curtis	Phyllis Welch
	Rita Johnson
Molly	Irene Hubbard
	Lyda Kane
Alan Green	Milo Boulton
Evelyn	Ethel Blume
Yvonne Caire	Ruth Yorke
Dr. Tony Chalmers	Alan Bunce
Granny	Mary Cecil
	Nell Harrison
	Vivia Ogden
Mrs. Manners	Vivia Ogden
Annette Rogers Sullivan	Franc Hale
Lanny	John Kane
Carolyn Prince	Elaine Kent
	Pat Holbrook
Jill Thropp	Margaret O'Connell
Janet Dioncheck	Mary Jane Higby
Ballard Brandon	James Krieger
Linda Holbrook	Stella Adler
Kingsley Mayo	David Jordan
Sheila Mayo	Linda Watkins
Robin	Edward Trevor
Curt Lansing	Alexander Kirkland
Roberta Lansing	Joan Banks

Jerry Marvin	Kingsley Colton
Ridgeway Tearle	Macdonald Carey
Dolores Winters	Florence Freeman
Marina Marinoff	Helene Dumas
Pat Grady	Don Beddoes
Judy	Alice Reinheart

Producers: Frank and Anne Hummert
Writer: Bill Sweets
Theme: "The Sweetest Story Ever Told" (sung, whistled, and played on the guitar by Stanley Davis)

John's Other Wife was first heard over NBC in 1936. "John Perry" owned a store. The "other wife" referred to his secretary. Hanley Stafford, the original "John Perry," was dropped from his role on the grounds that he was unable to project a "fatherly image." Later, of course, he became one of radio's most famous fathers—"Daddy Higgins"—in the "Baby Snooks" routines.

The Johnson Family

Comedy-Drama

CAST:

All roles: Jimmy Scribner

Directors: J. C. Lewis, Richard Lewis, Tom Slater
Theme: "Listen to the Mockingbird"

All the voices of the characters in this story of a Negro family were done by Jimmy Scribner. The series was first heard over Mutual in 1936.

The Johnson Wax Program: see *Fibber McGee and Molly.*

Jonathan Kegg

Courtroom Drama

CAST:

Jonathan Kegg, Amicus Curiae (Friend of the Court)
Lee Bowman
Carlton KaDell

Jonathan Trimble, Esq.

Serial Drama

CAST:

Jonathan Trimble	Gale Gordon
Alice Trimble	Irene Tedrow
Mildred	Jean Gillespie

Writer: Mort Green

Jones and Hare: see *The Happiness Boys.*

Joyce Jordan, Girl Interne

Serial Drama

CAST:

Joyce Jordan	Rita Johnson
	Ann Shepherd (Scheindel Kalish)
	Betty Winkler
	Elspeth Eric
	Gertrude Warner
Paul Sherwood	Myron McCormick
Dr. Hans Simons	Erik Rolf
Hope Alison	Charlotte Holland
Margot Sherwood	Lesley Woods
Chester Hedgerow	John Raby
Dr. Molly Hedgerow	Ethel Owen
	Eda Heinemann

Dr. Thomas Webster
Carlton Brickert
Inspector Carson — Ed Latimer
Dr. Rheinhardt — Stefan Schnabel
Roger Walton — Alan Devitt
Courtney Lee — Herbert Yost
Myra Lee — Pat Ryan
Dr. Clifford Reed
Raymond Edward Johnson
Sheila Brand — Kay Brinker
Ollie — Joe Julian
Dr. Alan Webster
Richard Widmark
Steve Welles — Frank Behrens
Martin Sparrowhill — Frank Behrens
Jane Belle — Virginia Kay
Dr. Andrews — Horace Braham
William Walter — Alan Devitt
Captain Clayton — Santos Ortega
Bill Winters — Bill Zuckert
Dorie Winters — Elspeth Eric
Granny Hewitt — Ruth McDevitt
Dawson Blakely — Les Tremayne
Iris Blakely — Elizabeth Watts
Tom Hughes — Jackie Grimes
Dr. Tracy — Irene Hubbard
Mike Malone — Charles Webster
Doria Van Dorn — Ginger Jones
Lydia Drake — Louise Fitch
Dr. Alexander Grey
Raymond Edward Johnson
Jimmy Malone — Edwin Bruce
Ernest Eden — Larry Robinson
Gregory Ogden — Boyd Crawford
Celia — Amanda Randolph
Diane Ogden — Virginia Dwyer
Edgar Jarvis — James Monks
Gloria Blaine — Ethel Blume
Dr. David Morgan
Michael Fitzmaurice
Anne Hill — Aileen Pringle
Vic Manion — Frank Lovejoy
Ada Manion — Vera Allen
Dr. Mildermaul — Ed Begley
Dean Russell — Larry Haines

Also: Mary Jane Higby
Announcer: Ken Roberts

Producer: Himan Brown
Directors: Ted Corday, Arthur Hanna, Mende Brown
Writers: Ralph Berkey, Henry Selinger, Julian Funt
Theme: "Poem"

Joyce Jordan, Girl Interne made its debut over CBS in 1938. In 1942 the name of the program was changed to *Joyce Jordan, M.D.;* Joyce practiced medicine in the town of "Preston."

Judy and Jane

Serial Drama

CAST:

Judy — Marge Calvert
Jane — Donna Reade
Dr. Bishop — Marvin Miller
Also: Ireene Wicker

Directors: Harry Holcomb, Anne Seymour, Jim Whipple

Judy and Jane was first heard over the Blue network in 1932. It originated in Chicago and was heard only in the Midwest. The program was sponsored by Folger's coffee.

The Judy Canova Show

Comedy

CAST:

Judy Canova — Herself
Aunt Aggie — Ruth Perrott
Verna Felton
Geranium, the maid
Ruby Dandridge

Pedro — Mel Blanc
Count Benchley Botsford — Joe Kearns
Brenda — Sharon Douglas
Roscoe Wortle — Mel Blanc
Neighbor — Gale Gordon
Mr. Hemingway — Hans Conried
William Boswell — Hans Conried
Joe Crunchmiller, the taxi driver — Sheldon Leonard
Patsy Pierce — Verna Felton
Mrs. Van Atwater — Ruth Perrott
Also: The Sportsmen Quartet
Orchestra: Bud Dant
Announcer: Howard Petrie

Director: Joe Rines
Writers: Fred Fox, Henry Hoople

Catch-phrase:

PEDRO. Pardon me for talking in your face, Señorita.

Sign-off Song:

JUDY CANOVA. "Goodnight, Sweetheart"

[or]

Go to sleep-y, little baby,
Go to sleep-y, little baby,
When you wake, you'll patty-patty-cake,
And ride a shiny little po-o-ny.

The Judy Canova Show was first heard over CBS in 1943.

Jumbo

Variety

CAST:

Claudius "Brainy" Bowers — Jimmy Durante
Mickey Considine — Gloria Grafton
Matt Mulligan — Donald Novis
Mr. Considine — Arthur Sinclair
Orchestra: Adolph Deutsch
Announcer: Louis Witten

Producer: Billy Rose

This super-colossal production was another of the spectacular ventures of the flamboyant Billy Rose. In 1935, while the stage play *Jumbo* was on at the Hippodrome Theater in New York, Rose conceived the idea of transferring it to radio as a weekly series. Each Tuesday night over NBC at 9:30, *Jumbo* was broadcast from the stage of the Hippodrome before a live audience of 4500, probably the largest regular studio audience in the history of radio. The plot was simple —two warring circus owners, Considine and Mulligan, their offspring as the romantic interest and for other complications, and Durante as the frantic press agent of the "Considine Wonder Show." *Jumbo* was sponsored by Texaco Fire Chief gasoline and appeared as a replacement for Ed Wynn's *Fire Chief* program.

Jungle Jim

Adventure

CAST:

Jungle Jim — Matt Crowley
Kolu — Juano Hernandez
Shanghai Lil — Franc Hale
Tiger Lil — Irene Winston
Tom Sun — Owen Jordan
Singh-Lee — Arthur Hughes
Van — Jack Lloyd
Also: Vicki Vola, Kenny Delmar
Announcers: Glenn Riggs, Roger Krupp

Producer-Writer: Jay Clark
Directors: Stuart Buchanan, Irene Fenton
Writer: Gene Stafford

This program was based on the character created by Alex Raymond.

Junior G-Men

Adventure

Junior G-Men presented the adventures of a young boy in battling crime. It made its debut over Mutual in 1936.

Junior Miss

Situation Comedy

CAST:

Judy Graves	Shirley Temple
Lois Graves	K. T. Stevens
	Barbara Eiler
	Peggy Knudsen
	Barbara Whiting
Harry Graves	Gale Gordon
	Elliott Lewis
Mrs. Graves	Sarah Selby
	Margaret Lansing
Hilda, the maid	Myra Marsh
Fuffy Adams	Priscilla Lyon
	Beverly Wills

Producer: Fran Van Hartesfeldt
Director: William Royal
Writers: Jack Rubin, Herbert Little, Jr., David Victor, Charlie Sinclair

This program, dealing with the problems of being a middle-class adolescent, was first heard over CBS in 1948 on Saturdays at 11:30 a.m.

Junior Nurse Corps

Serial Drama

CAST:

Clara Barton	Sunda Love
Major Drucker	Jess Pugh

Just Neighbors

Comedy

Featuring: Betty Caine, Helen Behmiller, Kathryn Card
Director: Gordon Hughes
Writer: William Hodapp

This series, which began on NBC in 1938, was originally called *The Three Flats.* It related the adventures of three chatty gals.

Just Plain Bill

Serial Drama

CAST:

Bill Davidson	Arthur Hughes
Nancy Donovan, Bill's daughter	Ruth Russell
David	Curtis Arnall
Kerry Donovan	James Meighan
Elmer Eeps	Joe Latham
Percy Blivens	Ray Collins
Grand Sutton	Bill Quinn
Wiki	Madeleine Pierce
	Sarah Fussell
Kathleen Chatton	Ara Gerald
Dr. Barton	Bill Lytell
Jonathan Hillery	Macdonald Carey
Edgar Hudson	Clayton "Bud" Collyer
Eric Marshall	Guy Sorel

Bessie
Ann Shepherd (Scheindel Kalish)
John Britton — William Woodson
Shirley King — Audrey Egan
Reba Britton — Charlotte Lawrence
Dorothy Nash — Teri Keane
Pearl Sutton
Ann Shepherd (Scheindel Kalish)
Humphrey Fuller — Charles Egleston
Ned Shepherd — Cliff Carpenter
Sylvia Bardine — Helen Walpole
Margaret Burns — Elizabeth Day
Sylvia Powers — Elaine Kent
Also: Anne Elstner
Announcers: André Baruch, Ed Herlihy, Roger Krupp, Fielden Farrington

---

Producers: Frank and Anne Hummert
Directors: Martha Atwell, Norman Sweetser, Gene Eubank, Arthur Hanna, Blair Walliser, Ed King
Writers: Jack Kelsey, Evelyn Hart, Barbara Bates, Peggy Blake, Robert Hardy Andrews
Sound Effects: Max Miller
Theme Player: Hal Brown; he played harmonica and guitar

Themes: "Darling Nellie Gray" (opening); "Polly Wolly Doodle" (closing)
Closing:
MUSIC. *"Polly Wolly Doodle" up and under . . .*
ANNOUNCER. Listen for *Just Plain Bill* on this station at this same time tomorrow. This is Roger Krupp saying good-by for *Just Plain Bill* and for the Whitehall Pharmacal Company, makers of Anacin and many other dependable, high-quality drug products.
MUSIC. *"Polly Wolly Doodle" up and out*

This was the story of a barber in the small town of "Hartville." It was first heard over CBS in 1932.

Juvenile Jury

Children's Panel

M.C.: Jack Barry
Jurors: Johnny McBride, Charlie Hankinson, Robin Morgan, Jerry Weissbard, Peggy Bruder, Glenn Mark Arthur, Dickie Orlan, Patsy Walker, Elizabeth Watson, Billy Knight, Laura Mangels
Announcer: John Scott
Producer: Dan Ehrenreich (later known as Dan Enright)

Juvenile Jury was first heard over Mutual in 1946. Five children served as jurors for each show. They were given problems for their reactions and solutions. The problems, submitted in writing or in person, concerned typical children's topics such as allowances, chores, etc. Guest stars appeared on the program—among them Eddie Cantor, Red Skelton, and Milton Berle.

K

Kaltenmeyer's Kindergarten

Children

CAST:

Professor August Kaltenmeyer D.U.N. (Doctor of Utter Nonsense) — Bruce Kamman
Izzy Finkelstein — Johnny Wolf
Yohnny Yohnson — Thor Ericson
Gertie Glump — Marian Jordan
Mickey Donovan — Jim Jordan
Percy Van Schuyler — Merrill Fugit
Chauncey, the bum — Sidney Ellstrom
Daisy Dean — Cecil Roy
"Tough Guy" Cornelius Callahan — Billy White

With: The Escorts and Betty–Betty Olson, Ted Claire, Cliff Petersen, Floyd Holm, Douglas Craig (accompanist and arranger)

Writer: Harry Lawrence

Kaltenmeyer's Kindergarten was first heard over NBC Blue in 1932. In 1940 the program's title became *Kindergarten Kapers* and the professor's name was changed to "Professor Ulysses S. Applegate" because of the anti-German feeling in the United States. Until the change, Bruce Kamman, as "Professor Kaltenmeyer," signed off with "Auf wiedersehen und adieu."

Kate Hopkins, Angel of Mercy

Serial Drama

CAST:

Kate Hopkins — Margaret MacDonald
Tom Hopkins — Clayton "Bud" Collyer
Robert Atwood — Raymond Edward Johnson
Jessie Atwood — Constance Collier
Diane Pers — Delma Byron
Elise — Peggy Allenby
Louise — Helen Lewis
Trudy — Templeton Fox

Director: Jack Hurdle
Writers: Chester McCracken, Gertrude Berg

This program was first heard over CBS in 1940.

The Kate Smith Show

Variety

Starring: Kate Smith
Host: Ted Collins
Orchestra: Jack Miller
Announcer: André Baruch
Directors: Bunny Coughlin, Bob Lee
Writers: Art S. Henley, Jean Holloway, Edward Jurist, Jay Bennett, Al Garry, Doris Gilbert
Theme: "When the Moon Comes Over the Mountain"
Opening:
KATE SMITH. Hello, everybody.
Closing:
KATE SMITH. Thanks for listening . . . good night, folks.

Kate Smith was known as "The Songbird of the South." The program featured music, drama, comedy, and radio sketches starring such people as Bert Lahr, Greta Garbo, John Barrymore, Grace George, Mary Boland, Edward G. Robinson, Helen Menken, Margaret Sullavan, Bert Lytell, and many others. The program also introduced *The Aldrich Family*, Abbott and Costello, and Henny Youngman, among others. Bert Parks was one of the "warm-up" announcers and applause-cuers. Miss Smith's singing of "God Bless America" is one of the best-remembered portions of the program.

The show, which made its debut over CBS in 1936, was also known as *The A&P Bandwagon*. Beginning in 1938, Miss Smith had a fifteen-minute, thrice-weekly program at noon on CBS. Ted Collins was with her on this show too, and he always began the program with "It's high noon in New York. . . ."

Kay Kyser's Kollege of Musical Knowledge

Variety-Quiz

CAST:

Quizmaster — Kay Kyser
Ish Kabibble — Mervyn Bogue
Also: Ginny Simms, Trudy Erwin, Sully Mason, Harry Babbitt, Georgia Carroll, Shirley Mitchell, The Town Criers,
The King Sisters (Alyce, Donna, Yvonne, and Louise)
Announcer: Verne Smith

Producer: Frank O'Connor
Directors: William Warwick, John Cleary, Harry Saz, Ed Cashman
Writers: Richard Dana, Martin Stark
Theme: "Thinking of You"

This popular Wednesday-night series on NBC made its debut in 1938 and featured musical numbers interspersed with quiz segments done in a light, humorous vein, using a mock college format. The various quiz segments were referred to as "midterms" and "final exams." The questions were frequently so easy that a broad hint from Kyser would tip the answer to the contestant, particularly for servicemen contestants, who never seemed to walk away empty-handed. After practically telling the contestant the answer, Kyser would shout, "How'd he get that?" In the event the contestant didn't get the answer, Kyser would call out, "Students?" and the audience would give the answer.

One segment was a true or false quiz using "right" or "wrong" as answers. When the answer was true and the contestant was incorrect, Kyser would exclaim, "That's right, you're wrong!" If the answer was false and the contestant was correct, he would declare, "That's wrong, you're right!"

Kyser was referred to on the program as "The Old Professor" or just "'Fes." The wearing of caps and gowns at the broadcast was obligatory, and even Verne Smith, the announcer, was called "Dean."

The Ken Murray Program

Comedy

Featuring: Ken Murray

CAST:

Oswald — Tony Labriola
Vocalist: Phil Regan
Also: Eve Arden, Shirley Ross, Marlyn Stuart
Orchestra: Lud Gluskin, Russ Morgan

Writers: Ken England, David Freedman
Catch-phrase:
OSWALD. Ooh, yeah!

The show made its debut in 1932. In his slot on Tuesday at 8:30 p.m. on CBS, Murray was sponsored by Lifebuoy Soap.

Kindergarten Kapers: see *Kaltenmeyer's Kindergarten*.

Kitchen Quiz: see *Women's Programs*.

Kitty Foyle

Serial Drama

CAST:

Kitty Foyle — Julie Stevens
Wyn Strafford — Clayton "Bud" Collyer

Writers: Doris Halman, Al Barker

Kitty Foyle was based on the novel by Christopher Morley. The program was first heard over CBS in 1942.

Kitty Keene

Serial Drama

CAST:

Kitty Keene — Beverly Younger, Fran Carlon
Bob Jones — Bob Bailey, Dick Wells
Jill — Dorothy Gregory, Janet Logan
Leddy Fowley — Cheer Brentson
Jefferson Fowley — Phil Lord
Anna Hajek — Louise Fitch
Dimples — Ginger Jones
Miss Branch — Josephine Gilbert
Norma Vernack — Angeline Orr
Clara Lund — Peggy Hillias
Pearl Davis — Loretta Poynton
Preacher Jim — Herbert Butterfield
Charles Williams — Carlton KaDell, Bill Bouchey, Ken Griffen
Buzzer Williams — Chuck Grant
Neil Perry — Stanley Harris
Humphrey Manners — Ian Keith

Creator-Writers: Day Keene and Wally Norman
Producer-Directors: George Fogle, Alan Wallace
Director: Win Orr
Writer: Lester Huntley
Theme: "None but the Lonely Heart" by Tchaikovsky

Kitty Keene originated in Chicago and was first on the air over Mutual in 1937.

Kitty Kelly: see *Pretty Kitty Kelly*.

Myrt and Marge. Left to right: Myrtle Vail, Ray Hedge, Donna Damerel, Jeanne Juvelier

The National Barn Dance. Uncle Ezra and the Hoosier Hot Shots

It Pays to Be Ignorant. Left to right: Harry McNaughton, Lulu McConnell, George Shelton, Tom Howard

Ozzie Nelson

Harriet Hilliard

Jessica Dragonette

Dwight Weist

Paula Winslowe

Vaughn de Leath

The Happiness Boys. Left to right: Billy Jones, Ernie Hare

Wendell Hall, "The Red Headed Music Maker"

Bill Griffis

Mary Jane Higby

Jerry Macy

Owen Jordan

Mel Allen

Charles Webster

First Nighter.
Olan Soule, Barbara Luddy

Les Tremayne and Barbara Luddy in *First Nighter,* 1941

Les Tremayne and Barbara Luddy reading a *First Nighter* script at the Hollywood Bowl, 1968

Anne Elstner as Stella Dallas. (*TV–Radio Mirror*)

Truth or Consequences.
At right: Eddie Cantor,
Ralph Edwards

Clicquot Club Eskimos.
At right: Harry Reser

Left to right: Jimmy
Wallington, Portland
Hoffa, Fred Allen

B. A. Rolfe

Clem McCarthy
(looking through
glasses)

Floyd Gibbons

Olivio Santoro

Baby Rose Marie

The Moylan Sisters

Kenny Baker

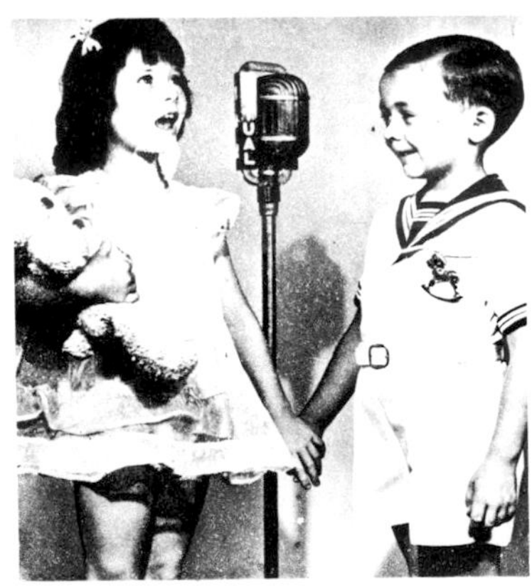

"Termite" Daniels,
Bobby Hookey

Milton Cross

Jay Jostyn (*left*) going over a *Mr. District Attorney* script with announcer Fred Uttal. (*Gary Wagner*)

Left to right: Ray Noble, Dale Evans, Don Ameche, Charlie McCarthy, Edgar Bergen. (*National Broadcasting Company*)

Ned Wever as Bulldog Drummond

Harold Peary as the Great Gildersleeve

Cornelius Westbrook
Van Voorhees;
Arthur Pryor, Jr.

Cavalcade of America. Left to right: Edwin Jerome, Karl Swenson, Jeanette Nolan, Ray Collins, Ted Jewett, Agnes Moorehead, John McIntire, Kenneth Delmar

"Uncle Don" Carney

Ed Sullivan

Ben Bernie

Life Can Be Beautiful. Left to right: Mitzi Gould, Ralph Locke, John Holbrook, Alice Reinheart

Second Husband. Left to right: Helen Menken, John Thomas, Virginia Dwyer

Joseph M. White, "The Silver Masked Tenor"

Arthur Hughes as "Just Plain Bill," making a Fourth of July speech

Jean Hersholt as Dr. Christian

Arthur Tracy,
"The Street Singer"

Ronald Liss

Blondie. Left to right: Arthur Lake, Penny Singleton, Hanley Stafford

Frank Knight

The Life of Riley. Left to right: John Brown, William Bendix

Athena Lorde

Lowell Thomas

Len Doyle

Joe Penner

Jan Miner

George Ansbro

Joseph Julian and Roger de Koven in a scene from *The O'Neills*

A recording session for *The Mysterious Traveler. Left to right:* Jack Amerine (sound), Bill Zuckert, Lon Clark, Roger de Koven, Ed Begley, Maurice Tarplin, Jim Wallington, Jackson Beck

Gangbusters. Left to right: Santos Ortega, Anne-Marie Gayer, Grant Richards, James McCallion. (CBS PHOTO)

The Aldrich Family. Left to right: Dickie Jones, Jackie Kelk. (CBS PHOTO)

Teddy Bergman (later known as Alan Reed) as *Joe Palooka*

John Nesbitt, Meredith Willson

Cliff Edwards ("Ukulele Ike")

Buck Rogers in the 25th Century. Left to right: Curtis Arnall (wearing gravity-defying inertron), Elaine Melchoir, William Shelley, Edgar Stehli (holding vibro-destructor ray), Adele Ronson

H. V. Kaltenborn

Gabriel Heatter

Tony Wons

David Ross

Bert Parks

Wally Butterworth

Roxy

Arthur Allen

Walter Damrosch

Walter Tetley

Curley Bradley

The Breakfast Club. Left to right: Eugenie Baird, Don Dowd, Don McNeill, Sam Cowling, Jack Owens

Frank Gallop

Graham McNamee,
Ed Wynn

Jimmy Durante

Weber and Fields

Bing Crosby

Jack MacBryde and
Walter Kinsella as,
respectively, Peewee and Windy

Vincent Lopez

Phil Cook

Frank Munn

Phil Harris,
Alice Faye

Frank Singiser

Rudy Vallee

Teri Keane,
Don Ameche

Countess Olga Albani

Amos 'n' Andy. Left to right:
Freeman Gosden,
Charles Correll

Al Jolson

Jeanette MacDonald

Little Jack Little

Frank Lovejoy

Sara Berner

Jack Arthur

Michael Fitzmaurice

Anna Appel and
Menasha Skulnik
in *Abie's Irish Rose*

Vicki Vola

Charlotte Manson

Frank Hummert

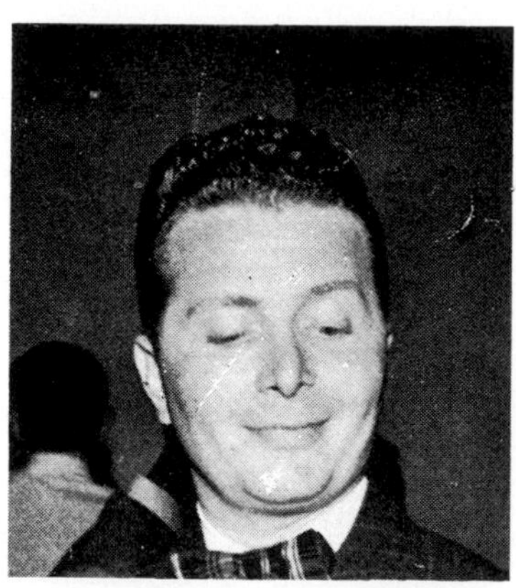

Henry Morgan

Anne Hummert

Walter Winchell

Harry Frankel
("Singin' Sam")

Maurice Tarplin
as *The Mysterious*
Traveler

Babe Ruth,
Graham McNamee

Mary Pickford

Eddie Cantor

Jim and Marian Jordan
as *Fibber McGee*
and Molly.

Bob Hope

The Columbia Workshop, with Orson Welles at far right

Boake Carter

Morton Downey (at right)

Arthur Godfrey

Will Rogers

Major Bowes

Left to right: Jimmy Wallington, George Jessel, Dave Rubinoff

"Evelyn and Her Magic Violin"

Floyd Buckley

Basil Ruysdael

"Tiny" Ruffner

Rolly Bester

A. L. Alexander

Joseph Curtin

Alice Frost

Ben Grauer

Ken Roberts

Paul Douglas

Russ Columbo

Julia Sanderson,
Frank Crumit

Ted de Corsia

Jim Boles

Let's Pretend, with
Nila Mack at center

The Railroad Hour. Left to right:
Gordon MacRae (star), Carmen
Dragon (musical director), Marvin Miller (announcer)

Gilbert Mack

Joe and Ethel Turp. Left to right: Jackson Beck, Patsy Campbell Larry Berns (producer- director)

Fred Waring with Jane Wilson on *The Chesterfield Supper* Club

Norman Brokenshire

Ted Husing

Alois Havrilla

Arthur Q. Bryan

Ed Thorgersen

Bret Morrison

The Dunninger Show. Left to right: George Wiest (producer), Roger Krupp (announcer), Joe Dunninger

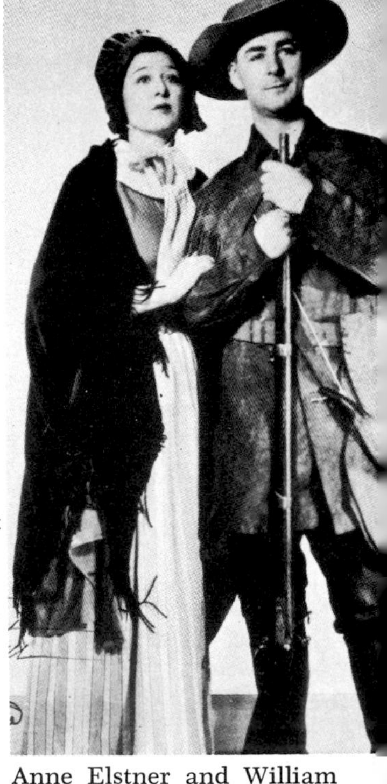

Anne Elstner and William Johnstone in *Wilderness Road*

Tom McCray (extreme right) and Ben Hawthorn (at microphone) among radio newsmen covering the 1936 flood in Hartford, Connecticut

Knickerbocker Playhouse

Drama

Featuring: Elliott Lewis
Also: Marvin Miller
Directors: Joe Ainley, Owen Vinson

Knickerbocker Playhouse was done in the style of *First Nighter*. It was first heard over NBC in 1940.

Kollege of Musical Knowledge: see *Kay Kyser's Kollege of Musical Knowledge.*

Kraft Music Hall

Variety

Host: Bing Crosby
Featuring: Bob Burns, The Arkansas Traveler; Jerry Lester, George Murphy
Regular Guests (about one year each): Mary Martin, singer; Connee Boswell, singer; Victor Borge, pianist-comedian; Peggy Lee, singer
With: The Music Maids and Hal, vocal group
Orchestra: Jimmy Dorsey (one year); John Scott Trotter
Announcers: Don Wilson (one year), Roger Krupp, Ken Carpenter
Directors: Cal Kuhl, Ezra MacIntosh, Ed Gardner, Bob Brewster
Writers: Carroll Carroll, David Gregory, Leo Sherin, Ed Helwick, Manny Mannheim

Kraft Music Hall, sponsored by the makers of Kraft dairy products, was first heard in 1934, starring Al Jolson with Paul Whiteman's orchestra and Deems Taylor. It was a two-hour show written by Carroll Carroll and heard locally in New York. It later went network with Paul Whiteman, Ramona, and Johnny Mercer. Many of the great names in jazz were featured on this program—Jack and Charlie Teagarden, Frank Trumbauer, Roy Bargy, Joe Venuti—and also Oscar Levant on the piano. The theme was "Rhapsody in Blue." Whiteman also presented guest stars from the New York theater, opera, sports, and vaudeville. Lou Holtz had a long run as a star comedian.

In 1936 the program moved to the West Coast, where Bing Crosby was the host for ten years. During that time countless people from all walks of life appeared with Crosby to sing and joke with him. Most listeners thought the show was ad-libbed but it was all written by Carroll Carroll, who had moved west to continue his job.

Still remembered are the station-break spots that featured Ken Carpenter as a student at KMH and Bing as Dr. Crosby, the dean. Each spot led into the sounding of the NBC chimes. When ASCAP pulled its music off the air, Crosby's theme, "Where the Blue of the Night Meets the Gold of the Day," had to be omitted. The *Kraft Music Hall* theme then became "Hail KMH," the fight song of the mythical school of the station breaks:

Hail KMH, hail, rain and snow
Onward to victory
Forward we will go
Stamping out our adversary
Like a dauntless dromedary
Tramples on its foe

Forever . . .
Hail KMH, our motto cry
Be brave and love each other
Wear the old school tie
Like an eagle loose aloft
Wave the pomegranate and puce aloft
Rah, rah, rah, rah, rah, rah, rah
With a hey-nonny-nonny-and-a-hotcha-cha
Hail K. . .M. . .H.

The final three notes were those of the NBC chimes. At that time they were struck manually.

When Bing left *Kraft Music Hall* in 1946, the program moved east and had a series of stars. The most notable of these was Al Jolson, who returned as host for two seasons while making a comeback in show business. His broadcasts featured Oscar Levant and Lou Bring's orchestra. Manny Mannheim and Charlie Isaacs became writers for the show, and Ken Carpenter continued as announcer.

While the program was out west, the summer shows featured such hosts as Bob Crosby, Frank Morgan, and Don Ameche; and for two summers starred Nelson Eddy and Dorothy Kirsten with Robert Armbruster's orchestra. (See also *The Bing Crosby Show*.)

L

Ladies Be Seated

Audience Participation

M.C.: Johnny Olson and Penny Olson (five years), Tom Moore (six months)
Producer: Philip Patton
Director: George Wiest
Writers: Bill Redford, Tom Dougall, Walt Framer

Ladies Be Seated was first heard over ABC in 1944.

Ladies' Fair

Audience Participation

M.C.: Tom Moore

This was first heard over Mutual in 1949.

Ladies' Programs: see *Women's Programs*.

Lady Esther Serenade

Music

Featuring: Bess Johnson as "Lady Esther"
Orchestra: Wayne King
Announcer: Phil Stewart

The Lady Next Door: see *Coast-to-Coast on a Bus.*

Lady of Millions

Drama

Featuring: May Robson
Announcer: Jackson Wheeler

LaGuardia: see *Mayor LaGuardia Reads the Funnies.*

The Lamplighter

Talk

Host: Jacob Tarshish

This was first broadcast on the Mutual network in 1935.

Land of the Lost

Children

CAST:

Red Lantern	Junius Matthews
	Art Carney
Isabel	Betty Jane Tyler
Billy	Ray Ives

Also: Jim Boles, Athena Lorde, Ann Thomas, Tom Eldridge, Kay Marshall, Lee Marshall
Announcer: Michael Fitzmaurice

Producer-Writer: Isabel Manning Hewson
Director: Cyril Armbrister
Theme: "Land of the Lost" (original music)

Land of the Lost was first heard over ABC in 1944. Red Lantern was a big, red fish who glowed under water. The children, Isabel and Billy, used him as their guide on each adventure. The episodes included meeting such characters as a sea horse or a lump of coal. The underwater characters sent messages by "shellaphone" and "shellagraph."

Lassie

Adventure

Imitator of dog noises: Earl Keen
Also: Betty Arnold, Marvin Miller
Announcer: Charles Lyon
Producers: Frank Ferrin, Harry Stewart
Director: Harry Stewart
Writer: Hobe Donovan
Organist: John Duffy

This was the story of a collie named Lassie. The real Lassie of movie fame was owned and trained by Rudd Weatherwax and did the actual barking in the radio series on cue from Weatherwax or his brother. Growls, whines, and pants were done by animal imitator Earl Keen. The many youngsters in the studio audience were fascinated by the on-cue barking and Keen's imitations. The series began over ABC in 1947.

Latitude Zero

Adventure

CAST:

Captain Craig McKenzie — Lou Merrill

Also: Bruce Payne, Charlie Lung, Jack Zoller, Ed Max, Anne Stone

---

Writers: Ann and Ted Sherdiman

These science-fiction adventures about a submarine and its captain had such characters as "Simba," "Brock Spencer," "Bert Collins," "Tibbs Canard," "Babyface Nelson," and the villains "Moloch" and "Lucretia."

Laugh Doctors

Comedy

Starring: Russell Pratt and Ransom Sherman

Lavender and New Lace

Variety

Harpischordist: Sylvia Marlowe
Vocalists: Felix Knight, Joan Brooks
Announcer: Glenn Riggs
Producer-Director: William Wilgus
Writer: Eddie Birnbryer

Lavender and Old Lace

Music

Featuring: Fritzi Scheff and Frank Munn, singers

This program was first heard over NBC in 1934.

Leave It to Joan

Situation Comedy

Starring: Joan Davis
Producer-Writer-Director: Dick Mack

Leave It to Mike

Situation Comedy

CAST:
Mike McNally — Walter Kinsella
Dinny, Mike's sweetheart — Joan Alexander
Mr. Berkeley, Mike's boss — Jerry Macy
Mrs. Berkeley — Hope Emerson
Also: Arthur Elmer, William Keene

Director: Roger Bower
Writer: Howard Merrill

Leave It to Mike made its debut over Mutual in 1945. It was broadcast from the Longacre Theatre on 48th Street in New York and ran for forty weeks.

Leave It to the Girls

Panel Discussion

Moderator: Elissa Landi, Paula Stone, Maggi McNellis
Guest Panelists: Constance Bennett, Robin Chandler, Binnie Barnes, Dorothy Kilgallen, Florence Pritchett, Lucille Ball, Eloise McElhone, *et al.*
Producer: Martha Rountree
Directors: Joan Sinclaire, Jean Wright

Listeners submitted ideas for discussion by the panel. After the panel had discussed the topic, which was often of a romantic nature, a male celebrity such as Burt Lancaster or George Jessel defended the men of America. The program was first heard over Mutual in 1945.

Let George Do It

Drama

CAST:

George Valentine — Bob Bailey
His secretary — Virginia Gregg
Also: Olan Soule

Writer: David Victor

Let's Dance

Music

Orchestra: Xavier Cugat, Benny Goodman, Kel Murray

Let's Pretend

Children's Drama

CAST:

Uncle Bill — Bill Adams
Animal Imitator — Harry Swan
Brad Barker

Featuring Child Actors: Miriam Wolfe, Patricia Ryan, Gwen Davies (Estelle Levy), Michael O'Day, Vivian Block, Bill Lipton, Jack Grimes, Kingsley Colton, Arthur Anderson, Bob Readick, Albert Aley, Sybil Trent, Robert Lee, Jimsey Sommers, Bobby and Billy Mauch, Julian Altman, Donald Hughes, Patricia Peardon, Jack Jordan, Billy and Florence Halop, Walter Tetley, Eddie Ryan, Jr., Lester Jay, Elaine Engler, Maury Benkoil, Ronald Liss, Sidney Lumet, Marilyn Erskine, Butch Cavell, Denise Alexander, Ivan Cury, Betty Jane Tyler, Alan Shea, Anne-Marie Gayer, Rita Lloyd, Dick Etlinger
Orchestra: Maurice Brown

Creator-Director: Nila Mack
Sound Effects: George O'Donnell, Arthur Strand

Opening:

CHILDREN'S CHORUS.
Cream of Wheat is so good to eat
That we have it every day.
We sing this song, it will make us strong
And it makes us shout hooray.
It's good for growing babies
And grown-ups too to eat.
For all the family's breakfast
You can't beat Cream of Wheat.

ANNOUNCER. Cream of Wheat—the great American family cereal—presents *Let's Pretend!*

The show was originally known as *The Adventures of Helen and Mary.* "Helen" and "Mary" were played by Estelle Levy and Patricia Ryan. In 1934 the title *Let's Pretend* was adopted. Miriam Wolfe was often cast as a witch, while Marilyn Erskine frequently played a fairy godmother.

CBS, as a matter of prestige, refused for years to permit commercials on *Let's Pretend.* However, in the 1940s they were finally forced to yield to economic pressure and sold it to what became its long-time sponsor—Cream of Wheat.

Liberty Baseball

Sports

The Liberty Broadcasting System

was launched in March 1948 and promptly became a major network. Its principal function was to re-create major league baseball games, though it also branched out into other sports as well as music and news. The baseball play-by-play announcers were Gordon McLendon (The Old Scotsman), Al Turner, Lindsey Nelson, Jerry Doggett, and Wes Wise. On days when there was no game, Liberty often re-created an old-time ballgame featuring players such as Babe Ruth, Ty Cobb, and Walter Johnson. The listener occasionally heard re-creations of games played in the nineteenth century. In such games the announcer might remark that a score had just come in by Pony Express; that the count was six balls and three strikes; that the young catcher Connie Mack was experimenting with the idea of wearing a mask while catching; or that the batter was ordering the pitcher to throw the next pitch a little lower. The broadcasts reached millions of listeners daily until the network went out of business in May 1952.

The Life and Love of Dr. Susan

Serial Drama

CAST:

Dr. Susan Chandler — Eleanor Phelps
Dr. Howard Chandler — Fred Barron
Miranda Chandler — Mary Cecil
Marilyn Chandler — Gloria Mann
Dickie Chandler — Tommy Hughes
Mrs. Joshua Waite — Allie Lowe Miles
Abby Bradford — Elspeth Eric
Nancy Chandler — Mary Mason
Dr. Halliday — Alexander Kirkland
Announcer: Frank Luther

Director: Ed Rice
Organist: Richard Leibert

Life Begins

Serial Drama

CAST:

Martha Webster — Bess Flynn
Richard Craig — Jimmy Donnelly
Winfield Craig — Carleton Young
Virginia Craig — Toni Gilman
Lucy Craig — Betty Philson
Alvin Craig — Ray Collins
Wilbur — Ralph Dumke
Dick Young — Donald Cook
Kay Smith — Jeanette Nolan
Gretchen Davidson
Aunt Ethel — Ethel Owen
Dolores King — Patricia Peardon
Peggy Smithgirl — Janet Rolands
Don Cavanaugh — Eddie Ryan
Jim Carroll — Tom Tully
Holly — Margaret MacDonald
Mrs. Riley — Agnes Moorehead
Also: Helene Dumas, Everett Sloane, Edgar Stehli, Charlotte Garrity

---

Director: Diana Bourbon
Writer: Bess Flynn

Life Begins was first heard over CBS in 1940. The title was later changed to *Martha Webster.*

Life Begins at 80

Panel Discussion

M.C.: Jack Barry

Producer: Dan Ehrenreich (later known as Dan Enright)

Life Begins at 80 was the counterpart of *Juvenile Jury*. It featured discussions by elderly people. The program was first on the air over Mutual in 1948.

Life Can Be Beautiful

Serial Drama

CAST:

Carol Conrad (Chichi) — Alice Reinheart, Teri Keane
David Solomon (Papa David) — Ralph Locke
Stephen Hamilton — Earl Larrimore, John Holbrook
Toby Nelson — Carl Eastman
Gyp Mendoza — Waldemar Kappel, Paul Stewart
Mrs. S. Kent Wadsworth — Adelaide Klein
Barry Markham — Richard Kollmar, Dick Nelson
Dr. Myron Henderson — Roger DeKoven
Nurse Kimball — Peggy Allenby
Hank Bristow — Ian Martin
Marybelle Owens — Ruth Yorke
Rita Yates — Mitzi Gould
Dr. Markham — Charles Webster
Mrs. Markham — Peggy Allenby
Nellie Conrad — Agnes Moorehead
Logan Smith — Clayton "Bud" Collyer
Maude Kellogg — Ruth Weston
Oscar Finch — Ed Begley
Douglas Norman — Sidney Smith
Nellie Gleason — Ethel Owen
Hank O'Hoolihan — John Moore
Al Douglas — Humphrey Davis
Also: Elsie Hitz, Minerva Pious, Gavin Gordon, Vinton Hayworth, Joe Julian
Announcers: Ralph Edwards, Don Hancock, Ed Herlihy, Ron Rawson, Bob Dixon

---

Producer-Director: Don Becker
Directors: Chick Vincent, Oliver Barbour
Writers: Carl Bixby, Don Becker
Sound Effects: Art Zachs
Organist: Herschel Leucke

Opening: As with most serial dramas, the opening for *Life Can Be Beautiful* changed many times over the years. At one time it was simply Papa David saying, "Come in. Come in. The door is open." A typical opening later in the program's history was:

MUSIC. *Theme*

ANNOUNCER. John Ruskin wrote this—"Whenever money is the principal object of life, it is both got ill and spent ill, and does harm both in the getting and spending. When getting and spending happiness is our aim, life can be beautiful!" *Life Can Be Beautiful* is an inspiring message of faith drawn from life, written by Carl Bixby and Don Becker, and brought to you by Spic and Span. No soap, no other cleaner, nothing in America cleans painted walls, woodwork, and linoleum like Spic and Span.

Life Can Be Beautiful was known to people in the radio industry as "Elsie Beebe," from the sound of the first letters of the show title. The program came to radio over CBS in 1938. Much of the action took place in "The Slightly Read Bookshop."

The Life of Mary Sothern

Serial Drama

CAST:

Mary Sothern — Linda Carlon, Minabelle Abbott, Betty Caine
Phyllis Stratford — Florence Golden
Danny Stratford — Jack Zoller, Joseph Julian, Leon Janney
Daddy Stratford — Charles Seel
Max Tilley — Jay Jostyn
Dr. John Benson — Jerry Lesser
Billie McDaniels — Jeanne Colbert
Jerome Sanders — Rikel Kent
Alice Sanders — Bess McCammon
Announcer: Ken Roberts

Director: Chick Vincent
Writer: Don Becker
Theme: "Just a Little Love, a Little Kiss"

The Life of Mary Sothern was first heard over Mutual in 1936.

The Life Of Riley

Situation Comedy

CAST:

Chester A. Riley — Lionel Stander, William Bendix
Mrs. Peg Riley — Grace Coppin, Paula Winslowe
Junior Riley — Jack Grimes, Scotty Beckett, Conrad Binyon, Tommy Cook
Babs Riley — Peggy Conklin, Sharon Douglas, Barbara Eiler
Digger O'Dell, The Friendly Undertaker — John Brown
Waldo Binny — Dink Trout
Uncle Buckley — Charlie Cantor
Uncle Baxter — Hans Conried

Producer-Writer: Irving Brecher
Directors: Al Kaye, Marx Loeb, Don Bernard
Writers: Ruben Ship, Ashmead Scott, Alan Lipscott, Robert Sloane, Leonard Bercovici

Catch-phrases:

RILEY. What a revoltin' development this is!

DIGGER O'DELL. You're looking fine, Riley. Very natural.

Life With Luigi

Situation Comedy

CAST:

Luigi — J. Carrol Naish
Rosa — Jody Gilbert
Pasquale — Alan Reed (Teddy Bergman)
Miss Spalding — Mary Shipp
Horowitz — Joe Forte
Schultz — Hans Conried
Petersen — Ken Peters

Director: Cy Howard
Writer-Director: Mac Benoff
Writer: Lou Derman
Sound Effects: Jack Dick
Theme: "Oh, Marie"

The full name of J. Carrol Naish was Joseph Patrick Carrol Naish. Although he was of Irish ancestry, he became identified with the Italian character Luigi. The program began over CBS in 1948.

The Light of the World

Religion

CAST:

The Speaker — Bret Morrison
Aram — Sanford Bickart
Josiah — Chester Stratton
Shallum — Humphrey Davis

Also: Eric Dressler, Louise Fitch, Mitzi Gould, Barbara Fuller, James Monks, Bill Adams, Jack Arthur, Peggy Allenby, James McCallion, Lynne Rogers, Iris Mann, Elaine Rost, Virginia Payne, Ernest Graves, Daniel Sutter, Florence Williams, *et al.*
Announcers: Stuart Metz, Ted Campbell
Creator-Producer: Don Becker
Producer-Director: Basil Loughrane
Directors: Don Cope, Oliver Barbour
Writers: Adele Seymour, Katharine Seymour, Noel B. Gerson, Margaret Sangster
Musical Director: Doc Whipple
Sound Effects: Jack Anderson

The Light of the World presented dramatizations of stories from the Bible. Countless performers appeared on the program, many of whom later became very famous. The voice of Bret Morrison opened the program with organ background and echo effect. The series was first heard over NBC in 1940.

Lights Out

Suspense Drama

Featuring: Betty Winkler, Sidney Ellstrom, Ted Maxwell, Raymond Edward Johnson, Templeton Fox, Lou Merrill, *et al.*
Creator: Wyllis Cooper
Writers: Wyllis Cooper, Arch Oboler, Ferrin N. Fraser

Opening:

ANNOUNCER. It . . . is . . . later . . . than . . . you . . . think!
[later]
Lights out . . . e-v-e-r-y-b-o-d-y!

Lights Out was originally a fifteen-minute program. It was eventually lengthened to a half-hour. The program was usually a late-night entry, at one time being heard at midnight and at another at 10:30 p.m., Wednesdays, on NBC.

Li'l Abner

Situation Comedy

CAST:

Li'l Abner — John Hodiak
Mammy Yokum — Hazel Dopheide
Pappy Yokum — Clarence Hartzell
Daisy Mae — Laurette Fillbrandt

Announcer: Durward Kirby

Producer: Wynn Wright
Director: Ted MacMurray
Writer: Charles Gussman

Li'l Abner featured the adventures of hillbilly characters in the village of "Dogpatch." It was based on the comic strip by Al Capp and first came to radio over NBC in 1939, originating in Chicago.

Lilac Time

Dance Instruction

Featuring: Arthur Murray
Vocalist: Carl Oxford

Arthur Murray described dance steps on this program.

Lincoln Highway

Drama

Narrator-M.C.: John McIntire
Directors: Don Cope, Maurice Lowell, Theodora Yates

Theme: (Composed and sung by Jack Arthur)
Hi there, neighbor,
Going my way
East or West on the Lincoln Highway?

Hi there, Yankee,
Give out with a great big "Thankee";
This is God's country.

Linda's First Love

Serial Drama

CAST:

Linda	Arline Blackburn
Danny	Karl Swenson

Also: Mary Jane Higby, many others
Announcers: Roger Forster, André Baruch

Director: Martha Atwell
Theme: "If You Are but a Dream"

The Line-up

Police Drama

CAST:

Police Lieutenant	Bill Johnstone
Police Sergeant	Wally Maher

This was first heard over CBS in 1950.

The Linit Show: see *The Fred Allen Show*.

Listen to This

Music and Conversation

CAST:

Dotty	Kay St. Germain
Johnny	Jack Brooks

Listening Post

Drama

Host: Bret Morrison
Also: Everett Sloane, Fredric March, Joan Tetzel, Myron McCormick, Martha Scott, Ethel Owen, Nancy Douglass, Clayton "Bud" Collyer, Mary Jane Higby
Directors: Henry Klein, James Sheldon
Writers: Ben Kagan, Gerald Holden, Noel B. Gerson

Listening Post presented dramatizations of stories from *The Saturday Evening Post*. It was first heard over ABC in 1944.

The Little Betsy Ross Girl Variety Program

Children's Variety

Featuring: Marion Loveridge, the Betsy Ross Girl; "Termite" Daniels, the Panty-Waist Glamour Girl; Billy Daniels, "Termite's" brother; Bobby Hookey, America's Youngest National Network Radio Comedian

All these youngsters graduated from *The Horn and Hardart Children's Hour.*

Little Italy

Serial Drama

CAST:

Nick — Ned Wever
Tony — Alfred Corn
(later known as Alfred Ryder)
Papa Marino — Himan Brown
Mrs. Marino — Ruth Yorke
Beatrice — Rose Keane

Producer-Writer-Director: Himan Brown

Little Italy was first heard over CBS in 1933.

Little Jack Little

Music

Featuring: Little Jack Little

The singer-pianist star of this program stood only five feet four inches tall and was billed as "Radio's Cheerful Little Earful." He was heard at various times over CBS in the early 1930s.

Little Ol' Hollywood

Hollywood Chatter

M.C.: Ben Alexander

This program was first heard over the Blue network in 1940.

Little Old New York

Variety

Starring: Jack Arthur
Director: Ed Whitney

This program featured music and light drama.

Little Orphan Annie

Adventure Serial

CAST:

Little Orphan Annie — Shirley Bell
Janice Gilbert
Joe Corntassle — Allan Baruck
Mr. Silo — Jerry O'Mera
Mrs. Silo — Henrietta Tedro
Daddy Warbucks — Henry Saxe
Stanley Andrews
Boris Aplon
Clay Collier (decoder inventor)
Hoyt Allen
Aha, the Chinese cook — Olan Soule
Voice of Sandy, the dog — Brad Barker
Also: Harry Cansdale, St. John Terrell, James Monks
Announcer: Pierre André

Director: Alan Wallace
Writers: Roland Martini, Ferrin N. Fraser, Day Keene and Wally Norman

---

Catch-phrase:
ANNIE. Leapin' lizards!

Little Orphan Annie was based on the comic strip by Harold Gray. "Mr. and Mrs. Silo" were Annie's parents by adoption. Obviously they were farmers. "Joe Corntassle" was the shy kid down the road who had a crush on Annie.

At the opening of the program "Uncle Andy"—announcer Pierre André—introduced the theme song:

Who's that little chatterbox?
The one with pretty auburn locks?
Who can it be?
It's Little Orphan Annie.
She and Sandy make a pair.
They never seem to have a care.
Cute little she,
It's Little Orphan Annie.
Bright eyes
Cheeks a rosy glow
There's a store of healthiness handy.
Pint-size
Always on the go
If you want to know
"Arf," goes Sandy.
Always wears a sunny smile.
Now wouldn't it be worth your while,
If you could be
Like Little Orphan Annie?

Other verses included:

Gather closer, girls and boys,
Mustn't make a bit of noise,
For we will hear—
Our Little Orphan Annie.
Everybody loves this miss.
A happy little girl is this.
Come lend an ear
To Little Orphan Annie.
She is bringing all her friends,
We will have a party that's dandy.
You'll meet each and every one,
Not to be outdone,
"Arf," says Sandy.
And before she goes away.
We know that everyone will say,
"She is a dear"—
Our Little Orphan Annie.

Little Orphan Annie's here,
The little girl so full of cheer,
Who doesn't know
Our Little Orphan Annie?
Be as quiet as a mouse,
Tell everybody in the house.
They'll want to know,
It's Little Orphan Annie.
Tell your mother and your dad,
You know something better than candy.
If you drink it once or twice,
You will think it nice—
Oooh - how dandy!
Later on we'll tell you more,
But now we have a treat in store—
On with the show,
And Little Orphan Annie.

As was the case with many of radio's themes, the lyrics varied from time to time. For example, the first verse listed above was taken from an actual broadcast and was not the same as the published sheet music, from which the other verses were taken.

The reference in the last verse of the theme song was to Ovaltine, the long-time sponsor of *Little Orphan Annie*. Among the premiums offered were an Ovaltine shake-up mug and a decoder for the daily clues given at the end of the broadcast.

The series was first heard over the Blue network in 1931.

Little Women

Serial Drama

CAST:

Jo — Elaine Kent
Amy — Pat Ryan
Mrs. March — Irene Hubbard
Meg — Joyce Hayward
Beth — Sammie Hill

This series was based on the novel by Louisa May Alcott.

Living Should Be Fun

Health

This durable series presented diet and health talks by Carlton Fredericks.

Lone Journey

Serial Drama

CAST:

Nita Bennett — Claudia Morgan, Betty Ruth Smith, Eloise Kummer
Wolfe Bennett — Lester Damon, Henry Hunter (Arthur Jacobson), Reese Taylor, Staats Cotsworth
Wolfe Bennett as a boy — Warren Mills
Mrs. Wolfe Bennett, Sr. — Nancy Osgood
Cullen Andrews — James Meighan, John Hodiak
Cecily Andrews — Dorothy Lowell
Lelia Matthews — Betty Caine, Genelle Gibbs
Jim Matthews — John Gibson, Frank Dane
Francesca Maguire — Nancy Marshall
Henry Newman — Clifford Soubier
Enor — Cameron Andrews, Bob Jellison
Mal Tanner — Wylie Adams, DeWitt McBride
Rollo St. Cloud — Dick Coogan
Mrs. Jessie King — Grace Valentine, Bess McCammon
Kyle King — Geraldine Kay
Jean — Norma Jean Ross
Lance McKenzie — John Larkin
Sydney Sherwood McKenzie — Charlotte Holland, Laurette Fillbrandt
Lansing McKenzie — Karl Weber
Lynne Alexander — Joan Alexander
Tao Smith — Oliver Cliff

Announcers: Durward Kirby, Henry Morgan, Nelson Case, Richard Stark

---

Directors: Axel Gruenberg, Ted MacMurray, Martin Magner
Writer: Sandra Michael

Lone Journey was first heard over NBC in 1940. It originated in Chicago.

The Lone Ranger

Western Adventure

CAST:

The Lone Ranger (John Reid) — George Seaton, Jack Deeds

Earle Graser
Brace Beemer
Tonto — John Todd
Dan Reid, The Lone Ranger's nephew — Ernie Stanley
James Lipton
Dick Beals
Butch Cavendish — Jay Michael
Thunder Martin — Paul Hughes
Announcer-Narrator — Harold True
Brace Beemer
Harry Golder
Charles Woods
Bob Hite
Fred Foy

Also: Rollon Parker, John Hodiak, Jack Petruzzi, Herschel Mayal, Ted Johnstone, Amos Jacobs (later known as Danny Thomas), Bob Maxwell, Frank Russell, Elaine Alpert

---

Creators: George W. Trendle, Fran Striker

Producer-Director-Writer: James Jewell

Directors: Al Hodge, Charles Livingstone

Chief Writer and Story Editor: Fran Striker

Writers: Felix Holt, Bob Green, Shelley Stark, Bob Shaw, Dan Beatty, Tom Dougall, Gibson Scott Fox

---

Theme: "William Tell Overture" by Rossini

Bridge Music: "Les Préludes" by Liszt

Opening:

MUSIC. *Theme up full and under . . .*

SOUND. *Hoofbeats fade in . . .*

RANGER. Hi-yo Silver!!!

SOUND. *Gunshots and hoofbeats . . .*

ANNOUNCER. A fiery horse with the speed of light, a cloud of dust and a hearty hi-yo Silver! The Lone Ranger!

MUSIC. *Theme up full and under . . .*

ANNOUNCER. With his faithful Indian companion, Tonto, the daring and resourceful masked rider of the plains led the fight for law and order in the early western United States. Nowhere in the pages of history can one find a greater champion of justice. Return with us now to those thrilling days of yesteryear . . .

SOUND. *Hoofbeats fade in . . .*

ANNOUNCER. From out of the past come the thundering hoofbeats of the great horse Silver. The Lone Ranger rides again!!!

RANGER. Come on, Silver! Let's go, big fellow! Hi-yo Silver! Away!

MUSIC. *Theme up full*

In 1930 George W. Trendle established a statewide radio network in Michigan with WXYZ Detroit as the key station for the Michigan Radio network. He began a search for a program dedicated to youth. In his mind he imagined a program that was action-packed without emphasis on violence, one that would entertain as well as quietly instruct and inspire, one that would have appeal to children but would also be logical and interesting to adults. Eventually Trendle decided on a story set in the pioneer days in the West and hired Fran Striker, a writer from Buffalo, New York, to create the hero. Trendle's instructions were that the hero must be realistic, serious, and soberminded, a man with a righteous purpose, a man who would serve as an example of good living and clean speech. The hero also had to be a man of mystery and be motivated by a burning desire to help the builders of the West and to do it, not for personal credit or gain, but purely for love of country.

The first broadcast of *The Lone Ranger* was on January 30, 1933. The show was scheduled for three complete half-hour adventures every week. To handle problems of production costs, Trendle called upon Allen H. Campbell, an advertising salesman for the Hearst organization. Campbell sold the program for broadcast not only in Detroit, but also in New York and Chicago. Campbell established a three-station hook-up with WXYZ feeding the program to WOR New York and WGN Chicago. The hook-up was called the Mutual Broadcasting System (MBS). The final broadcast on a nationwide basis was on September 3, 1954.

Brace Beemer narrated the program during the time that Earle Graser played the part of the Ranger. Graser was killed in an auto accident on April 8, 1941, and for a period of several broadcasts the Ranger was portrayed as being very ill and wasn't heard except for heavy breathing. After a sufficient time had passed, Beemer became the Ranger. Thus, there was no sudden change of voice for the Lone Ranger.

Tonto's horses were named White Feller, Paint, and Scout. Tonto's conversations with the Lone Ranger often included the phrase "Kemo Sabe"—which is translated "Faithful Friend." Another familiar part of the show was the closing, which usually involved someone asking, "Who was that masked man?"—and as the Lone Ranger and Tonto galloped off into the distance, the reply would come, "Why, don't you know? That man was . . . the Lone Ranger!"

Trendle and Striker also created *The Green Hornet*. There are some interesting parallels between the two programs, as noted in the listing for *The Green Hornet*.

Lonely Women

Serial Drama

CAST:

Marilyn Larimore	Betty Lou Gerson
Mrs. Schultz	Virginia Payne
Nora	Nanette Sargent
Judith Clark	Barbara Luddy
Judith Evans	Eileen Palmer
Helen	Florence Brower
Peggy	Harriette Widmer
Mr. Schultz	Murray Forbes
Bertha Schultz	Patricia Dunlap
George Bartlett	Reese Taylor
Jack Crandall	Les Tremayne
Edith Crandall	Muriel Bremner
Laura Richardson	Kay Campbell
Henry	Cliff Soubier
Virginia Marshall	Eunice Topper
Mr. Conway	John Barclay
Judge Carter Colby	Herb Butterfield
Mrs. Carter Colby	Muriel Bremner
John Murray	Willard Waterman

Announcer: Marvin Miller

Producer: Carl Wester
Director: Gil Gibbons
Writer: Irna Phillips

Lonely Women originated in Chicago and made its debut over NBC in 1942.

The Longines Symphonette

Music

Host: Frank Knight
Conductor: Mishel Piastro
Theme: "Moonlight Sonata" by Beethoven

The Longines Symphonette was sponsored by the Longines-Wittnauer Watch Company, makers of "The World's Most Honored Watch."

Look Your Best: see *Women's Programs*.

Lora Lawton

Serial Drama

CAST:

Lora Lawton	Joan Tompkins
	Jan Miner
Peter Carver	James Meighan
	Ned Wever
May Case, the secretary	Ethel Wilson
Iris Houston	Elaine Kent
Clyde Houston	James Van Dyk
Angus MacDonald	William Hare
Gail Carver	Marilyn Erskine
	Charita Bauer
Helene Hudson	Fran Carlon
Rex Lawton	Lawson Zerbe
Russell Gilman	Walter Greaza
Daniel	Alan MacAteer
Nannie	Kate McComb
Kevin	Paul McGrath
Octavia	Carol Summers

Producers: Frank and Anne Hummert
Directors: Martha Atwell, Arthur Hanna, Fred Weihe
Writers: Helen Walpole, Jean Carroll, Elizabeth Todd

"Lora Lawton" was a woman from the Midwest who moved to Washington, D.C., to become housekeeper for shipbuilder "Peter Carver." The program was first heard over NBC in 1943.

Lorenzo Jones

Serial Comedy-Drama

CAST:

Lorenzo Jones	Karl Swenson
Belle, his wife	Betty Garde
	Lucille Wall
Irma Barker	Nancy Sheridan
	Mary Wickes
	Grace Keddy
Judy	Colleen Ward
Nick	Elliott Reid
Frances	Helen Walpole
Millie	Ethel Owen
Jim Barker	John Brown
	Frank Behrens
Abby Matson	Jean McCoy
Sandy Matson	Joe Julian
Chester Van Dyne	Louis Hector
Mrs. Henry Thayer	Irene Hubbard
Clarence K. Muggins	Roland Winters
	Kermit Murdock
Margaret	Ann Shepherd (Scheindel Kalish)
Angus	Art Carney
Walter	Chester Stratton

Announcer: Don Lowe

Producers: Frank and Anne Hummert
Directors: Frank Hummert, Stephen Gross, Ernest Ricca

Writers: Theodore and Mathilde Ferro
Sound Effects: Frank Loughrane, Manny Segal
Organists: Rose Rio, Ann Leaf

Theme: "Funiculi, Funicula"
Opening:
ANNOUNCER. And now, smile a while with Lorenzo Jones and his wife Belle.

Lorenzo Jones made its debut over NBC in 1937. "Lorenzo" "worked" as a mechanic at "Jim Barker's" garage but spent most of his time inventing useless gadgets. In one of the stories, "Lorenzo" fell victim to amnesia and the program took on a serious overtone. The program was described by the announcer as "a story with more smiles than tears."

Louella Parsons: see *Hollywood Reporters*.

Lucky Smith

Adventure

CAST:
Detective Lucky Smith — Max Baer

Max Baer was a former heavyweight boxing champion of the world.

The Lullaby Lady

Music

The Lullaby Lady: Louise King
Evelyn Ames
Opal Craven
Margaret Gent

Lum and Abner

Comedy

CAST:

Lum Edwards	Chester Lauck
Abner Peabody	Norris Goff
Grandpappy Spears	Chester Lauck
Snake Hogan	Chester Lauck
Cedric Wehunt	Chester Lauck
Dick Huddleston, postmaster	Norris Goff
Doc Miller	Norris Goff
Squire Skimp	Norris Goff

Also: Edna Best, Zasu Pitts, Andy Devine, Cliff Arquette
Orchestra: Opie Cates
Announcers: Gene Hamilton, Del Sharbutt, Carlton Brickert, Lou Crosby, Wendell Niles, Gene Baker, Roger Krupp

Producer-Director: Larry Berns
Directors: Robert McInnes, Forrest Owen, Bill Gay
Writers: Jay Sommers, Betty Boyle, Roz Rogers, Wedlock and Snyder (Hugh Wedlock, Jr., and Howard Snyder)
Sound Effects: Dave Light, Harry Essman
Organist: Sybil Bock

The story was centered in the "Jot 'Em Down Store" in "Pine Ridge, Arkansas." Pine Ridge was originally a fictitious town, but in 1936 the real town of Waters, Arkansas, changed its name to Pine Ridge in honor of *Lum and Abner.*

The show started over NBC on April 26, 1931, and continued on radio for twenty-four years over NBC, CBS, ABC, and Mutual. Sponsors included Quaker Oats, Ford Motor Company, Horlick's Malted Milk, General Foods, Alka-Seltzer, and General Motors.

Luncheon at Sardi's

Interviews

M.C.: Bill Slater
Tom Slater
Producer-Director: Gary Stevens

The Lutheran Hour: see *Religion.*

Lux Radio Theatre

Drama

Hosts: Cecil B. DeMille (June 1, 1936, to January 22, 1945); William Keighley (December 1945 to June 6, 1955); Irving Cummings (occasionally as substitute)
Announcers: Mel Ruick, John Milton Kennedy, Ken Carpenter
Directors: Antony Stanford, Cecil B. DeMille, Frank Woodruff, Fred MacKaye, Earl Ebi
Writers: Charles S. Monroe, Sanford Barnett, Stanley Richards, Carroll Carroll, Ed James

"Lux . . . presents Hollywood!" was a familiar phrase to Monday-night radio listeners from June 1, 1936, to June 6, 1955. When this Blue network program was originally broadcast from New York on Sunday afternoons, beginning in 1934, under Antony Stanford's direction, it featured hour-long adaptations of Broadway plays starring Broadway actors. In 1936 Lever Brothers moved the show to Hollywood, where Cecil B. DeMille took over as host and director, and from then on *The Lux Radio Theatre* featured radio adaptations of famous motion pictures using movie stars as the leading actors. Sometimes the same actors who appeared in the radio version had appeared in the movie, but more often other stars assayed the roles.

The first program based upon a film starred Marlene Dietrich and Clark Gable in "The Legionnaire and the Lady," an adaptation of the motion picture *Morocco*. The following program was "The Thin Man," starring Myrna Loy and William Powell. Over the years Don Ameche appeared more than any other actor, playing leads in eighteen different productions. Fred MacMurray was next with seventeen appearances. Barbara Stanwyck starred in more productions than any other actress—fifteen. Claudette Colbert and Loretta Young tied for second with fourteen each.[1]

In 1945 DeMille relinquished his position as host-director under rather unusual circumstances. As required of all performers, DeMille was a member of the American Federation of Radio Artists (AFRA), the radio performers' union. In the fall of 1945 a proposition regarding closed-shop union rulings was to be voted on in the California election. AFRA was in favor of closed shops and assessed its members one dollar each to help support a campaign in this regard. DeMille, adamantly opposed to closed

[1] For a complete listing of the 387 productions broadcast under the aegis of Cecil B. DeMille, *see* Gene Ringgold, and DeWitt Bodeen, *The Films of Cecil B. DeMille.*

shops, refused to pay the assessment on the grounds that his payment of one dollar would nullify his opposition vote. AFRA ruled that anyone who did not pay the assessment would be suspended and thereby prevented from appearing on the air. Thus DeMille was banned from the air because he would not pay the one dollar or allow anyone else to pay it for him. After a year of on-the-air auditions of various possible hosts, William Keighley was selected as the new permanent host.

M

Ma and Pa

Comedy Dialogue

CAST:

Ma	Margaret Dee
Pa	Parker Fennelly

Ma and Pa was first heard over CBS in 1936.

Ma Perkins

Serial Drama

CAST:

Ma Perkins	Virginia Payne
Fay Perkins Henderson	Rita Ascot
	Marjorie Hannan
	Cheer Brentson
	Laurette Fillbrandt
	Margaret Draper
John Perkins	Gilbert Faust
Shuffle Shober	
	Charles Egleston (twenty-five years)
	Edwin Wolfe (two years)
Willie Fitz	Murray Forbes
Junior Fitz	Cecil Roy
	Arthur Young
	Bobby Ellis
Mr. Farnum	Ray Largay
Mrs. Farnum	Constance Crowder

Zenith Sambrini — Fran Carlon
Greta, the maid — Cheer Brentson
Evey Perkins Fitz — Dora Johnson
Laurette Fillbrandt
Kay Campbell (fifteen years)
Catherine Shaughnessey — Cheer Brentson
Josie — Louise Fitch
Dora — Mary Frances Desmond
C. Pemberton Toohey — Fred Howard
Forrest Lewis
Paul Henderson — Jonathan Hole
Walter Payne — Curtis Roberts
Miss Adams — Mary Marren Rees
Dr. Stevens — Curtis Roberts
Gary St. Denis — Rene Gekiere
John Adam Drayton — Duke Watson
Frank Fenton — Barry Drew
Dan Sutter
Mr. Silvus — Stuart McIntosh
Anton Julikak — Don Gallagher
Burton Wiley — Les Tremayne
Sonny Hallet — Billy Rose
Tommy Taylor — Dolph Nelson
Lula — Nanette Sargent
Russell — Barry Drew
Mr. Mortimer — Stanley Waxman
Judge Hartley — Billy Lee
Earl George
Mr. Erp — Glen Ransom
Eb Martin — Clare Baum
Zeke Hammill — Stanley Gordon
Mark Matthews — DeWitt McBride
Deborah Matthews — Betty Hanna
Susie Parker — Sylvia Leigh
Charley Brown — Ray Suber
Dr. Glassman — Carl Kroenke
Doris Fairchild — Kay Campbell
Timothy Gallagher — Forrest Lewis
Jessica Herringbone — Beryl Vaughn
Flossie Herringbone — Angeline Orr
Tweetsie Herringbone — Elmira Roessler
Phineas Herringbone — Herbert Butterfield
Mrs. Pendleton — Margaret Fuller
Bessie Flounce — Cecil Roy
Burt Carlon — Jack Petruzzi
Gary Curtis — Rye Billsbury
Augustus Pendleton — Maurice Copeland
Mathilda Pendleton — Beverly Younger
Paulette Henderson — Nanette Sargent
Judith Lockser
Stella Carlon Curtis — Marilou Neumayer
Gladys Pendleton — Virginia Payne
Patricia Dunlap
Helen Lewis
Jeff — Jack Brinkley
Forrest Lewis
Tom Wells — John Larkin
Casey Allen
Mr. Garrett — Wilms Herbert
Joseph — Joe Helgeson
Dr. Andrew White — Casey Allen
Hunkins — Murray Forbes
Gregory Ivanoff — McKay Morris
Rufus — Forrest Lewis
Sam Grim — Charles Egleston
Paulette — Judith Lockser
Esther — Lillian White
Andrew — Casey Allen
Lillian — Nancy Douglass

Announcers: Jack Brinkley, Dick Wells, "Charlie Warren,"[1] Marvin Miller, Dan Donaldson

[1] Owing to conflicts, Marvin Miller was forced to use the pseudonym "Charlie Warren" when he announced the program in Chicago. Dan Donaldson replaced Miller when the program moved to New York. Donaldson also used the name "Charlie Warren" during much of that time.

Creator: Robert Hardy Andrews
Producer: Lester Vail
Directors: Edwin Wolfe, George Fogle, Philip Bowman, Roy Winsor
Writers: Lee Gebhart, Natalie Johnson, Lester Huntley, Orin Tovrov
Musical Director: Doc Whipple
Sound Effects: Tommy Horan, Vincent Ronca, Wes Conant

Theme: "Ma Perkins" (original music)
Opening:
ANNOUNCER. And now . . . Oxydol's own Ma Perkins.

This serial drama was set in the town of "Rushville Center" where "Ma Perkins" operated a lumberyard. It made its debut over NBC on December 4, 1933, and was on the air for twenty-seven years for a total of 7065 broadcasts, with Virginia Payne playing "Ma" for the program's entire run. *Ma Perkins* had perhaps the best sponsor identification of all the "soap operas" through its long association with Oxydol.

Madison Square Garden Boxing

Sports

This was a long-running sports feature that began over NBC Blue in 1937. It was heard Friday nights at 10:00 and was sponsored originally by Adam Hats, later by Gillette.

Magazine of the Air

Music and Commentary

Featuring: B. A. Rolfe and His Orchestra
Theme: "Love's Own Sweet Song"

This program began in 1936. It was heard Monday, Wednesday, and Friday on CBS at 11:00 a.m. and presented music, guest speakers (such as Captain Tim Healy and Mrs. Martin Johnson), and a regular dramatic serial—"Trouble House," featuring Dorothy Lowell as Nancy Booth. (See also *Trouble House.*)

Maggi McNellis: see *Interviewers; Leave It to the Girls.*

The Magic Key

Music

M.C.: Milton Cross
Commentator: John B. Kennedy

The Magic Key was a concert series presenting world-famous musicians. It made its debut in 1936 sponsored by RCA. The program was originally on the air Sundays at 2:00 p.m.

The Magic of Speech

Education

Director-Writer: Vida Sutton

This program demonstrated ways of improving one's speech habits. It began on NBC in 1929 as a fifteen-minute broadcast on Thursday afternoons at 3:15.

The Magnificent Montague

Situation Comedy

CAST:

Edwin Montague, former Shakespearean actor — Monty Woolley
Lily Boheme Montague — Anne Seymour
Agnes, the maid — Pert Kelton

Writer: Nat Hiken
Organist: Jack Ward

This program was first heard over NBC in 1950.

Maisie

Situation Comedy

CAST:

Maisie — Ann Sothern
Bill — Elliott Lewis
Also: John Brown, Wally Maher, Norman Field, Donald Woods, Lurene Tuttle
Announcer: Ken Miles

Directors: Cal Kuhl, William Rousseau
Writer: Art Phillips

Maisie came to radio via CBS in 1945.

The Majestic Theater Hour

Variety

Featuring: The Two Black Crows (Moran and Mack)

This program began over CBS in 1927 as a sixty-minute broadcast on Sundays from 9:00 to 10:00 p.m. George Moran and Charlie Mack were already famous for their blackface comedy act.

Major Bowes and His Original Amateur Hour

Talent Contest

M.C.: Major Edward Bowes
Jay C. Flippen
Ted Mack
Announcers: Graham McNamee, Phil Carlin, Norman Brokenshire, Jimmy Wallington, Ralph Edwards, Dan Seymour, Tony Marvin, Warren Sweeney, Don Hancock
Producer: Lou Goldberg
Directors: Bob Reed, Lloyd Marx
Musical Supervisor: Lloyd Marx
Themes: "Stand By," "There's No Business Like Show Business"

Catch-phrase:

MAJOR BOWES. The wheel of fortune goes 'round and 'round and where she stops nobody knows.

Major Bowes and His Original Amateur Hour originated over WHN New York in 1934 and moved to

NBC on March 24, 1935, under the sponsorship of Chase and Sanborn. Jay C. Flippen replaced Bowes as M.C. of the WHN version while the Major appeared on the network. On September 17, 1936, the network show moved to CBS for Chrysler Corporation. It went to ABC under the sponsorship of Old Gold cigarettes on September 18, 1948. Both Flippen and Mack continued to use the wheel of fortune catch-phrase listed above. A gong was struck by the M.C. to indicate that the contestant had met defeat.

The Major Bowes Family Hour: see *The Family Hour.*

Major Hoople

Situation Comedy

CAST:

Major Hoople	Arthur Q. Bryan
Martha	Patsy Moran
Little Alvin	Franklin Bresee
Mr. Twiggs	Mel Blanc

Also: John Battle
Orchestra: Lou Bring
Walter Greene

Writer: Phil Leslie
Original Music: Lou Bring

Opening:

ORCHESTRA. *Laugh music . . . up and fade*

ANNOUNCER. He's not a sergeant . . . he's not a lieutenant . . . he's not a captain . . . he's a *major!* Yes, ladies and gentlemen, it's *Major Hoople!*

AUDIENCE. *Applause.*

ORCHESTRA. *Theme . . . up and fade*

ANNOUNCER. From out of the comic strip and into your homes, we bring you that overstuffed philosopher . . . Major Amos Hoople. His ever-loving but not too trusting wife, Martha . . . his precocious nephew, Little Alvin . . . and his star boarder and number-one complainer, Tiffany Twiggs.

ORCHESTRA. *Up and fade*

Closing:

ANNOUNCER. This radio version of Major Hoople was written by Phil Leslie . . . and featured in the leading roles Arthur Q. Bryan as Major Hoople, Patsy Moran as Martha, Franklin Bresee as Little Alvin, and Mel Blanc as Mr. Twiggs. Original music was by Lou Bring.

AUDIENCE. *Applause.*

ANNOUNCER. Major Hoople comes to you each week at this same time over most of these same stations. This program came to you from Hollywood. This is the Blue network.

Major Hoople was based on the newspaper comic character originated by Gene Ahern in "Our Boarding House." The above script excerpt was for the broadcast of Monday, October 5, 1942 (4:00–4:30 p.m. Pacific War Time).

The Make-Believe Ballroom

Music

Host: Martin Block

This was the first commercially successful record program, though its title had been used earlier in Los Angeles by Al Jarvis.

Martin Block scored a hit with *The Make-Believe Ballroom* in New York (on station WNEW) by referring to the various orchestras playing on the mythical stages in the "Crystal Studio" of WNEW during the radio coverage of the Hauptmann trial. Block generally devoted fifteen-minute segments of this two-hour program to an individual singer or orchestra's recordings. The best-remembered theme was "It's Make-Believe Ballroom Time," written by Martin Block and Mickey Stonner and recorded by Glenn Miller. Its lyrics included:

> It's Make-Believe Ballroom Time
> And free to everyone.
> It's no time to fret,
> Your dial is set
> For fun.
> Just close your eyes and visualize
> In your solitude.
> Your favorite bands are on the stands
> And Mister Miller puts you in the mood.

Malcolm Claire

Children's Stories

CAST:

The Old Witch, Whitewash, Spare Ribs, The Old Man — Malcolm Claire

---

Man Against Crime

Detective

CAST:

Mike Barnett, detective — Ralph Bellamy; Robert Preston[1]

Director: Paul Nickell
Writer: Lawrence Klee

This CBS series began its run on October 7, 1949.

The Man Behind the Gun

Adventure Drama

Featuring: Myron McCormick, William Quinn, Frank Lovejoy, Elizabeth Reller, Larry Haines, Paul Luther
Narrator: Jackson Beck
Producer-Director: William N. Robson
Writer: Ranald MacDougall
Musical Director: Van Cleave

The Man Behind the Gun was designed to build morale during World War II. The scripts were often based on actual events that had taken place in the various armed services. The series was first heard over CBS in 1943.

[1] Preston substituted for Bellamy from June 29, 1951 to August 3, 1951.

A Man Called X

Adventure

CAST:

Detective Ken Thurston
Herbert Marshall
His girl friend GeGe Pearson
Pagan Zeldschmidt, his side-kick
Leon Belasco

Producer: Jay Richard Kennedy
Directors: Jack Johnstone, William N. Robson
Writer: Milton Merlin

"Detective Thurston's" favorite hang-out was the "Café Tambourine" in Cairo, Egypt. The program began over ABC in 1944.

The Man from G-2

International Spy Adventure

CAST:

Major Hugh North
Staats Cotsworth
The girl Joan Alexander

The Man from G-2 was first heard over ABC in 1945.

The Man I Married

Serial Drama

CAST:

Evelyn Waring Vicki Vola
Gertrude Warner
Dorothy Lowell
Betty Winkler
Barbara Lee
Adam Waring Van Heflin
Clayton "Bud" Collyer
Phineas T. Grant Santos Ortega
Grandfather Grant Rikel Kent
Ella Hunt Frances Carden
Mr. Hunt Fred Irving Lewis
Teddy Hunt Jackie Grimes
Florence Weston Betty Worth
Mrs. Hempstead
Fanny May Baldridge
Frank Flippin Arnold Moss
Joe Billings Walter Vaughn
Ed Spalding
Raymond Edward Johnson
Aunt Matt Ethel Owen
Shelly Martin Spencer Bentley
Brooks Ed Jerome
Tippy John Gibson
Announcer: Howard Petrie

Director: Oliver Barbour
Writers: Carl Bixby, Don Becker
Theme: Original music by Don Becker

The Man I Married made its debut over NBC in 1939.

Mandrake the Magician

Adventure

CAST:

Mandrake
Raymond Edward Johnson
Lothar Juano Hernandez
Narda Francesca Lenni
Also: Laddie Seaman

Producer: Henry Souvaine
Director: Carlo De Angelo

MANDRAKE. Invoco legem magiciarum! [I invoke the law of magic.]

Mandrake the Magician was based on the comic-strip character created by Lee Falk and Phil Davis. The series was first heard over Mutual in 1940.

Manhattan at Midnight

Drama

Featuring: Alan Reed (Teddy Bergman), Ted de Corsia, Jeanette Nolan
Writer: Jay Bennett

This program was first heard over the Blue network in 1940.

Manhattan Merry-Go-Round

Music

Singers: Thomas L. Thomas, Rachel Carlay, Dennis Ryan, Marian McManus, Barry Roberts, Glenn Cross, Dick O'Connor, Rodney McClennan
Choral group: The Jerry Mann Voices, The Men About Town
Orchestra: Victor Arden and His Broadway Stage Band; Andy Sanella
Announcers: Ford Bond, Roger Krupp
Producers: Frank and Anne Hummert
Director: Paul Dumont

Theme: Although announcer Ford Bond unfailingly claimed the program presented lyrics "sung so clearly you can understand every word," we found it extremely difficult to decipher the third and fourth lines of the theme. After listening to recordings over and over, we found the lyrics to be as follows, with the third and fourth lines still uncertain:

Jump on the *Manhattan Merry-Go-Round*
We're touring alluring old New York town.
Broadway to Harlem a musical show
The orchestra tunes up to your radio.
We're serving music, fun, and laughter
A happy heart will follow after.
And we'd like to have you all with us
On the *Manhattan Merry-Go-Round.*

Opening:

ORCHESTRA AND CHORUS. *Theme, then under . . .*

FORD BOND. Here's the *Manhattan Merry-Go-Round* that brings you the bright side of life, that whirls you in music to all the big night spots of New York town to hear the top songs of the week sung so clearly you can understand every word and sing them yourself.

This program, heard Sundays at 9:00 p.m. over NBC, began in the early 1930s and was made up of a series of imaginary visits to night spots around Manhattan. The show became thoroughly identified with its long-time sponsor, Dr. Lyon's Tooth Powder (announcer Ford Bond always stressed the word "Powder" when he read the script). Many listeners, through the years, became curious as to what the "L" stood for in Thomas L. Thomas. It was a Welsh name—Llyfwny.

The March of Games

Quiz

Quizmaster: Arthur Ross
Drum Majorette: Sybil Trent
Producer: Nila Mack

The March of Time

Documentary

CAST:

Narrator	Ted Husing
	Harry Von Zell
	Westbrook Van Voorhis
Franklin D. Roosevelt	Bill Adams
	Art Carney
	Staats Cotsworth
Eleanor Roosevelt	
	Agnes Moorehead
	Nancy Kelly
	Jeanette Nolan
Josef Stalin	Edwin Jerome
Adolf Hitler	Dwight Weist
Benito Mussolini	Ted de Corsia
Winston Churchill	
	Maurice Tarplin
Neville Chamberlain	Peter Donald
King Farouk	Elliott Reid
Haile Selassie	Edwin Jerome
Huey Long	Jack Smart

Also: John McIntire, Georgia Backus, Martin Gabel, Karl Swenson, Gary Merrill, Adelaide Klein, Myron McCormick, Agnes Young, Everett Sloane, Kenny Delmar, Lotte Stavisky, Claire Niesen, *et al.*

Producer-Director: Arthur Pryor, Jr.
Assistant Producer: Tom Harrington
News Editor: Bill Geer
Directors: Don Stauffer, Homer Fickett, William Spier, Lester Vail
Musical Directors: Donald Voorhees, Howard Barlow
Writers: Richard Dana, Brice Disque, Jr., Carl Carmer, Paul Milton, Garrett Porter
Sound Effects: Mrs. Ora Nichols, Ronald Fitzgerald, Edward Fenton, Bob Prescott

---

Catch-phrases:
VAN VOORHIS. Time . . . marches on!
VAN VOORHIS. As it must to all men, death came this week to . . .

The first dramatized news story on *The March of Time* was broadcast over CBS in 1931—the renomination of "Big Bill" Thompson as mayor of Chicago.

Marie, the Little French Princess

Serial Drama

CAST:

Marie	Ruth Yorke
Richard	James Meighan

Also: Allyn Joslyn, Alma Kruger, Porter Hall
Announcer: André Baruch

Producer-Director: Himan Brown

This was one of the first nationally broadcast daytime "soap operas." "Marie" was a princess from a fictitious country who ran away to become a commoner.

Mark Trail

Adventure

CAST:

Mark Trail — Matt Crowley, John Larkin, Staats Cotsworth
Scotty — Ben Cooper, Ronald Liss
Cherry — Joyce Gordon
Announcers: Jackson Beck, Glenn Riggs

Director: Drex Hines
Writers: Albert Aley, Palmer Thompson, Elwood Hoffman, Gilbert Braun
Sound Effects: William B. Hoffman

Opening:

ANNOUNCER. Kellogg's Pep, the build-up wheat cereal with a prize in every package, invites you to share another thrilling adventure with . . . Mark Trail . . .
SOUND. *Burning forest*
ANNOUNCER. Battling the raging elements!
SOUND. *Wolf howl*
ANNOUNCER. Fighting the savage wilderness!
SOUND. *Horse hoofbeats*
ANNOUNCER. Striking at the enemies of man and nature!
MUSIC. *Sting*
ANNOUNCER. One man's name resounds from snow-capped mountains down across the sun-baked plains. Mark Trail!
MUSIC. *Sting*
ANNOUNCER. Guardian of the forests!
MUSIC. *Sting*
ANNOUNCER. Protector of wildlife!
MUSIC. *Sting*
ANNOUNCER. Champion of man and nature!
MUSIC. *Sting*
ANNOUNCER. Mark Trail!

This adventure series was based on the comic strip by Ed Dodd about an outdoorsman-conservationist. It was first heard over Mutual in 1950.

The Marlin Hurt and Beulah Show: see *Beulah*.

Marriage Club

Quiz

M.C.: Haven MacQuarrie

Marriage Club was first heard over CBS in 1940 on Saturdays at 8:00 p.m. for Wonder Bread.

Martha Deane: see *Women's Programs*.

Martha Tilton: see *The Curt Massey and Martha Tilton Show*.

Martha Webster: see *Life Begins*.

The Martin and Lewis Show

Comedy-Variety

Starring: Dean Martin and Jerry Lewis

The Martin and Lewis Show made its debut over NBC in 1949 and was heard originally Mondays at 10 p.m. Later the program was broadcast Friday evenings at 8:30. Dean Martin did the singing and Jerry Lewis was the comedian.

Martin Kane, Private Eye

Detective

CAST:

Martin Kane	William Gargan
Happy McMann	Walter Kinsella

Writer-Director: Ted Hediger
Sound Effects: Jack Keane, Jim Goode

This program was first heard over Mutual in 1949.

Marvin Miller, Storyteller

Documentary

Narrator: Marvin Miller
Producer: Joseph McCaughtry
Writer-Director: Larry Young

This was a syndicated series of five-minute programs (260 in all) recorded in 1948 and 1949. It was subtitled "Prelude to Greatness" and always dealt with a famous man who faced a crisis in his life or career and managed to solve it. The name of the man was never revealed until the last words of the program. Marvin Miller narrated and did all the voices.

In 1958 CBS ran another series using the same title. Miller again was the narrator and handled all the voices. This series was directed by Max Hutto, Harfield Weedin, Gene Webster, and Jack Rebney and written by Robert Turnbull, Marvin Miller, Elizabeth Dawson Miller, and Catherine Christopher. The scripts for this series were basically the ones used on Mutual's *Behind the Story.*

The Mary Ann Mercer Show: see *Aunt Jemima.*

Mary Lee Taylor: see *Women's Programs.*

Mary Margaret McBride: see *Interviewers; Women's Programs.*

Mary Marlin: see *The Story of Mary Marlin.*

Mary Noble: see *Backstage Wife.*

Mary Pickford and Buddy Rogers

Variety

Featuring: Mary Pickford and Buddy Rogers

Mary Pickford, "America's Sweetheart," and Buddy Rogers, "America's Boy Friend," an actor and bandleader, were husband and wife. Miss Pickford was the first major movie star to be identified by name. Previous actresses had been identified only by titles, such as "The Biograph Girl" (Florence Lawrence). Despite her vast experience as an actress, she developed a bad case of "mike fright" in her first radio appearances. NBC engineers camouflaged her microphone with a lampshade so that she would not be so conscious of it. The disguise worked, and the apparatus was dubbed "the Mary Pickford microphone." (See also *Parties at Pickfair.*)

Mary Small

Music

This fifteen-minute program, featuring child star Mary Small, made its debut over NBC Blue in 1934. (See also *Commercials.*)

Mary Sothern: see *The Life of Mary Sothern.*

Masquerade

Serial Drama

CAST:
Linda Leighton — Marguerite Anderson
Tom Field — Carlton KaDell
Thornton Drexel — Jack Edwards, Jr.
Joe — Conrad Binyon
Fred Nino — Ted Maxwell

Maude and Cousin Bill

Comedy Dialogue

CAST:
Maude — Maude Ricketts
Bill — Bill Ricketts
Also: Henry Rooter

Writer: Booth Tarkington

Maude and Cousin Bill was first heard over NBC Blue in 1932.

Maudie's Diary

Situation Comedy

CAST:
Maudie Mason — Mary Mason, Charita Bauer
Davy Dillon — Robert Walker
Pauly — Caryl Smith

Writer: Albert G. Miller

This series began over CBS in 1941.

Maverick Jim

Serial Drama

CAST:
Maverick Jim — Artells Dickson
Also: John Battle, Anne Elstner, Alice Frost

Writer: Stewart Sterling

Maverick Jim was among the earliest of radio programs with a Western setting. It was broadcast over WOR New York in the early 1930s.

Maxwell House Coffee Time

Comedy-Variety

CAST:
Starring: Frank Morgan, comedian
Singing M.C. — John Conte
Baby Snooks — Fanny Brice
Daddy Higgins — Jack Arthur, Alan Reed (Teddy Bergman), Hanley Stafford
Frank Morgan's niece — Cass Daley

Orchestra: Meredith Willson

Announcer: Robert Young
Writers: Paul Henning, Keith Fowler, Phil Rapp, Ed James
Theme: "You and I" by Meredith Willson

Catch-phrase:
CASS DALEY. I said it and I'm glad!

This program was first heard over NBC in 1937. (See also *Ziegfeld Follies of the Air.*)

Maxwell House Show Boat: see *Show Boat.*

Mayor LaGuardia Reads the Funnies

Talk

In 1945 Mayor Fiorello H. LaGuardia made radio history with his reading of the Sunday comics. This came about as a result of the strike by newspaper deliverers, which deprived the area of its prime source of Sunday recreation. Instead of the Mayor's usual weekly program on municipally owned station WNYC, *Talk to the People*, the Mayor read "Dick Tracy" and other Sunday comics to the kiddies. He embellished his reading with histrionics, vocal sound effects, and, most important, with comments on morality. He referred to Dick Tracy's slim figure and asked why his New York policemen couldn't be that trim.

WNYC donated its recordings of the programs of July 8, 1945, and July 15, 1945, to the Brooklyn Public Library, where they may still be heard.

Mayor of the Town

Comedy-Drama

CAST:

Mayor	Lionel Barrymore
Marilly	Agnes Moorehead
Butch	Conrad Binyon

Director: Jack Van Nostrand
Writers: Leonard St. Clair, Charles Tazewell, Howard Blake, Howard Breslin, Jean Holloway, Erna Lazarus

Mayor of the Town was first heard over CBS in 1942.

McGarry and His Mouse

Comedy-Detective

CAST:

Detective Dan McGarry	Roger Pryor Wendell Corey Ted de Corsia
Kitty Archer (the Mouse)	Shirley Mitchell Peggy Conklin Patsy Campbell
Mom Archer	Betty Garde
Sam	Carl Eastman
Bernice	Thelma Ritter
Uncle Matthew	Jerry Macy Jack Hartley

Orchestra: Peter Van Steeden
Announcer: Bert Parks

Writer: Milton J. Kramer

This was the story of a bumbling detective and his female companion, the "Mouse," based on a magazine series by Matt Taylor.

The Mediation Board: see *A. L. Alexander's Good Will Court.*

Meet Corliss Archer

Situation Comedy

CAST:

Corliss Archer	Janet Waldo
	Priscilla Lyon
	Lugene Sanders
Mr. Archer	Fred Shields
Mrs. Archer	Irene Tedrow
Dexter Franklin	Sam Edwards
	David Hughes
Little Raymond	Tommy Bernard
Mildred	Barbara Whiting

Also: Arlene Becker
Creator: F. Hugh Herbert
Director: Bert Prager
Writers: Carroll Carroll, F. Hugh Herbert, Jerry Adelman

Meet Corliss Archer made its debut over CBS in 1943.

Meet Me at Parky's

Comedy

CAST:

Nick Parkyakarkas	Harry Einstein
Cashier	Joan Barton
Prudence Rockbottom	Ruth Perrott
Orville Sharp	Sheldon Leonard

Also: Frank Nelson, Leo Cleary
Vocalists: Peggy Lee, Betty Jane Rhodes, Dave Street, Patty Bolton
Vocal group: The Short Order Chorus
Orchestra: Opie Cates
Announcer: Art Gilmore

Directors: Maurice Morton, Hal Fimberg
Writers: Hal Fimberg, Harry Einstein

Catch-phrase:
ORVILLE SHARP. Am I corr-eck-itt?

The action in *Meet Me at Parky's* was centered in a beanery owned by Nick Parkyakarkas. The program began over NBC in 1945.

Meet Mr. Meek: see *The Adventures of Mr. Meek.*

Meet the Meeks

Situation Comedy

Featuring: Forrest Lewis, Fran Allison, Beryl Vaughn, Cliff Soubier

Meet the Meeks made its debut over NBC in 1947.

Meet the Press

Interviews

Interviewers: Martha Rountree, Lawrence Spivak, Guest Reporters
Directors: Martha Rountree, Ray Hervey

This program featured interviews with people in the news, primarily political figures. It was founded in 1946 by Martha Rountree and Lawrence Spivak and was heard originally on Mutual.

The Mel Blanc Show

Comedy

CAST:
Starring: Mel Blanc

Betty Colby	Mary Jane Croft
Mr. Colby	Joe Kearns
Mr. Cushing	Hans Conried

Also: Jim Backus, Alan Reed (Teddy Bergman), Bea Benadaret, Earle Ross

Producer: Joe Rines
Director: Sam Fuller
Writer: Mac Benoff

This program was also known as *The Fix-It Shop* and *Mel Blanc's Fix-It Shop*.

Melody Puzzles

Quiz

M.C.: Fred Uttal
Orchestra: Harry Salter
Announcer: Ed Herlihy

Melody Puzzles was first heard over NBC Blue in 1937.

Melody Ranch: see *Gene Autry's Melody Ranch.*

Melody Treasure Hunt

Quiz

Featuring: Pat Ballard, Charlie Henderson

Mennen Shave Time

Situation Comedy

Featuring: Lou Parker, Ann Thomas
Director: Chet Gierlach

The Mercury Theatre on the Air

Drama

Host: Orson Welles
Producers: Orson Welles, John Houseman

The Mercury Theatre on the Air was a pioneer program of quality drama and experimental radio presentations. It made its debut over CBS in 1938. Orson Welles ("Your obedient servant") wrote, produced, directed, and starred on many of the broadcasts and developed such actors as Joseph Cotten, Everett Sloane, Agnes Moorehead, and the man Welles once called the greatest of all radio actors —Ray Collins. Various classics were dramatized, such as *Jane Eyre* by Charlotte Brontë.

On Sunday evening, October 30, 1938, *The Mercury Theatre on the Air,* as a Halloween stunt, presented Howard Koch's adaptation of H. G. Wells' *The War of the Worlds.* This dramatization of an invasion by space creatures at Grovers Mills, New Jersey, was so realistic that thousands of listeners were panic-stricken. Although disclaimers attesting to the fact that the broadcast was fictional were given on the program, such a furor ensued that the federal government was requested to take steps to insure that no such program could be broadcast again without making absolutely certain the listeners would understand it was fiction. Orson Welles played the lead in the Howard Koch (pronounced "Kotch") script: "Professor Richard Pearson of Princeton University."

The Mercury Theatre on the Air also performed a spectacular six-episode dramatization of Victor Hugo's *Les Misérables* with Welles as "Jean Valjean," Martin Gabel as "Javert," and Alice Frost as "Cosette." Others in the cast included Ray Collins, Richard Widmark, John McIntire, and Agnes Moorehead.

Opening:

ANNOUNCER. The Columbia Broadcasting System and its affiliated stations present Orson Welles and *The Mercury Theatre on the Air* in "The War of the Worlds" by H. G. Wells.

MUSIC. *Establish theme . . . then fade*

ANNOUNCER. Ladies and gentlemen, the director of *The Mercury Theatre* and star of these broadcasts—Orson Welles.

Closing:

MUSIC. *Establish theme . . . then under . . .*

ANNOUNCER. Tonight the Columbia Broadcasting System and its affiliated stations coast-to-coast has brought you "The War of the Worlds" by H. G. Wells . . . the seventeenth in its weekly series of dramatic broadcasts featuring Orson Welles and *The Mercury Theatre on the Air*. Next week we present a dramatization of three famous short stories. This is the Columbia Broadcasting System.

MUSIC. *Theme up full to conclusion*

Message of Israel: see *Religion*.

Metropolitan Opera Broadcasts

Music

Host: Milton Cross

This long-running series of broadcasts originated from the Metropolitan Opera House in New York. The première broadcast was on December 25, 1931, over NBC. Intermission features included interviews and "The Opera Quiz." The quiz was conducted by Olin Downes; musicologist Boris Goldovsky handled the interviews. Texaco began sponsorship of the broadcasts in 1940.

Meyer the Buyer

Comedy

CAST:

Meyer	Harry Hershfield
Mayor Mizznick	Teddy Bergman
Irma Mizznick	Adele Ronson
Lawyer Feldman	Paul Douglas
Mollie	Ethel Holt
Uncle Ben	Nick Adams
Beatrice	Dot Harrington
Milton Mizznick	Geoffrey Bryant

MGM Screen Test

Talent Show

M.C.: Dean Murphy
Orchestra: Ted Steele
Also: Charlotte Manson

Michael and Kitty

Mystery

CAST:

Michael	John Gibson
Kitty	Elizabeth Reller

Michael Shayne, Private Detective

Detective

CAST:

Michael Shayne	Jeff Chandler

This series was based on the character created by Brett Halliday (pseudonym of Davis Dresser).

The Mickey Mouse Theater of the Air

Children

CAST:

Mickey Mouse	Walt Disney
Donald Duck	Clarence Nash
Goofy	Stuart Buchanan
Minnie Mouse	Thelma Boardman
Clarabelle Cow	Florence Gill

Orchestra: Felix Mills
Also: Donald Duck's Swing Band, The Minnie Mouse Woodland Choir

Writer: Bill Demling

This program was based on characters created by Walt Disney. It was first heard over NBC in 1937.

Mickey of the Circus

Drama

CAST:

Mickey	Chester Stratton
Clara Gaines	Gretchen Davidson
Mamie	Betty Garde

Midstream

Serial Drama

CAST:

Charles Meredith	Hugh Studebaker
	Russell Thorson
	Sidney Ellstrom
Julia Meredith	Betty Lou Gerson
	Fern Persons
Midge	Mercedes McCambridge
	Laurette Fillbrandt
	Sharon Grainger
	Elia Braca
Stanley Bartlett	Bill Bouchey
David Meredith	Willard Farnum
Ruth Andrews	Connie Osgood
	Annette Harper
	Sylvia Jacobs
Howard Andrews (Ruth's brother)	Marvin Miller
Amy Gordon Bartlett	Josephine Gilbert

Jimmy Storey	Nina Klowden
	Lenore Kingston
Meredith Conway	Lesley Woods
Timothy Storey	Olan Soule
	Pat Murphy
Sandy Sanderson	Bob Jellison
John Elliott	Henry Hunter (Arthur Jacobson)
Bertha	Jane Green

Announcer: Gene Baker
Director: Gordon Hughes
Writer: Pauline Hopkins

Midstream made its debut over NBC in 1939. The program originated in Chicago.

The Mighty Show

Drama

CAST:

Ma Hutchinson	Agnes Moorehead
Jean Carter	Jay Meredith
Sally, the trapeze artist	Helen Lewis
Tex	Artells Dickson
Ruth, the knife thrower	Anne Boley

Also: Bradley Barker, Fred Irving Lewis, Elliott Reid

This drama was built around circus life.

Milligan and Mulligan

Comedy-Adventure

CAST:

Detective	Don Ameche
Comic side-kick	Bob White

Announcer: Tom Shirley

The Milton Berle Show

Comedy

Starring: Milton Berle
Also: Bert Gordon, Eileen Barton, Pert Kelton, Jack Albertson, Arnold Stang, Mary Shipp, Johnny Gibson, Roland Winters, Jackson Beck
Orchestra: Ray Bloch
Announcer: Frank Gallop
Writers: Martin A. Ragaway, Hal Block

The Milton Berle Show came to radio over NBC in 1939 and was sponsored by Quaker Oats.

Mimics: see *Animal Imitators, Baby Criers, Doubles, Mimics, and Screamers.*

Miracles of Magnolia

Serial Drama

Featuring: Fanny May Baldridge

This program was first heard over the Blue network in 1931.

Mirth and Madness

Comedy-Variety

Featuring: Jack Kirkwood, Lillian Lee, Don Reid, Jean McKean, Tom Harris, Billy Grey, Ransom Sherman, Lee Brodie, Mike McTooch, Herb Sheldon
Orchestra: Irving Miller, Jerry Jerome

Director: Joseph Mansfield
Writers: Jack Kirkwood, Ransom Sherman

———

Opening:
GREY. Hey, you!
KIRKWOOD. Are ya listenin'?
Theme: "Hi, Neighbor"

In Western sketches, Kirkwood would get shot and say, "Well, gal, I'm a-goin' fast. But before I go, I got somethin' to say . . ." Then he would go on and on and on.

Mirth and Madness was first heard over NBC in 1943.

Miss Hattie

Drama

Starring: Ethel Barrymore
Also: Dickie Van Patten

Modern Cinderella

Serial Drama

CAST:

Hope Carter — Rosemary Dillon, Laine Barklie
Larry Burton — Eddie Dean
Jimmy Gale — Ben Gage
Announcer: Roger Krupp

Modern Romances

Serial Drama

CAST:

Helen Gregory (Narrator) — Gertrude Warner

———

Directors: William Marshall, Joe Graham
Writers: Margaret Sangster, Ira Marion, Lillian Schoen, Don Witty
Organist: George Henninger

Modern Romances made its debut over the Blue network in 1936.

Mollé Mystery Theater: see *Mystery Theater.*

Molly of the Movies

Serial Drama

CAST:

Molly — Gene Byron
Also: Ray Jones, Betty Caine

Molly of the Movies made its debut over Mutual in 1935.

Moon Dreams

Music and Poetry

Narrator: Marvin Miller
Vocalist: Warren White
Orchestra: Del Castillo, Ivan Eppinoff (later known as Ivan Scott)
Producer: Carl Kraatz
Director: John Holbrook
Writers: Ken Krippene, Marvin Miller

Moon Dreams was a syndicated series of fifteen-minute programs recorded in 1946 and 1947.

Moon River

Music and Poetry

Narrator: Harry Holcomb

Palmer Ward
Charles Woods
Don Dowd
Jay Jostyn
Peter Grant, et al.

Creator: Edward Byron

Theme: "Caprice Viennois" by Fritz Kreisler

Bridge Music under Poems: "Clair de Lune" by Debussy

Opening:

NARRATOR.

Moon River,
A lazy stream of dreams
Where vain desires forget themselves
In the loveliness of sleep.
Moon River,
Enchanted white ribbon
Twined in the hair of night,
Where nothing is but sleep,
Dream on . . . Sleep on . . .
Care will not seek for thee.
Float on . . . Drift on . . .
Moon River, to the sea.

Closing:

NARRATOR.

Down the valley of a thousand yesterdays
Flow the bright waters of Moon River.
On and down, forever flowing, forever waiting
To carry you down to the land of forgetfulness,
To the kingdom of sleep . . . to the realm of . . .

Moon River,
A lazy stream of dreams
Where vain desires forget themselves
In the loveliness of sleep.
Moon River,
Enchanted white ribbon
Twined in the hair of night,
Where nothing is but sleep,
Dream on . . . Sleep on . . .
Care will not seek for thee.
Float on . . . Drift on . . .
Moon River, to the sea.

This was a nationally famous program of music and poetry from WLW Cincinnati.

Moonshine and Honeysuckle

Serial Drama

CAST:

Clem	Louis Mason
Peg Leg Gaddis	Claude Cooper
"Cracker" Gaddis	Anne Elstner

Also: Virginia Morgan, Jeanie Begg, John Milton, Anne Sutherland, Sara Haden

Director: Henry Stillman
Writer: Lula Vollmer

Moonshine and Honeysuckle, one of the early serial dramas, was first heard over NBC in 1930.

The Mormon Tabernacle Choir

Music and Talks

The Morman Tabernacle Choir broadcasts each Sunday from the Mormon Tabernacle located on Temple Square in Salt Lake City, Utah—as it has done since 1929. It is the oldest continuous nationwide network series in American radio. The choir is composed of 375 singers from all walks of life—farmers, housewives, bankers, teachers, etc.—all of whom are unpaid professionals.

Originally the broadcasts were carried over NBC by the local affiliate, KSL. In 1932, KSL switched to CBS affiliation, and the broadcast went with it. The original director of the choir was Professor Anthony C. Lund of Brigham Young University. The producer and announcer was Earl J. Glade. In 1935, with the death of Professor Lund, J. Spencer Cornwall was appointed choir director and held that position until 1957. In that same year Richard L. Evans took over the job of producing, directing, and announcing the programs. Both Cornwall and Evans were the voices who gave "The Spoken Word" each week, a message of inspiration and stimulation. Among the organists were Alexander Schreiner and Frank Asper. (See also *Religion.*)

Mortimer Gooch

Comedy-Serial Drama

CAST:

Mortimer Gooch	Bob Bailey
Betty Lou	Louise Fitch

Mortimer Gooch was first heard over CBS in 1936.

Morton Downey: see *The Coke Club.*

Mother and Dad

Comedy Dialogue

CAST:

Mother	Charme Allen
Dad	Parker Fennelly

Mother and Dad was first heard over CBS in 1943.

Mother of Mine

Serial Drama

CAST:

Mother Morrison	Agnes Young
John	Donald Cook
Helen	Ruth Yorke
Anne	Pattee Chapman
Pop Whitehouse	Arthur Allen
Pete	Jackie Kelk
Paul Strong	Paul Nugent

Mother of Mine was first heard over the Blue network in 1940.

The Moylan Sisters

Music

Featuring: The Moylan Sisters
Accompanist: Morty Howard
Announcer: Don Lowe
Producer-Writer: Isaac Clements
Director: Robert Smith

Theme:

We feed our doggie Thrivo,
He's very much alive-o,
Full of pep and vim!
If you want a happy pup,

You'd better hurry up—
Buy Thrivo, for him!

This fifteen-minute, Sunday-afternoon program featured Marianne (the elder by three years) and Peggy Joan Moylan and a pianist. It made its debut over NBC Blue in 1939. The script described the two sisters' unique ability to sing three-part harmony. The girls were billed as "The Angels of the Airwaves." The creator of the familiar Thrivo jingle was Elizabeth Zindel. For a long time the program was followed immediately on the Blue network by *Olivio Santoro*.

Mr. Ace and Jane: see *Easy Aces*.

Mr. and Mrs.

Comedy

CAST:

Joe — Jack Smart
Vi — Jane Houston

Themes: "Mean to Me," "Home, Sweet Home"

This program, which was first heard over CBS in 1929, was based on the comic strip by Clare Briggs. A later program with the same title but not based on the comic strip originated over KNX Los Angeles. The latter featured Eddie Albert as "Jimmie" and Georgia Fifield as "Jane." The script was written by Ralph Rogers.

Mr. and Mrs. North

Mystery-Adventure

CAST:

Jerry North — Joseph Curtin
Pamela North — Alice Frost
Susan, the Norths' niece — Betty Jane Tyler
Bill Weigand, chief detective — Staats Cotsworth, Frank Lovejoy, Francis DeSales
Sergeant Mullins — Walter Kinsella
Mahatma McGloin, the driver — Mandel Kramer
Orchestra: Charles Paul
Announcer: Joseph King

Producer-Director: John Loveton
Writers: Michael Morris, Jerome Epstein, Hector Chevigny, Louis Vittes, Robert Sloane
Sound Effects: Al Hogan, Jerry McCarthy, Al Binnie
Theme: "The Way You Look Tonight"

Oft-heard phrase:
PAM. Look out, Jerry! He's got a gun!

Mr. and Mrs. North was based on characters created by Frances and Richard Lockridge. The series made its debut over NBC in 1942.

Mr. Anthony: see *The Goodwill Hour*.

Mr. Chameleon

Adventure

CAST:

Mr. Chameleon — Karl Swenson
Dave Arnold, Mr. Chameleon's assistant — Frank Butler
Commissioner — Richard Keith
Orchestra: Victor Arden
Announcers: Roger Krupp, Howard Claney

Producers: Frank and Anne Hummert
Director: Richard Leonard
Writer: Marie Baumer
Sound Effects: Jack Amerine

"Mr. Chameleon" was a master of disguise who used his art to apprehend criminals. He began solving crimes over CBS in 1948.

Mr. District Attorney

Drama

CAST:

District Attorney — Dwight Weist
Raymond Edward Johnson
Jay Jostyn
Miss Edith Miller — Vicki Vola
Harrington — Walter Kinsella
Len Doyle
Miss Rand — Eleanor Silver
Arlene Francis
Policeman — Walter Kinsella
Voice of the Law, opening
Maurice Franklin
Jay Jostyn

Also: Frank Lovejoy, Paul Stewart, Thelma Ritter
Orchestra: Harry Salter, Peter Van Steeden
Announcers: Ed Herlihy, Fred Uttal

Creator-Director: Edward Byron
Producer: Phillips H. Lord
Writers: Edward Byron, Harry Herman, Finis Farr, Jerry McGill, Jerry Devine, Robert J. Shaw
Sound Effects: John Powers

Opening:

ANNOUNCER. Mr. District Attorney . . . champion of the people . . . defender of truth . . . guardian of our fundamental rights to life, liberty, and the pursuit of happiness.

MUSIC. *Bridge*

D.A. (*FILTER*) And it shall be my duty as District Attorney not only to prosecute to the limit of the law all persons accused of crimes perpetrated within this county but to defend with equal vigor the rights and privileges of all its citizens.

Mr. District Attorney, a popular Wednesday-night feature on NBC for many years, was first heard in 1939. The loyal sponsor of the program was Bristol-Myers, makers of "Ipana for the smile of beauty and Sal Hepatica for the smile of health" —a double-barreled slogan for a toothpaste and a laxative.

Mr. Fix-It

Home Repair

CAST:

Mr. Fix-It — Jim Boles
Typical Domestic Couple
Loretta Ellis, Art Van Horn

The Typical Domestic Couple dramatized home-repair situations. Mr. Fix-It offered his advice on repairing sundry items. He would also suggest that listeners write in for a book on home repair by Hubbard Cobb.

Mr. Keen, Tracer of Lost Persons

Mystery-Adventure

CAST:

Mr. Keen — Bennett Kilpack
Phil Clarke

Arthur Hughes
Miss Ellis — Florence Malone
Mike Clancy — Jim Kelly
Announcers: Larry Elliott, James Fleming

Producers: Frank and Anne Hummert
Director: Richard Leonard
Writers: Barbara Bates, Lawrence Klee, Robert J. Shaw, Charles J. Gussman, Stedman Coles, David Davidson
Musical Director: Al Rickey
Sound Effects: Jack Amerine
Organist: John Winters
Theme: "Someday I'll Find You"

Catch-phrase:
MIKE CLANCY. Saints preserve us, Mr. Keen!

This program was first heard over NBC Blue in 1937.

Mr. Meek: see *The Adventures of Mister Meek.*

Mr. President

Drama

CAST:
The President — Edward Arnold

Producer-Director: Dick Woollen
Producer: Robert Jennings
Directors: Joe Graham, Dwight Hauser, Leonard Reeg
Writers: Jean Holloway, Ira Marion
Sound Effects: Fred Cole

Each week Edward Arnold portrayed a different American President. The identity of the President was not revealed until the end of the program. The series began over ABC in 1947.

Mrs. Miniver

Serial Drama

CAST:
Mrs. Miniver
Judith Evelyn (first few shows only)
Gertrude Warner
Mr. Miniver
Karl Swenson (first few shows only)
John Moore

Producer-Director: Nila Mack
Writers: Carl Bixby, Margaret Lerwerth

This program was based on the novel by Jan Struther.

Mrs. Wiggs of the Cabbage Patch

Serial Drama

CAST:
Mrs. Wiggs — Betty Garde
Eva Condon
Pa Wiggs — Robert Strauss
Billy Wiggs — Andy Donnelly
Mr. Stebbins — Joe Latham
Mr. Bob — Frank Provo
Bill Johnstone
Miss Hazy — Agnes Young
Alice Frost
Lucy Redding — Marjorie Anderson
Announcer: George Ansbro

Producers: Frank and Anne Hummert

Mrs. Wiggs of the Cabbage Patch, based on the novel by Alice Caldwell

Rice, was heard over NBC beginning in September 1936 after a brief run on CBS.

The Munros

Family Dialogue

CAST:

Gordon Munro	Neal Keehan
Margaret Munro	Margaret Heckle

Murder and Mr. Malone

Adventure

CAST:

Mr. Malone	Frank Lovejoy

Director: William Rousseau
Writer: Craig Rice

The program was first heard over ABC in 1946.

Murder Is My Hobby

Adventure

CAST:

Detective Barton Drake — Glenn Langan

Writer: Richard Wilkinson

Murder Is My Hobby was first on the air over Mutual in 1945.

Murder Will Out

Mystery-Adventure

Featuring: William Gargan

Producer-Writer-Director: Lew X. Lansworth

Music: see *Big Band Remotes; Musicians; Orchestra Leaders; Singers.*

The Music Appreciation Hour

Music

Featuring: Dr. Walter Damrosch

Opening:

DAMROSCH. Good morning, my dear young people.

This program began over the Blue network in 1928.

Music from the House of Squibb

Music

Guest stars: Burl Ives, Regina Resnik, Jan Peerce, Richard Tucker
Orchestra: Lyn Murray
Chorus: Van Alexander
Director: Chet Gierlach

This program originated from Liederkranz Hall in New York City.

Music That Satisfies

Musical-Variety

Featuring: Arthur Tracy ("The Street Singer"); The Boswell Sisters (Connee, Vet, and Martha); Ruth Etting
Announcer: Norman Brokenshire

This 1932 musical program was sponsored by Chesterfield over the NBC Red network.

The Musical Comedy Hour

Music and Comedy

CAST:

Vivian, The Coca-Cola Girl — Jessica Dragonette

The Musical Steelmakers

Music

M.C.: John Wincholl

The Singing Millmen—William Stevenson, William Griffiths, tenors; Glynn Davies, bass; Walter Schane, baritone

The Steele Sisters—Betty Jane Evans, Margaret June Evans, Harriet Drake, Lois Mae Nolte

Mary Bower, harpist

Regina Colbert, vocalist

The Musical Steelmakers grew out of an industrial program presented each week on WWVA Wheeling (West Virginia). The series started on November 8, 1936, and featured people employed by a local steel corporation. John Wincholl, for example, was an accountant in the general offices. J. L. Grimes was credited with putting together the particular program that caught on with the listeners; this led to a network series over Mutual in 1938 from Wheeling's Capitol Theater. The Steele Sisters, incidentally, were not all sisters; the group was originally a trio, then became a quartet.

Musicians

Music comprised an important segment of radio entertainment. Among the well-known musicians of radio's Golden Age were organist Jesse Crawford ("The Poet of the Organ"); violinist-composer Emery Deutsch; pianist-composer George Gershwin; singer-pianist Art Gillham ("The Whispering Pianist"); pianist-composer-orchestra leader Johnny Green; guitarist Tito Guizar (also a singer); xylophonist Yoichi Hiraoka; violinist Jules Lande ("The Troubadour of the Violin"); violinist Florence Richardson; Honey Chile Robinson (a precocious child pianist); Shandor (a Gypsy violinist); Eddie South (a violinist billed as "The Dark Angel of the Violin"); Alec Templeton (a blind pianist-composer); singer-violinist Anthony Trini ("The Romantic Fiddler"); singer-pianist Happy Jack Turner; and pianist Leo Zollo.

There were also many teams and groups of musical performers who turned up on various radio programs. Among the most prominent were Bennett and Wolverton (singer-pianist Betty Bennett and guitarist Joe Wolverton); the piano team of Braggiotti and Fray (Mario Braggiotti and Jacques Fray); Borrah Minevitch and His Harmonica Rascals; the piano team of Muriel and Vee (Muriel Pollack and Vee Lawnhurst); and Carson Robison and His

Buckaroos, a Western music group comprised of Carson Robison, John and Bill Mitchell, and Pearl Pickens, who was actually Mrs. Bill Mitchell. (See also *Big Band Remotes; Orchestra Leaders; Singers.*)

The Mutual Forum Hour: see *American Forum of the Air.*

My Best Girls

Situation Comedy

CAST:

Jill Bartlett	Lorna Lynn
Linda Bartlett	Mary Shipp
Penny Bartlett	Mary Mason
Russell Bartlett	Roland Winters

Director: Wesley McKee
Writer: John D. Kelsey

My Favorite Husband

Situation Comedy

CAST:

Liz Cooper	Lucille Ball
George Cooper, the husband	Lee Bowman (initial performance only)
	Richard Denning
Katie, the maid	Ruth Perrott
Rudolph Atterbury	Gale Gordon

Writer-Director: Jess Oppenheimer
Writers: Madelyn Pugh, Bob Carroll, Jr.
Sound Effects: Clark Casey

My Favorite Husband was based on characters created by Isabel Scott Rorick in the novel *Mr. and Mrs. Cugat.* The program made its debut over CBS in 1948.

My Friend Irma

Situation Comedy

CAST:

Irma Peterson	Marie Wilson
Jane Stacy	Cathy Lewis
	Joan Banks
Mr. Clyde	Alan Reed (Teddy Bergman)
Al	John Brown
Prof. Kropotkin	Hans Conried
Richard Rhinelander III	Leif Erickson
Mrs. Rhinelander	Myra Marsh
Mrs. O'Reilly	Gloria Gordon

Orchestra: Lud Gluskin
Vocal group: The Sportsmen Quartet

Director: Cy Howard
Writers: Parke Levy, Stanley Adams, Roland MacLane
Sound Effects: James Murphy
Theme: "Friendship"

Catch-phrase:

JOHN BROWN (*on telephone*). Hello, Joe. Al.

My Friend Irma related the amusing adventures of a classic "dumb blonde." It made its debut over CBS in 1947.

My Good Wife

Situation Comedy

Featuring: John Conte, Arlene Francis

My Son and I

Serial Drama

CAST:

Connie Vance — Betty Garde
Buddy Watson, her son — Kingsley Colton
Aunt Minta Owens — Agnes Young
Kent Davis — Alan Hewitt

This serial was first heard over CBS in 1939.

My True Story

Drama

Featuring: Guest Actors
Announcer: Glenn Riggs
Directors: Martin Andrews, Charles Warburton, George Wiest
Writer: Margaret Sangster
Organist: Rosa Rio
Theme: "My True Story" by Hathaway

There were no regular running characters on *My True Story;* various performers appeared on the program, which was first heard over ABC in the 1940s.

Myrt and Marge

Serial Drama

CAST:

Myrt — Myrtle Vail
Marge — Donna Damerel Fick, Helen Mack
Jack Arnold — Vinton Hayworth, Santos Ortega
Clarence Tiffingtuffer — Ray Hedge
Billie de Vere — Eleanor Rella
Midgie — Betty Jane Tyler
Edna Seymour — Lucy Gilman
Jimmie Kent — Michael Fitzmaurice
Mr. Arnold — Charles Webster
Mrs. Arnold — Frances Woodbury
Brellerton White — Alan Devitt
Bill Boyle — Arthur Elmer
Thaddeus Cornfelder — Cliff Arquette
Paul Hargate — Jackson Beck
Lee Kirby — Santos Ortega, Dick Sanaver
Randy Greenspring — Roger DeKoven
Pete Vanessi — Teddy Bergman
Pop Nunally — Joe Latham
Jim Barnett — Raymond Edward Johnson
Anthony Link — Matt Crowley
Paula Kirby — Lucille Fenton
Tad Smith — Robert Walker
Lizzie Lump — Marjorie Crossland
Barney Belzer — Maurice Tarplin
Max Woodard — Wendell Holmes
Chris — Warren Mills
Mrs. Armstrong — Jeanne Juvelier
Biddy, the cop — Vincent Coleman
Francis Hayfield — Karl Way, Ed Begley
Agatha Folsom — Violet Le Claire
Sanford Malone — Reg Knorr
Phyllis Rogers — Dorothy Day
Jimmy Minter — Ray Appleton
Leota Lawrence — Sunda Love
Darrell Moore — Ken Griffin
Maggie — Marie Nelson
Helmi — Edith Evanson
Dr. Burr — Henry Saxe
Rex Marvin — Gene Morgan
Brad — Cliff Bunston
Detective O'Toole — John C. Daly

Also: Henrietta Tedro, James Van Dyk, Olan Soule, Joseph Curtin
Announcers: David Ross, Tom Shirley, André Baruch

Producer-Director: Bobby Brown
Directors: Lindsay MacHarrie, John Gunn
Writers: Myrtle Vail, Cliff Thomas
Organists: John Winters, Rosa Rio, Eddie House
Theme: "Poor Butterfly"

This series had its première over CBS in 1931 and originated in Chicago. *Myrt and Marge* was the story of a hard-boiled trouper (Myrt) who made it her business to protect the innocence of a newcomer to backstage life (Marge). In 1932 the public learned through an "exclusive" magazine article that Donna Damerel Fick (Marge) was actually the daughter of Myrtle Vail (Myrt) although they were sisters in the script. Donna Damerel Fick died on February 15, 1941, and was replaced by Helen Mack.

The Mysterious Traveler

Adventure

CAST:
The Mysterious Traveler — Maurice Tarplin
Also: Bill Zuckert, Lon Clark, Roger DeKoven, Ed Begley, Jackson Beck, *et al.*
Announcer: Jimmy Wallington

Director: Jock MacGregor
Writers: Robert A. Arthur, David Kogan
Sound Effects: Jack Amerine, Jim Goode, Ron Harper

"The Mysterious Traveler" warned his audience to keep a hypo handy for emotional emergencies. He closed with, "I take this same train every week at this time." The program made its debut over Mutual in 1943.

Mystery in the Air

Mystery

Featuring: Peter Lorre

CAST:
Stonewall Scott — Jackson Beck
Tex — Geoffrey Bryant

Producer: Ken MacGregor

Mystery Theater

Mystery

Host: Bernard Lenrow

CAST:
Inspector Hearthstone of the Death Squad — Alfred Shirley

Producers: Frank and Anne Hummert
Directors: Martha Atwell, Ernest Ricca, Frank K. Telford, Day Tuttle, Kenneth W. Macgregor, Henry Howard
Writers: Frank Hummert, Edward Francis, Lawrence Menkin, Bill Wyman, Joseph Russell, Jay Bennett, Peter Lyon, Charles Tazewell
Sound Effects: Charles Grenier

Mystery Theater was first heard over NBC in 1943 as *Mollé Mystery Theater* (sponsored by the makers of Mollé shave cream). Bernard Lenrow was featured on the Mollé version. When the title was changed, the format was altered and the character of Hearthstone was added. Later the title was changed to *Hearthstone of the Death Squad.*

N

Name the Movie

Musical Quiz

M.C.: Marvin Miller
Singing host: Clark Dennis
Vocalist: Peggy Mann
Vocal group: The Starlighters
Orchestra: Edward Gilbert
Director: Charles Herbert
Writer: Fred Heider

On *Name the Movie,* which ran on ABC in 1949, servicemen were used as contestants eligible to win prizes by identifying movies. A top movie star appeared on the program each week. It was sponsored by Revere cameras after they dropped *The Jo Stafford Show.*

National Amateur Night

Amateur Talent

M.C.: Ray Perkins

Ray Perkins blew a whistle to indicate that the performer had failed.

The National Barn Dance

Country and Western Music

M.C.: Joe Kelly ("The Man in Overalls")

CAST:

Uncle Ezra, The Old Jumping Jenny Wren, Ezra P. Waters — Pat Barrett
Arkie, the Arkansas Woodchopper — Luther Ossiebrink
Pokey Martin — Hoyt Allen
Lulubelle and Scotty — Myrtle Cooper and Scotty Wiseman
Spare Ribs — Malcolm Claire
With: Maple City Four–Art Janes, Pat Patterson, Fritz Meissner, Al Rice
Cumberland Ridge Runners–Slim Miller, Karl Davis, Hartford Connecticut Taylor, Hugh Cross, John Lair, Red Foley
The Hoosier Hot Shots, The Rural Rhythm Boys and Their Tin Pan Band–Paul ("Hezzie") Trietsch, zither, whistle, washboard; Ken Trietsch, banjo, guitar; Gabe Ward, clarinet; Frank Kettering, bass fiddle
Louise Massey and The Westerners –Louise Massey, Curt Wellington, Milt Mabie, Dott Massey (sister of Louise), Allen Massey (their brother)
Verne, Lee and Mary Trio–Verne Hassell, Leone Hassell, Evelyn Wood
Dinning Sisters–Jean and Ginger (twins) and Lou

Also: Little Georgie Gobel
Bob Hastings ("The Twelve-Year-Old Boy Soprano")
Linda Parker, The Sunbonnet Girl
Sally Foster ("Little Blue-eyed Sally")
Eddie Peabody, banjoist
Pat Buttram, The Sage of Winston County, Alabama
Bob Ballantine, harmonica player
Otto and His Novelodeons
The Tune Twisters
Janie and Connie, singers
Tom and Don, The Hayloft Harmony Boys
Captain Stubby and the Buccaneers
Marvin Miller
Joe Parsons, bass
The Hill Toppers
And: Bob Atcher, Henry Burr, Lucille Long, Bill O'Connor, Jane Kaye, Dean Brothers, Hal O'Halloran, Tiny Stokes, Red Blanchard, Skip Farrell, Florence Folsom, Danny Duncan
Orchestra: Glenn Welty
Announcer: Jack Holden

Producer-Writers: Peter Lund, Jack Frost
Producers: Walter Wade, Ed Freckman
Director: Bill Jones

Catch-phrases:
UNCLE EZRA. This is station E-Z-R-A, the powerful little five-watter down in Rosedale.
UNCLE EZRA. Give 'em a toot on the tooter, Tommy.

Hoosier Hot Shots Intro.: Are you ready, Hezzie? (*slide whistle*)

Opening:
JOE KELLY. Hello, hello, everybody, everywhere.

This was one of the few radio shows to charge admission. It was originally broadcast from Chicago's Eighth Street Theater but moved later to the Civic. It made its debut on September 30, 1933, and was heard Saturday nights at 10:30 on NBC.

The National Farm and Home Hour

Variety

M.C.: Everett Mitchell
Forest Ranger: Don Ameche
Raymond Edward Johnson
Orchestra: Harry Kogen and The Homesteaders
Also: Jack Baus and The Cornbusters; The Cadets (a male quartet); Mirandy of Persimmon Holler
Supervisor: W. E. Drips
Producer: Herbert Lateau

Theme: "The Stars and Stripes Forever" by John Philip Sousa
Opening:
MITCHELL. It's a beautiful day in Chicago!

This program was first heard over the Blue network in 1928 for Montgomery Ward. Later the program was presented by the United States Department of Agriculture.

The National Radio Pulpit: see *Religion.*

National Spelling Bee

Education

Spelling Master: Paul Wing

National Vespers: see *Religion.*

NBC Symphony

Music

The NBC Symphony Orchestra was formed in 1936 under the conductorship of Maestro Arturo Toscanini and performed each week over the NBC network. The Maestro was coaxed out of retirement in Italy after David Sarnoff of NBC made up his mind that such a program could make a great contribution by bringing fine music to the masses. Every effort was made to gather together the world's finest musicians, and NBC raided the country's leading musical organizations in an effort to build the ninety-piece orchestra. The special radio studio constructed at Rockefeller Center in New York for the orchestra was known as "8H." It was described as the world's only "floating" studio because of its unique construction.

Dr. Frank Black appeared frequently as conductor of the NBC Symphony. Ben Grauer was the announcer on most of the broadcasts.

The Nebbs

Situation Comedy

Featuring: Gene and Kathleen Lockhart

Also: Conrad Binyon, Bill Roy, Dink Trout, Dick Ryan, Ruth Perrott

Announcer: Tommy Dixon

The Nebbs was based on the comic strip by Sol Hess.

Ned Jordan, Secret Agent

Adventure

CAST:

Ned Jordan — Jack McCarthy

Director: Al Hodge

"Ned Jordan" was a railroad detective.

Nell Vinick: see *Women's Programs.*

Nelson Olmsted: see *Stories by Olmsted.*

Nero Wolfe: see *The Adventures of Nero Wolfe.*

The Networks

In the early days of radio, stations in various parts of the country began broadcasting independently of one another. Among the earliest stations broadcasting regularly were those which eventually became WWJ Detroit and KDKA Pittsburgh. The station claiming the record as the oldest in the United States is KCBS San Francisco, which was broadcasting regularly as a 15-watt school station in 1909 and is still on the air.

It wasn't long, however, before the independent stations began to provide programing for one another, and eventually they joined together in what came to be known as networks. In 1926 General Electric, Westinghouse, and RCA formed the National Broadcasting Company with David Sarnoff as its leading organizer; and the next year Arthur Judson, a concert artists' manager, formed the Columbia Broadcasting System along with George A. Coats and J. Andrew White. In 1934 the Mutual Broadcasting System was formed and became the largest of the networks. The difference, however, was that Mutual owned no stations whereas NBC and CBS owned and operated many of their own network stations.

During the late 1930s the Federal Communications Commission (FCC) launched an investigation into "chain broadcasting" and the possible monopolistic tendencies therein. NBC at that time owned two separate networks, the Red network and the Blue network. Simultaneously with the release of the FCC's report, recommending the end of multi-network ownership, NBC decided to sell NBC Blue. The sale of this network in 1943 to Edward J. Noble, the owner of Life Savers, eventually led to the formation of the American Broadcasting Company. After that, the Red network became simply NBC.

There were several regional networks too—among them the Don Lee network in California, The Yankee network in New England, and the Liberty Broadcasting System, which was set up primarily to carry sports broadcasts. The "regionals" were mostly formed to act as convenient clearing houses for sales packages and with some exceptions didn't do anywhere near the volume of programing as the big four networks.

A New Penny

Drama

Starring: Helen Hayes
Leading Man: Joseph Bell
Writer: Edith Meiser

The New York Times Youth Forum: see *Dorothy Gordon.*

News and Newscasters

There were literally hundreds of newscasters, both locally and nationally, who brought the news of the world into our homes. Thus radio, particularly during World War II, made a major contribution toward keeping Americans informed.

Among the most famous newscasters and reporters were Gabriel Heatter, whose opening line, "Ah, there's good news tonight!" reassured millions of Americans each evening; Floyd Gibbons, who pioneered on-the-spot remote news broadcasts (his trademark was a white patch worn over his left eye); Boake Carter ("Cheerio!"); Elmer Davis, whose flat, unemotional, midwestern voice seemed to offer a reasonable perspective on the news; Paul Harvey ("Good . . . night!"); Edwin C. Hill with "The Human Side of the News"; H. V. (Hans von) Kaltenborn, whose clipped speech was parodied by President Truman following the commentator's inaccurate forecast of a Dewey victory in the 1948 election; Fulton Lewis, Jr. (". . . and that's the top of the news as it looks from here"); Herbert Morrison, who described the historic explosion of the German dirigible Hindenburg on May 6, 1937; Drew Pearson, whose outspoken comments often made headlines themselves (his announcer introduced him with, "And now, Drew Pearson, whose predictions have proved to be eighty-four per cent accurate!"); and Lowell Thomas, who started in radio in 1930, substituting for Floyd Gibbons, and who signed off each night with "So long . . . until tomorrow."

Edward R. Murrow deserves some special attention. In the late thirties his nightly broadcasts from London ("This is London . . .") brought news of the impending war in Europe, and Americans were alerted by his commentary to the threat of Nazi Germany. Murrow's social conscience and broadcasting acumen helped to launch such successful news documentaries as *Hear It Now,* which brought a new dimension to radio's comments on the news of the day.

Other well-known commentators and newscasters were: Cedric Adams; Martin Agronsky; Robert Allen, who teamed with Drew Pearson for a time; H. R. Baukhage (Hilmar Robert Baukhage), who always opened with "Baukhage talking"; Morgan Beatty; Cecil Brown; Clellan Card, who often impersonated people he quoted, such as FDR, Churchill, etc.; Sheila Carter (Boake Carter's sister); Henry Cassidy; W. W. Chaplin; Raymond Clapper; Upton Close; Charles Collingwood; Bob Considine; John Charles Daly, whose voice we heard announcing the Japanese attack on Pearl Harbor; Alex Dreier; George Fielding Eliot; Cedric Foster; Pauline Frederick, who was one of the few successful female commentators (the others were Lisa Sergio and Dorothy Thompson); Arthur Gaeth; Don Gardiner ("Monday Morning Headlines"); Earl Godwin; Peter Grant; Taylor Grant; Royal Arch Gunnison; John Gunther (also a distinguished author); Arthur Hale; Richard Harkness; Joseph C. Harsch; George Hayes; Sam Hayes; Bill Henry; George Hicks; Edwin C. Hill; Richard C. Hottelet; Quincy Howe; John B. Hughes; General Hugh S. Johnson; John B. Kennedy; Alan Kent; Walter Kiernan; David Lawrence; Larry Lesueur; Ian Ross MacFarlane, who worked without a script as he was partially blind; John MacVane; Robert McCormick; Merrill "Red" Mueller; Fulton Oursler; Leon Pearson; Elmer Peterson; George C. Putnam; Q.E.D. (his actual identity was never revealed); Quentin Reynolds; Cesar Saerchinger; Eric Sevareid; William L. Shirer; Frank Singiser; George Sokolsky; Robert St. John; Johannes Steel; Paul Sullivan ("Good night . . . and thirty"); Raymond Gram Swing; Henry J. Taylor; Cal Tinney (a sort of latter-day Will Rogers); Robert Trout, who brought us the news of D-Day in Europe; Clifton Utley; Arthur Van Horn; Hendrik Willem Van Loon (also a well-known author); John W. Vandercook; Albert Warner; Major J. Andrew White; Frederick William Wile; and Wythe Williams.

News of Youth

Dramatized News

"Scoop," the narrator: Laddie Seaman

News of Youth was a fifteen-minute, three-times-a-week dramatized news broadcast somewhat in the style of *The March of Time,* but aimed at a teen-age audience.

Next, Dave Garroway: see *Reserved for Garroway.*

Nick Carter, Master Detective

Detective

CAST:

Nick Carter, Master Detective — Lon Clark
Patsy Bowen — Helen Choate, Charlotte Manson
Sergeant Mathison (Matty) — Ed Latimer
Scubby, the reporter — John Kane
Also: John Raby, Bill Lipton, Raymond Edward Johnson, Bryna Raeburn
Announcer: Michael Fitzmaurice

Producer-Writer-Director: Jock MacGregor
Writers: David Kogan, Milton J. Kramer, John McGreevey, Ferrin N. Fraser, Norman Daniels, Alfred Bester
Sound Effects: Adrian Penner, Mario Siletti
Organist: Hank Sylvern

Opening:

MUSIC. *Fanfare up and under for . . .*
ANNOUNCER. *Nick Carter, Master Detective!*
MUSIC. *Up full then under for . . .*
ANNOUNCER. Today's Nick Carter adventure . . . "The Case of the Stray Bullet Murder!"
CAST. *Brief teasing scene*
MUSIC. *Three chords*
ANNOUNCER. Now, another intriguing, transcribed adventure with Nick Carter, Master Detective . . . presented by the Mutual network. In a moment, "The Case of the Stray Bullet Murder!" But first . . .

Closing:

ANNOUNCER. *Nick Carter, Master Detective,* is produced and directed by Jock MacGregor. Copyrighted by Street and Smith Publications, Incorporated, it is presented each week at this time by the Mutual network. Lon Clark is starred as "Nick," Charlotte Manson is featured as "Patsy," and Ed Latimer plays "Matty." Others in today's cast were John Raby, Bill Lipton, and Bryna Raeburn. This program is fictional and any resemblance to actual persons, living or dead, or to actual names or places, is purely coincidental.
MUSIC. *Theme up to close*
ANNOUNCER. Join us again next week for "The Case of the Forgotten Murder," another intriguing, transcribed adventure with *Nick Carter, Master Detective!* This program came from New York.

Nick Carter, Master Detective was first heard over Mutual in 1943. (See also *Chick Carter, Boy Detective.*)

Night Beat

Adventure

CAST:

Lucky Stone — Frank Lovejoy

Announcer: Don Rickles

This was the story of a newspaper columnist who combed Chicago's streets looking for material.

Night Shift with Rayburn and Finch

Music and Talk

Gene Rayburn and Dee Finch were the hosts on this program; they played records, held interviews, and traded quips.

A Night with Horace Heidt

Talent Contest

Host: Horace Heidt

Accordionist Dick Contino became famous on this program after winning many weeks in a row.

No School Today: see *Big Jon and Sparkie.*

Noah Webster Says

Quiz

M.C.: Haven MacQuarrie
Director: Andrew Love

Listeners submitted a list of five difficult words. Two dollars was paid for each list used on the program and for each correct answer.

Nobody's Children

Drama

CAST:

Narrator — Walter White, Jr.
Matron — Georgia Fifield

Also: Robert Mitchell Boys' Choir
Guest Stars: James Cagney, Robert Montgomery, Joe E. Brown, Jack Benny, Fay Bainter, Bob Hope, Gene Autry, Barbara Stanwyck
Announcer: Bill Kennedy

Nobody's Children was first heard over Mutual in 1939 and originated from KHJ Los Angeles. Orphans appeared on the program accompanied by a guest star, and many of the orphans were adopted by listeners as a result of the broadcasts.

Nona from Nowhere

Serial Drama

CAST:

Nona — Toni Darnay
Pat Brady — James Kelly
Vernon Dutell — Karl Weber
Thelma Powell — Mitzi Gould
Gwen Parker — Florence Robinson

Producers: Frank and Anne Hummert

This was first heard over CBS in 1949.

Nora Drake: see *This Is Nora Drake.*

Norman Corwin

Drama

Norman Corwin wrote, produced, and directed several series, but a good portion of his work was broadcast as what today would be called "specials," single programs put on as the occasion demands and usually preempting a regularly scheduled broadcast. Among these were "We Hold These Truths" (1941), "On a Note of Triumph" (V-E Day, May 8, 1945), "14 August" (August 14, 1945), and "The Undecided Molecule" (July 17, 1945). (See also *Columbia Presents Corwin; Passport for Adams.*)

ON A NOTE OF TRIUMPH

CAST:

Narrator	Martin Gabel
Nazi	George Sorel
Nazi	Ludwig Donath
Mother	Lucille Kibbee
Selassie	Peter Witt
Interpreter	Joseph Worthy
Singers	Johnny Bond Trio

Music: Score composed by Bernard Herrmann; conducted by Lud Gluskin; song "Round and Round Hitler's Grave" composed by Millard Lampell, Woodie Guthrie, Pete Seeger, and Norman Corwin

Production: Directed by Norman Corwin; sound by Berne Surrey; studio engineer–Gary Harris; production assistants–Charles Lewin and Lou Ashworth

14 AUGUST

CAST:

Soliloquist	Orson Welles

A repeat broadcast was heard on the following Sunday under the title "God and Uranium." Olivia de Havilland assisted Orson Welles on this broadcast, and Norman Corwin directed both productions in addition to writing them.

THE UNDECIDED MOLECULE

CAST:

Judge	Groucho Marx
Interpreter	Robert Benchley
Prosecutor	Vincent Price
Clerk	Norman Lloyd
Miss Anima	Sylvia Sidney
Defense Counsel	Keenan Wynn
Spokesman for the Vegetables	Keenan Wynn
Spokesman for the Animals	Keenan Wynn
Conductor	Keenan Wynn
V.P. in Charge of Physiochemistry	Elliott Lewis

Writer-Director: Norman Corwin
Music: Composed by Carmen Dragon; conducted by Lud Gluskin

N.T.G. and His Girls

Variety

M.C.: Nils Thor Granlund
Orchestra: Harry Salter
Director: Herb Polesie
Writer: Carroll Carroll

Nils Thor Granlund, a well-known Broadway producer, had talented chorus girls as the guests on his show. Six or seven appeared on each broadcast, and each girl told a little about herself and then played an instrument, sang, or gave a dramatic reading. There were also "special guests," ex-chorus girls who had made it on Broadway.

Of Human Bondage

Drama

CAST:
Dr. Philip Carey — Raymond Edward Johnson
Mildred Rogers — Jessica Tandy

Director: Carlo De Angelo

This program was based on the novel by Somerset Maugham.

Of Men and Books

Literary Discussion

Moderator: Professor John T. Frederick
John Mason Brown

Of Men and Books presented discussions and reviews of books with guest literary figures such as J. B. Priestley, Bellamy Partridge, Arna Bontemps, Edmund Gilligan, Ludwig Bemelmans, Paul Engel, and Lin Yutang. It was heard on CBS from 1941 to 1948.

Official Detective

Detective

CAST:

Detective Dan Britt — Ed Begley, Craig McDonnell
Police Sergeant — Louis Nye
Also: Chuck Webster, Bill Zuckert, Allan Stevenson

Director: Wynn Wright
Writers: Jack Bentkover, William Wells
Sound Effects: Al April

Opening:

MUSIC. *Organ up and under . . .*

ANNOUNCER. *Official Detective!* Dedicated to the men who guard your safety and protect your home—your police department!

This program first appeared on the Mutual network in 1946.

The O'Flynns

Serial Drama

CAST:

Captain Flynn O'Flynn — Milton Watson

This program was about the world of opera. It began over CBS in 1934.

Og, Son of Fire

Prehistoric Adventure

CAST:

Og — Alfred Brown
Nad — Patricia Dunlap
Ru — James Andelin
Big Tooth — Reg Knorr
Also: Jess Pugh, Karl Way

Writer: Irving Crump (author of the original Og stories)
Sound Effects: Herb Johnson, Louie Wehr

This program was first heard over CBS in 1934.

The Old Curiosity Shop

Drama

Keeper of The Old Curiosity Shop: David Ross
Orchestra: Howard Barlow
Writer: David Ross

The Old Curiosity Shop was a program of the early 1930s. It presented stories concerning various items in the shop. The program opened with a conversation between the keeper and his daughter, in which the girl would ask her father to tell her the story about a particular item in the shop. The keeper's narration would then lead into the actual drama.

The Old-Fashioned Revival Hour: see *Religion.*

The Old Gold Paul Whiteman Hour

Music

Starring: Paul Whiteman and His Orchestra

Paul Whiteman, "The King of Jazz," broadcast this show on Tuesdays from 9:00 to 10:00 p.m. over CBS in the late 1920s and early 1930s. He also appeared over the years for other sponsors, such as Woodbury Soap. His announcers included Douglas Browning and Alan Kent.

The Old Gold Show

Variety

CAST:

John Bickerson — Don Ameche
Blanche Bickerson — Frances Langford
Also: Frank Morgan
Orchestra: Carmen Dragon
Announcer: Marvin Miller

Producers: Mann Holiner, Frank Woodruff
Writer-Director: Phil Rapp

This weekly half-hour program was first heard over CBS in 1947 and ran for two seasons. It filled the time-slot occupied previously by *Songs by Sinatra, Songs for Sinatra,* and *Rhapsody in Rhythm.* Frank Morgan performed his famous monologues full of exaggeration, with Marvin Miller as his foil and the object of his wrath.

The Old Skipper

Children

The Old Skipper: Don Hix

Olivio Santoro

Music

Starring: Olivio Santoro, The Boy Yodeler
Announcer: Glenn Riggs

Theme: (Sung to the tune of "Ta-Ra-Ra-Boom-De-Ay")
Scrapple o-del-ay-de-ay
Comes from Phil-a-del-phi-ay.
Eat Philadelphia Scrapple, friends,
With that advice my story ends.

Olivio Santoro played the guitar, sang, and yodeled. His program was fifteen minutes long and followed *The Moylan Sisters* (which see). The program was first heard over the Blue network in 1940.

Omar the Mystic

Adventure

CAST:

Omar the Mystic — M. H. H. Joachim
Mr. Kimball — Ralph Schoolman
Mrs. Kimball — Ethel Everett
The Kimballs' daughter — Mrs. Ralph Schoolman
Zaidda — Ethel Everett
Also: Edward MacDonald, Jeff Sparks

Opening:
SOUND. *The stroke of a gong*

Omar the Mystic was first heard over Mutual in 1935.

One Man's Family

Serial Drama

CAST:

The Parents

Henry Barbour J. Anthony Smythe
(April 29, 1932–May 8, 1959)
Fanny Barbour Minetta Ellen
(April 29, 1932–July 8, 1955)
Mary Adams
(February 13, 1956–May 8, 1959)

The Children

Paul Barbour Michael Raffetto
(April 29, 1932–July 8, 1955)
Russell Thorson
(July 28, 1955–May 8, 1959)
Hazel Barbour Bernice Berwin
(April 29, 1932–August 29, 1943)
Claudia Barbour Kathleen Wilson
(April 29, 1932–August 29, 1943)
Floy Margaret Hughes
(played the part when Miss Wilson was ill)
Barbara Fuller
(October 14, 1945–May 8, 1959)
Laurette Fillbrandt
(played the part ten times during July, August, and September 1949)
Clifford Barbour Barton Yarborough
(April 29, 1932–December 27, 1951)
Jack Barbour Page Gilman
(April 29, 1932–May 8, 1959)

The Children's Spouses

Bill Herbert Bert Horton
Dan Murray Wally Maher
Russell Thorson
Bill Bouchey
Ken Peters
Ann Waite Helen Musselman
Irene Franklyn Naomi Stevens
Janet Waldo
Johnny Roberts Frank Provo
Captain Nicholas Lacey (Nicky)
Walter Paterson
Tom Collins
Dan O'Herlihy
Ben Wright
Betty Carter Jean Rouverol
Virginia Gregg

The Grandchildren

Teddy Barbour Winifred Wolfe
Jeanne Bates
William Herbert Murray (Pinky)
Richard Svihus
Dix Davis
Billy Idelson
Eddie Firestone, Jr.
Tommy Bernard
George Pirrone
Henry Herbert Murray (Hank)
Conrad Binyon
Dickie Meyers
Billy Idelson
Margaret Herbert Murray
Dawn Bender
Andy Barbour (Skipper)
Mary Lansing
Henry Blair
Michael Chapin
David Frankham
Joan Roberts Ann Shelley
Mary Lou Harrington
Penny Lacey Anne Whitfield
Elizabeth Sharon Ann Barbour
Mary Lansing
Jill Oppenheim
Susan Luckey
Marilyn Steiner
Susan Odin
Mary Lou Barbour Mary Lansing
Mary McGovern
Jane Barbour Jana Leff
Susan Luckey
Susan Odin

Abigail Barbour	Leone Ledoux
Deborah Barbour	Leone Ledoux
Constance Barbour	Leone Ledoux

The Grandchildren's Spouses

Elwood Giddings	Tyler McVey
Roderick Stone	Marvin Miller
Ross Farnsworth	Victor Perrin
Raymond Borden	Robert Bailey
Lois Holland	Sharon Douglas
Sidney Lawrence	James McCallion
Greta Steffanson	Sharon Douglas

The Great-grandchildren

Paul John Farnsworth (the only great-grandchild with lines)	Leone Ledoux

Friends and Neighbors

Judge Glenn Hunter	George Rand
	Charles McAllister
	Lloyd Corrigan
	Norman Fields
	Jay Novello
	Herb Butterfield
Dr. Fred Thompson	Frank Cooley
	Cy Kendall
	William Green
	Earl Lee
	Emerson Treacy
Beth Holly	Barbara Jo Allen
Christine Abbott	Mary Jane Croft
Ben	Forrest Lewis
	Earl Lee
Wayne Grubb	Jack Edwards, Jr.
Tracy Baker	Sam Edwards
Rev. McArthur	Frank Cooley
	Francis X. Bushman
	Marvin Miller
	Maurice Manson
Nicolette Moore	Jeanette Nolan
Cousin Consider	Marvin Miller

Announcers: William Andrews, Ken Carpenter, Frank Barton

Also: Visitors played by themselves—Loretta Young, Petty Officer Third Class Francesca Ritter, Sir Charles Mendl

---

Creator-Writer: Carlton E. Morse

Directors: Carlton E. Morse (most of the time), Michael Raffetto, Clinton Twiss, Charles Buck, George Fogle

Writers: Harlan Ware (1944–59), Michael Raffetto (occasionally in the early days, regularly 1949–55)

Organists: Paul Carson, from the begining through May 11, 1951; Sybil Chism, May 14, 1951–March 26, 1954; Martha Green, March 29, 1954–May 7, 1954; the music was pre-taped from then on

Themes: "Destiny Waltz" by Sydney Barnes (used as theme 1932–41); "Patricia" by Paul Carson (used as theme 1941–59)

Introduction:

ANNOUNCER. *One Man's Family* is dedicated to the mothers and fathers of the younger generation and to their bewildering offspring. Tonight we present Chapter One of Book Six, entitled "Three Months Between." [Other sample chapter titles: "Clifford Throws a Party," "Christmas Eve at the Barbours'," "Paul Meets the Widow," "The Gathering of the Leaves."]

One Man's Family made its debut on radio on Friday, April 29, 1932, from 9:30 to 10:00 p.m. PST, over NBC stations in San Francisco, Los Angeles, and Seattle. Two or three weeks later the rest of the western

NBC network was added. The program began broadcasting on the entire NBC network on May 17, 1933, and was the first serial to originate in San Francisco for the entire network. In order to bring the rest of the country up to date, the network broadcasts from May 17, 1933, until January 5, 1934, were devoted to presenting a somewhat condensed version of the Barbour family story from its beginning.

The format consisted of thirty-minute programs, broadcast once a week, through Sunday, June 4, 1950. Then the programs were fifteen minutes in length, five days a week, from June 5, 1950, through May 8, 1959, the last broadcast. In the book-chapter identification, the last broadcast was Chapter 30 of Book 134. There were 3256 episodes in all, not counting repeats for different time zones.

Measured by the calendar, *One Man's Family* was the longest-running serial drama in American radio. It told the week-to-week (and later day-to-day) story of the Barbour family, who lived in the Seacliff section of San Francisco.

Henry and Fanny Barbour had five children:

Paul, a World War I aviator, was the all-knowing oldest brother to whom all the others took their problems; he was a writer and lived in an attic with his adopted daughter Teddy.

Hazel was almost an old maid when she married dairy farmer *Bill Herbert*; they had twin sons, *Hank* and *Pinky*, and a daughter. Some years after Bill died she married *Dan Murray*.

Claudia was a rebel until her second husband, *British Army Captain Nicholas Lacey*, tamed her to only occasional flare-ups; they were aboard a ship that was torpedoed during World War II, but were rescued and interned in a German concentration camp until after the war.

Cliff, Claudia's twin, was a kind of ne'er-do-well, unable to make up his mind about anything serious. His only period of tranquillity was during his marriage to his second wife, Irene, who was killed in an automobile accident. When actor Barton Yarborough died in 1951, the authors sent Cliff to Scotland, where he became successful in business and married for a third time.

Jack, the baby, married the girl down the block while he was still in college and ultimately showed signs of being the one who would succeed Father Barbour as head of the family. He and *Betty* had six daughters, three of them triplets.

In its last years the series was built around the lives of Hazel's twin sons, *Hank* and *Pinky*. Hank was the solid one who always did the right thing, while Pinky was in and out of trouble most of the time.

The cast over the years included many actors and actresses who were already or were later to become well known, most of them playing relatively small roles. They include Edgar Barrier, Hans Conried, Dick Crenna, Rosemary De Camp, Ted de Corsia, Larry Dobkin, Betty Lou Gerson, Vivi Janniss, Jack Kruschen, Lyn Lauria, Richard Legrand, Elliott Lewis, John McIntire, Howard McNear, Ruth Perrott, Hal Peary, Cameron Prud'Homme, Isabel Randolph, Alice Reinheart, Anne Stone, Gil Stratton, Jr., D. J. Thompson, Les Tremayne, Lurene Tuttle, Luis Van Rooten, Theodor von Eltz, and Barbara Jean Wong.

Marvin Miller played more roles than any other actor in the series; he played twenty different parts, sometimes two or more of them in the same broadcast.

The O'Neills

Serial Drama

CAST:

Mrs. O'Neill	Kate McComb
Eileen Turner	Arline Blackburn
Eddie Collins O'Neill	Jimmy Donnelly
Peggy O'Neill Kayden	Betty Caine
	Violet Dunn
	Claire Niesen
	Betty Winkler
Janice Collins O'Neill	Janice Gilbert
Danny O'Neill	Jimmy Tansey
Morris Levy	Jack Rubin
Mrs. Trudy Bailey	Jane West
Monte Kayden	Chester Stratton
Tillie	Gee Gee James
Mrs. Turner	Effie Lawrence Palmer
Mr. Turner	Alfred Swenson
Barbara Grayson	Adele Harrison
Mr. Collins	Santos Ortega
Harold Wilkinson	John McGovern
Mr. Coleman	Joseph Julian
Grandpa Hubbell	Roy Fant
Mrs. Collins	Marjorie Anderson
Dr. Bruce Kingsley	David Gothard
Lester Lewis	James Van Dyk
Skip Martin	Lawson Zerbe
Mrs. Mitchell	Vivia Ogden
Basil	Burford Hampden
Sally Scott O'Neill	Helen Claire
Mr. Tasek	John Anthony
Mrs. Tasek	Gladys Thornton
Jack Vernon	Charles Carroll
Mayme Gordon	Ethel Everett
Mrs. Carson	Charme Allen
Mrs. Kayden	Josephine Hull
Bob Winton	James Boles
Judge Scott	Julian Noa
Mr. Fielding	Harry Neville
Mrs. Scott	Linda Carlon
Ginger Raymond	Jessie Fordyce
Jean	Selena Royle

Also: Roger DeKoven
Announcer: Ed Herlihy
Directors: Jack Rubin, Carlo De Angelo
Writers: Jane West, Jack Rubin
Theme: "Londonderry Air"

The O'Neills was first heard over CBS in 1934.

The Open Door

Serial Drama

CAST:

Dean Eric Hansen	Dr. Alfred T. Dorf
Liza Arnold	Barbara Weeks
	Florence Freeman
Tommy	Edwin Bruce
Ivan Jones	Martin Blaine
Corey Lehman, Dean Hansen's secretary	Charlotte Holland
Hester Marleybone	Ethel Intropidi
Charlotte Marleybone	Jane Houston
Stephanie Cole	Joan Alexander
David Gunther	Alexander Scourby

Writers: Sandra Michael, Doria Folliott
Theme: "Sim Sala"

This program was first heard over CBS in 1943. "Eric Hansen" was the "Dean of Students" at "Jefferson University."

Opera: see *Metropolitan Opera Broadcasts.*

The Orange Lantern

Mystery

CAST:

Botak, a Javanese adventurer
Arthur Hughes

Also: Peggy Allenby, Agnes Moorehead, John McGovern, Bill Shelley, Bruno Wick

---

Director: Joseph Bell
Writer: Innes Osborn
Original Music: Sven von Hallberg

The Orange Lantern began over NBC Blue in 1932. It was regarded as NBC's answer to *Fu Manchu* in the network competition of that era.

Orchestra Leaders

One of the most important facets of radio was music. Orchestras were hired not only for musical broadcasts and the big variety shows but even for dramatic programs. In such an unmusical program as *Mr. District Attorney,* for example, the orchestra was important in providing unobtrusive but vital musical backgrounds and bridges. In addition to those in the program listings and those included in *Big Band Remotes,* the following orchestra leaders appeared frequently on radio:

Irving Aaronson, Don Alberto, Mario Antabal, Jeno Bartal, Leon Belasco (also an actor and dialectician), Maximilian Bergere, Fred Berrens, Charles Boulanger, Del Campo (also a singer), Reggie Childs, Jolly Coburn, Emil Coleman, Bernie Cummins, Ben Cutler, Eli Dantzig, Jack Denny, Angelo Ferdinado, Felix Ferdinado, Max Fransko, Fran Frey (also a singer), Richard Gasparre, Emerson Gill, Jean Goldkette, Edwin Franko Goldman, Arthur Jarrett, Johnnie Johnson, Merle Johnston, Roger Wolfe Kahn, Al Katz, Al Kavelin, Alexander Kirilloff, Bennie Krueger, Frank La Marr, Eddie Lane, Enric Madriguera, Dolphe Martin, Don Marton, Marti Michel, Kel Murray, Leon Navara, Nick Orlando, Lee Perrin, Mischa Raginsky, Don Redmond, Joe Reichman, Leo Reisman, Freddie Rich, Sam Robbins, Willard Robison (also a singer, known as "The Evangelist of Rhythm"), Buddy Rogers (also an actor), Luis Russel, Paul Sabin, Harold Sanford, Scotti, Ben Selvin, Irving Selzer, Ray Sinatra, Ted Steele (also a singer), Harold Stern, Paul Tremaine, Anson Weeks, Fess Williams, Frank Wine-Gar, Gleb Yellin, and Horacio Zito.

Among the many famous symphony conductors were Arturo Toscanini and Dr. Frank Black, who led the NBC Symphony Orchestra; and Alexander Smallens, who was long associated with programs sponsored by Ford. See also *Big Band Remotes; Musicians; Singers.*

Original Amateur Hour: see *Major Bowes and His Original Amateur Hour.*

Orphan Annie: see *Little Orphan Annie.*

Orphans of Divorce

Serial Drama

CAST:

Michael	James Meighan
Gregory Pearson	Louis Hall
Nora Worthington	Margaret Anglin Effie Palmer
Cyril Worthington	Richard Gordon
Juliet Worthington	Claire Wilson
Joan Worthington	Patricia Peardon
Dick Worthington	Warren Bryan
Barbara	Geraldine Kay
Alex Pratt	James Krieger
Annie	Vivia Ogden

Also: Charita Bauer, Richard Keith, Joseph Julian, Henry M. Neely

---

Producers: Frank and Anne Hummert
Theme: "I'll Take You Home Again, Kathleen"

Orphans of Divorce was first heard over the Blue network in 1939.

Orson Welles: see *The Columbia Workshop; The Mercury Theatre on the Air; The Black Museum.*

Our Barn

Children

This was a Saturday-morning children's program directed by Madge Tucker and written by Jean Peterson. It was on NBC and featured many of the cast members from *Coast-to-Coast on a Bus.*

Our Gal Sunday

Serial Drama

CAST:

Sunday	Dorothy Lowell Vivian Smolen
Lord Henry Brinthrope	Karl Swenson Alistair Duncan
Jackie	Jay Jostyn
Lively	Robert Strauss Joe Latham Roy Fant
Mrs. Sedgewick	Irene Hubbard
Bill Jenkins	Carleton Young
Slim Delaney	Van Heflin
Lanette	Charita Bauer
Fred Castleson	Spencer Bentley
Elaine	Vicki Vola
Dwight	Louis Hall
Lord Percy	Eustace Wyatt
Oliver Drexton	Santos Ortega
Barbara Hamilton	Kay Brinker
Lieutenant Nevils	John McGovern
Jack	Tom Gunn
Rose Hunt	Florence Robinson
Madelyn Travers	Joan Tompkins
Vivian Graham	Delma Byron
Gann Murray	Hugh Marlowe
Prudence Graham	Anne Seymour

Lonnie — Alastair Kyle
John Grinnell
Charlotte Abbott — Elaine Kent
Irene Galway — Fran Carlon
Hilda Marshall — Ara Gerald
Peter Galway — Joe Curtin
Kathy — Ruth Russell
Lawrence Shieffield — Clyde North
Pearl Taggart — Ann Shepherd (Scheindel Kalish)
St. John Harris — John Raby
Steve Lansing — John McQuade
Victor Maldstone — James Monks
Susan Robinson — Venezuela Jones
Countess Florenze — Ara Gerald
Lile Florenze — Inge Adams
Anna — Jay Meredith
Leona Kenmore — Charlotte Lawrence
Aunt Alice — Katherine Emmet
Fred Davis — Louis Neistat
Announcers: Art Millett, James Fleming, John A. Wolfe, Bert Parks, Charles Stark, John Reed King

---

Producers: Frank and Anne Hummert
Directors: Frank and Anne Hummert, Stephen Gross, Arthur Hanna
Writers: Jean Carroll, Helen Walpole
Sound Effects: John McCloskey

Theme: "Red River Valley"
Opening:

ANNOUNCER. *Our Gal Sunday* . . . the story of an orphan girl named Sunday, from the little mining town of Silver Creek, Colorado, who in young womanhood married England's richest, most handsome lord, Lord Henry Brinthrope. The story asks the question—Can this girl from a mining town in the West find happiness as the wife of a wealthy and titled Englishman?

Our Gal Sunday, which evolved from an earlier CBS program called *Rich Man's Darling,* made its debut on March 29, 1937, and was heard over CBS consistently at 12:45 p.m. It was sponsored variously by Anacin, Standard Brands, and American Home Products. The program's locale was the state of Virginia; "Lord Brinthrope's" manor was "Black Swan Hall."

Our Miss Brooks

Situation Comedy

CAST:

Miss Brooks, Madison High School English teacher — Eve Arden
Philip Boynton, the bashful biology instructor — Jeff Chandler
Osgood Conklin, the principal — Gale Gordon
Walter Denton — Dick Crenna
Harriet Conklin, the principal's daughter — Gloria McMillan
Stretch Snodgrass — Leonard Smith
Mrs. Davis, the landlady — Jane Morgan
Announcer: Verne Smith

Producer: Larry Berns
Director-Writer: Al Lewis
Musical Director: Wilbur Hatch
Sound Effects: Bill Gould

Our Miss Brooks was first heard over CBS in 1948.

Ozzie and Harriet: see *The Adventures of Ozzie and Harriet.*

P

Paducah Plantation

Variety

The Old Southern Colonel: Irvin S. Cobb, humorist

Pages of Romance

Serial Drama

Featuring: Peggy Allenby, Ned Wever, Allyn Joslyn, Eunice Howard, Teddy Bergman, Hugh Rennie, Alma Kruger, John McGovern

Pages of Romance was first heard over NBC Blue in 1932.

Painted Dreams

Serial Drama

Producer: Frank Hummert
Theme: "I'm Yours"

This serial drama on WGN Chicago is regarded as that station's first true "soap opera." It evolved from a program called *Sue and Irene,* which was sponsored by Super Suds and starred Irna Phillips as "Sue" and Ireene Wicker as "Irene." Miss Phillips and Miss Wicker also handled all the other roles on the show at first. *Painted Dreams* was originally written by Miss Phillips, who took the role of "Mother Monahan"; Bess Flynn later became the program's writer and also played "Mother Monahan." Ireene Wicker played the daughter and several other roles. Also appearing in the cast were Lucy Gilman, Kay Chase, Alice Hill, and Olan Soule.

The Palmolive Beauty Box Theater

Musical-Variety

Featuring: Jessica Dragonette, Benny Fields

CAST:

Baby Snooks	Fanny Brice
Daddy	Hanley Stafford
Olive Palmer[1]	Virginia Rea

Director: Kenneth W. MacGregor

This was one of the early variety programs, first heard over NBC in 1934. Jessica Dragonette was a major star of early radio. She was known variously as "The Little Angel of Radio" and "Vivian, the Coca-Cola Girl." (See also *The Musical Comedy Hour; Ziegfeld Follies of the Air.*)

Parade of Progress

Drama

Starring: Charlotte Manson

[1] This was a "house name" used on Palmolive programs.

The Parker Family

Situation Comedy

CAST:

Richard Parker — Michael O'Day, Leon Janney
Mr. Parker — Jay Jostyn
Mrs. Parker — Linda Carlon-Reid, Marjorie Anderson
Nancy Parker — Mitzi Gould
Elly — Pat Ryan
Grandpa Parker — Roy Fant
Announcer: Hugh James

Creator-Producer: Don Becker
Directors: Oliver Barbour, Chick Vincent
Writers: Ed Wolfe, Chick Vincent, Ben Kagan, Priscilla Kent, Vera Oldham

The Parker Family was first heard over the Blue network in 1939.

Parkyakarkas: see *Meet Me at Parky's*; *The Eddie Cantor Show*.

Parties at Pickfair

Variety

Starring: Mary Pickford

CAST:

Alvin, the butler — Eric Snowden
Also: Mary Jane Higby, Bret Morrison, Ted Osborne, Lou Merrill, James Eagles
Singers: Paul Turner Singers
Orchestra: Al Lyons

Creator-Producers: Nat Wolff, Marion Parsonette
Director: Eric Snowden
Writer: Jerry Cady

This short-lived program originated from the fabulous Hollywood home of Mary Pickford, "Pickfair," and pretended to be an actual celebrity-studded party. It was sponsored by an amalgam of ice dealers who were trying to stave off mechanical refrigeration. Their slogan was "Cold *alone* is not enough!"

The Passing Parade

Documentary

Host-Narrator: John Nesbitt
Orchestra: Meredith Willson
Writer-Director: John Nesbitt

Opening:

MUSIC. *Theme up full and under . . .*

ANNOUNCER. *The Passing Parade!* . . . Your favorite stories as told by your favorite storyteller . . . a man whose voice is familiar to millions of theatergoers and radio listeners. Here's John Nesbitt to bring you some stories of *The Passing Parade!*

MUSIC. *Theme up full ending on dissonant note and into dramatic music*

Passport for Adams

Drama

CAST:

Doug Adams — Robert Young, Myron McCormick

Perry Quisinberry (Quiz)
Dane Clark
Paul Mann

Director: Norman Corwin
Writers: Ranald MacDougall, Norman Corwin

In this series a New York news syndicate, "Consolidated Syndicate," sent "Doug Adams," a small-town ("Centerville") editor, and "Quiz Quisinberry," a New York photographer, around the world to report on the people of countries friendly to the Allies. The program was on the air in 1943 and 1944. Among the places visited by Doug and "Quiz" were Belém, Monrovia, Tel Aviv, Marrakesh, and Moscow.

Pat Novak, for Hire

Adventure

CAST:

Pat Novak — Jack Webb
Jocko Madigan — Tudor Owen
Inspector — John Galbraith

Writer: Richard Breen

(See also *Johnny Modero, Pier 23.*)

Paul Whiteman: see *Big Band Remotes: The Old Gold Paul Whiteman Hour; Radio Hall of Fame.*

Peewee and Windy

Comedy

CAST:

Peewee — Jack MacBryde
Windy — Walter Kinsella

Director: Paul Dumont
Writer: Pete Clarke
Composer and Conductor: Joe Rines

This program was about the adventures of two young sailors on shore leave. It was heard over NBC in the early 1930s and was sponsored by Hickok belts and suspenders.

Penthouse Party

Conversation

Hostesses: Gladys Glad
Ilka Chase

People Are Funny

Audience Participation

M.C.: Art Baker
Art Linkletter
Producer-Director: John Guedel
Writers: Art Linkletter, John Guedel, Jack Stanley, John Murray

People Are Funny, a program with stunts very much in the mold of those on *Truth or Consequences,* was first heard over NBC in 1942.

People's Platform

Discussion

Moderator: Lyman Bryson
Chef: Louis Heuberger

For this program, four guests were invited to dinner at the CBS studio. Under the centerpiece of flowers was a concealed microphone. After dinner, Bryson would lead the guests into the subject chosen for the broadcast, and the results were spontaneous and informal. The guests consisted of one big name, an expert on the subject, a woman, and an "average" man.

The Pepper Pot: see *The Breakfast Club*.

Pepper Young's Family

Serial Drama

CAST:

Larry (Pepper) Young — Curtis Arnall, Lawson Zerbe, Mason Adams
Peggy, Pepper's sister — Elizabeth Wragge
Sam Young — Jack Roseleigh, Bill Adams, Thomas Chalmers
Mary Young — Marion Barney
Nick Havens — John Kane
Ted Hart, football coach — Alan Bunce
Sally — Maureen McManus
Linda Benton Young — Eunice Howard
Biff Bradley — Laddie Seaman, Elliott Reid, Tony Barrett
Edie Gray Hoyt — Jean Sothern
Butch — Madeleine Pierce
Pete Nickerson — Arthur Vinton
Gil — Larry Haines
Lou Scott — Fred Herrick
Min — Joanna Ross
Mrs. Curt Bradley — Grace Albert
Ginny Taylor — Virginia Kaye
Edith Hoyt — Cecil Roy
Hal Trent — Madeleine Pierce
Jerry Feldman — Leon Janney
Mr. Smiley — George Hall
Curt Bradley — Edwin R. Wolfe
Hastings — James Krieger
Molly O'Hara — Katharine Stevens
Marcella the Menace — Jean McCoy
Carter Trent — Bert Brazier, James Krieger, Stacy Harris, Michael Fitzmaurice, Chester Stratton, Bob Pollock
Ivy Trent — Irene Hubbard
Horace Trent — Charles Webster
Andy Hoyt — Blaine Cordner
Anna — Annette Sorell
Hank — G. Swaye Gordon
Hattie Williams, the maid — Greta Kvalden
Mr. Jerome — Richard Gordon

Announcers: Alan Kent, Martin Block, Richard Stark
Directors: Chick Vincent, John Buckwalter, Ed Wolfe
Writer: Elaine Sterne Carrington
Musical Director: William Meeder
Sound Effects: Ross Martindale

Theme: "Au Matin"

Opening:

ANNOUNCER. *Pepper Young's Family* . . . the story of your friends, the Youngs, is brought to you by Camay, the mild beauty soap for a smoother, softer complexion.

This series made its debut over NBC Blue in 1936, evolving from *Red Adams, Red Davis* (1932) and *Forever Young.* "The Youngs" lived in "Elmwood." (See also *Red Davis.*)

The Perfect Fool: see *The Fire Chief.*

Perry Mason

Serial Drama

CAST:

Attorney Perry Mason — Bartlett Robinson, Santos Ortega, Donald Briggs, John Larkin
Della Street — Gertrude Warner, Jan Miner, Joan Alexander
Paul Drake — Matt Crowley, Charles Webster
Sergeant Dorset — Arthur Vinton
Lieutenant Tragg — Mandel Kramer, Frank Dane
Peg Neely — Betty Garde
The Judge — Maurice Franklin
Mary Blade — Mary Jane Higby
Announcers: Richard Stark, Bob Dixon

Producers: Tom McDermott, Leslie Harris
Directors: Arthur Hanna, Carlo De Angelo, Carl Eastman, Hoyt Allen, Ralph Butler
Writers: Irving Vendig, Erle Stanley Gardner, Dan Shuffman, Eugene Wang
Musical Director: Paul Taubman
Sound Effects: Jim Lynch

Perry Mason was based on the stories by Erle Stanley Gardner and was first heard over CBS in 1943.

Peter Lind Hayes and Mary Healy: see *Interviewers.*

Peter Quill

Mystery-Drama

CAST:

Peter Quill — Marvin Miller
Gail Carson — Alice Hill
Captain Roger Dorn — Ken Griffin

Writer-Director: Blair Walliser

Opening:

EERIE VOICE. Peeeeeeterrrrrr Quillllll. . . . !

This program was first heard over Mutual in 1940 as a weekly half-hour series. It ran until 1941. "Quill" was a mysterious scientist-detective-adventurer who caught criminals, saboteurs, traitors, and spies. He was aided by the romantic team of "Gail" and "Captain Dorn." Miller did the opening by wailing into the strings of a piano while the sostenuto pedal was held down.

Peter Salem: see *The Affairs of Peter Salem.*

The Phil Baker Show

Comedy

Starring: Phil Baker

CAST:

Beetle — Ward Wilson, Sid Silvers
Bottle — Harry McNaughton
Ferdinand — Ward Wilson
Mrs. Sarah Heartburn — Agnes Moorehead

Also: Artie Auerbach, Oscar Bradley, Mabel Albertson
Orchestra: Frank Shields, Hal Kemp
Vocal group: The Seven G's
Announcer: Harry Von Zell

Writers: Arthur Phillips, Hal Block, Sam Perrin, Phil Baker
Theme: "Rolling Along" by Phil Baker

Phil Baker, a vaudeville comedian and accordionist, appeared on his own variety program from 1933 to 1940. The show was also known as *The Armour Hour*, and Baker was often introduced as "The Armour Star Jester." "Bottle" was his very British butler and "Beetle" was a heckling stooge.

After a two-year rest, Baker returned to radio as quizmaster of *Take It or Leave It* (which see) and became equally successful with that format.

The Phil Cook Show

Variety

Featuring: Phil Cook

Phil Cook was a popular radio personality of the 1930s who sang, chatted, and played the ukulele. He often sang the news in rhyme ("I see by the papers . . ."). He appeared for Quaker Oats on the Blue network in 1930 and was known as "The Quaker Oats Man."

The Phil Harris and Alice Faye Show: see *The Fitch Bandwagon.*

Philco Radio Time: see *The Bing Crosby Show.*

Philip Marlowe: see *The Adventures of Philip Marlowe.*

Philip Morris Playhouse

Drama

Featuring: Ray Collins, Charlie Cantor, Teddy Bergman, Bill Johnstone, John McIntire, Jeanette Nolan, Ann Thomas, Barbara Weeks, Ward Wilson, Raymond Edward Johnson, *et al.*
Orchestra: Russ Morgan, Johnny Green, Ray Bloch
Directors: William Spier, Jack Johnstone, Charles Martin

One of the most famous programs in this dramatic series sponsored by Philip Morris was Edgar Allan Poe's "The Tell-Tale Heart" starring Luther Adler. (See also *Commercials.*)

Phillips: see *The Guiding Light.*

Philo Vance

Detective

CAST:
Philo Vance — Jackson Beck, José Ferrer
District Attorney Markham — George Petrie
Vance's secretary — Joan Alexander, Frances Farras

Sergeant Heath — Humphrey Davis

Producer: Frederic W. Ziv
Director: Jeanne K. Harrison
Writers: Robert J. Shaw, Kenny Lyons
Organist: Henry Sylvern

Plantation Party

Music and Comedy

CAST:

The Duke of Paducah	Whitey Ford
Tom	Bud Vandover
Dick	Marlin Hurt
Harry	Gordon Vandover

Plantation Party, first heard over the Blue network in 1938, was sponsored by Bugler tobacco.

Play Broadcast

Comedy Quiz

M.C.: Bill Anson

CAST:

Jack the Crackpot and other comedy voices	Marvin Miller
Home Economist	June Baker

Orchestra: Harold Stokes

Announcer: Guy Savage
Director: Lou Jacobson

This weekly half-hour program, heard over Mutual from 1940 to 1941, presented wild comedy sketches designed to provide clues to studio contestants.

The Poet Prince

Poetry Readings

Featuring: Anthony Frome (Abraham Feinberg) as "The Poet Prince"

Poet's Gold

Poetry

Narrator: David Ross
Orchestra: Victor Bey
Theme: "Clair de Lune" by Debussy

Point Sublime

Comedy-Variety

Featuring: Cliff Arquette, Mel Blanc

Catch-phrase: Ain't we the ones?

This program was first heard over ABC in 1947.

Policewoman

Adventure

CAST:

The policewoman	Betty Garde

This program was based on Mary Sullivan's file of police records. It was first heard over ABC in 1946.

Pond's Program

Talk

Featuring: Mrs. Franklin D. Roosevelt
Orchestra: Leo Reisman
Vocalist: Lee Wiley

This program, sponsored by Pond's, presented talks by Mrs. Roosevelt in addition to music. It began over NBC in 1932.

Popeye the Sailor

Children

CAST:

Popeye	Det Poppen
	Floyd Buckley
Olive Oyl	Olive La Moy
	Mae Questel
Matey, a newsboy adopted by Popeye	Jimmy Donnelly
Wimpy	Charles Lawrence

Also: Don Costello, Everett Sloane, Jean Kay
Orchestra: Victor Erwin's Cartoonland Band
Announcer: Kelvin Keech

Popeye the Sailor was based on the comic strip created by E. C. Segar. The program was first heard on radio, sponsored by Wheatena, over NBC in 1935.

Portia Faces Life

Serial Drama

CAST:

Portia Blake Manning	Lucille Wall
Dickie Blake	Raymond Ives
	Larry Robinson
	Alastair Kyle
	Edwin Bruce
Arline Manning	Joan Banks
Kirk Roder	Carleton Young
Walter Manning	Myron McCormick
	Bartlett Robinson
Dr. Stanley Holton	Donald Briggs
Miss Daisy	Henrietta Tedro
	Doris Rich
Lambert	Walter Vaughn
Bill Baker	Richard Kendrick
	Les Damon
John Parker	Bill Johnstone
Buck	Ken Lynch
Dr. Byron	Peter Capell
Eric Watson	John Larkin
Clint Morley	Santos Ortega
Joan Ward	Ginger Jones
Lilli	Cora B. Smith
Mark Randall	Lyle Sudrow
Leslie Palmer	Luise Barclay
Arline Harrison	Nancy Douglass
Amelia Blake	Ethel Intropidi
Elbert Gallo	Karl Swenson
Kathy Marsh	Marjorie Anderson
	Esther Ralston
	Selena Royle
	Rosaline Greene
	Anne Seymour
	Elizabeth Reller
Meg Griffin	Alison Skipworth
Phillip Coolidge	James Van Dyk
Susan Peters	Nancy Douglass

Also: Barry Sullivan

Announcers: George Putnam, Ron Rawson

Producers: Don Cope, Tom McDermott
Directors: Hoyt Allen, Mark Goodson, Beverly Smith, Paul Knight
Writers: Mona Kent, Hector Chevigny
Sound Effects: Wes Conant

Opening:
ANNOUNCER. *Portia Faces Life . . .* a story reflecting the courage, spirit, and integrity of American women everywhere . . .

"Portia" was a very successful lawyer. She was obviously named for Shakespeare's heroine in *The Merchant of Venice*. The program was first heard over CBS in 1940.

Pot O' Gold

Quiz

Hosts: Rush Hughes
Ben Grauer
Orchestras: Horace Heidt and His Musical Knights; Tommy Tucker
Vocalists: Amy Arnell, Don Brown
Guests: Cole Porter, other songwriters
Creator-Producer: Edward Byron
Director: Paul Dudley
Writer: John Tackaberry

Catch-phrase:
GRAUER. Hold it, Horace . . . stop the music!

Phone calls were made to listeners, giving them an opportunity to win money by answering questions correctly. The program first came to radio in 1939 over NBC.

Prairie Folks

Serial Drama

CAST:

Torwald Nielson	Erik Rolf
Smiley	Parker Fennelly
Mrs. Anna Nielson	Helen Warren
Adam Bassett	Morris Carnovsky
Curtis Bassett	Cliff Carpenter
Hansi	Kingsley Colton
Eldora Wilkins	Nell Converse
Arne Anders	Joe Helgeson
Mrs. Arne Anders	Josephine Fox

Prairie Folks told the story of settlers in Minnesota in the 1870s.

Pratt and Sherman: see *Laugh Doctors.*

Press Club

Adventure

CAST:

Mark Brandon	Marvin Miller

Director: George Fogle

Press Club first appeared on CBS in 1944 and told the story of reporter Mark Brandon. Marvin Miller was supported by a different cast each week.

Pretty Kitty Kelly

Serial Drama

CAST:

Kitty Kelly	Arline Blackburn
Michael Conway	Clayton "Bud" Collyer

Bunny Wilson	Helen Choate
Kyron Welby	Bartlett Robinson
Mr. Welby	Dennis Hoey
Mrs. Welby	Ethel Intropidi
Dennie Pierce	Richard Kollmar
The Doctor	Charles Webster
Patrick Conway	Charles Slattery
Mrs. Mogram	Florence Malone
Jack Van Orpington	Richard Kollmar
Slim	Artells Dickson
Grant Thursday	John Pickard
Dr. Orbo	Louis Hector
Isabel Andrews	Lucille Wall
Inspector Grady	Howard Smith
Mr. Astrakhan	Luis Van Rooten
Mrs. Murger	Charme Allen
Narrator	Matt Crowley

Writer: Frank Dahm
Theme: "Kerry Dance"

Pretty Kitty Kelly made its debut over CBS on March 15, 1937, at 5:45 p.m. as a Monday-through-Friday serial drama, sponsored by Wonder Bread. The story began when a young girl claiming to be "Kitty Kelly of Dublin, Ireland," was accused of being a gun moll and murdering "Inspector Conway."

Princess Pat Players

Drama

This dramatic series was first heard over NBC Blue in 1933.

The Private Lives of Ethel and Albert: see *Ethel and Albert*.

Professor Quiz

Quiz

Quizmaster: Craig Earl
Announcer: Robert Trout
Director: Ed Fitzgerald

Professor Quiz was first heard over CBS in 1936. (See *Quiz Shows*.)

The Prudential Family Hour

Music

Commentator: Deems Taylor
Featuring: Gladys Swarthout, contralto; Ross Graham, baritone; Jack Smith, pop singer
Orchestra: Al Goodman
Announcer: Frank Gallop
Writer: William N. Robson
Theme: "Intermezzo"

Opening:

ORCHESTRA AND CHORUS. *Chord blending to hum*

ANNOUNCER. *The Prudential Family Hour!*

ORCHESTRA AND CHORUS. *Theme up full*

This music program was sponsored by the Prudential Insurance Company. It was first heard over CBS in 1941 as a forty-five-minute broadcast on Sundays at 5:00 p.m. (See also *The Family Hour*.)

Pursuit

Adventure-Drama

CAST:

Chief Inspector Peter Black of Scotland Yard	Ted de Corsia
	John Dehner

Producer-Director: William N. Robson
Sound Effects: Clark Casey, Berne Surrey

Closing:
ANNOUNCER. *Pursuit* . . . and the pursuit is ended!

Pursuit first appeared on CBS in 1949.

Pursuit of Happiness

Variety

M.C.: Burgess Meredith

Pursuit of Happiness was a CBS series of the 1940s featuring music and drama.

Quality Twins

Comedy

Featuring: Ed East, Ralph Dumke

Queen for a Day

Audience Participation

M.C.: Jack Bailey
Announcer: Gene Baker
Directors: James Morgan, Bud Ernst, Lee Bolen
Writer: Jack Bailey
Sound Effects: Arthur Fulton

Women selected from the studio audience explained why they wanted a specific item. The winner was picked by studio applause, crowned "Queen for a Day," and given not only the gift she asked for, but many others. The long-running program made its debut over Mutual in 1945.

Quick as a Flash

Quiz

M.C.: Ken Roberts
Win Elliot
Bill Cullen
Dramatic Cast: Santos Ortega, Jack-

son Beck, Elspeth Eric, Julie Stevens, Charles Webster, Joan Alexander, Mandel Kramer, Raymond Edward Johnson
Orchestra: Ray Bloch
Announcers: Frank Gallop, Cy Harrice
Director: Richard Lewis
Writers: Louis M. Heyward, Mike Sklar, Eugene Wang
Sound Effects: Al Cooney, Adrian Penner

A group of studio contestants were pitted against one another. Each contestant was assigned a different colored flash of light, which he activated by pressing a buzzer in front of him. If he thought he knew the answer he pressed the buzzer. If he answered correctly he won the round, but if the answer was wrong he was disqualified until the next round. The final round was a mystery featuring a guest detective such as "Nick Carter," "The Falcon," etc. The first contestant to spot the clue that solved the mystery won the round. Occasionally no one could unravel it, so the guest detective gave the solution himself.

The makers of Helbros watches were long time sponsors of the program. It was first heard over Mutual in 1944.

Quiet, Please

Adventure

Narrator: Ernest Chappell
Producer-Writer-Director: Wyllis Cooper
Sound Effects: Bill McClintock
Theme: Second Movement of Franck's Symphony in D Minor

Quiet, Please was first heard over Mutual in 1947.

The Quiz Kids

Quiz

M.C.: Joe Kelly
Announcers: Fort Pearson, Roger Krupp
Producer: Louis G. Cowan
Directors: Jack Callahan, Riley Jackson, Forrest Owen, Ed Simmons, Clint Stanley
Writers: John Lewellen, Maggie O'Flaherty

The Quiz Kids was one of the best-known programs of its era. M.C. Joe Kelly posed difficult questions for a panel of exceptionally intelligent youngsters. The questions were tough even by adult standards. For example, the very first question asked of the panel on the première broadcast on June 28, 1940, was: "I want you to tell me what I would be carrying home if I brought an antimacassar, a dinghy, a sarong, and an apteryx."

The youngsters, all under sixteen years of age, comported themselves quite well with such questions. However, lest parents of today make comparisons with their own offspring, it should be pointed out that, many years after the final broadcast, it was revealed that the panelists were given advance knowledge of some of the questions. Nevertheless, the youngsters on the show displayed great wit and intelligence and provided inspiration for many schoolchildren throughout the United States.

That first broadcast of *The Quiz Kids* was as a summer replacement for a program starring the blind pianist-composer Alec Templeton, Friday nights on NBC. In the fall *The Quiz Kids* switched to the Blue network on Wednesday evenings and later moved back to NBC on Sunday afternoons. The Quiz Kids appearing on the first broadcast were seven-year-old Gerard Darrow, Joan Bishop (thirteen), Van Dyke Tiers (thirteen), Mary Ann Anderson (fourteen), and Charles Schwartz (thirteen).

Chronologically, the first fifty Quiz Kids, in addition to the preceding, were: Lois Jean Ashbeck, George Coklas, Cynthia Cline, Joan Alizier, Virginia Booze, Richard Kosterlitz, Linda Wells, Lloyd Wells, Mary Clare McHugh, Marvin Zenkere, Clem Lane, Jr., Emily Anne Israel, Robert Walls, Jack Beckman, Davida Wolffson, Edith Lee James, Richard Williams, Geraldine Hamburg, Jack Lucal, Paul Kirk, Tim Osato, Muriel Deutsch, Elizabeth Wirth, Lucille Eileen Kevill, Barbara Hutchinson, Gloria Jean (a guest), Jack French, Gloria Hunt, Arthur Haelig, Richard Frisbie, Frank Mangin, Jr., William Wegener, Claude Brenner, Lois Karpf, Sheila Brenner, Pat Chandler, Corinne Shapira, Sally Bogolub, Joan McCullough, Nancy Bush, Joann Cohen, Lois Jean Hesse, Nanni Kahn, Nancy Coggeshall, and Inez Fox.

Later Quiz Kids included Harve Bennett Fischman, Ruth Duskin, Joel Kupperman, Patrick Owen Conlon, Ruel (Sparky) Fischman, Lonny Lunde, Sheila Conlon, Gunther Hollander, André Aerne, Nancy Wong, Norman D. (Skippy) Miller, Richard Weixler, John C. Pollock, Rochelle Liebling, Naomi Cooks, and Robert Burns.

Quiz of Two Cities

Quiz

Producer: Dan Enright
Director: Ray Kremer

Two cities, represented by studio contestants, were pitted against each other on this quiz program. The rival cities were New York *vs.* Chicago, Minneapolis *vs.* St. Paul, San Francisco *vs.* Los Angeles, etc. The M.C. in New York was Michael Fitzmaurice. He would conduct the quiz in New York, then switch to Chicago for that city's turn.

Quiz Shows

Quiz shows were consistently ranked among the most popular programs. *Professor Quiz* and *Uncle Jim's Question Bee* are generally regarded as being the first major quiz programs on the air. A number of others soon filled the airwaves, including *Take It or Leave It*, *Vox Pop*, *Dr. I. Q.*, *Double or Nothing*, *Quick as a Flash*, *Quiz of Two Cities*, *Quizzer Baseball*, and *Spelling Bee*. Some used straight question-and-answer formats, but many had such production values as an M.C. who could handle comedy interviews with the contestants. Stars such as Phil Baker, Garry Moore, Bob Hawk, and Groucho Marx excelled at this, and the actual quiz became secondary to the interview.

Music was the basis for many quiz shows, such as *Kay Kyser's Kollege of Musical Knowledge* and *Beat the Band.* There were also some rather esoteric formats, such as *Grand Slam,* which was based on the rules of bridge. Youngsters got their chance to shine intellectually on *The Quiz Kids.* Then there was *It Pays To Be Ignorant,* a fully scripted comedy quiz that was a take-off on the panel quiz *Information, Please!* The prizes on radio quiz shows didn't involve immense jackpots until *Stop the Music* came along in 1948, offering a dazzling jackpot for the listener correctly identifying the "Mystery Melody."

Most quiz shows were legitimate, and the M.C. often had to admonish the studio audience with, "No help from the audience, please." However, some programs took the liberty of telling contestants prior to air time how to answer certain questions so as to provoke a laugh. For instance, one contestant on *Give and Take* was told in advance to respond to the question, "What is the difference between bailing out of an airplane and bailing out of a boat?" by declaring, "Well, you better not use a bucket when you bail out of an airplane!"

Quizzer Baseball

Quiz

CAST:

The Pitcher	Budd Hulick
The Umpire	Harry Von Zell

R

Radio Bible Class: see *Religion.*

Radio City Playhouse

Drama

Featuring: Guest Stars
Announcer: Fred Collins
Producer: Richard McDonough
Director: Harry Junkin
Sound Effects: Jerry McGee, John Powers

In one memorable program in this NBC series, John Larkin played a scientist and Bill Lipton a jet pilot who experiments with speed, crashes through the time barrier, and suffers a loss of age. When the pilot and wreckage are finally discovered, the pilot is an infant almost smothered in the uniform. Unfortunately, the show was on the air the same evening as an Air Force defense drill. Many listeners had not heard about the drill, and when they saw lights searching the skies for "the enemy" and were bombarded by the sounds of jet aircraft, they assumed the radio show was describing the real thing. The broadcast was in a documentary style so it was easy to jump to the wrong conclusion. The program marked the end of such realistic radio scripts.

Radio Hall of Fame

Music

Featuring: Martha Tilton, Georgia Gibbs, Paul Whiteman, The Merry Macs, Virginia Rees

Radio Reader's Digest

Drama

M.C.: Richard Kollmar
Les Tremayne
Narrator: Conrad Nagel
Producers: Anton M. Leader, Carl Schullinger
Director: Robert Nolan
Writers: Martin Magner, Robert Nolan, William N. Robson, Henry Denker, Josephine Lyons, Peggy Lou Mayer, Ralph Berkey, James Erthein, Carl Bixby
Musical Director: Van Cleave

Radio Reader's Digest was first broadcast over CBS in 1942.

The Radio Rogues: see *Animal Imitators, Baby Criers, Doubles, Mimics, and Screamers.*

Radio's Court of Honor

Drama

CAST:
Don Towne — Fred Uttal

The Railroad Hour

Music and Drama

Starring: Gordon MacRae
Orchestra: John Rarig, Carmen Dragon
Announcer: Marvin Miller
Directors: Ken Burton, Fran Van Hartesfeldt, Murray Bolen
Writers: Jean Holloway, Jerry Lawrence, Bob Lee
Choral Director: Norman Luboff

Theme: "I've Been Working on the Railroad"
Opening:
MARVIN MILLER. Ladies and gentlemen, *The Railroad Hour!*

This popular Monday-night NBC program was sponsored by the Association of American Railroads. It had a brief run as a forty-five-minute program on ABC before turning up on NBC in 1948 in a thirty-minute format. It was a high-budget series and survived until 1954.

The Railroad Hour presented famous musical comedies as well as original stories with music. The guests opposite Gordon MacRae were top names, such as Jo Stafford, Rise Stevens, and Jane Powell. During the summer a standard female vocalist was vis-à-vis MacRae—some years it was Dorothy Warenskjold, others Lucille Norman. A large dramatic cast was also used on the program, with announcer Marvin Miller often doubling in acting roles and even singing occasionally.

Rainbow House

Children

M.C.: "Big Brother" Bob Emery
Featuring: The Dolphe Martin "Vocal Orchestra"
Director: Bob Emery

Rainbow House was first heard over Mutual in 1942 as a fifteen-minute program on Saturday mornings at 10:00. The "Vocal Orchestra" was a children's choir.

Raising Your Parents

Children's Panel

M.C.: Milton Cross
Producer: Dan Golenpaul

Raising Your Parents featured a panel of children who discussed parents.

The Raleigh Room

Music

Starring: Hildegarde
Musical Director: Harry Sosnik

This pianist-songstress was known as "The Incomparable Hildegarde" (Hildegarde Loretta Sell). The program was sponsored by Raleigh cigarettes. (See also *Beat the Band.*)

Rate Your Mate

Interview-Quiz

M.C.: Joey Adams

With Joey Adams egging them on, a married or engaged couple estimated each other's ability to answer questions. If a wife, for example, rated her husband's answer correctly, they would win even though her husband's answer was actually wrong. The program was first heard over CBS in 1950.

The Ray Bolger Show

Variety

Starring: Ray Bolger
Also: Elvia Allman, Harry Lang, Verna Felton, Jeri Sullavan
Orchestra: Roy Bargy

Real Folks

Drama

This was one of radio's first dramatic series. It started on NBC in 1928.

Real Stories from Real Life

Serial Drama

Producers: Frank and Anne Hummert
Director: Ernest Ricca

This was first heard over Mutual in 1945.

Red Adams: see *Red Davis.*

Red Davis

Serial Drama

CAST:

Red Davis	Burgess Meredith
Red's sister	Elizabeth Wragge
Sam Davis	Jack Roseleigh
Mother	Marion Barney
Clink	John Kane
Connie Rickard	Jean Sothern
Luda Barclay	Eunice Howard

This serial drama later became *Forever Young* and then *Pepper Young's Family*. The original title had been *Red Adams*, but when Beech-Nut Gum sponsored it, the name was changed to *Red Davis* so there would be no mention of "Adams," a Beech-Nut rival. (See also *Pepper Young's Family*.)

Red Hook–31

Farm

Featuring: Woody and Virginia Klose
Director: Woody Klose

These farm broadcasts came from "Echo Valley Farm."

Red Ryder

Western Adventure

CAST:

Red Ryder	Reed Hadley
	Carlton KaDell
	Brooke Temple
Little Beaver	Tommy Cook
	Henry Blair

Producer-Writer-Director: Paul Franklin
Sound Effects: Monte Frazer, Norm Smith, Bob Turnbull

Catch-phrase:
LITTLE BEAVER. You betchum, Red Ryder.
Opening:
MUSIC. *Sting*
SOUND. *Hoofbeats*
ANNOUNCER. From out of the West comes America's famous fighting cowboy—Red Ryder!

This series was based on the comic strip by Fred Harman.

The Red Skelton Show

Comedy

CAST:

Junior, The Mean Widdle Kid	Red Skelton
Clem Kadiddlehopper	Red Skelton
Deadeye	Red Skelton
Willy Lump-Lump	Red Skelton
J. Newton Numskull	Red Skelton
Bolivar Shagnasty	Red Skelton
Junior's Mommy	Harriet Hilliard
	Lurene Tuttle
Daisy June	Harriet Hilliard
	Lurene Tuttle
Calamity Jane	Harriet Hilliard
Mrs. Willy Lump-Lump	Harriet Hilliard
	GeGe Pearson
Sara Dew	GeGe Pearson
Mrs. Bolivar Shagnasty	GeGe Pearson
Mrs. J. Newton Numskull	GeGe Pearson
Junior's Grandmother	Verna Felton
Mademoiselle Levy	Marlin Hurt

Also: "Wonderful" Smith, Tommy Mack
Vocalists: Ozzie Nelson, Harriet Hilliard, Anita Ellis
Vocal quartet: The Four Knights
Orchestra: Ozzie Nelson, David Rose
Announcers: John Holbrook, Truman Bradley, Marvin Miller, Rod O'Connor, Pat McGeehan

Producer: Jack Simpson

Director: Keith McLeod
Writers: Edna Skelton, Jack Douglas, Ben Freedman, Johnny Murray
Sound Effects: Clark Casey, Jack Robinson, Tiny Lamb

Catch-phrases:

JUNIOR. If I dood it, I gets a whipping. I dood it!

DEADEYE (*Authoritatively*). Whoa, horse! (Then *pleadingly*) Oh, come on, horse, whoa!

CLEM. W-e-e-e-ll, Daisy June!

JUNIOR. Hello, Fatso.

ANNOUNCER. Junior, why do you call me Fatso?

JUNIOR. I calls them the way I sees them.

JUNIOR (*Sobbing*). I hurt my widdle self.

MOTHER. Bless your little heart.

JUNIOR (*recovering abruptly*). Yeah. Bwess my widdle heart.

The Red Skelton Show made its debut in 1941 over NBC, where it had a long run Tuesday nights at 10:30.

Reg'lar Fellers

Children

CAST:

Jimmie Dugan	Dickie Van Patten
Dinky Dugan	Dickie Monahan
Washington Jones	Orville Phillips
Puddinhead Duffy	Ray Ives
Aggie Riley	Patsy O'Shea
Victor	Skippy Homeier
Daisy	Joyce Van Patten

Director: Joseph Hill

This program was based on the comic strip by Gene Byrnes.

Religion

In the very early days of radio Sunday was devoted mainly to religious programs or programs of serious intellectual content. In fact, many stations in those days were owned and operated by religious groups or individual churches, and the general feeling among broadcasters was that it was not appropriate to have any other kind of programing on Sunday. *The Fitch Bandwagon* has generally been credited with being one of the first big variety shows to break into the Sunday line-up. Eventually religious programing was relegated to Sunday mornings for the most part.

Several religious personalities emerged as early radio "stars." Billy Sunday, a former professional baseball player who became the foremost evangelist of his day, preached with great fervor on radio. His program first appeared over CBS in 1929 and was called *The Back Home Hour.* Another noted figure was Elder Michaux, whose full name was Solomon Lightfoot Michaux (pronounced "Me-Shaw"). The theme used by this Negro preacher was "Happy Am I." But the most famous—and most controversial—religious personality of the day was Father Coughlin.

The Reverend Charles E. Fuller presided over *The Old-Fashioned Revival Hour.* In its early days it was broadcast from the Hollywood Women's Club, with a studio audience of only fifty persons. In 1940, in order to accommodate the large crowds, the Reverend Fuller rented the 4400-seat

Long Beach Municipal Auditorium in Long Beach, California. By 1943 he was the biggest buyer of time on the Mutual network for his religious broadcasts. The program's theme was "Heavenly Sunshine."

Toward the end of radio's Golden Age, Billy Graham, the stirring evangelist from North Carolina, became a familiar voice on radio on *The Hour of Decision*. He applied the Bible to modern times instead of dwelling upon its historical aspects. His theme was "How Great Thou Art." *The Hour of Decision* was first heard nationally over ABC in 1950.

Among the other long-running religious broadcasts were:

The National Radio Pulpit—a series featuring the Reverend S. Parkes Cadman, first broadcast nationally over NBC in 1926. In the 1930s the Reverend Ralph Sockman was featured.

National Vespers—a program conducted by the Reverend Harry Emerson Fosdick; it began over NBC in 1927.

The Catholic Hour—featuring guest speakers and music of the Church; it began on NBC in 1929.

The Mormon Tabernacle Choir, which began in 1929 and featured a sermon referred to as "The Spoken Word."

The CBS Church of the Air—a series that began in 1931.

Religion in the News—a discussion of religious topics conducted by Walter Van Kirk; it began over NBC in 1933.

Message of Israel—a pioneer Jewish religious series founded by Rabbi Jonah B. Wise in 1934 over NBC.

The Gospel Hour—a series featuring religious speakers and music; it was first heard over Mutual in 1936.

The Lutheran Hour—a program of religious speakers and sacred music, featuring for many years the Reverend Walter A. Maier; it began in 1938 over Mutual.

Radio Bible Class—a series first broadcast nationally over Mutual in 1940.

Young People's Church of the Air—first presented over Mutual in 1940.

The Voice of Prophecy—first broadcast nationally over Mutual in 1941.

The Hour of Faith—a series first heard nationally over ABC in 1942.

The Back to God Hour—a religious broadcast first heard nationally over Mutual in 1948.

(See also *The Eternal Light; Father Coughlin; The Greatest Story Ever Told; The Light of the World; The Mormon Tabernacle Choir.*)

Religion in the News: see *Religion*.

Renfrew of the Mounted

Adventure

CAST:

Inspector Douglas Renfrew of the Royal Canadian Mounted Police — House Jameson

Carol Girard — Joan Baker

Animal sounds: Brad Barker

Announcer: Bert Parks

Creator-Writer: Laurie York Erskine

Opening:
SOUND. *Wind noise*
ANNOUNCER (*shouting*). Renfrew! Renfrew of the Mounted!
SOUND. *Wolf howl*

This program was first heard over CBS in 1936.

Report to the Nation

News

Featuring: Guest Correspondents
Writers: Joseph Liss, Earle C. McGill

This was a documentary program presenting reports from CBS news correspondents, along with dramatizations of events in the news. The series began in 1940.

Reserved for Garroway

Music and Conversation

Host: Dave Garroway
Vocalists: Connie Russell, Jack Haskell
Also: Art Van Damme Quintet

This program originated in Chicago and was also known as *Dial Dave Garroway* and *Next, Dave Garroway.*

RFD America

Farm

M.C.: Ed Bottcher

RFD America was first heard over Mutual in 1947.

RFD #1

Farm

Featuring: Irene Beasley

This program featured songs and talk for farm listeners.

Rhapsody in Rhythm

Music

Featuring: Johnny Johnston and Peggy Lee, vocalists
Vocal group: The Pied Pipers

This was heard over CBS briefly in 1947, filling the time-slot occupied earlier by *Songs by Sinatra* and *Songs for Sinatra.*

Rich Man's Darling

Serial Drama

CAST:

Packy O'Farrell	Karl Swenson
Peggy O'Farrell	Peggy Allenby
Gregory Alden	Edwin Jerome
Claire Van Roon	Ethel Remey

Announcer: Art Millett

Rich Man's Darling made its debut over CBS in 1936. The following year it evolved into the better-known *Our Gal Sunday.*

Richard Diamond, Private Detective

Detective

CAST:

Richard Diamond — Dick Powell
Lieutenant Levinson — Ed Begley
Also: Virginia Gregg

This was first heard over NBC in 1949.

Richard Lawless

Adventure

CAST:

Richard Lawless — Sidney Smith, Kevin McCarthy

This adventure series was set in seventeenth-century England.

Richard Willis: see *Women's Programs*.

The Right to Happiness

Serial Drama

CAST:

Carolyn Kramer Nelson — Claudia Morgan, Eloise Kummer
Doris Cameron — Selena Royle, Constance Crowder, Irene Hubbard
Fred Minturn — Charles Webster, Art Kohl, Hugh Studebaker
Mr. Kramer — Julian Noa
Mrs. Kramer — Leora Thatcher
Bill Walker — Reese Taylor
Louise Sims — Sarajane Wells
Dwight Kramer — Frank Behrens, Ed Prentiss, David Gothard
Adele Carmody — Sunda Love
Mary — Mary Patton
Dr. Richard Campbell — Les Damon, Alexander Scourby
Susan Wakefield — Charita Bauer, Rosemary Rice
Ginny — Anne Sterrett
Arnold — Ian Martin
"The Past"[1] — Marvin Miller
Ted Wakefield — Jimmy Dobson, Billy Redfield
Constance Wakefield — Violet Heming, Luise Barclay
Alex Delavan — Staats Cotsworth
Miles Nelson — Gary Merrill, John Larkin
Jane Browning — Ginger Jones
Rose Kransky — Ruth Bailey
Terry Burke — Carlton KaDell
Emily Norton — Alice Yourman
Ed Norton — Jerry Macy
Also: Bill Lipton, Elizabeth Lawrence, Sarah Fussell, Ethel Owen, Bill Quinn, Gertrude Warner, J. Ernest Scott, Peter Capell, Joseph Bell, Maurice Franklin, Helene Dumas, Anne Sargent, Walter Greaza
Announcers: Ron Rawson, Michael Fitzmaurice, Hugh Conover

[1] "The Past" was a haunting conscience-voice device used regularly on the program from 1941 to 1944. Irna Phillips later used the same device on *Today's Children* and *The Guiding Light*.

Producers: Paul Martin, Carl Wester, Kathleen Lane, Fayette Krum
Directors: Frank Papp, Charles Urquhart, Arthur Hanna, Gil Gibbons
Writers: Irna Phillips, John M. Young
Sound Effects: Frank Loughrane, Manny Segal
Musical Director: William Meeder

Opening:

ANNOUNCER. And now—Ivory Soap's own story—*The Right to Happiness.*

MUSIC. *Chords and music under . . .*

ANNOUNCER. Happiness is the sum total of many things—of health, security, friends, and loved ones. But most important is a desire to be happy and the will to help others find their right to happiness as well.

MUSIC. *Chords*

ANNOUNCER. *The Right to Happiness . . .*

MUSIC. *Chords*

ANNOUNCER. A very human story . . .

The Right to Happiness was first heard over the Blue network in 1939. It originated in Chicago.

Riley: see *The Life of Riley.*

Rin-Tin-Tin

Adventure

Owner of Rin-Tin-Tin, the Wonder Dog: Francis X. Bushman
Also: Lee Duncan

This program began over the Blue network in 1930. It featured stories of the bravery of Rin-Tin-Tin and other dogs. Rin-Tin-Tin was actually owned by Lee Duncan.

The Rise of the Goldbergs: see *The Goldbergs.*

The Road of Life

Serial Drama

CAST:

Dr. Jim Brent	Ken Griffin
	Matt Crowley
	Don MacLaughlin
	David Ellis
	Howard Teichmann
Nurse paging Dr. Brent at opening of broadcast	Jeannette Dowling
	Angel Casey
Dr. Winslow	Jack Roseleigh
	Percy Hemus
Helen Gowan Stephenson	Peggy Allenby
	Betty Lou Gerson
	Muriel Bremner
	Janet Logan
Arthur Reads	Carlton KaDell
Mrs. Evans	Hope Summers
	Doris Rich
Mary Hot	Vivian Fridell
Dr. Reginald Parsons	Reese Taylor
	Jack Petruzzi
Fred	Lawson Zerbe
	Frank Dane
Mrs. Brent	Effie Palmer
Julia	Olive Parker
Sylvia Bertram	Joan Winters
	Lois Zarley
Paula Harwood	Mary Mareen
Ted Fenton	Marvin Miller
Janet Mercer	Eloise Kummer
Adele Corlis	Betty Arnold

Mrs. Chapman	Dorothy Francis
Morton Blair	Ray Suber
George Jeffries	Marvin Miller
Dr. Ralph Thompson	Sidney Breese
Dr. Bill Evans	Harry Elders
	Lee Young
	Bill Griffis
Tom Stephenson	Robert Griffin
Marion Baxter	Barbara Fuller
Verna Roberts	Barbara Fuller
Dorothy Reads	Lillian White
Grandpa Sutter	Hugh Studebaker
Ray Sawyer	Frank Behrens
Dr. Grant Frasier	Dick Post
	Willard Waterman
	Robert Duane
Clifford Foster	Dick Foster
Dale Humphrey	Bob Bailey
Hartley Knowlton	Stanley Gordon
Jack Felzer	Russell Thorson
Butch Brent	Donald Kraatz
	Roland Butterfield
	Lawson Zerbe
	David Ellis
	Bill Lipton
Francie Brent (Mrs. John Brent)	Elizabeth Lawrence
Auntie	Evelyn Varden
	Dorothy Sands
Mr. Overton	Charles Dingle
Mrs. Overton	Abby Lewis
Jocelyn	Barbara Becker
Linden Wake	Bret Morrison
Junior Stephenson	Dick Holland
	Cornelius Peeples
	Jack Bivens
Carol Evans Martin	Lesley Woods
	Barbara Luddy
	Louise Fitch
	Marion Shockley
Sally Barnett	Doris Mead
	Nanette Sargent
	Viola Berwick
Miss Todd	Mary Patton
Dr. Burke	Ralph Camargo
Claudia Wilson	Sarajane Wells
Mrs. Hurley	Hellen Van Tuyl
George Hurley	Arthur Kohl
Miss Radcliff	Eva Parnell
Miss Bradley	Gladys Heen
Alice Jamison	Angeline Orr
Frank Roberts	Leslie Spears
Joe Buckley	Arthur Hern
Daley	John Briggs
Isobel Daley	Mary Patton
Alice Randall	Terry Rice
Dr. Carson McVicker	Charlotte Manson
Frank Dana	John Larkin
Dr. Yates	Guy Sorel
Nurse Lanier	Grace Lenard
Faith Richards	Vicki Vola
	Beryl Vaughn
Miss Boyle	Ethel Everett
Elizabeth	Nanette Sargent
Maggie Lowell	Julie Stevens
	Helen Lewis
Frances Brent	Eileen Palmer
Jim Brent's father	Joe Latham
Dr. Miller	Sam Wanamaker
Mary Holt	Dale Burch
Frank Dana	Lyle Sudrow
Society Doctor	John Anthony
Night Nurse	Peggy Allenby
Eloise Cummings	Ethel Wilson

Announcers: Clayton "Bud" Collyer, Ron Rawson, George Bryan

Producers: Carl Wester, Walt Ehrgott, Kay Lane, Fayette Krum

Directors: Charles Schenck, Charles Urquhart, Walter Gorman, Stanley Davis, Gil Gibbons

Writers: William Morwood, John M. Young, Irna Phillips, Howard Teichmann

Sound Effects: Manny Segal

Organist: Charles Paul

Theme: First Movement of Tschaikovsky's Sixth Symphony (Pathétique)
Opening:
SOUND. *Hospital Bell*
NURSE. Dr. Brent . . . call surgery. Dr. Brent . . . call surgery.

The Road of Life, though remembered as a drama of doctors and nurses, was once billed as "the story of an Irish-American mother and her troubles raising her children." The series began over CBS in 1937 and originated in Chicago.

The Robert Burns Panatela Program

Comedy-Variety

Starring: George Burns and Gracie Allen
Orchestra: Guy Lombardo and His Royal Canadians
Director: Herschel Williams
Writers: Carroll Carroll, Willy Burns, John P. Medbury, George Burns, Harry Conn

The Robert Burns Panatela Program began over CBS in 1932 and featured thirty minutes of comedy and music. Because Burns and Allen and the Lombardo band were frequently in different places, this was one of the very first variety shows to integrate music and talk originating in widely separated locations. The show rapidly rose to a highly ranked position among network programs following an all-network search for Gracie's "missing brother."

This was basically a publicity gimmick to help build the audience. Conceived by Bob Taplinger, head of publicity for CBS, the idea was for Gracie to start talking about her "missing brother" on the program, then plant stories in the newspapers, and finally actually walk into the middle of other radio programs looking for her brother. This was unheard of at the time, but the idea worked and garnered a great deal of free publicity in the short ten days that it lasted. The final touch was having Gracie appear on Rudy Vallee's program on the rival NBC. NBC said she couldn't mention her brother on that show, but Vallee did, and NBC took the show off the air. More publicity ensued from that. Through it all, Gracie's real brother simply wanted to get lost! (See also *Burns and Allen.*)

Robinson Crusoe Jr.

Children's Adventure

CAST:

Robinson Brown Jr.	Lester Jay
Julie	Toni Gilman
Jinky	Michael O'Day
Friday	Arthur Bruce
The Twins	Billy and Bobby Mauch
Katie, the maid	Jean Sothern
Binnacle Barnes, the sailor	Cal Tinney

This was the story of a rich little boy and his less fortunate playmates who were shipwrecked on a mythical island. It was first heard over CBS in 1934.

Roger Kilgore, Public Defender

Drama

CAST:

Roger Kilgore — Santos Ortega
Raymond Edward Johnson

Writer: Stedman Coles

Rogue's Gallery

Detective

CAST:

Richard Rogue — Dick Powell
Barry Sullivan

Producer: Charles Vanda
Directors: Clark Andrews, Dee Engelbach, Jack Lyman
Writer: Ray Buffum

Rogue's Gallery was first heard over Mutual in 1945.

Romance

Serial Drama

Voice of Romance: Doris Dalton

The Romance of Evelyn Winters: see *Evelyn Winters*.

The Romance of Helen Trent

Serial Drama

CAST:

Helen Trent — Virginia Clark
Betty Ruth Smith
Julie Stevens
Philip King — David Gothard
Mrs. Ward Smith — Hilda Graham
Monica Ward Smith
Audrey McGrath
Tony Griffin — Louis Krugman
Agatha Anthony — Marie Nelson
Katherine Emmet
Bess McCammon
Alice Carroll — Ginger Jones
Drew Sinclair — Reese Taylor
Jeanette McNeil — Vivian Fridell
Margot Burkhart — Alice Hill
Mrs. Kelvin — Selena Royle
Mr. Kelvin — William Thornton
Lucia Lang — Loretta Poynton
Nancy Granger — Lucy Gilman
Dick North — Les Mitchel
Roy Gabler — John Larkin
Ginger Leroy — Bernice Silverman
Bernice Martin
Florence Robinson
Karl Dorn — Alan Hewitt
Tweed Parker — Sarah Burton
Violet — Cora B. Smith
Brook Forrester — Karl Weber
Frank Chase — Whitfield Connor
Chuck Blair — John Walsh
Lisa Valentine — Nanette Sargent
Douglas — Spencer Bentley
Dr. Fleming — Reese Taylor
Gordon Decker — Bill Bouchey
Gil Whitney — Marvin Miller
David Gothard
William Green
Cherry Martin — Marilyn Erskine
Marjorie Claiborne
Charlotte Manson
Nancy — Patsy O'Shea
Bud — George Ward
Sylvia Hall — Alice Goodkin
Buggsy O'Toole — Ed Latimer
Cynthia Carter — Mary Jane Higby
Jeff Brady — Ken Daigneau
Harriet Eagle — Amzie Strickland

Tember Adams	Lesley Woods
Rita Harrison	Cathleen Cordell
Nick Collins	Klock Ryder
Norman Hastings	Lauren Gilbert
Eric Stowell	Olan Soule
Agnes	Linda Reid
Francine	Mitzi Gould
Dolly McKinley	Doris Rich
Curtis Bancroft	Bartlett Robinson
Lydia Brady	Helene Dumas
Jonathan Hayward	Bret Morrison
Mrs. Dunlop	Hope Summers
Barbara Sue	Mary Frances Desmond
Chris Wilson	Carlton KaDell
Lois Colton	Peggy Wall
Marcia	Donna Reade
Hiram Weatherbee	Klock Ryder
Nina Mason	Patricia Dunlap
Clara Blake	Janet Logan

Also: Les Tremayne, Don MacLaughlin, Ed Prentiss, Grant Richards, Karl Weber, John Hodiak, James Meighan, Jay Barney

Announcers: Don Hancock (Chicago), Pierre André (Chicago), Fielden Farrington (New York)

Producers: Frank and Anne Hummert

Producer-Director: Stanley Davis

Directors: Ernest Ricca, Blair Walliser, Richard Leonard, Les Mitchel

Writers: Ruth Borden, Martha Alexander, Ronald Dawson, Marie Banner

Sound Effects: James Lynch

Theme: "Juanita" (hummed by Stanley Davis, Lawrence Salerno)

Opening: These lines, of course, varied. For a time they were—

ANNOUNCER. *The Romance of Helen Trent* . . . who sets out to prove for herself what so many women long to prove, that because a woman is thirty-five . . . or more . . . romance in life need not be over . . . that romance can live in life at thirty-five and after.

[later]

ANNOUNCER. *The Romance of Helen Trent* . . . the story of a woman who sets out to prove what so many other women long to prove in their own lives . . . that romance can live on at thirty-five . . . and even beyond.

"Helen Trent," many of whose lovers met violent death, was a fashion designer. The series began over CBS in 1933. Virginia Clark and Betty Ruth Smith played the lead in Chicago. When the show moved to New York in 1944, Julie Stevens took over the part and played it until the program left the air.

Roosevelt: see *Fireside Chats*.

Roosty of the AAF

Adventure

CAST:

Roosty	William Tracy

This was first heard over Mutual in 1944.

Rosa Rio Rhythms

Music

Starring: Rosa Rio, organist

Theme: "Sunrise Serenade"

This program featured the well-known organist of many famous radio programs in her own daily presentation of music.

Rosemary

Serial Drama

CAST:

Rosemary Dawson — Betty Winkler
Peter Harvey — Sidney Smith
Mr. Dennis — Ed Latimer
Dick Phillips — James Van Dyk
Joyce Miller — Helen Choate
Tommy Taylor — Jackie Kelk
Patti Dawson — Jone Allison, Patsy Campbell
Lieutenant George Schuyler — Michael Fitzmaurice
Mr. Martin — John Gibson
Dr. Jim Cotter — Bill Adams, Charles Penman
Mother Dawson — Marion Barney
Dr. Greer — Guy Repp
Audrey Roberts — Lesley Woods, Joan Alexander
Bill Roberts — George Keane
Jessica — Joan Lazer
Lefty Higgins — Larry Haines
Mrs. Kenyon — Ethel Wilson
Brad Boyden — Woody Parker
Jane — Elspeth Eric
Marie — Marie De Wolfe

Announcers: Joe O'Brien, Fran Barber, Bob Dixon

Producer: Tom McDermott
Directors: Carl Eastman, Hoyt Allen, Leslie Harris, Theodora Yates, Ralph Butler, Charles Fisher
Writer: Elaine Sterne Carrington
Sound Effects: Jerry Sullivan
Musical Director: Paul Taubman

Rosemary made its debut over NBC in 1944.

Roses and Drums

Historical Dramas

CAST:

Captain Gordon Wright, the Yankee Captain — Reed Brown, Jr.
Captain Randy Claymore, the Rebel Captain — John Griggs
Betty Graham — Betty Love, Helen Claire

Also: Florence Williams, Pedro de Cordoba, De Wolf Hopper, Osgood Perkins, Walter Connolly, Guy Bates Post, Mrs. Richard Mansfield, Jack Roseleigh
Orchestra: Wilfred Pelletier

Director: Herschel Williams

Roses and Drums featured dramatizations with a Civil War background. Professor M. W. Jernegan of the University of Chicago edited and checked the scripts for historical accuracy. The program made its debut over CBS in 1932 and lasted until March 29, 1936. The roses of the title signified love and romance, and the drums symbolized progress, war, and adventure. In the final episode, "Betty Graham" married "Captain Wright," the Yankee, after having been wooed by him and "Captain Claymore," the Southerner.

Roxy's Gang

Music

Host: Roxy (Samuel L. Rothafel)
Featuring: James Melton, tenor; Jan

Peerce, tenor; Leonard Warren, baritone; Harold Van Duzee, tenor; William (Wee Willie) Robyn, tenor; Alva (Bomby) Bomberger, baritone; Douglas Stanbury, baritone; Peter Hanover, bass; Frank Moulan, character actor and Gilbert and Sullivan specialists; Beatrice Belkin, coloratura; Caroline Andrews, coloratura; Betsy Ayres, soprano; Gladys Rice, soprano; Florence Mulholland, contralto; Adelaide De Loca, contralto; Julia Glass, piano soloist; Yasha Bunchuk, cellist; Maria Gambarelli, dancer; Patricia Bowman, dancer

Roxy Male Quartet—George Reardon, John Young, Fred Thomas, Frank Miller

Announcer: Phil Carlin

Coach-Pianist-Arranger: Leo Russotto

Roxy's Gang was broadcast from the Capitol Theatre, the Roxy Theatre, and Radio City Music Hall during its tenure on the air. It was the first radio show to broadcast from a theater. Roxy led the orchestra although he couldn't read music. All he needed to know was the general tempo—fast or slow—and he'd take it from there. He would honor musical requests and dedications, and he closed the show with "Good night . . . pleasant dreams . . . God bless you." His was the first show on radio to broadcast a complete symphony, a complete opera, and a complete oratorio. His initial network appearance with his gang was over NBC Blue in 1927.

Roy Rogers

Western Adventure

Starring: Roy Rogers

Featuring: Dale Evans, Gabby Hayes

Also: Pat Brady, Marvin Miller

With: Foy Willing and the Riders of the Purple Sage, vocal group
Sons of the Pioneers, vocal group[1]

Announcer: Lou Crosby

Producer-Director: Tom Hargis

Producer: Art Rush

Directors: Fran Van Hartesfeldt, Ralph Rose

Writer: Ray Wilson

Roy Rogers, the self-styled "King of the Cowboys," had several programs featuring music and Western adventure. In 1944 his sponsor was Goodyear Tire and Rubber; the show presented Rogers and the Sons of the Pioneers. In 1948 his program featured himself, Dale Evans (his wife), and Foy Willing and the Riders of the Purple Sage. It was sponsored by Quaker Oats and Mother's Oats. The theme was "Smiles Are Made out of Sunshine," and the commercial jingle had such lines as "Delicious, nutritious, makes you ambitious." One of the premium offers was for a branding-iron ring with the Double R Bar brand. This program was heard on Sunday nights. Then Post Sugar Crisp became the sponsor, and later Dodge automobiles (1953–55). Pat Brady replaced Gabby Hayes during the Post series and the theme was "It's Roundup Time on the Double R Bar." "Happy Trails" was the theme when Dodge became the sponsor.

[1] See p. 284.

Ruby Valentine: see *We Love and Learn.*

The Rudy Vallee Show

Variety

Starring: Rudy Vallee
Guest Stars: John Barrymore, Ethel Barrymore, Eva Le Gallienne, Helen Hayes, Walter Huston, *et al.*
With: Sara Berner as Conchita ("Vot else?") Shapiro; Dr. R. E. Lee, spokesman for Fleischmann's Yeast
Announcers: Jimmy Wallington and Carol Hurst, Marvin Miller
Directors: Gordon Thompson, Tony Stanford, Art Daly, Howard Wiley, Jim Wright
Writers: George Faulkner, Bob Colwell, A. L. Alexander, Henrietta Feldstein, Sid Zelinka, Sam Silver, R. Marks, Carroll Carroll

Catch-phrase:
RUDY VALLEE. Heigh-ho, everybody!

Rudy Vallee was host and producer of *The Fleischmann Hour,* which began broadcasting in 1929 and ended on September 28, 1939. During this time Vallee proved himself a pioneer of radio variety programs and also pointed the way for radio drama, situation comedy, and documentaries. His program showed careful attention to production detail, good writing, and quality performers. Beatrice Lillie, Ezra Stone, Edgar Bergen, Tommy Riggs, Carmen Miranda, Eddie Cantor, Milton Berle, Phil Baker, Alice Faye, Olsen and Johnson, Bob Burns, Lou Holtz, and many others made their première appearances on the air on his show.

Among the program segments that later became programs in their own right were *The Aldrich Family* and *We, the People.* The program also was the first to use stars of the theater in dramatic sketches written especially for radio rather than in scenes from Broadway plays, which had been the custom up until then. Later, Vallee was the star of *The Sealtest Hour* which co-starred John Barrymore. In 1945 and 1946 Vallee starred in a show from Hollywood carried by NBC and sponsored by Drene Shampoo. It was on this version that Marvin Miller served as commercial announcer. He also took part in comedy sketches. The directors of this series were Art Daly, Howard Wiley, and Jim Wright. Vallee was associated with many songs—foremost of them was "My Time Is Your Time." He is also remembered for his frequent salutes to Maine and his affection, in the early days, for a cheerleader's megaphone.

Rumpus Room

Audience Participation

M.C.: Johnny Olson

S

The Sad Sack

Comedy

The Sad Sack: Herb Vigran
Announcer: Dick Joy

This CBS program was based on the comic strip by George Baker.

Safety Legion Time

Children

CAST:

The Story Lady	Colleen Moore
Captain Jack	Jess Kirkpatrick

The Saint

Adventure

CAST:

Simon Templar, the Saint	
	Edgar Barrier
	Brian Aherne
	Vincent Price
	Tom Conway
	Barry Sullivan
Louie	Larry Dobkin
The Inspector	John Brown
Happy	Ken Christy
Patricia Holmes	Louise Arthur

Also: Tom Collins, Theodor von Eltz, Joe Forte
Announcer: Dick Joy

Producer: Leslie Charteris
Director: Bill Rousseau

The Saint was based on the character created by Leslie Charteris. It made its debut over NBC in 1944.

The Sal Hepatica Revue: see *The Fred Allen Show.*

The Salad Bowl Revue: see *The Fred Allen Show.*

Salute to Youth

Variety

This was a program of the early 1940s dedicated to recounting the achievements of young Americans. The National Youth Orchestra, conducted by Raymond Paige, provided the music.

Sam 'n' Henry: see *Amos 'n' Andy.*

Sam Spade

Detective

CAST:

Sam Spade	Howard Duff
	Steve Dunne
Effie	Lurene Tuttle

Also: June Havoc, Cathy Lewis
Announcer: Dick Joy

Director: William Spier
Writers: Gil Doud, Bob Tallman
Musical Director: Lud Gluskin

This program, set in San Francisco, made its debut over CBS in 1946 and was later heard over ABC and NBC. Its faithful sponsor was Wildroot Cream-Oil.

"Sam Spade" was based on the character created by Dashiell Hammett. Listeners may recall that his license number was 137596 and that he ended each program by dictating a report on the case to "Effie" and then saying, "Period. End of report." He referred to his cases as "capers."

Sam Spade was replaced by a program known as *Charlie Wild, Private Eye.*

Sara's Private Caper

Comedy-Mystery

Sara: Sara Berner
Also: Bob Sweeney, Ed Fields, Herb Vigran

Saturday Night Serenade

Music

Featuring: Jessica Dragonette, Bill Perry, Emil Coty Serenaders, Vic Damone, Hollace Shaw
Orchestra: Gustave Haenschen, Howard Barlow
Producer-Writer-Director: Chick Martini

Saturday Night Serenade was first presented over CBS in 1936.

Saturday Night Swing Club

Music

M.C.: Paul Douglas
Ted Husing

Saturday's Child

Serial Drama

CAST:

Ann Cooper	Doris Kenyon

Scarlet Queen

Mystery

Featuring: Elliott Lewis

This mystery series was set on the high seas.

Scattergood Baines

Serial Drama

CAST:

Scattergood Baines	Jess Pugh Wendell Holmes
Hippocrates Brown	John Hearne
Pliny Pickett	Francis "Dink" Trout
Clara Potts	Catherine McCune
Ed Potts	Arnold Robertson
J. Wellington Keats	Forrest Lewis
Agamemnon	Forrest Lewis
Erne Baker	Forrest Lewis
Mr. Martin	Arnold Robertson
Dr. Chancellor	Burton Wright
Eloise Comstock	Louise Fitch
Beth Reed	Norma Jean Ross

Mirandy	Viola Berwick
Lorinda	Viola Berwick
Jimmy Baines	Chuck Grant
Spotty	Patty Conley
Verne Sanders	Bob Bailey
Barbara Calkins	Barbara Fuller
Geraldine Quinton	Dorothy Gregory
Mrs. Black	Eileen Palmer
Bob	George Wallace
Margie	Jean McCoy
"Hands" Bannister	Marvin Miller
Arturo Valdi	Marvin Miller

Announcers: George Walsh, Roger Krupp

Director: Walter Preston

Scattergood Baines originated in Chicago and was first heard over CBS in 1938.

School of the Air of the Americas: see *The American School of the Air.*

Science in the News

Science

Narrator: Olan Soule
Director: James Whipple

Science in the News was produced in Chicago by the University Broadcasting Council and was heard on NBC. It began in 1946.

Scotland Yard's Inspector Burke

Detective

CAST:

Inspector Burke	Basil Rathbone

Scramby Amby

Quiz

M.C.: Perry Ward
Orchestra: Charles Dant
Announcer: Larry Keating

Contestants had to unscramble words written on a blackboard. For example: NOCLUES=COUNSEL; ATACLIP=CAPITAL.

The program was first heard over ABC in 1944.

Screamers: see *Animal Imitators, Baby Criers, Doubles, Mimics, and Screamers.*

Screen Guild Theater

Drama

M.C.: Roger Pryor
Orchestra: Oscar Bradley

This program, sponsored for many years by Gulf, made its debut over CBS in 1938 and featured Hollywood stars in radio adaptations of motion-picture screenplays. Among the productions were "The Tuttles of Tahiti" with Charles Laughton and Jon Hall; "Dark Angel" with Merle Oberon, Ronald Colman, and Donald Crisp; "Design for Scandal" with Carole Landis and Robert Young; "Altar Bound" with Bob Hope, Jack Benny, and Betty Grable; "Liberty's Lady" with Loretta Young; and

"Bachelor Mother" with Henry Fonda, Laraine Day, and Charles Coburn. Other stars who appeared included Barbara Stanwyck, Clark Gable, Anna Lee, and Lucille Ball.

The Sea Hound

Adventure

CAST:

Captain Silver	Ken Daigneau
Jerry	Bobby Hastings
Carol Anderson	Janice Gilbert
Kukai	Alan Devitt
Tex	Walter Vaughn

Director: Cyril Armbrister
Writers: Floyd Miller, Frank C. Dahm

The Sea Hound was first heard over ABC in 1942.

The Sealtest Hour: see *The Rudy Vallee Show.*

Sealtest Village Store: see *Village Store.*

Second Honeymoon

Audience Participation

Featuring: Bert Parks, Dick Todd
Director: George Wiest
Writer: Don Witty

This show was first heard over ABC in 1948.

Second Husband

Serial Drama

CAST:

Brenda Cummings	Helen Menken
Grant Cummings (the second husband)	Joe Curtin
Milton Brownspun	Ralph Locke
Bill Cummings	Carleton Young
Ben Porter	Jay Jostyn
Marion Jennings	Arlene Francis
Edwards, the butler	William Podmore
Fran Cummings	Janice Gilbert Charita Bauer
Dick Cummings	Tommy Donnelly Jackie Grimes
Louise McPherson	Ethel Wilson
Irma Wallace	Joy Hathaway
Valerie Welles	Jacqueline De Wit
Marcia	Judy Blake
Peter	Dick Nelson
Dr. Mark Phillips	Vinton Hayworth

Also: Lois Hall, James Meighan, Colleen Ward, Virginia Dwyer, Nancy Bashein, John Thomas, Skippy Homeier, Peter Donald, Stefan Schnabel
Announcer: André Baruch

Producers: Frank and Anne Hummert
Writers: Helen Walpole, Nancy Moore, Elizabeth Todd

Second Husband made its debut over CBS in 1937 as a thirty-minute, evening program for Bayer Aspirin. Later it became a leading daytime serial drama. It was originally on the air Tuesdays at 7:30 p.m. In 1942 it moved to 11:15 a.m., Monday through Friday, as a fifteen-minute serial.

The Second Mrs. Burton

Serial Drama

CAST:

Terry, the second Mrs. Burton — Sharon Douglas, Claire Niesen, Patsy Campbell, Teri Keane
Mrs. Burton, the first Mrs. Burton — Evelyn Varden, Ethel Owen
Louise — Patsy Campbell
Stan Burton — Dwight Weist
Brad Burton — Dix Davis, Karl Weber, Ben Cooper, Larry Robinson
Marion — Anne Stone, Joan Alexander
Stanley — Gary Merrill
Marian Sullivan — Joan Alexander, Cathleen Cordell
Lillian Anderson — Elspeth Eric
Jim Anderson — King Calder
Greg Martin — Alexander Scourby
Mrs. Miller — Doris Rich
Don Cornwell — Robert Readick
Judge Watson — Craig McDonnell
Van Vliet, the lawyer — Rod Hendrickson
Rev. Cornwell — Bartlett Robinson
Dr. Jack Mason — Staats Cotsworth, Les Tremayne
Suzette Acheson — Helen Coulé
Jane Waters — Lois Holmes
Elizabeth Miller — Betty Caine
Wendy Burton — Madaline Lee

Announcers: Harry Clark, Hugh James
Producer-Director: Ira Ashley
Producer: Lindsay MacHarrie
Directors: Beverly Smith, Viola Burns, Stuart Buchanan
Writers: Priscilla Kent, Martha Alexander, John M. Young, Hector Chevigny
Sound Effects: Jim Dwan
Organist: Chet Kingsbury, Richard Leibert

The "first Mrs. Burton" was the "second Mrs. Burton's" mother-in-law. The program was first heard over CBS in 1945.

Secret City

Mystery

CAST:

Ben Clark — Billy Idelson

This was first heard over the Blue network in 1941.

Secret Three

Serial Drama

Featuring: Murray McLean

Seeley and Fields

Music

Starring: Blossom Seeley and Benny Fields

This song-and-patter team made frequent appearances on radio.

Sergeant Preston of the Yukon: see *Challenge of the Yukon.*

Serial Dramas: see *Soap Operas.*

Service to the Front

Drama

Producer-Directors: Bob Brown, Ted Robertson
Writers: Frank and Doris Hursley

This was a World War II program broadcast by CBS in behalf of the U.S. Army. It was first heard in 1944.

Seth Parker

Music and Serial Drama

CAST:
Seth Parker — Phillips H. Lord
Lizzie Peters — Sophia M. Lord (Mrs. Phillips H. Lord)
Ma Parker — Effie Palmer, Barbara Bruce
Jane — Joy Hathaway, Erva Giles
Captain Bang — Raymond Hunter
Cefus Peters — Bennett Kilpack
Laith Pettingal — Bennett Kilpack
George, the Captain's brother — Edward Wolters
Dr. Tanner — William Jordan
John — Richard Maxwell
Singers and neighbors: Gertrude Foster, James Black, John Kulik, Norman Price, Edwin Dunham

---

Accompanist: Polly Robertson

This program of small-town humor and hymn singing was an early show of great popularity. It was written and created by Phillips H. Lord; the setting for the stories was "Jonesport, Maine." The program was heard over NBC at 10:30 p.m. on Sundays. It made its debut in 1933.

The Shadow

Mystery-Drama

CAST:
Lamont Cranston, The Shadow — Robert Hardy Andrews, Orson Welles, Bill Johnstone, Bret Morrison (1944–56)
Margot Lane — Agnes Moorehead, Marjorie Anderson, Gertrude Warner, Grace Matthews, Lesley Woods
Commissioner Weston — Dwight Weist, Arthur Vinton, Kenny Delmar, Santos Ortega, Jimmy LaCurto, Ted de Corsia
Shrevie — Keenan Wynn, Alan Reed (Teddy Bergman), Mandel Kramer
Also: Everett Sloane, Bob Maxwell
With: John Barclay, Blue Coal's Distinguished Heating Expert
Announcers: André Baruch, Carl Caruso, Sandy Becker, Ken Roberts

---

Directors: Dana Noyes, Harry Ingram, John Cole, Chick Vincent, Bill Sweets, Wilson Tuttle
Writers: Peter Barry, Max Ehrlich, Alonzo Deen Cole, Stedman Coles, Joe Bates Smith, Nick Kogan, Robert Arthur, Jerry McGill, Bill Sweets

Organists: Rosa Rio, Elsie Thompson, Charles Paul

Theme: "Omphale's Spinning Wheel" ("Le Rouet d'Omphale," Opus 31) by Saint-Saëns

Opening:

MUSIC. *"Spinning Wheel"—fade under . . .*

THE SHADOW. (*Filter*). Who knows what evil lurks in the hearts of men? The Shadow knows! (*Laughs*)

MUSIC. *Theme up . . . segue bright theme*

ANNOUNCER. Once again your neighborhood Blue Coal dealer brings you the thrilling adventures of The Shadow . . . the hard and relentless fight of one man against the forces of evil. These dramatizations are designed to demonstrate forcibly to old and young alike that crime does not pay!

MUSIC. *Theme up . . . segue to neutral background*

ANNOUNCER. The Shadow, mysterious character who aids the forces of law and order, is in reality Lamont Cranston, wealthy young man-about-town. Several years ago in the Orient, Cranston learned a strange and mysterious secret . . . the hypnotic power to cloud men's minds so they cannot see him. Cranston's friend and companion, the lovely Margot Lane, is the only person who knows to whom the voice of the invisible Shadow belongs. Today's drama . . . "The Lady in Black."

Closing:

ANNOUNCER. *The Shadow* program is based on a story copyrighted by Street and Smith Publications. The characters, names, places, and plot are fictitious. Any similarity to persons living or dead is purely coincidental. Again next week The Shadow will demonstrate that . . .

THE SHADOW. (*Filter*). The weed of crime bears bitter fruit. Crime does not pay. The Shadow knows! (*Laughs*)

"The Shadow" made his first appearance on a program for Street & Smith's *Detective Story* magazine, which, of course, featured dramatizations of stories from the magazine. A young writer named Harry Charlot came up with the idea of the announcer being "The Shadow." Dave Chrisman and Bill Sweets of Ruthrauff and Ryan Advertising Agency carried the idea still further and had him become a narrator—an ethereal, disembodied voice that knew everything. The first actor to play the part was James LaCurto, who gave it up within a few weeks to appear on Broadway. He was succeeded by Frank Readick, who did the part for several years. The program became so successful that in order to copyright the idea Street & Smith began publishing a new magazine called *The Shadow*. Later the "Lamont Cranston" character was developed and became the model for such celebrated crime-fighters as "Superman," "Batman," and "Captain Marvel," who also lived two lives. By the time the series appeared on Mutual in 1936, "The Shadow" was no longer just the narrator but the principal character in the show.

Sheilah Graham: see *Hollywood Reporters*.

Shell Chateau

Variety

M.C.: Al Jolson
Wallace Beery
Smith Ballew
Edward Everett Horton
Vocalist: Nadine Connor
Nadine Connor's spoken voice: Mary Jane Higby
Orchestra: Victor Young
Directors: Herb Polesie, Cal Kuhl
Writers: Bob Colwell, Ed Rice, Carroll Carroll
Theme: "About a Quarter to Nine"

Shell Chateau was a program created especially to star Al Jolson. While it remained essentially a variety program, it changed in character slightly with each successive M.C.

The Sheriff

Western Adventure

CAST:
Mark Chase, Sheriff of Canyon County, California — Bob Warren, Robert Haag, Donald Briggs
Cassandra Drinkwater (Cousin Cassie) — Olyn Landick (a man)
Also: Helen Claire

Directors: Walter Scanlan, John Wilkinson, Florence Ortman

The Sheriff was heard Friday evenings on ABC. (See also *Death Valley Days.*)

Sherlock Holmes

Detective

CAST:
Sherlock Holmes — Richard Gordon, Louis Hector, Basil Rathbone, Tom Conway, Ben Wright, John Stanley
Dr. Watson — Leigh Lovel, Nigel Bruce, Eric Snowden, Alfred Shirley, Ian Martin
Moriarty — Louis Hector
With: Mr. Bell, who interviewed Sherlock Holmes and always suggested they have a cup of G. Washington coffee — Joseph Bell
Also: Agnes Moorehead, Harry Neville, Lucille Wall, Bill Shelley, Junius Matthews

Producer: Edna Best
Directors: Basil Loughrane, Joseph Bell, Tom McKnight, Glenhall Taylor
Writers: Edith Meiser, Bruce Taylor (pseudonym of Leslie Charteris) and Dennis Green, Bruce Taylor and Anthony Boucher, Howard Merrill, Max Ehrlich
Sound Effects: Bill Hoffman
Musical Director: Graham Harris
Theme: "March of the Ancestors"—based on a theme from *Ruddigore* by Gilbert and Sullivan

This program was based on the stories by Sir Arthur Conan Doyle. It was first heard over NBC in 1930. As in the original writings, Holmes frequently remarked to his friend, "Elementary, my dear Watson."

Show Boat

Variety

CAST:

Captain Henry — Charles Winninger, Frank McIntire
Captain Barnet Barnett — Carlton Brickert
Aunt Maria — Irene Hubbard
Mammy — Hattie McDaniel
Molasses 'n' January — Pat Padgett and Pick Malone
Mary Lou — Muriel Wilson (singing voice), Rosaline Greene (speaking voice)

Also: Winifred Cecil, Annette Hanshaw, Lanny Ross, Conrad Thibault, Jules Bledsoe, Frank Willoughby, Ross Graham, Sam Hearn, Edmund "Tiny" Ruffner, Jack Haley, Virginia Verrill, Warren Hull, Nadine Connor, Dick Todd, Helen Jepson, Honey Dean

Show Boat Four–Scrappy Lambert, Randolph Weyant, tenors; Leonard Stokes, baritone; Robert Moody, bass

Louise Massey and The Westerners[1]

Orchestra: Donald Voorhees, Al Goodman

Director: Kenneth W. MacGregor

Writers: Sam Perrin, Arthur B. Phillips

Catch-phrase:

CAPTAIN HENRY. It's only the beginnin', folks!

[1] See p. 218.

Show Boat, which made its debut over NBC in 1932, was a pioneer variety program. At one point the sponsor, Maxwell House coffee, tired of the show-boat locale and decided that as part of the plot the show boat would burn up, forcing the troupe to a tent-show locale. Simultaneously and coincidentally, *The Gibson Family* program had the same idea of establishing a tent-show because the Gibson youngsters were stage-struck. The Gibsons beat *Show Boat* to it, and *Show Boat* continued to travel the river. *Show Boat* was eventually replaced by *Hollywood Good News,* produced in conjunction with MGM. For the first two years Allyn Joslyn was tenor Lanny Ross's speaking voice. (See also *Hollywood Good News; The Gibson Family.*)

Sidewalk Interviews: see *Vox Pop.*

Silver Eagle, Mountie

Adventure

CAST:

Jim West — Jim Ameche
Joe Bideaux — Mike Romano, Jack Lester
Inspector Argyle — John Barclay, Jess Pugh
Doc — Clarence Hartzell
Narrator — Ed Prentiss, Bill O'Connor

Also: Dennis Price, Dick Moore, Bill Windom, Maurice Copeland, Don Gallagher, Art Peterson, Charles Flynn, Everett Clarke, Harry Elders, Jim Goss, George Cisar, Jack Bivens, Alexander McQueen, Howard Hoffman, Art Van Harvey,

Stanley Gordon, Cornelius Peeples, Johnny Coons, Sam Siegel, Paul Barnes, Art Hern, Clare Baum, Norman Gottschalk, Pat Murphy, Lester Podewell, Kurt Kupfer, Leo Curley, Frank Dane, Jim Bannon, Eloise Kummer, Fern Persons, Sondra Gair, Alma Platts, Beverly Younger, Geraldine Kay, Elmira Roessler, Vera Ward, Viola Berwick, Ilka Diehl, Sally Hughes, Leonore Allman, Nancy Brougham, Laurette Fillbrandt

Announcers: Ken Nordine, Ed Cooper

Producer-Writer-Director: James Jewell

Director: Bob Woolson

Writers: James Lawrence, Gibson Scott Fox, Thomas Elvidge, Richard Thorne, John T. Kelly

Musical Director: Richard Dix

Opening:

ANNOUNCER. (*Cold-echo*). The Silver Eagle!

SOUND. *Wolf . . . fade in galloping hoofs*

ANNOUNCER. A cry of the wild . . . a trail of danger . . . a scarlet rider of the Northwest Mounted, serving justice with the swiftness of an arrow . . .

SOUND. *Arrow effect . . . thud*

ANNOUNCER. The Silver Eagle!

RECORD. *Theme:* "Winged Messenger"

SOUND. *Blizzard . . . dog team fade in and out behind . . .*

ANNOUNCER. The untamed North . . . frontier of adventure and peril! The lone, mysterious North . . . where one man, dedicated to the motto of the Canadian Northwest Mounted Police, faces danger and death to bring in the lawless and maintain the right . . . the most famous Mountie of them all . . . The Silver Eagle!

RECORD. *Swell . . . fade out behind*

Although this ABC program was not on the air until after 1950, which would put it outside the scope of this book, it has been included because it was a radio milestone; when it went off the air on March 10, 1955, it virtually marked the end of top-flight radio adventures. It made its debut from Chicago on July 5, 1951.

Silver Eagle, Mountie was created by James Jewell, who was dubbed "Dean of the Adventure Stories," having also produced *The Lone Ranger* and *The Green Hornet* from their inception until 1938. At that time he moved from WXYZ to WWJ (Detroit stations), where he originated and directed the series titled *The Black Ace*, which introduced Danny Thomas in his first running comedy role in radio. Jewell's next writing and directing assignment was *Jack Armstrong, the All-American Boy* (1943–51).

Silver Theatre

Drama

Featuring: Guest Stars

Host: Conrad Nagel

Announcers: John Conte, Dick Joys, Roger Krupp

Writer: Joseph Russell

Opening:

ORCHESTRA. *Opening signature*

CONTE. International Silver Company presents the *Silver Theatre!*

ORCHESTRA. *Musical progression*

CONTE. Starring Lee Tracy and Shirley Ross in "Love Is Where You Find It"—directed by Conrad Nagel.

ORCHESTRA. *Musical progression*

CONTE. Brought to you in behalf of two of the greatest names in silverware . . . International Sterling, world famous solid silver . . . and 1847 Rogers Brothers, America's finest silver *plate!*

ORCHESTRA. *Theme . . . fade to background*

NAGEL. Good afternoon, ladies and gentlemen . . . this is Conrad Nagel greeting you from the stage of the *Silver Theatre* in Hollywood and bringing you the twenty-fourth in our new series of dramatic productions. But before we raise the curtain on today's performance, we'd like to announce that next week *Silver Theatre* will star Henry Fonda and Gail Patrick. Among the many brilliant stars whose names already grace our guest book for future dates are Rosalind Russell, Joan Crawford, Douglas Fairbanks, Jr., Helen Hayes, and others.

ORCHESTRA. *Curtain raiser*

Silver Theatre was first heard in 1938 over CBS. The script sample is from the broadcast of March 5, 1939—3:00–3:30 p.m. Pacific Standard Time.

The Silvertown Cord Orchestra: see *The Goodrich Silvertown Cord Orchestra.*

The Simpson Boys of Sprucehead Bay

Drama

CAST:

The Simpson Boys
Arthur Allen and Parker Fennelly

This story was set in rural New England. (See also *Snow Village.*)

The Sinclair Minstrel Show

Music

CAST:

Interlocutor: Gene Arnold
Gus Van
Spare Ribs Malcolm Claire
Sinclair Minstrel Men—Bill Childs, Cliff Soubier, Fritz Clark
Sinclair Quartet—Pat Patterson, Art Janes, Al Rice, Fritz Meissner
Orchestra: Harry Kogen

The show was originated by Gene Arnold, who first played the "Interlocutor." The Sinclair Quartet was called the Maple City Four on other shows.

Sing It Again

Music and Quiz

M.C.: Dan Seymour
Vocalists: Alan Dale, Patti Clayton, Bob Howard

Also: The Riddlers
Orchestra: Ray Bloch
Directors: Bruno Zirato, Jr., Lester Gottlieb, Rocco Tito
Writer: Johanna Johnston
Sound Effects: Jim Rinaldi

Sing It Again was first heard over CBS in 1948.

Singers

In addition to the many singers whose names appear in the cast lists, there were a number of other familiar voices that were not associated with any particular show. Among them were:

Sopranos Berenice Ackerman, Countess Olga Albani, Durelle Alexander, Josephine Antoine, Marion Claire, Vivienne Della Chiesa, Jean Dickenson, Eileen Farrell, Helen Jepson, Maria Jeritza, Ruth Lyon, Jeanette MacDonald, Lucy Monroe (famous for her renditions of "The Star-Spangled Banner"), Grace Moore, Lily Pons, Rosa Ponselle, Jane Powell, Bidu Sayao (from Brazil), and Jean Tennyson.

Contraltos Rose Bampton, Ruth Carhart, and Madame Ernestine Schumann-Heink.

Baritones John Barclay, Clyde Barrie, Jack Berch ("I'm a-whistlin' . . . are ya listenin'?"), Phil Brito, Walter Cassel, Jerry Cooper, Nelson Eddy, Wilbur Evans, Michael Loring, Everett Marshall, Barry McKinley (also an orchestra leader), Tommy McLaughlin, Robert Merrill, Vaughn Monroe (famous for singing "Racing with the Moon" and also an orchestra leader), Titta Ruffo, Whispering Jack Smith, John Charles Thomas ("Good night, Mother"), and Jerry Wayne.

Tenors Ron Alley, Gene Austin ("The Whispering Tenor"), Jimmy Brierly, Donald Dame, Tito Guizar (also a guitarist), Nino Martini, Johnny Marvin ("The Lonesome Singer of the Air"), Richard Maxwell, John McCormack, Bill Perry, Phil Regan, Lanny Ross, The Silver Masked Tenor (played by Joseph M. White, whose identity was kept secret from listeners), and Smiling Jack Smith ("The Singer with the Smile in His Voice").

Other vocalists included Juan Arvizu (a Latin-American personality), Eileen Barton, Vera Barton, Betty Bennett, Beverly (Beverly Freeland), Irene Bordoni, Roy Brower (often sang under the name of Ornamental Johnson), Carol Bruce, Julietta Burnett, Del Campo, Mindy Carson, Bernice Claire, Rosemary Clooney, Harry Cool, Don Cornell, Diane Courtney, Vic Damone, Vaughn de Leath (one of the first women to sing on the air, known as "The Original Radio Girl"), Honey Deane, Will Donaldson, Phil Duey, Laura Deane Dutton, Cliff Edwards ("Ukulele Ike"), Ruth Etting, Fran Frey (also an orchestra leader), Sylvia Froos, Patsy Garrett, Connie Gates, Bob Gibson, Art Gillham (also a pianist), Hazel Glenn, Ray Heatherton, Jackie Heller, Sarita Herrera, Peter Higgins, Burl Ives (a folk singer), Alice Joy ("Radio's Dream Girl"), Jane Joy, Helen Kane ("Boop Boop Bedoop"), Irving Kaufman ("Lazy Dan"), Jane Kaye, Ralph Kirbery ("The Dream Singer"), Evelyn Knight, Peg LaCentra, Bill Lawrence, Linda Lee, Peggy

Lee, Margo, Howard Marsh, Tony Martin, Mary McCoy, Edward McHugh ("The Gospel Singer"), Johnny Mercer (also a well-known composer of popular music), Helen Morgan, Edith Murray, Gertrude Niesen, Donald Novis, Olive Palmer, Jack Parker, Ramona, Leah Ray, Virginia Rea, Doris Rhodes, Lillian Roth, Genevieve Rowe, Olive Shea (also a noted actress), Sally Singer, Amanda Snow, Ted Steele (also an orchestra leader), Tamara (Tamara Drasin), Mel Tormé ("The Velvet Fog"), Arthur Tracy ("The Street Singer"), Anthony Trini (also a violinist), Sophie Tucker ("The Last of the Red-Hot Mamas"), Happy Jack Turner (also a pianist), Vera Van, Lee Wiley, and Willard Robinson (also an orchestra leader, known as "The Evangelist of Rhythm").

Certainly the best known of all the vocal quartets was The Ink Spots. The original members of this Negro group were tenor Ivory (Deek) Watson, bass Orville (Hoppy) Jones, baritone Charlie Fuqua, and tenor Slim Greene. Later members included Bill Kenny, Herb Kenny, Billy Bowen, and Harold Frances. Bill Kenny, who joined the group in 1934 when Slim Greene died, provided the high tenor voice that became a trademark of The Ink Spots. During a recording of "If I Didn't Care," Orville Jones is said to have forgotten the tune and resorted to reciting the lyrics, a technique that became another trademark of the group.

Among the other famous vocal quartets were The Baker Boys (Will Donaldson, Frank Luther, Jack Parker, and Phil Duey—known for their "Yo ho, yo ho, yo ho"); The Cavaliers (tenors Morton Bowe and Jack Keating; baritone John Seagle, bass Stanley McClelland, and pianist-arranger Lee Montgomery); The Charioteers (tenors Wilfred Williams and Eddie Jackson, baritone Ira Williams, bass Howard Daniel, and pianist James Sherman); The Deep River Boys (Vernon Gardner, George Lawson, Edward Ware, and Harry Douglass); The Four Southern Singers (brothers Owen, Robert, and James Ward and Annie Laurie, the wife of James); Maple City Four (Art Janes, Fritz Meissner, Pat Patterson, and Al Rice); The Martins Quartet (Ralph Blane, Hugh Martin, and sisters Phyllis and Jo-Jean Rogers); The Mills Brothers (brothers John, Jr., Herbert, Donald, and Henry —when John, Jr., died in 1935 their father, John, Sr., took his place); and The Southernaires Quartet (bass William Edmondson, baritone Jay Stone Toney; tenor Homer Smith, soloist Lowell Peters).

Among radio's other singing groups were The Andrews Sisters (Patty, Maxene, and LaVerne); The Boswell Sisters (Connee—originally spelled Connie—Vet, and Martha); The DeMarco Sisters (Lily, Mary, and Ann); The Dinning Sisters (Lou and twins Jean and Ginger); The Double Daters (Chuck Goldstein, Helen Carroll, Ruth Doring, and Ray Charles); The Fontane Sisters (Geri, Marge, and Bea); The King Sisters (Donna Driggs, Louise Driggs, Alyce Driggs, and Yvonne Driggs); The King's Guards (Ken Darby, Bud Linn, and Jon Dodson—later known as The King's Men, which added Rad Robinson); The King's Jesters (John Ravencroft, Fritz Bastow, and George

Howard); The Landt Trio (Dan, Earl, and Jack Landt—"Sing along with the Landt Trio"); The McGuire Sisters (Dorothy, Phyllis, and Christine); The Merry Macs (Joe, Ted, and Judd McMichael, Cheri McKay, and Helen Carroll); The Modernaires (originally comprised of Chuck Goldstein, Harold Dickinson, Bill Conway, and Ralph Brewster—later members included Paula Kelly, Virginia Maxey, Marian Hutton, Mel Tormé, Alan Copeland, Francis Scott, and Johnny Drake); The Pickens Sisters (Jane, Helen, and Patti Pickens); The Pied Pipers (John Huddleston, Jo Stafford, Chuck Lowry, Allen Storr, and Lee Gotch); The Revelers (James Melton, Wilfred Glenn, Lewis James, Elliott Shaw, Frank Parker, and Robert Simmons); The Rhythm Boys (originally Bing Crosby, Al Rinker, and Harry Barris—later Ice Switzler, Al Dary, George MacDonald, and Ray Kulz); The Satisfiers (Art Lambert, Helen Carroll, Bob Lange, and Kevin Gavin); The Smoothies (a trio including at various times Charlie Ryan, Babs Ryan, Little Ryan, Babs Stewart, Daisy Bernier, and Lilyan Perron); The Tastyeast Jesters (Dwight "Red" Latham, Guy Bonham, and Wamp Carlson); The Three Debutantes (Betty, Margery, and Dot); The Three Marshalls (Peggy, Kay, and Jack Marshall—actually Peggy and Kay Marshall and Hugh Martin); and Tom, Dick and Harry (Bud Vandover as Tom, Marlin Hurt as Dick, and Gordon Vandover as Harry).

There were also a number of singing twosomes: Betty and Buddy (Betty Barton and Buddy Arnold); The Blossom Sisters (Helen and Dorothy Blossom); The Delmore Brothers (Alton and Rayburn); The Eberly Brothers (Bob Eberly and Ray Eberle —the latter changed the last letter of his surname); The Frazee Sisters (Jane and Ruth Frazee); The Gold Dust Twins (Goldy and Dusty, played by Harvey Hindermyer and Earle Tuckerman); The Lane Sisters (Priscilla and Rosemary Lane); and The Luther-Layman Singers (Frank Luther and Zora Layman).

(See also *Big Band Remotes; Musicians; Orchestra Leaders;* and individual listings for variety and musical programs.

Singin' Sam, the Barbasol Man

Music

Starring: Harry Frankel as "Singin' Sam"

Theme: (Sung to the tune of "Tammany")

Barbasol, Barbasol,
No brush, no lather,
No rub-in,
Wet your razor, then begin.

"Singin' Sam" was one of radio's earliest singing stars. His first network program began on CBS in 1930.

Singing Bee

Music

Featuring: Welcome Lewis (4′10″ female singer)

The Singing Lady

Children's Stories and Songs

The Singing Lady: Ireene Wicker
Announcer: Bob Brown
Producer-Writer: Ireene Wicker
Directors: Charles Warburton, Charles Bishop
Musical Director: Milton Rettenberg

The Singing Lady made its debut over WGN Chicago in 1931 and went on the NBC Blue network six months later. The program was on the air for over twenty years with Kellogg's cereals as its long-time sponsor. Miss Wicker changed her first name from Irene to Ireene after an astrologer told her it would bring her good luck.

Singo

Musical Quiz

Starring: Welcome Lewis
With: Art Gentry, vocalist
Announcer: George Ansbro

On *Singo,* listeners could send in a combination of any three song titles which told a story or asked a question. The prize was four dollars. The contestant had to include the name of a serviceman or servicewoman with whom he would split the prize money. The "Daily Double Duet," sung by Welcome Lewis and Art Gentry, paid off double to the winner.

Sisters of the Skillet

Comedy

Starring: Ed East, Ralph Dumke

The Six-Shooter

Western Adventure

Starring: Jimmy Stewart

Although *The Six-Shooter* did not turn up on radio until 1952, it is included here because of its significance: it was a last, desperate effort by a radio network (NBC) to maintain interest in adventure drama by employing a major Hollywood movie star in the leading role.

The Sixty-Four-Dollar Question: see *Take It or Leave It.*

Skipper Jim

Children

CAST:

Skipper Jim	James Sarsfield

Skippy

Children

CAST:

Skippy	Franklin Adams, Jr.
Socky	Francis Smith
Jim Lovering	St. John Terrell

Producers: Frank and Anne Hummert
Producer-Director: David Owen

Writers: Robert Hardy Andrews, Roland Martini

This program was based on the comic strip by Percy Crosby. It first appeared over NBC in 1931.

Sky Blazers

Aviation Adventure

Narrator: Colonel Roscoe Turner, ace flier
Producer: Phillips H. Lord

Sky Blazers was first heard over CBS in 1939.

Sky King

Aviation Adventure

CAST:

Sky King	Jack Lester
	Earl Nightingale
	Roy Engel
Penny	Beryl Vaughn
Clipper	Jack Bivens
Sky King's foreman	Cliff Soubier

Writers: Abe Burrows, Roy Winsor

Sky King was first heard over ABC in 1947 from Chicago. It related the adventures of a rancher-pilot.

The Smackouts

Comedy

Starring: Jim and Marian Jordan

The Jordans performed these comedy skits before they and writer Don Quinn created the characters "Fibber McGee and Molly" (which see).

Smalltown Boys: see *Snow Village.*

Smile Time

Comedy

CAST:

Featuring:	Steve Allen
	Wendell Noble
Junie	June Foray
Manuel Labor	Wendell Noble
Claude Horribly	Steve Allen

Producer-Writer-Directors: Steve Allen, Wendell Noble
Theme:
It's Smile Time,
Time to chase your blues away.

Organist: Skitch Henderson

Smile Time, a midday hit in the 1940s, was on Mutual for two years. "Manuel Labor" was a Mexican who appeared on the show frequently. "Claude Horribly" was a character who greatly resembled Edgar Bergen's "Mortimer Snerd." One of the regular features was a satire of other programs, such as "Young Dr. Magoon" (*Young Dr. Malone*); "Life Can Be Blaah" (*Life Can Be Beautiful*); and "Dr. Ice Cube" (*Dr. I. Q.*).

The Smilin' Ed McConnell Show: see *The Buster Brown Gang.*

Smilin' Jack

Aviation Adventure

CAST:

Smilin' Jack	Frank Readick

This adventure series was based on the comic strip by Zack Mosley.

The Smith Brothers

Music

CAST:

Trade — Billy Hillpot
Mark — Scrappy Lambert

The Smith Brothers were a popular song-and-patter team in the early days of radio. They took their names from the words "Trade" and "Mark" which appeared under the respective pictures of the bearded Smith Brothers on the cough-drops package. The cough-drop makers sponsored their earliest network program over NBC in 1926.

The Smith Family

Situation Comedy

This program was first heard in 1925 over WENR Chicago and featured the vaudeville team of Jim and Marian Jordan, who later became "Fibber McGee and Molly." *The Smith Family* was one of radio's first situation-comedy serials.

Snow Village

Drama

CAST:

Dan'l Dickey — Arthur Allen
Hiram Neville — Parker Fennelly
Wilbur — John Thomas
Margie — Jean McCoy
Hattie — Agnes Young
Wilbur Z. Knox (Grandsir) — Arthur Allen
Grammie — Elsie Mae Gordon
Carrie — Katherine Raht

Writer: William Ford Manley

Snow Village was first heard in 1930. The story was set in rural New England. Arthur Allen and Parker Fennelly did several shows that were basically the same—New England characters in a New England village: *Four Corners, U.S.A.; Gibbs and Finney, General Delivery; The Simpson Boys of Sprucehead Bay; Smalltown Boys; The Stebbins Boys;* and *Uncle Abe and David.*

So This Is New York: see *Duffy's Tavern.*

So You Want to Lead a Band?

Music

Starring: The Sammy Kaye Orchestra ("Swing and Sway with Sammy Kaye")
Director: John Cleary
Writers: Bill Mogle, Marian Stearn

Audience members were invited to lead the band.

Soap Operas

Soap operas were so called because these serial dramas, aimed mainly at the daytime women's audience, were often sponsored by one soap product or another. The usual form was a fifteen-minute broadcast on Monday through Friday somewhere between 10:00 a.m. and 4:30 p.m., at which point the "soaps" gave way to the children's adventure serials. The contents of the "soap operas" rarely varied—marital difficulties, terminal illnesses, amnesia, long-lost relatives, and all the other horrors of real life seemed to settle endlessly on the soap opera heroes and heroines. The sympathetic characters were almost always given Anglo-Saxon names, while the villains often had names with a "foreign" ring.

Determining the first "soap opera" is a difficult task, but our research has shown that the prototypes were *Clara, Lu, 'n' Em; Painted Dreams; The Stolen Husband;* and *Marie, The Little French Princess*—any one of which could well lay claim to being the "first" one on the air. A program called *Henry Adams and His Book,* produced by Patt Barnes over WHT Chicago in 1925, has also been considered a prototype of serial dramas. During the late 1920s and early 1930s, these and other programs featured continuing stories about continuing characters. Many were simply read by an actor playing all the parts, but eventually there evolved the system of actors and actresses, organists and sound effects, that became the familiar method of production. The category of "soap opera" is somewhat arbitrary when you consider that *Vic and Sade* was most often broadcast as a fifteen-minute, Monday-through-Friday, daytime program, but it was no more a "soap opera" than was, say, *The Fred Allen Show.*

Most of the serial dramas were broadcast from Chicago or New York, and some of them proved to be programs of great longevity. Indeed, many actresses made a career of playing one character every day for many years: Virginia Payne as "Ma Perkins," Anne Elstner as "Stella Dallas," Mary Jane Higby as "Joan Field Davis" in *When a Girl Marries.* Among the male performers, Arthur Hughes, regarded as one of the most gifted actors in the business, spent nearly all of his career in the role of "Bill Davidson" on *Just Plain Bill.*

The production team of Frank and Anne Hummert turned out more major "soap operas" than any other producer. Of the nearly two hundred serial dramas listed in this book, the Hummerts produced, among others, *Amanda of Honeymoon Hill, Backstage Wife, David Harum, Evelyn Winters, Front Page Farrell, John's Other Wife, Just Plain Bill, Lora Lawton, Lorenzo Jones, Mrs. Wiggs of the Cabbage Patch, Nona from Nowhere, Orphans of Divorce, Our Gal Sunday, Real Stories from Real Life, The Romance of Helen Trent, Second Husband, Skippy, Stella Dallas, The Stolen Husband, Young Widder Brown*—a remarkable record indeed. The Hummerts also produced a number of programs well outside the realm of "soap operas," such as *Manhattan Merry-Go-Round* and *Mr. Chameleon.*

Few people came to know the Hummerts intimately. Most of those associated with this husband-and-wife team regarded them as a stern, Victorian couple who expected their employees to adhere to a rigid moral code. Employing many writers and directors who worked in conditions not unlike a sweatshop, the Hummerts personally supervised every story outline, all the scripts and character development, and every aspect of the on-the-air production. The success of their serials attests to their meticulous craftsmanship.

(For information on Irna Phillips, the prolific writer of "soap operas," see *The Guiding Light*.) (See also Bibliography: Stedman, *The Serials*.)

Society Girl

Serial Drama

CAST:

Bryn Clark Barrington — Charlotte Manson
Russ Barrington — Philip Reed
Dexter Hayes — Jim Backus
Bryn's brother — Carleton Young

Also: Guest Celebrities
Director: Ted Cott
Writers: David Davidson, Jerome Ross
Organist: Ted Steele

The story of *Society Girl* was set in New York City. The program was first heard over CBS in 1939.

Song of the Stranger

Adventure

CAST:

Pierre Varnay, the Stranger — Bret Morrison

Writer: Doris Halman

The Song Shop

Music

Featuring: Kitty Carlisle and Alice Cornett, vocalists

Songs by Sinatra

Music

Starring: Frank Sinatra
Vocal group: The Pied Pipers
Orchestra: Axel Stordahl
Also: Guest Vocalists
Announcer: Marvin Miller
Producer-Director: Mann Holiner
Writer: Frank Wilson

This program was heard over CBS from 1945 to 1947 and was sponsored by Old Gold cigarettes. See also *The Frank Sinatra Show; Songs for Sinatra; Your Hit Parade.*

Songs for Sale

Music and Comedy

Host: Jan Murray
Richard Hayes
Vocalist: Rosemary Clooney
Orchestra: Ray Bloch

This program featured amateur songwriters whose music was performed by professionals. It was first heard over CBS in 1950.

Songs for Sinatra

Music

Starring: Frank Sinatra

This program began over CBS in 1947 as a replacement for *Songs by Sinatra.*

Songs of the B-Bar-B

Music and Comedy

CAST:
Bobby Benson — Ivan Cury
Windy Wales, the handyman — Don Knotts
Tex Mason — Herb Rice
Tex Fletcher
Al Hodge
Tex Ritter
Announcer: "Cactus" Carl Warren

Writer: James McMenemy

This program was the music and comedy version of *Bobby Benson's Adventures* (which see).

Sons of the Pioneers

Western Music

Sons of the Pioneers was a well-known vocal group led by Bob Nolan, the composer of "Tumblin' Tumbleweeds." The others in the group were Pat Brady, Hugh Farr, Karl Farr, and Lloyd Perryman.

Sorry, Wrong Number: see *Suspense.*

Sound-Effects Men

Clearly the unsung heroes were the sound-effects men. Without these diligent, uniquely talented individuals (who have been classified somewhere between performers and technicians since they were a little of both), radio comedy and drama would have been considerably less effective, if not impossible. Their work was, in general, taken for granted by directors and casts. To the listeners of dramatic scenes, they didn't exist—at least they didn't exist if they were doing their jobs properly. The principal assignment was to create the appropriate mood and environment for various scenes. For example, a scene in a city might be introduced by traffic noises, while a rural scene might call for the sound of chirping crickets. Other commonly used, artificially created sounds were thunder, ocean roar, lapping water, horses' hoofbeats, coyote howls, gunfire, singing birds, office typewriters, marching soldiers, frying foods, various automobile and airplane effects, opening and closing doors and footsteps.

Footstep effects are a good example of the lengths to which the more imaginative sound-effects men would go for authenticity. A woman's footsteps would be made to sound different from those of a man so the listener wouldn't become confused. The speed of the walk would be important too, so the listener would know at once whether the character was sneaking, running, or just strolling leisurely. In action, the late Gene Twombly would slip on his special "walking" shoes—tight-fitting and with wooden soles and heels—and, standing in one spot on a board, seem almost to tap dance as he produced the effects of one man walking or two men running or "a fat lady in a tight girdle walking up stairs." As one of Jack Benny's sound-effects men, Gene was not allowed to do Benny's footsteps until he had practiced for many months and finally passed the approval of Benny himself.

In most instances the sound was unobtrusive and subtle. On comedy shows, however, the sound-effects man was often required to exaggerate for comic effect. Easily the most famous of all comedy sound effects was the weekly routine opening of Fibber McGee's hall closet (for details, see *Fibber McGee and Molly*). The horrendous cacophony of sirens and alarms when Jack Benny opened his vault and Mel Blanc's vocal sound effects as Benny's Maxwell automobile are other well-remembered comic sound effects.

As mentioned, occasionally a sound effect was produced vocally, but usually the reliance was on mechanically or manually produced effects; half-coconut shells pounded rhythmically in a small box of dirt for a posse of cowboys; a large balloon filled with bird shot shaken vigorously for thunder; and a huge wooden tank of water in which a plunger was inserted when a dive into water was required. Simultaneously a three or four turntable amplifier would be employed to play records of rain, waves lapping, automobiles and airplanes, and other effects not possible otherwise. The need for an unusual effect called for great imagination on the part of the creators. One of the most famous occurred on *Lights Out* where the writer described a man being turned inside out. The sound-effects men solved this one by slowly and excruciatingly removing a tight rubber glove from one hand while the other man crunched strawberry boxes to represent the breaking bones.

The importance of the sound-effects men became obvious when a cue was missed or the effect was not convincingly performed. In such instances the scene could be ruined, and, particularly in the years when shows were live, such a slip might destroy the scene and cause the director to explode in anger or send the cast into fits of laughter. One of the most famous of these "fluffs" was when, in a dramatic moment, a sound-effects pistol jammed briefly, causing this sequence:

ACTOR. You swine! I'm going to take this pistol and shoot you. Take this!

SOUND. *Silence*

ACTOR (*thinking quickly*). My gun . . . it's jammed! Luckily I have this knife and I'll stab you with it. Take this!

SOUND. *Gunshot, loud and clear*

Sound-effects men—and that expression is not totally accurate as a few women learned the trade, notably Ora Nichols—were part of one of the pioneer radio unions, AGRAP (American Guild of Radio Announcers and Performers, which also included directors in its membership).

Among the busiest men in sound effects, in addition to those listed under specific programs, were Jack Amerine, Ed Blainey, Joe Cabibbo, Fred Cole (the penguin in the Kools commercials), Manny Cramer, Keene Crockett, Ralph Curtis, Jerry De Carlo, Jimmy Dwan, Ray Erlenborn, Harry Essman, Ronald Fitzgerald, Agnew Horine, Elliott Grey, Ray Kelly, Gene Twombly, Harold Johnson, Jr., Fred Knoepfke, Billy Gould, Bud Tollefson, Ed Ludes, Ray Kremer, Edward Fenton, Ross Martindale, Jack Wormser, Lloyd J. Creekmore, Ross Murray, William McClintock, Harry Nelson, Kjell Pederson, John Powers, Bob Prescott, William B. Hoffman, Clem Waters, Ted Slade, Jimmy Rinaldi, Jim Rogan, Terry Ross, Zale Dillon, Fritz Street, Walter Gustafson, Vic Rubi, James Flynn, Harry Saz, and Max Uhlig.

The Sparrow and the Hawk

Adventure

CAST:

Lieutenant-Colonel Spencer Mallory, The Hawk — Michael Fitzmaurice
His nephew Barney Mallory, The Sparrow — Donald Buka
Laura Weatherby — Susan Douglas
Tony — Joe Julian
The Hawk's mother — Mary Hunter

Director: Richard Sanville
Writers: Carl Alfred Buss, Larry Menkin

This was a dramatic adventure serial concerning a teen-age aviator and his uncle, a former lieutenant-colonel in the Army Air Corps. The program was first heard over CBS in 1945.

Speak Up, America

Educational Quiz

The Wordmaster: Vincent Pelletier

Special Agent

Adventure

CAST:

Insurance Investigator Alan Drake — James Meighan
His assistant — Lyle Sudrow

Special Delivery

Serial Drama

CAST:

Tiny Woodward — Marian Randolph
Aunt Mary — Irene Hubbard

This story concerned life in a small college town.

Spelling Bee

Quiz

M.C.: Paul Wing

Spelling Bee was first heard over the Blue network in 1937 on Saturdays at 8:30 p.m.

The Spike Jones Show

Music and Comedy

Starring: Spike Jones and His City Slickers, musical satirists
Featuring: Dorothy Shay, "The Park Avenue Hillbilly"
Also: Doodles Weaver, George Rock, Dick and Freddy Morgan

Spin to Win

Quiz

M.C.: Warren Hull

This was first heard over NBC Blue in 1940.

Sports and Sportscasters

Sports were an important element of network radio from the earliest days on. Even now, many fans insist they enjoyed the radio descriptions of great sports events more than they enjoy watching them today on television, which somehow doesn't always capture the glamour and excitement created by the great sportscasters in those early days. The standard events covered by radio included the World Series, the All-Star baseball game, the Army-Navy and post-season football bowl games, the Kentucky Derby, championship boxing matches (in Joe Louis's heyday they were among the greatest of all audience draws), and the Indianapolis 500.

In the early days staff announcers were frequently assigned to describe sporting events as routinely as they might be sent to cover a news story or broadcast a band remote. Then these announcers gave way to specialists with a thorough knowledge of sports. Eventually the networks began to hire famous sports personalities, such as Tom Harmon, dubbed "Old Number 98," his uniform number at Michigan, where he was an All-America halfback; Harold "Red" Grange, the Illinois All-America halfback known as "The Galloping Ghost"; and Jerome "Dizzy" Dean, the great pitcher for the Cardinals and Cubs and the bane of English teachers for his ungrammatical expressions ("He slud into third" and "They throwed him out at second"). In 1932, long before the networks employed these athletes, a former Cleveland Indians outfielder named Jack Graney broadcast Cleveland games, thereby becoming the first well-known athlete to become a sportscaster.

On April 11, 1921, Pittsburgh sportswriter Florent Gibson described over KDKA Pittsburgh the lightweight boxing match between Johnny Ray and Johnny Dundee—the first live sports event ever broadcast. On July 2, 1921, Major J. Andrew White, a news commentator, relayed the description of the Dempsey–Carpentier fight from Boyle's Thirty Acres in Jersey City, New Jersey. The bout was broadcast over WJY. However, the listeners heard not White's voice but that of technician J. O. Smith, who repeated White's description into the microphone. (Dempsey won with a fourth-round KO.) On August 5, 1921, Harold Arlin did the first broadcast of a baseball game. It was carried over KDKA Pittsburgh. (The Pirates beat the Phillies 8–5.) Arlin was also the first sportscaster to describe a football game and a tennis match.

Among the other early sportscasters were Truman Bradley, Pat Flanagan, Tom Manning, Hal Totten, Ty Tyson, and Gunnar Wiig. But the most renowned of all was Graham McNamee, who was also a top-flight program announcer. (He served as a foil for Ed Wynn on *The Fire Chief.*) McNamee pioneered many of the sportscasting techniques and expressions that are still in use today. He is properly known as "the father of sportscasting."

Ted Husing is also in a class by himself and is regarded by many fans as the greatest of all sportscasters. Clem McCarthy stands foremost as the top horse-racing sportscaster of his day. It wouldn't have been an important horse race if Clem McCarthy was not at the mike to growl into the microphone his familiar, terse greeting: "Racing fans!"

The most controversial sportscaster of radio's Golden Age was Bill Stern. His emotionally charged, piercing delivery made him ideally suited for play-by-play action, but he had a tendency toward exaggeration and overdramatization. A common complaint was that a fan watching the game while listening to Stern describing it over a portable radio would not recognize it as the same game. A routine pass play, for example, often generated this excited description: "There goes a long, *long*, LONG, LONG pass!!!" A player dropping a pass would often evoke such compassion as: "He *had* it and he *dropped* it! How do you think that boy feels now?" During broadcasts of Notre Dame games he often remarked: "There's a little lady listening to this game today," a reference to the widow of Notre Dame's immortal coach Knute Rockne. When the ball rested at midfield Stern occasionally interjected: "Please don't ask me *whose* fifty-yard line!" His vivid imagination carried over to his highly rated *Sports Newsreel* program, where he elevated Dwight Eisenhower to the All-America roster, revealed that Pope Pius XII had been a baseball player in his youth, made super sports stars of countless prominent politicians, actors, and other celebrities who had, in fact, only dabbled in athletics, and on one occasion related the story of a baseball player who suffered a fatal heart attack between third base and home and was dead when he scored the winning run! Despite such flagrant fictionalization, Stern created tremendous interest in sports, particularly college football. He was clearly the most listened-to sportscaster of his day. Those who criticized his lack of concern for veracity admitted to his great talent as an entertainer, and few questioned his knowledge of sports, his energy, sense of timing, and announcing skill.

A number of sportswriters became well known as sports commentators. Among them were Bob Considine (also a noted news commentator); Grantland Rice (his All-America selections were considered by many fans to be the most authentic of all); Halsey Hall; and Bill Corum, who appeared at countless World Series and prizefight broadcasts to make succinct comments on the action in his gravel-voice. Certainly the most prominent boxing announcer was Don Dunphy, who became famous for his ringside descriptions of championship fights.

Several sportscasters (including Ford Bond, Ed Thorgersen, Paul Douglas, Bill Slater, and Mel Allen) served as program announcers in addition to covering sports. Allen eventually specialized in sports, and for many years this native of Birmingham, Alabama, was "The Voice of the Yankees." He was also a fixture on broadcasts of the World Series and the Rose Bowl. His catch-phrase "How *about* that?"—which he often used following an outstanding play—became a household expression.

Among the other famous sportscasters of radio's Golden Age were Sam Taub, Walter Lanier "Red" Barber ("The Ol' Redhead"), Jim Britt, Bill Munday, Gordon McLendon (see *Liberty Baseball*), Sam Balter, Bill Brandt, Russ Hodges, Bob Elson (*"He's* out," Bob would say casually following a close play at first base), Stan Lomax, Arch MacDonald, Quin Ryan, Jack Drees, Joe Foss, Jack Brickhouse, Bert Wilson ("I don't care who wins just so it's the Cubs"), Harry Wismer, and Van Patrick.

Many sponsors picked up the tab for broadcasting sporting events, but, without question, the most consistent sports advertiser was the Gillette Safety Razor Company, whose commercials were a part of countless sports broadcasts that made up *The Gillette Cavalcade of Sports.*

The Sports Newsreel Starring Bill Stern: see *The Colgate Sports Newsreel Starring Bill Stern.*

The Squeaking Door: see *Inner Sanctum.*

Stage Door Canteen

Variety

M.C.: Bert Lytell
Orchestra: Raymond Paige
Writer: Frank Wilson

The radio studio from which *Stage Door Canteen* was broadcast was designed to resemble an actual canteen for servicemen. Members of the orchestra wore busboy aprons. Countless celebrities visited the program—among them, Alexander Woollcott, Jeanette MacDonald, Merle Oberon, and Wendell Willkie. The program, suggested by actress Helen Menken, had its première over CBS in July 1942.

Starring Boris Karloff

Mystery

Starring: Boris Karloff

Stars over Hollywood

Drama

Featuring: Basil Rathbone, Alan Hale, Sr., Brenda Marshall, Brenda Joyce, Ann Rutherford
Orchestra: Del Castillo
Announcers: Frank Goss, Marvin Miller (1944–45)
Directors: Les Mitchel, Don Clark, Paul Pierce
Sound Effects: Jack Dick

This was a Saturday-morning series of original dramas. It was first broadcast over CBS in 1941.

The Stebbins Boys

Drama

CAST:

Esly	Parker Fennelly
John	Arthur Allen

This had its première over NBC in 1931. (See also *Snow Village*.)

The Steelmakers: see *The Musical Steelmakers*.

Stella Dallas

Serial Drama

CAST:

Stella Dallas	Anne Elstner
Stephen Dallas	Frederick Tozere
Helen Dallas	Julie Benell
Laurel Dallas Grosvenor ("Lolly Baby")	Joy Hathaway
	Vivian Smolen
Dick Grosvenor	Carleton Young
	Macdonald Carey
	Spencer Bentley
	George Lambert
	Michael Fitzmaurice
Charlie Martin	Frank Lovejoy
	Tom Tully
Beatrice Martin	Mary Jane Higby
Sam Ellis	Mandel Kramer
Nellie Ellis	Barbara Barton
Mr. Bruce	Harold Vermilyea
Vera Johnson	Helene Carew
Lewis Johnson	Raymond Bramley
Ada Dexter	Helen Claire
Dr. Ramey	Luis Van Rooten
Thomas	Henry M. Neeley
Agatha Griswold	Ara Gerald
Gus Grady	Walter Kinsella
Bob James	Albert Aley
	Warren Bryan
Mercedes	Joan Lorring
Ora Mount	Elizabeth Morgan
Lester	Hal Studer
Hilda	Dorothy Sands
Claude Duff	Paul Potter
Morgan Ford	Richard Gordon
Madge Harte	Elaine Kent
Fletcher	Kenneth Daigneau
Mrs. Grosvenor	Jane Houston
Minnie Grady	Grace Valentine
Ed Munn	Arthur Vinton
Philip Baxter	Bill Smith
Dr. Alan Simms	John Brewster
Merle Chatwin	Ethel Everett
Madeline Carter	Nancy Sheridan
Jerry	William Quinn
Jack	Peter Donald

Also: Ed Begley, Raymond Edward Johnson

Announcers: Ford Bond, Howard Claney, Frank Gallop, Jack Costello, Jimmy Wallington, Roger Krupp

---

Producers: Frank and Anne Hummert

Directors: Richard Leonard, Ernest Ricca, Norman Sweetser

Writers: Helen Walpole, Frank and Anne Hummert

Organist: Richard Leibert

Sound Effects: Agnew Horine

Themes: "How Can I Leave You?" "Memories" was played for a period of six weeks only, to satisfy a sponsor

Opening:

ANNOUNCER. We give you now . . . *Stella Dallas* . . . a continuation on the air of the true-to-life story of mother love and sacrifice, in which Stella Dallas saw her own beloved daughter Laurel marry into wealth and society and, realizing the differences in their tastes and worlds, went out of Laurel's life. These episodes in the later life of Stella Dallas are based on the famous novel of that name by Olive

Higgins Prouty . . . and are written by Frank and Anne Hummert.

Closing:

ANNOUNCER. This chapter in the later life of Stella Dallas is written by Frank and Anne Hummert and is based on the famous character created by Olive Higgins Prouty in her great novel. *Stella Dallas* will be on the air at this same time Monday. This is Howard Claney speaking and reminding you to buy Savings Bonds.

The first broadcast of *Stella Dallas* was over NBC on October 25, 1937. Anne Elstner, who portrayed Stella, a seamstress in a little Boston shop, commuted to New York five days a week from Stockton, New Jersey, but missed only two broadcasts in the eighteen and a half years the program was on the air.

Stepmother

Serial Drama

CAST:

Kay Fairchild, the stepmother — Sunda Love, Janet Logan, Charlotte Manson
John Fairchild, Kay's husband — Francis X. Bushman, Bill Green, Charles Penman, Willard Waterman
Peggy Fairchild — Peggy Wall, Barbara Fuller
Mrs. Fletcher — Edith Davis
Adella Winston — Cornelia Osgood
Genevieve Porter — Ethel Owen, Donelda Currie, Betty Arnold
Leonard Clark — Ken Christy
Reginald Brooks — Marvin Miller
Bud Fairchild — Cornelius Peeples
David Houseman — Harry Elders
Mother Fairchild — Bess McCammon
Edith Wood — June Meredith
Pat Rority — Stan Gordon
Boss McKinney — Stan Gordon
Mattie, the maid — Edith Davis, Guila Adams
Bert Weston — John Larkin, Robert Guilbert
Jim — Robert Guilbert
Billy Fairchild — Elmira Roessler, Jane Gilbert
Andy Clayton — Forrest Lewis, Don Gallagher
Ginnie Sawyers — Dorothy Gregory
Jamie O'Connor — Dick Ahearne
Luella Hayworth — Betty Hanna
Pop — Francis "Dink" Trout
Gerald Lowe — Karl Weber

Announcer: Roger Krupp

Directors: Les Weinrot, Art Glad
Writer: Roy Maypole, Jr.

Stepmother was first heard over CBS in 1937 from Chicago.

The Stolen Husband

Serial Drama

This early prototype of "soap operas" was created by Robert Hardy Andrews and produced by Frank and Anne Hummert in 1931. Originally the story was simply read by one actor who played all the parts, but eventually a full cast was assembled to do the roles.

Stoopnagle and Budd

Comedy

CAST:

Colonel Lemuel Q. Stoopnagle — F. Chase Taylor
Budd — Wilbur Budd Hulick
Girl stooges — Joan Banks, Alice Frost

Vocalist: Gogo DeLys
Orchestra: Donald Voorhees, Peter Van Steeden
Announcer: Harry Von Zell

Theme: "Chopsticks" (described as being "played on the mighty gas-pipe organ")

This zany comedy team was first heard over CBS at 8:15 p.m., three times a week, and later on Thursdays at 7:30 p.m. With Budd as straight man, the Colonel would tell him about his inventions, such as a twelve-foot pole for people he wouldn't touch with a ten-foot pole. This was also known as *The Gloom Chasers.*

Stop and Go

Quiz

M.C.: Joe E. Brown

Stop Me If You've Heard This One

Comedy

M.C.: Roger Bower
Also: Milton Berle, Jay C. Flippen, Harry Hershfield
Orchestra: Horace Heidt
Director: Mitch Benson
Writer: Ray Harvey

This program featured joke-telling by prominent comedians. It was first heard over Mutual in 1947.

Stop That Villain

Comedy Quiz

M.C.'s: Jack Bailey and Marvin Miller
Writer-Director: Hobart Donovan

This program made its debut over Mutual in 1944. One of the M.C.'s (Jack Bailey) was the villain who tried to upset and distract the studio contestants and make them give wrong answers. The other (Marvin Miller) was helpful, steering contestants to the correct answers.

Stop the Music

Musical Quiz

M.C.: Bert Parks
Vocalists: Kay Armen, Dick Brown
Orchestra: Harry Salter
Also: Happy Felton
Director: Mark Goodson
Writer: Howard Connell

On this program, which made its debut over ABC in 1948, musical selections were played. If the number was sung, the vocalist hummed the song title but sang the rest of the lyrics clearly. Meantime, a telephone call was placed to a home somewhere in the United States. When the connection came through, a telephone bell was sounded and Bert Parks called out, "Stop the Music!" If the person at home could name the selection, a prize was awarded. In addition, contestants had a chance to guess the "Mystery Melody" for a giant jackpot.

Stop the Music was an immediate success; so much so that Fred Allen, who was on at the same time, announced a bond guaranteeing $5000 to anyone who was called by *Stop the Music* while listening to *The Fred Allen Show*.

Stories by Olmsted

Drama

Story-teller: Nelson Olmsted
Director: Norman Felton

All the characters in these stories were portrayed by the narrator, Nelson Olmsted.

Stories of the Black Chamber

Drama

CAST:

Bradley Drake, Chief of the American Black Chamber	Jack Arthur
Steve, his aide	Paul Nugent
Betty Lee Andrews	Helen Claire
Paradine, the master spy	Gale Gordon
Joyce Carraway, Paradine's assistant	Rosaline Greene
Thornton Oliver	Morgan Farley

The Story of Bess Johnson

Serial Drama

CAST:

Bess Johnson	Bess Johnson
Mr. Jordan	Joseph Curtin
Mrs. Jordan	Irene Winston
Mrs. Townsend	Agnes Moorehead
Natalie Holt	Nancy Marshall
Barbara Bartlett	Mitzi Gould
Wally Scudder	Donald Briggs
Dr. Franklin	Eric Dressler
Arthur Bartlett	Walter Vaughn
Patricia Jordan	Adrienne Marden
Whitney Lewis	Bill Johnstone

Writer: William Sweets

In March 1941 *Hilltop House* became *The Story of Bess Johnson* on NBC. The Bess Johnson character and the actress who played her moved to become superintendent of a boarding school. (See also *Hilltop House*.)

The Story of Bud Barton: see *The Barton Family*.

The Story of Mary Marlin

Serial Drama

CAST:

Mary Marlin	Joan Blaine
	Anne Seymour
	Betty Lou Gerson
	Muriel Kirkland
	Eloise Kummer
	Linda Carlon
Sally Gibbons	Anne Seymour
	Elinor Harriot

Henry Matthews
Raymond Edward Johnson
Bill Taylor — Gene Morgan
Daniel Burke — Gene Burke
Frances Moran Matthews
Bess Johnson
David Post — Carlton Brickert
Arthur Jacobson
Joe Marlin — Robert Griffin
Campbell B. Campbell — Clare Baum
Eve Underwood — June Meredith
Annie, the maid — Judith Lowry
Betty Caine
Bunny Mitchell — Fran Carlon
Templeton Fox
Frazier Mitchell — Phil Lord
Fred Sullivan
Doc Sharpe — Murray Forbes
Mac McKenna — John C. Daly
Miss Wood — Charlotte Learn
Barbara Crayley — Mary Jane Higby
Jay Meredith
Abner Peabody — William A. Lee
Maria — Patsy O'Shea
Henrietta Dorne — Betty Lou Gerson
Peter Fortune — Jess Pugh
Michael Dorne — Harvey Hays
Francis X. Bushman
Never-Fail Hendricks — Frank Dane
William A. Lee
Sarah Jane Kane — Helen Behmiller
Charme Allen
Robert Malloy — Bob Bailey
Rufus Kane — Rupert LaBelle
Timothy — Frankie Pacelli
Hennessy, head nurse — Joan Vitez
Cynthia Adams — Loretta Poynton
Marge Adams — Constance Crowley
Isabel Randolph
Jonathan — Bret Morrison
Bob White
Philo Sands (Sandy) — Barry Drew
Arthur Adams — DeWitt McBride
Bob Fiske
Tanya — Olga Rosenova
Davey Marlin — Jerry Spellman
Bobby Dean Maxwell
Dolores Gillen
Dennie McKenzie
Eddie Firestone, Jr.
Bill Lipton
Peter Hujaz — Arthur Peterson
Arnold, the butler — Arthur Kohl
Robert White
Joe Post — Arthur Jacobson
Oswald Ching — Peter Donald
Giles Henning — Arnold Moss
Franklin Adams — Bill Adams
Penny — Judy Blake
Tootie — Rosemary Garbell
Grandma — Joan Blaine
George Crabbe — Billy Lee
Parker — Earl George
Olga — Sharon Grainger
Irina and Lina Troyer (twins)
Gerta Rozan
Mrs. Hopkins — Eunice Howard
Caroline — Lucille Husting
Edith — Marjorie Hannan
Eugene — Murray Forbes
McKenna — Bob Fiske
Nora — Isabel Randolph
Elizabeth Fortune — Judith Lowry
Eric Cunningham — Bob White
Sheri Velentine — Elinor Harriot
Pietro Franchoni — Frank Dane

Announcers: Truman Bradley, Les Griffith, Nelson Case, John Tillman

---

Creator-Writer: Jane Crusinberry
Directors: Basil Loughrane, Don Cope, Kirby Hawkes, Ed Rice
Pianists: Joe Kahn, Allan Grant
Theme: "Clair de Lune" by Debussy

"Mary Marlin" was a senator who was, naturally, very active in politics. When the program originated from Chicago the title role was played successively by Joan Blaine, Anne Seymour, and Betty Lou Gerson. When it was broadcast from New York, Anne Seymour again took over the role, followed by Muriel Kirkland, Eloise Kummer, and Linda Carlon. The program made its debut on WMAQ Chicago on October 3, 1934, and went to the full NBC network at 5:00 p.m. on January 1, 1935.

The Story of Ruby Valentine: see *We Love and Learn.*

Story to Order

Children

These dramas, written and narrated by Lydia Perera, were written to order. Children would write in and suggest three subjects to be woven into an original story.

Straight Arrow

Western Adventure

CAST:

Straight Arrow — Howard Culver

Director: Ted Robertson
Writer: Sheldon Stark
Sound Effects: Tom Hanley, Ray Kemper

Opening:

MUSIC. *Indian rhythm up and under . . .*

ANNOUNCER. N-A-B-I-S-C-O
Nabisco is the name to know.
For a breakfast you can't beat
Try Nabisco Shredded Wheat.

MUSIC. *Up full and out*

ANNOUNCER. Keen eyes fixed on a flying target . . . a gleaming arrow set against a rawhide string . . . a strong bow bent almost to the breaking point . . . and then . . .

SOUND. *Bowstring released followed by musical shimmer, then sound of arrow reaching target*

ANNOUNCER. *Straight Arrow!*

MUSIC. *Up and under . . .*

ANNOUNCER. Nabisco Shredded Wheat presents *Straight Arrow*, a new and thrilling adventure story from the exciting days of the Old West. To friends and neighbors alike, Steve Adams appeared to be nothing more than the young owner of the Broken Bow cattle spread. But when danger threatened innocent people and when evildoers plotted against justice, then Steve Adams, rancher, disappeared and . . . in his place . . . came a mysterious, stalwart Indian wearing the dress and warpaint of a Comanche, riding the great golden palomino—Fury. Galloping out of the darkness to take up the cause of law and order throughout the West comes the legendary figure of . . . Straight Arrow!

This series first appeared over Mutual in 1948.

Strange as It Seems

Drama

Narrator: Gayne Whitman
Patrick McGeehan
Creator-Producer: Cyril Armbrister

This program featured dramatizations of the newspaper cartoon series by John Hix. It was first heard over CBS in 1939.

The Strange Dr. Karnac

Mystery

CAST:

Dr. Karnac, a sleuth James Van Dyk
His assistant Jean Ellyn

The Strange Dr. Weird

Chiller Drama

CAST:

Dr. Weird Maurice Tarplin
Announcer: Dick Willard

Director: Jock MacGregor
Writer: Robert A. Arthur

These fifteen-minute chillers were sponsored by Adam Hats while on the Mutual network.

The Strange Romance of Evelyn Winters: see *Evelyn Winters.*

Strange Wills

Drama

CAST:

Investigator Warren William
Also: Lurene Tuttle, Howard Culver, Marvin Miller
Orchestra: Del Castillo

Producer: Carl Kraatz
Director: Robert M. Light

This syndicated series had its première in 1946. It dramatized unusual bequests and hunts for missing heirs.

Streamliner's Show

Comedy

Featuring: Arthur Fields, Fred Hall
Orchestra: Jerry Sears

Strike It Rich

Audience Participation

M.C.: Todd Russell
Warren Hull
Announcer: Ralph Paul
Producer-Writer-Director: Walt Framer
Directors: Larry Harding, Jack Tyler

This quiz program featured contestants who tried to win prizes and gifts because of their hardships, which they enumerated in the course of the program. One of the features of the program was "The Heartline," a large red heart set up on the stage. When it was lit up, a phone would ring and the M.C. would inform the audience that a call had come from a manufacturer or someone at home offering gifts to the contestants. The program was first heard over CBS in 1947.

Studio One

Drama

Producer-Director: Fletcher Markle
Director: Robert J. Landry
Writer: Vincent McConnor

Studio One presented hour-long dramatizations of literature, often from the classics. It was first broadcast on CBS in 1947.

Sue and Irene: see *Painted Dreams*.

Sunday Mornings at Aunt Susan's

Drama

CAST:

Aunt Susan — Elaine Ivans
Also: Harry Swan, Artells Dickson, Vivian Block, Albert Aley

Director: Nila Mack

This hour-long CBS family potpourri was broadcast on Sunday mornings in the mid-thirties.

Superman

Adventure Serial

CAST:

Superman, alias Clark Kent, mild-mannered reporter for The Daily Planet — Clayton "Bud" Collyer, Michael Fitzmaurice
Lois Lane, girl reporter — Joan Alexander
Editor Perry White — Julian Noa
Jimmy Olsen, office boy — Jackie Kelk
Beanie, office boy — Jackson Beck
Batman — Stacy Harris, Gary Merrill, Matt Crowley
Robin — Ronald Liss
Narrator — Jackson Beck, George Lowther, Frank Knight
Also: Mandel Kramer, George Petrie, Robert Dryden, Guy Sorel

Producer-Writer-Directors: Robert and Jessica Maxwell, George Lowther
Directors: Allen DuCovny, Mitchell Grayson
Writer: B. P. Freeman
Sound Effects: Jack Keane

Catch-phrase:
SUPERMAN. Up, up and a-way!

Opening:
ANNOUNCER. Kellogg's Pep . . . the super-delicious cereal . . . presents . . . *The Adventures of Superman!* Faster than a speeding bullet!
SOUND. *Rifle bullet ricochet*
ANNOUNCER. More powerful than a locomotive!
SOUND. *Locomotive effect*
ANNOUNCER. Able to leap tall buildings at a single bound!
SOUND. *Burst of wind, level and fluctuate behind announcer and voices . . .*
ANNOUNCER. Look! Up in the sky!
VOICE 1. It's a bird!
VOICE 2 (*female*). It's a plane!
VOICE 3 (*big*). It's Superman!

"Superman" was "a strange visitor from another planet" ("Krypton") who fought criminals and disguised himself as mild-mannered "Clark Kent," reporter for "The Daily Planet," a large metropolitan newspaper in the city of Metropolis. The actor who played "Superman" used a relatively high-pitched tone for "Clark Kent" and then a deep, powerful tone for "Superman." The voice change usually occurred in the middle of the line: "This looks like a job—for Superman!" "Batman" and "Robin" occasionally appeared as guests. *Superman* was based on the comic strip created by Jerry Siegel and Joe Shuster. The series first came to radio via the Mutual network in 1940.

Superstition

Drama

The Voice of Superstition: Ralph Bell
Director: Robert Sloane
Writers: Robert Sloane, Albert Aley

This was a thirty-minute fantasy drama of the mid-forties broadcast on ABC.

Surprise Package

Audience Participation

M.C.: Jay Stewart

Surprise Party

Audience Participation

M.C.: Stu Wilson
Director: Dave Young

Suspense

Drama

CAST:

The Man in Black	Joe Kearns
Narrator	Paul Frees

Guest Stars: Cary Grant, Ida Lupino, Agnes Moorehead, Lucille Ball, Orson Welles, Brian Donlevy, *et al.*
Announcer: Truman Bradley
Producers: Charles Vanda, Elliott Lewis
Directors: William Spier, Norman Macdonnell, John Peyser, Tony Leader
Writers: Joseph Russell, Sigmund Miller, Robert Richards, Joseph L. Greene, Ferrin N. Fraser
Sound Effects: Ross Murray, Jack Sixsmith, Dave Light, Gus Bayz

These tales were "well calculated to keep you in—Suspense." One of the most popular productions was "Sorry, Wrong Number," starring Agnes Moorehead. It was repeated many times by popular request. This series began over CBS in 1942.

Sweeney and March

Comedy

Starring: Bob Sweeney, Hal March
Vocalist: Patsy Bolton
Orchestra: Irving Miller
Directors: Sterling Tracy, Manny Mannheim
Writers: Bob Sweeney, Hal March, Manny Mannheim, John Hayes

Sweeney and March was first heard over CBS in 1947.

Sweet River

Serial Drama

Writer: Charles Jackson

This program was first broadcast on ABC in 1943 and originated in Chicago. It was also heard for a time on NBC.

T

Take a Card

Quiz

Featuring: Wally Butterworth, Margaret (Honey) Johnson

Take a Number

Audience Participation

M.C.: Red Benson
Director: Bob Monroe

Take It or Leave It

Quiz

M.C.: Phil Baker
Bob Hawk
Garry Moore
Jack Paar
Eddie Cantor (1950)
Directors: Harry Spears, Betty Mandeville
Writer: Edith Oliver

On this program, later known as *The Sixty-four Dollar Question*, contestants could quit or keep trying until they reached the question that paid sixty-four dollars. The program was first heard over CBS in 1940.

A Tale of Today

Serial Drama

CAST:

Joan Houston Allen	Joan Blaine
	Betty Caine
	Luise Barclay
Harriet Brooks	Isabel Randolph
	Ethel Owen
Dot Houston	Laurette Fillbrandt
Billy Houston	Frank Pacelli
Beulah	Harriette Widmer
Dick Martin	Willard Farnum
Robert Houston	Harvey Hays
	Carlton Brickert
Dr. Robert Gardner	Robert Griffin
Johnny Ward	Bob Jellison
Sally	Norma Peterson
David Allen	Ed Prentiss
	Raymond Edward Johnson
Sandra Hall	Sunda Love
Michael Denby	Ed Prentiss
Flora Little	Mercedes McCambridge

Director: Howard Keegan
Writer: Gordon Saint Clair
Theme: "Coronation March" from Meyerbeer's opera *The Prophet*

This weekly serial drama was heard on Sundays from 4:30 to 5:00 p.m. on NBC, but it followed the same format as other "soap operas" in all other respects. It was the "interesting story of the Houston family, filled with poignant drama and typical American appeal," as one publicity release described it.

Tales of Fatima

Adventure

Narrator and Star: Basil Rathbone

Talk to the People: see *Mayor LaGuardia Reads the Funnies.*

Tarzan

Jungle Adventure

CAST:

Tarzan — James Pierce
Jane Porter — Joan Burroughs

Opening:

VOICE. *Jungle call*

ANNOUNCER. From the heart of the jungle comes a savage cry of victory. This is Tarzan . . . lord of the jungle!

MUSIC. *Up and under . . .*

ANNOUNCER. From the black core of dark Africa . . . land of enchantment, mystery, and violence . . . comes one of the most colorful figures of all time. Transcribed from the immortal pen of Edgar Rice Burroughs . . . Tarzan, the bronzed, light son of the jungle!

This program was based on the stories by Edgar Rice Burroughs.

Tea Time at Morrell's

Variety

M.C.: Don McNeill
Featuring: Gale Page, Charles Sears
Orchestra: Joseph Gallichio

This program was broadcast Thursdays at 2:00 p.m. over NBC. The half-hour was sponsored by the John Morrell Company, makers of Red Heart dog food. It began in 1936.

The Ted Mack Family Hour: see *The Family Hour.*

Ted Malone's Poetry: see *Between the Bookends.*

The Telephone Hour

Music

Guest Artists: Jascha Heifetz, violinist; Ezio Pinza, basso; Marian Anderson, contralto; Lily Pons, soprano; José Iturbi, pianist; Grace Moore, soprano; James Melton, tenor; Nelson Eddy, tenor; Helen Traubel, soprano; Robert Casadesus, pianist; *et al.*
With: Raymond Edward Johnson as Alexander Graham Bell
Orchestra: Donald Voorhees and the Bell Telephone Orchestra
Announcers: Floyd Mack, Dick Joy (West Coast)
Director: Walter McGill
Writers: Norman Rosten, Mort Lewis
Theme: "The Bell Waltz"

The Telephone Hour began its long run over NBC in April 1940.

Tell It Again

Children's Drama

Narrator: Marvin Miller
Writer-Director: Ralph Rose

Tell It Again made its debut over CBS in 1948 and ran for two years as a sustaining (unsponsored) half-hour, Sunday-morning series dramatizing great works of literature for older children. Among the works presented were *Les Misérables, Don Quixote, The Hunchback of Notre Dame, Moby Dick,* and *Robin Hood.*

Tena and Tim

Comedy

CAST:

Tena — Peggy Beckmark
Tim — George Cisar, James Gardner
Mrs. Hutchinson — Gladys Heen

Director: Harry Holcomb
Writer: Peggy Beckmark

This program was first heard over CBS in 1944.

Tennessee Jed

Western Adventure

CAST:

Tennessee Jed Sloan — Johnny Thomas, Don MacLaughlin
Sheriff Jackson — Humphrey Davis
The Deputy — Jim Boles
Indian Chief — Juano Hernandez
Masters, the gambler — Raymond Edward Johnson
Narrator — Court Benson
Also: John McGovern, George Petrie
Announcer: Court Benson

Producer: Paul DeFur
Director: Bill Hamilton
Writers: Ashley Buck, Howard Carraway, Tom Taggert

Theme Singer: Elton Britt

Opening:

ANNOUNCER. There he goes, Tennessee! Get him!

SOUND. *Rifle shot and ricochet*

ANNOUNCER. Got him! D-e-a-a-a-d center!

Tennessee Jed was first heard over ABC in 1945.

Terry and Mary

Children's Serial Drama

Writer: Robert Hardy Andrews

Terry and Ted

Children's Adventure

CAST:

Terry — Lester Jay
Chico — Jerry Macy

This was first heard over CBS in 1935.

Terry and the Pirates

Adventure

CAST:

Terry Lee — Jackie Kelk, Cliff Carpenter, Owen Jordan
Patrick Ryan — Clayton "Bud" Collyer, Larry Alexander, Warner Anderson, Bob Griffin
The Dragon Lady — Agnes Moorehead, Adelaide Klein, Marion Sweet

Burma	Frances Chaney
Connie	Cliff Norton
	Peter Donald
	John Gibson
Flip Corkin	Ted de Corsia
Hotshot Charlie	Cameron Andrews
Captain Goodhue	John Moore
Eleta	Gerta Rozan

Also: Charles Cantor, William Podmore, Mandel Kramer
Announcer: Douglas Browning

Directors: Wylie Adams, Marty Andrews, Cyril Armbrister
Writer: Al Barker

Opening:
SOUND. *Stroke of a gong*
ANNOUNCER. (*Chinese chatter, actually nonsense syllables that sounded Chinese*). *Terry and the Pirates!*
MUSIC. (*Kelvin Keech sang the theme and played the ukulele*)

This program was based on the comic strip by Milton Caniff. It was first heard over NBC in 1937.

Tex and Jinx: see *Interviewers.*

The Texaco Star Theater

Variety

The Texaco Star Theater featured various performers over the years, usually in variety programs. Among the most famous were Ed Wynn ("The Fire Chief") and Fred Allen. In the 1940s the format consisted of a half-hour of variety from Hollywood followed by a half-hour of drama from New York. Here are two sample programs:

May 1, 1940: Variety from Hollywood, 9:00 to 9:30 p.m.
M.C.: Ken Murray
Vocalists: Kenny Baker
Frances Langford
Orchestra: David Broekman
Also: Irene of "Tim and Irene"
Guest Stars
Announcer: Jimmy Wallington

Drama from New York, 9:30 to 10:00 p.m.

THE MILKY WAY

Newsboy	Cecil Secrest
Joe Holland	Dwight Weist
Gabby Sloan	Don Costello
Spider Higgins	Tony Burger
Anne Westley	Audrey Christie
Speed McFarland	Jack Arthur
Burleigh Sullivan	Joe E. Brown
Mae Sullivan	Sylvia Field

Announcer: Larry Elliott

Director: Antony Stanford
Original music composed and conducted by: Lehman Engel

May 29, 1940: Variety from Hollywood, 9:00 to 9:30 p.m. (Same variety cast as above.)

Drama from New York, 9:30 to 10:00 p.m.

THE FRONT PAGE

Hildy Johnson	Lee Tracy
Walter Burns	Jack Arthur
McCue	John MacBryde
Bensinger	Cecil Secrest
Murphy	Raymond Bramley
Mollie Malloy	Betty Worth
Sheriff Hartman	Edwin Cooper

Peggy Grant	Frances Fuller
Earl Williams	Milton Herman
Mr. Pincus	Bernie Suss

Announcer: Larry Elliott

Director: Antony Stanford
Music (as above): Lehman Engel

Among the writers who contributed to *The Texaco Star Theater* were Paul Conlan, Bob Phillips, Ed James, and Frank Phares.

Thanks for Tomorrow

Serial Drama

Starring: Mary Jane Higby, Peter Capell

CAST:

Aunt Agatha	Vera Allen
Amah	Wynne Gibson
Chinese houseboy	Edgar Stehli

Announcer: Ed Herlihy

Director: Paul Roberts
Writer: LeRoy Bailey

This was the story of a blind pianist (played by Mary Jane Higby). When the script called for her to play the piano, Paul Taubman served as pianist.

Thanks to the Yanks

Quiz

M.C.: Bob Hawk
Director: Kenneth W. MacGregor

This show had its première over CBS in 1942.

That Brewster Boy

Situation Comedy

CAST:

Joey Brewster	Eddie Firestone, Jr. Arnold Stang Dick York
Jim Brewster, the father	Hugh Studebaker
Jane Brewster, the mother	Constance Crowder
English teacher	Ruth Perrott
Minerva	Jane Webb
Nancy Brewster	Louise Fitch Patricia Dunlap
Phil Hayworth	Bob Bailey
Herbert Clark	Bob Jellison
Chuck	Billy Idelson
Lefty Harper	Eddie Goldberg
Pee Wee	Jerry Spellman
Mark Brown	Dickie Van Patten
Janey Brown	Marilyn Erskine

Announcer: Marvin Miller (1941–44)

Director: Owen Vinson
Writer: Louis Scofield

That Brewster Boy was first heard over NBC in 1941 from Chicago. It was replaced by *Those Websters* on March 9, 1945.

Thatcher Colt

Detective

CAST:

Thatcher Colt	Hanley Stafford

This program was first heard over NBC in 1936.

Theater of Today: see *Armstrong Theater of Today.*

The Theatre Guild on the Air

Drama

Host: Lawrence Langner
Orchestra: Harold Levey
Spokesman for United States Steel: George Hicks
Announcer: Norman Brokenshire
Producer: George Kondolf
Executive Director: Armina Marshall
Director: Homer Fickett
Sound Effects: Wes Conant, Bill McClintock

The Theatre Guild on the Air, also known as *The United States Steel Hour,* was a series of radio adaptations of successful Broadway plays. The series began over CBS in 1943 and was heard originally on Thursdays at 10:00 p.m. Among the many plays presented were *Strange Interlude, The Silver Cord, I Remember Mama, Dead End,* and *Payment Deferred.* Two sample cast lists follow:

ON BORROWED TIME
Original Play by Paul Osborn
Based on the novel by Lawrence Edward Watkins
Radio Adaptation by Paul Peters

Narrator	Dwight Weist
Trixie	Brad Barker
Susan	Anne Burr
Jim	James Monks
Gramps	Walter Huston
Pud	Sarah Fussell
Mellett	Ian MacAllaster
Granny	Leona Roberts
Mr. Brink	Glenn Anders
Demetria	Dorothy Sands
Marcy	Frances Heflin
A boy up a tree	Peter Griffith
Dr. Evans	Frank Lovejoy
Mr. Pilbeam	Cameron Prud'Homme
Workman	Ian MacAllaster
Sheriff	John Girard
A bartender	James Monks
Grimes	Edwin Jerome

THREE MEN ON A HORSE
Original Play by John Cecil Holm and George Abbott
Radio Adaptation by Arthur Miller

Erwin	Stuart Erwin
Patsy	Sam Levene
Mabel	Shirley Booth
Audrey	Betty Breckenridge
Clarence	J. Scott Smart
Harry	Frank Lovejoy
Frankie	George Tyne
Charlie	Millard Mitchell
Mr. Carver	Edwin Jerome
Delivery boy	James McCallion

Announcer: James McCallion

There Was a Woman

Drama

Featuring: Raymond Edward Johnson
Also: Betty Caine
Announcer: Les Griffith
Writers: Les Fogely, Ranald MacDougall

This was a weekly NBC series that

dramatized the fact that behind so many famous men there was a woman who helped make them great.

The Thin Man

Detective

CAST:

Nick Charles — Lester Damon, Les Tremayne, Joseph Curtin, David Gothard
Nora Charles — Claudia Morgan
Ebenezer Williams, Sheriff of Crabtree County — Parker Fennelly
Announcers: Ron Rawson, Ed Herlihy

Producer-Director: Himan Brown
Writers: Milton Lewis, Eugene Wang, Robert Newman, Louis Vittes
Sound Effects: Hal Reid

This program was based on the character created by Dashiell Hammett. It came to radio over NBC in 1941.

Think Fast

Panel Quiz

Moderator: Mason Gross
Panelists: David Broekman, Leon Janney, Eloise McElhone, George Hamilton Combs
Frequent guest panelist: John Lardner

Think Fast was first heard over ABC in 1949.

This Day Is Ours

Serial Drama

CAST:

Eleanor MacDonald — Joan Banks, Templeton Fox
Curtis Curtis — Jay Jostyn
Pat Curtis — Patricia Dunlap
Wong — Alan Devitt
Eugene Snell — Julian Noa
Frank Allison — House Jameson
Catherine Allison — Agnes Moorehead
Miss Farnsworth — Effie Palmer
Mrs. Simpson — Leslie Bingham
Also: Frank Lovejoy
Announcer: Mel Allen

Director: Chick Vincent
Writers: Carl Bixby, Don Becker
Theme: Original music composed by Don Becker

This program made its debut over CBS in 1938.

This Is Life

Drama

CAST:

Victor Powell — Vincent Pelletier
Announcer: Marvin Miller

Director: Burke Herrick

This was a fifteen-minute program for Hecker Products, broadcast Monday, Wednesday, and Friday over Mutual from 1941 to 1943. It offered help to the audience by reading letters to locate missing relatives or lost possessions, sought aid for charity organizations, etc.

This Is New York: see *Duffy's Tavern.*

This Is Nora Drake

Serial Drama

CAST:

Nora Drake — Charlotte Holland, Joan Tompkins, Mary Jane Higby
Arthur Drake — Everett Sloane, Ralph Bell
Dorothy Stewart — Elspeth Eric
Tom Morley — Bob Readick
Dr. Sergeant — Lester Damon
George Stewart — Leon Janney
Peg Martinson — Lesley Woods, Joan Alexander, Mercedes McCambridge
Dr. Ken Martinson — Alan Hewitt
Andrew King — Roger DeKoven
Suzanne Turrie — Joan Lorring
Rose Fuller — Irene Hubbard
Gillian Gray — Charlotte Manson
Charles Dobbs — Grant Richards
Carol Douglas — Charlotte Manson
Dr. Jensen — Arnold Robertson

Also: Doug Parkhirst

Announcers: Ken Roberts, Bill Cullen

Directors: Arthur Hanna, Dee Engelbach, Charles Irving
Writer: Milton Lewis
Sound Effects: Jerry Sullivan, Ross Martindale
Organist: Charles Paul

This show made its debut over NBC in 1947.

This Is Your Enemy

Drama

This was an OWI (Office of War Information) World War II series describing the enemy's military and civilian outrages.

This Is Your FBI

Drama

CAST:

Jim Taylor — Stacy Harris
Narrator — Frank Lovejoy

Also: Karl Swenson, Geoffrey Bryant, James Van Dyk, Helen Lewis, Elspeth Eric, Santos Ortega, Mandel Kramer, Joan Banks

Announcers: Milton Cross, Carl Frank, Larry Keating

Producer-Director: Jerry Devine
Writer: Jerry D. Lewis
Sound Effects: Virgil Reime, Monte Frazer

These were dramatized cases taken from the files of the Federal Bureau of Investigation. FBI Director J. Edgar Hoover appeared on the première broadcast over ABC on April 6, 1945.

This Is Your Life

Biography

M.C.: Ralph Edwards
Director: Axel Gruenberg
Writer: Jerry Devine

On this program, which made its debut over NBC in 1948, Ralph Edwards related the life stories of the honored guests. Important people from the subject's life, such as teachers, employers, friends, and relatives, appeared on the program to surprise him. The producers of the program went to great lengths to keep the subject in the dark about his appearance on the show until the last possible minute. Usually he would be invited out for an evening with friends and then driven to the studio.

This Life Is Mine

Serial Drama

CAST:

Bob Hastings — Michael Fitzmaurice
Charlie Dyer — Tony Barrett
Also: Betty Winkler, Paul McGrath

Director: Marx Loeb
Writers: Addy Richton, Lynn Stone

The première broadcast of *This Life Is Mine* was over CBS on March 22, 1943.

Those Bartons: see *The Barton Family*.

Those Happy Gilmans

Family Adventure

CAST:

Gordon Gilman — Bill Bouchey
Mrs. Gilman — Edith Adams
Stanley Gilman — John Hench
Phyllis Gilman — Joan Kay
Wheezy — Cornelius Peeples
Aunt Bessie — Henrietta Tedro

This was first heard over NBC in 1938.

Those We Love

Serial Drama

CAST:

John Marshall — Hugh Sothern, Oscar O'Shea, Francis X. Bushman
Kathy Marshall — Nan Grey
Kit Marshall (Kathy's twin) — Richard Cromwell, Bill Henry
Aunt Emily Mayfield — Alma Kruger
Dr. Leslie Foster — Donald Woods
Amy Foster — Priscilla Lyon, Ann Todd
Elaine Dascomb — Jean Rogers, Helen Wood
David Adair — Bob Cummings
Ed Neely — Lou Merrill
Jerry Payne — Victor Rodman
Dr. Lund — Franklin Parker
Allan McRae — Owen Davis, Jr.
Lynn Royce — Gavin Gordon
Abner — Eddie Walker
Peggy Edwards — Lurene Tuttle
Lydia Dennison — Anne Stone
Mrs. Emmett — Mary Gordon
Ellis — David Kerman
Martha Newbury, the cook — Virginia Sale
Lile Kilgore — Sally Creighton
Steve Blackman — Gene O'Donnell
Roy Meadows — Gale Gordon
Rodney Kilgore — Gale Gordon

Rags, the dog — Lee Millar
Announcer: Dick Joy

Writers: Agnes Ridgway, Ruth A. Knight

Those We Love was first heard over the Blue network in 1937. It was later broadcast over CBS.

Those Websters

Situation Comedy

CAST:

George Webster (Dad) — Willard Waterman
Mrs. Webster (Mom) — Connie Crowder
Billy Green — Arthur Young, Gil Stratton, Jr.
Billy's sister — Joan Alt
Jeep — Jerry Spellman
Belinda Boyd — Jane Webb
Announcer: Charles Irving

Producers: Joe Ainley, Les Weinrot
Writers: Priscilla Kent, Albert G. Miller, Frank and Doris Hursley

The program was set in the town of "Spring City." It made its debut over CBS as a replacement for *That Brewster Boy* on March 9, 1945.

The Three Flats: see *Just Neighbors.*

Three Sheets to the Wind

Adventure

Starring: John Wayne

Thurston, the Magician

Adventure

Featuring: Cliff Soubier, Carlton Brickert
Announcer: William Kephart

This program was also known as *Howard Thurston, the Magician.* It was first heard over NBC Blue in 1932.

Tillie the Toiler

Situation Comedy

CAST:

Tillie — Caryl Smith
Mac — Billy Lynn
Mr. Simpkins — John Brown
Tillie's mother — Margaret Burlen

Based on the comic strip by Russ Westover.

The Tim and Irene Show

Variety

CAST:

Tim — Tim Ryan
Irene — Irene Noblette
Uncle Happy — Teddy Bergman

Tim Healy's Stamp Club: see *Captain Tim Healy's Stamp Club.*

Time Flies

Adventure

Featuring: Frank Hawks, flying ace
Also: Allyn Joslyn

Time Flies was so-called because the sponsor was the Elgin Watch Company. "Time Flies" was also the name of Frank Hawks's racing plane, which set many records while sponsored by the watch company.

Time for Love

Drama

CAST:

Dianne La Volta, International Chanteuse — Marlene Dietrich

Producer: Marlene Dietrich
Directors: Murray Burnett, Ernest Ricca

Time to Smile: see *The Eddie Cantor Show.*

The Timid Soul

Comedy

CAST:

Casper Milquetoast, The Timid Soul — Billy Lynn
Madge, his wife — Cecil Roy
The druggist — Jackson Beck

Based on the comic strip by H. T. Webster.

T-Man

Adventure

CAST:

Treasury Agent — Dennis O'Keefe
Announcer: Bob Lemond

Tobacco Auctioneers: see *Auctioneers.*

Today's Children

Serial Drama

CAST:

Kathryn Carter — Helen Kane
Don Carter — Forrest Lewis
Aunt Martha — Judith Lowry
Ralph Santo — Michael Romano
Nancy Matthews — Harriet Cain
Helen Marshall — Ethel Owen
Bob Brewer — Robert Griffin, Olan Soule
John Bartlett — Rupert LaBelle
Mr. Schultz — Murray Forbes
Mrs. Schultz — Virginia Payne
Bertha Schultz — Patricia Dunlap
Terry Moran — Fred Von Ammon
Lucy Moran — Lucy Gilman
Henry Matthews — Raymond Edward Johnson
Joan Young — Margaret Fuller
Liza — Edith Adams
Michael Gregory — Michael Romano
Jack Marsh — Seymour Young, Frank Pacelli
Junior Matthews — Donald Weeks
John Murray — Willard Waterman
Robert Marshall — Parker Wilson
Jerry Ryan — Robert O'Malley
Gloria Marsh — Gale Page

Richard Coles	Bob Bailey
Arthur Donnelly	Ed Prentiss
Kay Crane	Irna Phillips
Bobby Moran	Frank Pacelli
Jen Burton	Laurette Fillbrandt
Judge Colby	Herb Butterfield
Catherine Colby	Nanette Sargent
Eileen Moran	Fran Carlon
	Ireene Wicker
Bill Taylor	Gene Morgan
Bob Crane	Walter Wicker
Frances Moran Matthews	
	Bess Johnson
	Sunda Love
Tony	Edwin Rand
Julie Johnson	Lucy Gilman
Marilyn	Betty Lou Gerson
Naomi	Jo Gilbert
Peter Piper	Clarence Hartzell
Italo Lagorro	Milton Herman
Mary	Lois Kennison
Therese	Betty Moran
Keith Armour	Wilms Herbert
Candice Drake	Jeanne Bates
"The Past"[1]	Marvin Miller
David Lagorro	Jack Edwards, Jr.
Walter Drake	Joe Forte
Charlotta Lagorro Armour	
	Gale Page
	Marjorie Davies
Katherine Norton	Irna Phillips
Dick Crane	Willard Farnum
Patty Moran	Fran Carlon
Dorothy Moran	Jean McGregor
Mother Moran	Irna Phillips

Producer: Carl Wester
Directors: Axel Gruenberg, Bob Dwan
Writer: Irna Phillips
Theme: "Aphrodite"

[1] See explanatory note under *The Right to Happiness.*

Today's Children made its debut over NBC Blue in 1933. It was originally the story of German-born citizens who came to America to live. The program originated in Chicago, then moved to Hollywood in 1947.

Tom, Dick and Harry: see *The Affairs of Tom, Dick and Harry; Plantation Party.*

Tom Mix

Western Adventure

CAST:

Tom Mix	Artells Dickson
	Russell Thorson
	Jack Holden
	Curley Bradley
The Old Wrangler	Percy Hemus
Jimmy	Andy Donnelly
	George Gobel
	Hugh Rowlands
Jane	Winifred Toomey
	Jane Webb
Amos Q. Snood	Sidney Ellstrom
Pecos Williams	Curley Bradley
Sheriff Mike Shaw	Leo Curley
	Hal Peary
	Willard Waterman
William Snood	Cornelius Peeples
Calamity	Bob Jellison
Wash	Vance McCune
	Forrest Lewis
Judge Parsons	Arthur Peterson
Chris Acropolous	Carl Kroenke
Professor Wallace	Phil Lord
Sheriff	DeWitt McBride
Pat Curtis	Patricia Dunlap
Lee Loo, the Chinese cook	
	Bruno Wick

The Ranch Boys—Shorty Carson, Jack Ross, Curley Bradley
Announcers: Don Gordon, Les Griffith, Franklyn Ferguson

Producer: Al Chance
Directors: Charles Claggett, Clarence L. Menser
Writers: George Lowther, Roland Martini, Charles Tazewell
Theme: "When It's Round-up Time in Texas and the Bloom Is on the Sage"

Tom Mix was a popular cowboy movie star of the 1930s. However, he did not play himself in this radio series which originated in Chicago and made its debut over NBC in 1933. Instead, the actors listed above took his part.

Radio's "Tom Mix" lived on the "T-M Bar Ranch" in "Dobie Township." As in the films, his horse was Tony, the Wonder Horse, who often played a part in rescuing Tom from bad guys. Tom's friends and cohorts were "Straight Shooters," and one of the main moral points of the program was that "Straight Shooters always win."

Premiums were offered to listeners by the sponsor, Ralston, if box-tops and money were sent to Checkerboard Square, St. Louis, Missouri.

"Amos Q. Snood" was the Scrooge of Dobie and was known for his "Pink Pills for Pale People." "The Old Wrangler" would spout such homilies as, "Well, I'll be a lop-eared kangaroo with big black eyes, if it isn't round-up time!"

Tommy Riggs and Betty Lou

Comedy

CAST:

Tommy Riggs — Himself
Betty Lou — Tommy Riggs
Wilbur, Betty Lou's moronic boy friend — Wally Maher
Mrs. McIntyre — Verna Felton
Vocalist: Anita Kurt
Announcer: Don Wilson

Writers: Sam Perrin, Jack Douglas, George Balzer

Tommy Riggs was a ventriloquist; his alter-ego was "Betty Lou," his niece in the skits. "Betty Lou" was not a dummy, only a voice. The program began over NBC in 1938. (See also *Comedy and Comedians.*)

Tomorrow's Tops

Teen-age Talent

Hostess: Margo Whiteman (daughter of Paul Whiteman)

Tony Wons' Scrapbook

Poetry

Featuring: Tony Wons
Theme: "Träumerei" by Schumann

This poetry-reading program, first heard over CBS in 1930, acquired a large following. Tony Wons was especially popular with women, who seemed to appreciate his romantic style.

Topper: see *The Adventures of Topper.*

The Town Crier

Interviews

Featuring: Alexander Woollcott
Opening:
SOUND. *Bell Ringing*
WOOLLCOTT. Hear ye! Hear ye!

First heard over CBS in the early 1930s.

Town Hall Tonight: see *The Fred Allen Show.*

Town Meeting of the Air: see *America's Town Meeting.*

Treasury Agent

Drama

CAST:
Joe Lincoln, Chief Treasury Agent — Raymond Edward Johnson

Producer: Phillips H. Lord
Director: Leonard Bass

Treat Time

Music and Drama

Starring: Buddy Cole, singer
Narrator: Marvin Miller
Orchestra: Caesar Petrillo
Directors: Lee Strahorn, Jim Whipple

Treat Time was a fifteen-minute, daytime series for Armour heard over CBS from 1941 to 1942. Romantic sketches and vignettes on composers' lives were used to lead into Buddy Cole's songs.

Trouble House

Serial Drama

CAST:

Martha Booth	Anne Elstner
Bill Mears	Carleton Young
Ted Booth	Elliott Reid
Ann Lowery	Joan Madison
Phoebe	Elsie Mae Gordon
Harvey, the hired man	Jerry Macy
John	Ray Collins
Dr. Clem Allison	Gene Leonard
Nancy Booth	Dorothy Lowell

Writer: Elaine Sterne Carrington

(See also *Magazine of the Air.*)

True Confessions

Serial Drama

Starring: Bess Johnson
Also: Ned Wever, Charlotte Manson, Richard Widmark, Alfred Ryder (Alfred Corn), Lucille Wall, *et al.*
Creator-Writer: Bill Sweets
Producer: Roy Winsor
Director: Ernest Ricca

This series was presented by *True Confessions* magazine.

True Detective Mysteries

Mystery

CAST:

Narrator — John Shuttleworth
John Shuttleworth — Dick Keith
Also: Mandel Kramer, Johnny Thomas

Writer-Director: Murray Burnett
Sound Effects: Jim Goode

These stories were based on true incidents reported in *True Detective* magazine. John Shuttleworth, the editor, narrated the program; his role in the story itself was taken by Dick Keith. The series began over CBS in 1929.

True or False

Quiz

M.C.: Dr. Harry Hagen
Eddie Dunn
Bill Slater
Announcer: Glenn Riggs
Director: Jeanne Harrison
Writers: Ed Rice, Milton Cassel, Phil Davis

This was first heard over NBC Blue in 1938.

The True Story Hour with Mary and Bob

Drama

CAST:

Mary — Nora Stirling
Bob — William Brenton
Cecil Secrest
David Ross
Also: Lucille Wall, Elsie Hitz, Arthur Vinton, Virginia Morgan, Ned Wever, *et al.*
Orchestra: Howard Barlow
Announcers: Ted Husing, Paul Douglas

Writer-Director: Bill Sweets

This was radio's first full-hour dramatic series. It ran on CBS for four and a half years after making its debut in January 1928. A *New York Telegram* radio poll in October 1929 showed that the program ranked second only to *Roxy's Gang* among listeners.

True Story Theater

Drama

Featuring: Henry Hull

These stories were selected from *True Story* magazine.

Truth or Consequences

Quiz

M.C.: Ralph Edwards
Announcers: Clayton "Bud" Collyer, Mel Allen, Jay Stewart, Milton Cross, Ed Herlihy, Harlow Wilcox, Ken Carpenter
Directors: John Guedel, Al Paschall, Ed Bailey
Writers: Carl Jampel, George Jeske, Phil Davis, Bill Burch, Esther Allen, Ralph Edwards

Sound Effects: Bob Prescott, Lloyd Creekmore
Theme: "Merrily We Roll Along"

Catch-phrases:

EDWARDS (*after sending a contestant off on an embarrassing mission*). Aren't we devils?

EDWARDS (*after asking the question preceding the stunt*). No snitching in the audience!

EDWARDS (*after contestant missed the question*). You did not tell the truth so you must pay the consequences!

Opening:

AUDIENCE. *Laughter*

ANNOUNCER. Hello, there. We've been waiting for you. It's time to play Truth . . .

ORGAN. *Glissando*

ANNOUNCER. . . . or Consequences!

SOUND. *Razzing buzzer twice*

MUSIC. *Theme*

This program was the radio version of the old parlor game in which contestants must pay the consequences if they don't tell the truth. It made its debut over NBC in 1940. The questions were usually very silly and were seldom answered correctly, as it was almost expected that the contestant would rather participate in whatever stunt was planned than collect the money for a correct answer to the question. If the studio contestant didn't answer the question in the required time, Bob Prescott, the sound-effects man, activated Beulah the Buzzer, indicating that the consequence would have to be paid. The contestant was then launched into some kind of elaborate stunt, which might prove humorous, embarrassing, or sometimes sentimental—as when long-lost relatives were reunited through the designs of the stunt.

The program conducted some of radio's most famous contests, including "Mr. Hush" (Jack Dempsey), "Miss Hush" (Clara Bow), and "The Walking Man" (Jack Benny). Clues were offered concerning the identity of the foregoing celebrities, and a huge jackpot was eventually awarded to the winner of each contest. In another elaborately publicized stunt, the town of Hot Springs, New Mexico, changed its name to Truth or Consequences, New Mexico. (For a description of the elaborate warm-up for this program, see *Announcers.*)

Tune Detective

Music

M.C.: Sigmund Spaeth

Sigmund Spaeth exposed various tunes as being lifted from older melodies. The program began over the Blue network in 1931.

Twenty Questions

Quiz

M.C.: Bill Slater
Jay Jackson
Panelists: Fred Van Deventer, Florence Rinard (Mrs. Fred Van Deventer), Bobby Van Deventer, Nancy Van Deventer, Herb Polesie
Mystery Voice: Jack Irish, Bruce Elliott, Frank Waldecker
Ronson Girl: Charlotte Manson

Announcer: Frank Waldecker
Directors: Gary Stevens, Del Crosby

The panel had to identify the given subject within twenty questions after being told if it was animal, vegetable, or mineral. The Mystery Voice gave the answers to the home audience. *Twenty Questions* made its debut over Mutual in 1946.

Twenty Thousand Years in Sing Sing

Crime Stories

CAST:

Warden Lewis E. Lawes of Sing Sing — Himself
Guy Sorel
Mr. Stark (who interviewed the Warden before each story began) — Joseph Bell
Announcer: Kelvin Keech

Directors: Joseph Bell, Arnold Michaelis

This series was first heard over the Blue network in 1933.

The Twin Stars Show

Variety

The Twin Stars: Rosemarie Broncato and Helen Claire

The Two Black Crows

Comedy

The Two Black Crows: George Moran and Charles Mack

(See also *The Eveready Hour; The Majestic Theater Hour.*)

Two on a Clue

Mystery

CAST:

Jeff Spencer — Ned Wever
Debby Spencer — Louise Fitch
Mrs. Grover — Kate McComb
Mickey — Ronald Liss
Sergeant Cornelius Trumbull — John Gibson
The Midget — Athena Lorde
The Professor — Jim Boles
Announcer: Alice Yourman

Writer-Director: Harry Ingram
Writer: Louis Vittes

Two on a Clue was first heard over CBS in 1944.

Two Thousand Plus

Science Fiction

This program was first broadcast over Mutual in 1950 in response to a growing interest in science fiction.

U

Uncle Abe and David

Drama

CAST:

Uncle Abe	Arthur Allen
David	Parker Fennelly

Uncle Abe and David was first heard over NBC in 1930. (See also *Snow Village.*)

Uncle Charlie's Tent Show

Music and Variety

Uncle Charlie: Charles Winninger
Vocalists: Lois Bennett, soprano
Conrad Thibault, baritone
Orchestra: Donald Voorhees

Uncle Don

Children

Uncle Don: Don Carney (Howard Rice)
Announcers: Joe Bolton, Jeff Sparks, Jack Barry, Barry Gray, Henry Morgan, Frank Knight, Norman Brokenshire, Floyd Neal, Arthur Hale, Charles Kribling
Creator-Writer: Don Carney
Writer: Bill Treadwell

Themes:

"Hello, Little Friends, Hello"
(to the tune of "My Caroline")
Hello nephews, nieces, mine.
I'm glad to see you look so fine.
How's Mama? How's Papa?
But tell me first just how you are.
I've many, many things to tell you, on the radio.
This is Uncle Don, Your Uncle Don,
Hello, little friends, hello."

"Hibbidy Gits"
Hibbidy gits, hass hah,
Rainbow ree, Sibonia,
Skividee, hi-lo-dee,
Horney-ka-dote, with an alikazon,
Sing this song with your Uncle Don.

"Uncle Don" broadcast locally to children in some eighteen nearby states over WOR in New York for twenty-one years. Although the program had only one brief year (1938–39) as a network program, it is a classic among children's programs and is fondly remembered, somehow even by people who never heard it.

Uncle Don made its debut in September 1928, from 6:00 to 6:30 p.m., and continued in that time-slot until February 9, 1949. "Uncle Don" also read the funnies on Sundays at various times. The program was a combination of original stories and songs, advice, personal messages, birthday announcements, and lots of commercials. "Uncle Don" told stories about a typical girl and boy, "Susan Beduzen" and "Willipus Wallipus," and he sang songs about such unsavory children as "Meanwells," "Slackerminds," "Talkabouts," "Stuckups," and "Cryterions." A typical birthday greeting would congratulate a child (whose mother had written in with the pertinent facts), chide him for some bad habit (thumb-sucking and swearing were the biggest crimes), and then tell him he would find a present under the couch or behind the radio.

"Uncle Don" frequently arrived at the studio in his imaginary autogyro, which he called a "puddle-jumper." On Monday nights he would have a parade of "Earnest Savers," who had accounts at the Greenwich Savings Bank—or at least small tin banks that he gave out as a premium.

He held "The Uncle Don Healthy Child Contest" and had an "Uncle Don Talent Quest" for several years which included a trip to Hollywood and a screen test for the winners. He was a tireless worker for various charitable causes and frequently entertained in children's wards at hospitals and in the homes of extremely sick children. For them, and frequently on radio, he played his favorite song, "The Green Grass Grew All Around, All Around."

The program set a much-imitated standard for "kiddie" shows. Don Carney broke new ground in radio broadcasting, and among his many "firsts" were: personally checking out sponsors and their products before accepting them for the program; sampling sponsors' products on the air; and accepting free merchandise for his own use from non-sponsors in exchange for free plugs.

The one story about "Uncle Don" that has been told the most never even happened. The story alleges that he signed off the broadcast one night and then, thinking he was off the air, said, "I guess that'll hold the little bastards." Supposedly this went out over the air, and he was taken off the air for a period of time. None of it is true, even though you can find people today who swear they heard it, and even though there is a recording of so-called "on-the-air mistakes" that alleges to include this infamous fluff. It simply never happened. A columnist in Baltimore, where *Uncle Don* was not heard, made up the story to fill space on an otherwise dull news day. And the story just grew and grew.

To add to the confusion, two other radio performers are supposed to have said the same thing—John Daggett, who played "Uncle John" on KHJ Los Angeles, and John Keough, who played "Big Brother" on KPO San Francisco. If true, apparently Daggett wasn't fired while Keough was. And there it stands. (See Bibliography: Treadwell, Bill. *Head, Heart, and Heel.*)

Uncle Ezra's Radio Station

Comedy Drama

CAST:

Uncle Ezra — Pat Barrett
Cecilia — Nora Barrett (Pat's wife)

This popular series, sponsored by Alka-Seltzer, began in 1934 and was heard three nights a week over NBC. It originated in Chicago. Uncle Ezra, who also starred on *The National*

Barn Dance, broadcast "from station E-Z-R-A, the powerful little five-watter down in Rosedale."

Uncle Jim's Question Bee

Quiz

Uncle Jim: Jim McWilliams
Bill Slater

This program was first heard over the Blue network in 1936. It is generally regarded as being one of radio's first major quiz programs, along with the better-known *Professor Quiz*.

Uncle John: see *Uncle Don*.

Uncle Remus

Children

Uncle Remus: Fred L. Jeske

This program was based on the stories of Joel Chandler Harris.

Uncle Walter's Dog House

Family Adventure-Comedy

CAST:

Uncle Walter	Tom Wallace
Father	Charles Penman
Mother	Kathryn Card
Margie	Beryl Vaughn

Also: Marvin Miller

Director: Watson Humphries

This program had its première over NBC in 1939. It was a thirty-minute show originating in Chicago and sponsored by B&W (Walter Raleigh pipe tobacco).

Uncle Wiggily

Children

Uncle Wiggily: Albert Goris

In this children's series "Uncle Wiggily" related stories for his young audience.

Under Arrest

Adventure

CAST:

Captain Drake	Craig McDonnell
	Joe Di Santis

Also: Betty Garde, John Larkin, Patsy Campbell, Lester Damon, Kermit Murdock, Sid Raymond, Vicki Vola, Bryna Raeburn
Announcer: Ted Brown

Creator-Producer: Wynn Wright
Director: Martin Magner
Writer: William Wells

Under Arrest was first heard over Mutual in 1938.

The United States Steel Hour: see *The Theatre Guild on the Air*.

Universal Rhythm

Music and Conversation

M.C.: Frank Crumit

The University of Chicago Round Table

Discussion

Directors: John Howe, George Probst

This long-running public-affairs program arose from a suggestion made by someone that the spirited luncheon conversation at the faculty club of the University of Chicago, which took place across the traditional large, round oaken tables, might be of interest to radio listeners. An inquiry was directed to NBC, which responded that it might be worth a try. On February 1, 1931, three professors sat around a card table at WMAQ Chicago discussing the Wickersham Commission report on prohibition. The public responded enthusiastically, and within two years NBC was carrying the show weekly, on Sunday afternoon, on the network. For more than twenty-four years the *Round Table* was the most popular discussion program on the air, consistently beating commercial shows in the ratings. At its peak it was carried by ninety-eight network and twenty educational stations and ranked among the nation's ten most popular radio shows. It drew as many as 16,000 letters in response to a provocative broadcast. Over 21,000 persons subscribed to the transcripts, which totaled nearly half a million copies annually. Programs were rebroadcast in Canada and England. Countless professors, writers, and public figures appeared on the broadcast, which had a relaxed, informal atmosphere.

A number of important firsts were scored by the *Round Table*. It was the first regular network program to be produced entirely without a script; it was the first regular network program to win a Peabody Award; and it was the first program to establish beyond all doubt the existence of deep public interest in non-commercial programing.

The final radio broadcast on the *Round Table* on June 12, 1955, was devoted to a discussion of the use of mass communications by the academic world, to clarify the issues of our society for the general public.

V

Valiant Lady

Serial Drama

CAST:

Joan Hargrave-Scott, the Valiant Lady — Joan Blaine, Joan Banks, Florence Freeman
Jim Barrett, Joan's father — Richard Gordon, Bill Johnstone, Gene Leonard
Mike Hagen — Teddy Bergman, Parker Fennelly
Mr. Wright — Teddy Bergman
Paul Morrison — Raymond Edward Johnson
Emma Stevens (Stevie) — Judith Lowry
Agnes Westcott — Linda Carlon
Estelle Cummings — Elsie Mae Gordon
Clarissa Clarke — Ethel Intropidi
Edward Curran — Adelaide Klein
Mr. Collins — Dwight Weist
Mr. Barclay — Maurice Tarplin
Grace Wilson — Jeannette McGrady
Norman Price — Albert Hayes
Mr. Carson — Bernard Lenrow
Judge Kruger — Jerry Macy
Mr. Trent — Sidney Slon
Dr. Lilienthal — Milton Herman
Billy — Kingsley Colton, Jackie Grimes
Abbey Trowbridge — Ethel Owen
Dudley Trowbridge — Shirling Oliver
Carla Scott — Elsa Grsi
Emilio — Luis Van Rooten
Mrs. Scott — Charme Allen
Dr. Lanson — James Trantor
Oliver — Jackie Kelk
Lafe Simms — Lawson Zerbe
Thomas R. Clark — Charles Webster
Jeffrey Clark — Lawson Zerbe
Margie Cook — Jean Ellyn
Mrs. Evans — Kate McComb
Nelson, the butler — A. T. Kaye
Eleanor Richards — Elspeth Eric
Mr. Richards — Everett Sloane
Lester Brennan — Everett Sloane
Jolly Rogers — Clifford Stork, Craig McDonnell
Pamela Stanley — Ethel Intropidi
Dr. Abendroth — William Shelley
Dr. Alec Gordon — Eric Dressler
Myra Gordon — Irene Winston
Mrs. Scott, Truman's mother — Charlotte Garrity
Dr. Truman "Tubby" Scott — Charles Carroll, Bartlett Robinson, Martin Blaine
Monica Brewster — Cathleen Cordell
Colin Kirby — Ned Wever
Amy Bingham — Elaine Kent
Pixie Jefferys — Joan Lazer
Dr. Christopher Ellerbe — Frank Lovejoy
Norman Price, Sr. — John Brewster

Directors: Roy Lockwood, Ernest Ricca, Rikel Kent

Writers: Addy Richton and Lynn Stone, Lawrence Klee, Howard Teichmann

Theme: "Estrellita"

Valiant Lady was first heard over NBC in 1938.

The Vaseline Program: see *Dr. Christian.*

The Vass Family

Variety

Featuring: The Vass Family

The members of the Vass Family were Fran, Weezy (Louise), Jitchy (Virginia), Sally, and Emily. The program was first heard over NBC in 1934.

Ventriloquists: see *Comedy and Comedians.*

Vic and Sade

Comedy Serial

CAST:

Vic Gook — Art Van Harvey
Sade Gook — Bernardine Flynn
Rush Gook, their son — Billy Idelson, Johnny Coons, Sid Koss
Uncle Fletcher — Clarence Hartzell
Dottie Brainfeeble — Ruth Perrott
Chuck Brainfeeble — Carl Kroenke
Russell Miller, nephew — David Whitehouse
L. J. Gertner, City Water Inspector — Johnny Coons

(CHARACTERS MENTIONED ON THE SHOW):

Ruthie Stembottom, Sade's friend who went to all the washrag sales at Yamelton's Department Store
Jake Gumpox, the garbage man
The Brick-Mush Man
Smelly Clark
Blue-Tooth Johnson
Mr. Buller
Ishigan Fishigan of Sishigan, Michigan (who occasionally called long distance)
Robert and Slobbert Hink (identical twins who sent Vic and Sade postcards)
Harry Dean (who hung out around the Inter-Urban Station)
Chief of Police Cullerson
Lolita Sterienzi, Vic's secretary

Orchestra: Walter Blaufuss
Announcers: Ralph Edwards, Ed Herlihy, Bob Brown, Glenn Riggs, Jack Fuller, Roger Krupp
Creator-Writer: Paul Rhymer
Directors: Clarence Menser, Earl Ebi, Charles Rinehardt, Roy Winsor

---

Themes: "Oh, You Beautiful Doll," "Shine On, Harvest Moon," "Chanson Bohémienne"

Opening:

ANNOUNCER. And now, folks, get ready to smile again with radio's home folks, Vic and Sade, written by Paul Rhymer.

"Vic and Sade" were a married couple who lived "in the little house halfway up in the next block," in "Crooper, Illinois, forty miles from Peoria." "Vic," "Sade," "Rush," and "Uncle Fletcher" were the regularly featured characters on the show, with the others appearing occasionally, and with the "invisible characters" referred to frequently. "Vic" (whose full name was "Victor R. Gook") worked for "Plant No. 14" of the "Consolidated Kitchenware Company." "Uncle Fletcher" is best remembered for his nasal, rambling reminiscences about his friends and acquaintances, usually ending with, ". . . later died." He used to hang out at the "Bright Kentucky Hotel" and often watched the trains go by. His response to practically everything was "Fine."

Occasionally the announcer gave a credit at the conclusion of the show: "Sade's gowns by Yamelton's Department Store, Crooper, Illinois."

The program was first heard over the Blue network in 1932 and originated in Chicago. (See also *Comedy and Comedians*.)

The Victor Borge Show

Variety

Starring: Victor Borge, comedian-pianist
Also: Pat Friday Singers
Henry Russell Chorus
Orchestra: Billy Mills
Announcer: Harlow Wilcox

Victor Lindlahr

Health Talks

Featuring: Victor Lindlahr

In this series of talks Victor Lindlahr discussed ways of attaining and maintaining good health. He first appeared on Mutual in 1936.

Village Store

Variety

CAST:
Owner Jack Haley
Blossom Blimp Verna Felton
Penelope (Penny) Cartwright Sharon Douglas
Also: Joan Davis, Eve Arden
Vocalist: Dave Street

Producer: Bob Redd
Writer: Si Wills

This program was also known as *At the Village Store* and *Sealtest Village Store.*

The Voice of Broadway

Broadway Gossip

Starring: Dorothy Kilgallen, columnist
Announcer: Allan Stuart

The Voice of Experience

Advice

The Voice of Experience: Dr. Marion Sayle Taylor

"The Voice of Experience" began dispensing advice over CBS in 1933.

The Voice of Firestone

Music

Guest artists: Margaret Speaks, Richard Crooks, *et al.*

Orchestra: Howard Barlow
Announcer: Hugh James
Writer-Director: Edwin L. Dunham
Theme: "If I Could Tell You"

This NBC program made its debut on December 24, 1928, and was sponsored by the Firestone Tire and Rubber Company. It had one of the longest runs in the history of radio.

The Voice of Prophecy: see *Religion.*

Vox Pop

Quiz and Interview

M.C.'s: Parks Johnson and Jerry Belcher
Wally Butterworth (replaced Belcher)
Warren Hull (replaced Butterworth)
Announcers: Dick Joy, Roger Krupp
Directors: Rogers Brackett, Herb Moss, John Bates
Writer: Rogers Brackett

Vox Pop was originally called *Sidewalk Interviews* and made its debut under that name over NBC in 1935. *Vox Pop* was also heard later over CBS.

Walter Damrosch: see *The Music Appreciation Hour.*

Walter Winchell

News and Commentary

Starring: Walter Winchell, "Your New York Correspondent"
Announcers: Ben Grauer, Richard Stark
Opening:
WINCHELL. Good evening, Mr. and Mrs. North and South America and all the ships at sea . . . let's go to press!

Walter Winchell built up one of the highest-rated programs in radio history. Usually working in the studio with his hat on and operating a code-signal key to accent his dramatic, rapid-fire style of newscasting, he was heard by literally millions of American families on his Sunday-evening broadcast. During his tenure on the air he not only reported the news; he influenced the news with his tips and hints to prominent people.

Winchell had several sponsors. While Jergens Lotion was the sponsor the program was called *The Jergens Journal,* and Winchell wished his audience "lotions of love." Richard Stark was the announcer when Richard Hudnut was the sponsor, and Winchell introduced him with, "Now, here's Richard Stark for Richard Hudnut." Under Lucky Strike sponsorship, Winchell appeared on *The Lucky Strike Magic Carpet.*

Wanted

True Crime Stories

Narrator: Fred Collins

Wanted used the actual voices of the people involved in the crimes—the criminals, the victims, arresting officers, etc.

The War of the Worlds: see *The Mercury Theatre on the Air.*

Warden Lawes: see *Twenty Thousand Years in Sing Sing.*

Warm-Ups: see *Announcers.*

Watanabe and Archie: see *Frank Watanabe and Honorable Archie.*

Watch the Fords Go By: see *Al Pearce and His Gang.*

Way Down East

Serial Drama

Featuring: Agnes Moorehead, Van Heflin

The Wayne and Shuster Show

Comedy-Variety

Starring: Johnny Wayne and Frank Shuster
Vocalist: Georgia Day

We Are Always Young

Serial Drama

Starring: William Janney
Featuring: Linda Watkins, Margalo Gilmore, Jessie Royce Landis
Producer-Director: Robert Shayon
Writers: Ashley Buck, Nicholas Cosentino

This was the story of a composer who worked as a cab-driver until his music was successful.

We Are Four

Serial Drama

CAST:

Nancy Webster	Marjorie Hannan
Lydia Webster	Alice Hill
Priscilla	Sally Smith
Pat	Carl Boyer
Tony Webster	Charles Flynn
Carl Maritz	Reuben Lawson
Arthur Blaine	Olan Soule

Announcer: Ed Smith

Director: Ed Smith
Writer: Bess Flynn
Theme: "Diane"

We Are Four was on the air for two and a half years, from 1935 to 1938.

We Love and Learn

Serial Drama

CAST:

Bill Peters	Frank Lovejoy
Andrea Reynolds	Joan Banks
	Betty Worth
Mrs. Van Cleve	Grace Keddy
Harrington, the butler	Bill Podmore
Abraham Lincoln Watts (Mr. Bones)	Juano Hernandez
Taffy Grahame	Mitzi Gould
Paul	Norman Rose
Kit Collins	Don MacLaughlin
Jim	Cliff Carpenter
Frank Harrison	Horace Braham
The Minister	José Ferrer
Dr. West	Robert Dryden
Dixie	Ann Thomas
Thelma	Sybil Trent
Carlo	Carlo De Angelo
Mr. Cahill	Charles Webster
Mickey	Lesley Woods
Mrs. Carlton	Charme Allen
Mrs. Wicks	Ethel Everett
Susan	Eleanor Sherman
Laura	Sarah Burton
Peter	Norman Rose
Madame Sophie	Barbara Weeks
	Lilli Darvas

Also: George Coulouris, Betty Caine
Announcers: Dick Dunham, Fielden Farrington, Adele Ronson

Producer: John Clark
Producer-Writer: Don Becker
Directors: Oliver Barbour, Carl Eastman, Chet Gierlach
Writers: Martin Stern, John Clark
Sound Effects: Arthur Zachs
Organist: Herschel Leucke
Theme: Original music composed by Don Becker

We Love and Learn made its debut over CBS in 1942. It was originally titled *As the Twig Is Bent.* In 1955 the locale was changed from a dress shop to a Harlem beauty parlor, and the show became the first Negro "soap opera" with an all-Negro cast in radio. The title was then changed to *The Story of Ruby Valentine;* the cast was comprised of Juanita Hall, Viola Dean, Earl Hyman, and Ruby Dee. The pianist was Luther Henderson.

We, the Abbotts

Serial Drama

CAST:

John Abbott	John McIntire
Emily Abbott	Betty Garde
	Ethel Everett
Jack Abbott	Cliff Carpenter
Linda Abbott	Betty Jane Tyler
	Betty Philson
Barbara Abbott	Audrey Egan
Hilda, the maid	Adelaide Klein
Isabel Kenyon	Kay Brinker
Madelyn	Esther Ralston

Writer: Bess Flynn

We, the Abbotts was first broadcast over CBS in 1940.

We, the People

Human-Interest Stories

Host: Gabriel Heatter
Eddie Dowling

Milo Boulton
Dwight Weist
Burgess Meredith
Danny Seymour

Orchestra: Oscar Bradley
Producer: Phillips H. Lord
Directors: David Levy, Lindsay MacHarrie, James Sheldon
Writers: Arthur Henley, Richard Dana, Ruth Barth, Ted Adams, Leonard Safir, Paul Adams, Laurence Hammond, Paul Gardner
Sound Effects: Byron Winget
Theme: From Brahms' First Symphony

This was first heard over the Blue network in 1936. (See also *The Rudy Vallee Show.*)

Welcome Traveler

Audience Participation

M.C.: Tommy Bartlett

Bartlett recruited travelers passing through Chicago's train, plane, and bus terminals. The program was first heard over ABC in 1947.

Welcome Valley

Drama

Host: Edgar Guest, poet

CAST:

Emmy Ferguson	Judith Lowry
Esther Ferguson	Betty Winkler
Grace Ferguson	Isabel Randolph
Sheriff Luke Ferguson	Cliff Arquette
Jeffrey Barker	Art Van Harvey
Dr. Haines	Hal Peary
Dolores Dumont	Joan Blaine
Mathilda Barker	Bernardine Flynn
Teenie	Lucy Gilman
Bill Sutter	Raymond Edward Johnson
Bob Drainard	Robert Griffin

Also: Sidney Ellstrom, Johnny Ames, Joseph Richardson Jones, Ted Maxwell, Don Briggs

Director: Ted Sherdiman
Writers: Irna Phillips, Edith Meiser

Welcome Valley was first broadcast in January 1935, sponsored by the Household Finance Corporation, over NBC Tuesdays at 9:30 p.m.

Wendy Warren

Serial Drama

CAST:

Wendy Warren	Florence Freeman
Newscaster	Douglas Edwards
Gil Kendal	Les Tremayne
Mark Douglas	Lamont Johnson
Mother Kendal	Vera Allen
Adele Lang	Jane Lauren
Charles Lang	Horace Braham
Jean	Meg Wylie
Nona Marsh	Anne Burr
Estelle	Lotte Stavisky
Parkes	Guy Spaull
Dorrie	Tess Sheehan
Don Smith	John Raby
Sam Warren	Rod Hendrickson
Anton Kamp	Peter Capell
Bill Flood, the announcer	Hugh James

Directors: Don Wallace, Tom McDermott, Hoyt Allen, Allan Fristoe
Writers: Frank Provo, John Picard
Musical Director: Clarke Morgan
Sound Effects: Hamilton O'Hara

This program made its debut over CBS in 1947; it was also known as *Wendy Warren and the News.* The program opened with "Wendy" and newscaster Douglas Edwards doing a show. When they signed off the broadcast, the drama began.

What Makes You Tick?

Psychological Quiz

Host: John K. M. McCaffery
Producer-Writer-Director: Addison Smith
Directors: Art Henley, Henry Dick, Dick Charles
Writer: Edward Ettinger

The studio contestant rated himself in response to ten questions, such as "How aggressive are you?" then two psychologists gave their appraisal of the contestant and compared their individual answers with his. The program began over CBS in 1948.

What Would You Have Done?

Drama-Quiz

M.C.: Ben Grauer
Announcer: Jack Costello

What's My Name?

Quiz

Starring: Wilbur Budd Hulick, Arlene Francis
Producer: Edward Byron

What's My Name? was first heard over Mutual in 1938.

What's the Name of That Song?

Musical Quiz

M.C.: Dud Williamson
Bill Gwinn
Director: Loyal Hays

A songfest was conducted in the studio prior to airtime to uncover people with reasonably good singing voices as contestants. Those selected were asked during the broadcast to listen to excerpts from three tunes. If a contestant could identify one of the three played during his turn at the microphone, he received five dollars. He could earn additional money by singing the first line and still more by singing the entire song. The program was first heard over Mutual in 1944.

At this type of Hollywood broadcast, contestants were often accosted outside the studio doors by operators of nearby recording studios who offered to sell them a recording of their participation on the program for five dollars. Naturally, most of the contestants were excited at the opportunity to hear themselves on the air, and with money still in the winning contestants' hands, the operators did a thriving business.

When A Girl Marries

Serial Drama

CAST:

Joan Field Davis
Noel Mills (6 months)
Mary Jane Higby (18 years)
Harry Davis — John Raby

	Robert Haag
	Whitfield Connor
	Lyle Sudrow
Lillie, the maid	Georgia Burke
Sammy	Dolores Gillen
Phil Stanley	Michael Fitzmaurice
	Richard Kollmar
	Staats Cotsworth
	Karl Weber
	Paul McGrath
Dr. Samuel Tilden Field	Ed Jerome
Eva Topping Stanley	Irene Winston
Stella Field	Frances Woodbury
Mrs. Stanley	Ethel Owen
Little Rudy Cameron	Madeleine Pierce
Angie	Mary Jane Higby
	Wynne Gibson
Sylvia Field	Joan Tetzel
	Jone Allison
	Toni Darnay
Anne Davis (Mother Davis)	Marion Barney
Tom Davis	William Quinn
Dr. Wiggins	John Milton
Professor Kilpatrick	Edgar Stehli
Madison, the butler	Eustace Wyatt
Betty McDonald	Eunice Hill
	Helene Dumas
Ella Ashby	Gladys Thornton
Mr. Cameron	Maurice Tarplin
Chick Norris	John Kane
Steve Skidmore	Jack Arthur
	King Calder
Kathy Cameron	Anne Francis
	Rosemary Rice
Irma Cameron	Jeannette Dowling
Lola	Audrey Egan
Betty Skidmore	Gertrude Warner
Police Officer Connolly	Peter Capell
John Hackett	Joe Latham
Whitey	Kay Renwick
Mother Field	Ethel Wilson

Announcers: Frank Gallop, Charles Stark, Dick Stark, Dennis King, Hugh James, George Ansbro, Don Gardiner, Wendell Niles

---

Directors: Kenneth W. MacGregor, Maurice Lowell, Theodora Yates, Tom McDermott, Oliver Barbour, Olga Druce, Charles Fisher, Art Richards, Scott Farnworth, Warren Somerville, Tom Baxter

Writers: Elaine Sterne Carrington, LeRoy Bailey

Organists: Richard Leibert, John Winters, Rosa Rio

Theme: "Drigo's Serenade"

Opening:

ANNOUNCER. *When A Girl Marries* . . . this tender, human story of young married love . . . is dedicated to everyone who has ever been in love . . .

When A Girl Marries went on the air over CBS on May 29, 1939.

Which Is Which?

Quiz

M.C.: Ken Murray

This made its debut over CBS in 1944.

Whispering Streets

Serial Drama

Hope Winslow (Narrator)	Gertrude Warner
	Bette Davis

The Whistler

Mystery-Drama

CAST:

The Whistler — Bill Forman, Marvin Miller, Everett Clarke

Announcer: Marvin Miller

Producer-Director: George Allen
Directors: Sherman Marks, Sterling Tracy
Sound Effects: Berne Surrey, Gene Twombly
Musical Director and Original Music Score: Wilbur Hatch. Dorothy Roberts did the whistling.

Opening:

THE WHISTLER. I am The Whistler. And I know many things, for I walk by night. I know many strange tales hidden in the hearts of men and women who have stepped into the shadows. Yes . . . I know the nameless terrors of which they dare not speak.

"The Whistler" was identified by the mournful whistling of the theme music. He never actually participated in the dramas. He observed the actions of the participants and commented on the ironies of life.

The original version of this long-running program was heard in the Pacific and Mountain zones over CBS as a half-hour, Sunday-evening broadcast for Signal Oil. Bill Forman was "The Whistler" in that version, with Marvin Miller as the announcer (1945–54). Miller also played the part for six months while Forman served in the Army. The director in that period was George Allen, and Wilbur Hatch conducted the orchestra. Hatch also wrote the catchy theme.

For a short time the series was produced independently and simultaneously in Chicago, with Everett Clarke as "The Whistler" and Sherman Marks as director. For another brief period it was a CBS sustainer, except in the West, with Sterling Tracy as director. The two-octave range of the theme made it an extremely difficult assignment for whistlers, and the only person who ever mastered it was a girl, Dorothy Roberts.

Whiz Quiz

Quiz

M.C.: Johnny Olson

Who Said That?

Quiz

M.C.: Robert Trout
Writer: Fred Friendly
Sound Effects: Jerry McGee

Who Said That? was first heard over NBC in 1948.

Wife Saver: see *Women's Programs.*

Wilderness Road

Serial Drama

CAST:

Daniel Boone — Ray Collins

Ann Weston	Vivian Block
Sam Weston	Lon Clark
Peter Weston	Jimmy Donnelly
David Weston	James McCallion
John Weston	Chester Stratton
Mary Weston	Anne Elstner
Simon Weston	William Johnstone
Bunch	John Mitchell

Also: Parker Fennelly

Director: Richard Sanville
Writers: Richard Stevenson, William K. Clarke, Ronald Dawson

This program featured the hardships and struggles of a pioneering American family, "the Westons," during the latter half of the eighteenth century. It was first heard over CBS in 1936.

Wings for the Martins

Drama

Starring: Adelaide Klein, Ed Latimer
Director: Philip Cohen

Wings for the Martins dramatized social problems involved in the rearing of families. It began over the Blue network in 1938.

Wings of Destiny

Drama

CAST:

Steve Benton	Carlton KaDell John Hodiak
Peggy Banning	Betty Arnold
Brooklyn, the mechanic	Henry Hunter (Arthur Jacobson)

Announcer: Marvin Miller

Director: Mel Williamson

Airplanes were awarded to contest winners on this program, which began over NBC in 1940. It originated in Chicago and was sponsored by B & W Wings cigarettes.

Winner Take All

Quiz

M.C.: Bill Cullen
Clayton "Bud" Collyer
Ward Wilson
Directors: Frank Dodge, Mark Goodson, Bill Todman
Sound Effects: Jerry Sullivan

Winner Take All began over CBS in 1946.

The Witch's Tale

Drama

Host: Alonzo Deen Cole

CAST:

Old Nancy	Adelaide Fitz-Allan Miriam Wolfe Martha Wentworth

Also: Mark Smith, Marie Flynn, Don MacLaughlin
Directors: Alonzo Deen Cole, Roger Bower
Writer: Alonzo Deen Cole

Opening:

SOUND. *Howling wind, tower clock tolling*

ANNOUNCER. *The Witch's Tale!*

SOUND. *Eerie music up and under, howling wind in background . . .*

ANNOUNCER. The fascination for the eerie . . . weird, blood-chilling tales told by Old Nancy, the Witch of Salem, and Satan, the wise black cat. They're waiting, waiting for you now . . .

SOUND. *Eerie music up*

The Witch's Tale had its première over Mutual in 1934.

The Wizard of Oz

Children

CAST:

Dorothy	Nancy Kelly

The Wizard of Oz made its debut over NBC in 1933. The stories were based on the books by L. Frank Baum.

Woman from Nowhere

Drama

Starring: Irene Rich
Announcer: Marvin Miller
Director: Gordon Hughes

Woman from Nowhere was heard over CBS. The show's sponsor, Ralston, based its pitch on the fact that famous movie star Irene Rich, though a "mature" woman, kept her beauty and glamorous figure by eating Ry-Krisp.

Woman in White

Serial Drama

CAST:

Karen Adams Harding, the Woman in White	Luise Barclay
	Betty Ruth Smith
	Betty Lou Gerson
	Peggy Knudsen
John Adams	Willard Farnum
	Harry Elders
Rosemary Hemingway	Irene Winston
	Genelle Gibbs
Thomas Hawkins	Phil Lord
Betty Adams	Toni Gilman
	Louise Fitch
Alice Day	Ruth Bailey
Roy Palmer	Frank Behrens
Sybella Mayfield	Lois Zarley
Bob Banning	C. Henry Nathan
Aunt Helen Spalding	Henrietta Tedro
Bryant Chandler	David Gothard
Dr. Lee Markham	Macdonald Carey
	Marvin Miller
Uncle Bill	Finney Briggs
Dr. Kirk Harding	Karl Weber
Mrs. Grey	Kathryn Card
Gladys	Sarajane Wells
Frank Fenton	Sidney Ellstrom
Janet Munson Adams	Edith Perry
	Lesley Woods
	Barbara Luddy
Tim Barnes	Eddie Firestone, Jr.
Crandall Barnes	Jack Swingford
	Robert Griffin
Myra Walker	Betty Ruth Smith
Dr. Torrance	Ian Keith
Mr. Munson	Herb Butterfield
Linda Munson	Gail Henshaw
	Alma Dubus
Dad Munson	Bob Dryenforth
Dave Talbot	Lester Damon
	Bret Morrison
Anna	Jeanne Juvelier
Sister Elaine	Connie Crowder
Alice Craig	Ruth Bailey
Kenneth Craig	Bill Bouchey
Ruth Craig	Beverly Ruby
Leonard Huntley	Les Tremayne
Dr. Paul Burton	Kenneth Griffin
Eileen Homes	Sarajane Wells

Dr. Bradley — Harry Elders
Helen Bradley — Muriel Bremner
Amelia Jameson — Cheer Brentson
Alice Hendricks — Beverly Taylor
Dr. Purdy — Hugh Studebaker
Dr. Wilton — Maurice Copeland
Dr. Jack Landis — Harry Elders
Robert Latting
Annie Marie Templeton
Louise Arthur

Producer: Carl Wester
Directors: Al Ulrich, Howard Keegan, Robin Black, Owen Vinson
Writers: Irna Phillips, Herbert Futran, Robert Futran

Woman in White related the romance of a nurse and a young surgeon. It made its debut over NBC in 1937 from Chicago. In 1948 the show moved to Hollywood.

A Woman of America

Serial Drama

CAST:
Prudence Dane — Anne Seymour
Florence Freeman
Wade Douglas, wagonmaster
James Monks
Slim Stark — Kenneth Lynch
Peg Hall — Nancy Douglass
Fanny Carlysle — Louise Larabee
Emilio Prieto — Jackson Beck
John Dane — Larry Robinson
Caleb Jackson — Ed Jerome
Emmie Hatfield — Irene Hubbard
Linda — Coletta McMahon
Tommy — Richard Leone
Walter Carlin — Bartlett Robinson
Madeleine — Helene Dumas
Johnny — Ogden Miles
Sylvia — Fran Carlon

Producer: Don Cope
Writers: Della West Decker, Doria Folliott

A Woman of America was unique in that the entire locale and motif were altered after it had been on the air. Originally it was a Western serial drama with Anne Seymour in the role of "Prudence Dane." In the later version "Prudence" was the editor of a modern-day newspaper. Her part was then played by Florence Freeman. The program made its debut over NBC in 1943.

Woman of Courage

Serial Drama

CAST:
Martha Jackson, the Woman of Courage — Selena Royle
Alice Frost
Esther Ralston
Jim Jackson — Albert Hecht
Tommy Jackson — Larry Robinson
Lucy Jackson — Joan Tetzel
George Harrison — Horace Braham
Lillian Burke — Enid Markey
Mrs. Sullivan — Dora Merande
Joseph Benedict — John Brewster
Susan Benedict — Claire Howard
Red — Carl Eastman
Tommy Lewis — Larry Robinson
Cora — Tess Sheehan
Mrs. Humphries — Joan Alexander

Writer: Carl Alfred Buss

Woman of Courage was first heard over CBS in 1939.

Women and Children First: see *Joe and Mabel.*

Women's Programs

A large segment of each broadcast day was allotted to women's programs. The fifteen-minute serial dramas or "soap operas" made up the great bulk of such programs, but there were also many lecture and conversation programs for the ladies. The most listened-to personality was Mary Margaret McBride, who had her own programs on which she chatted with her audience and interviewed celebrities. She also appeared as "Martha Deane," which was a house name belonging to WOR New York. The program featured homemaking discussions as well as interviews. Bessie Beattie and Marion Young Taylor later took over the role of "Martha Deane."

Betty Crocker was one of radio's earliest recipe programs. It began on NBC in 1926. Various actresses, including Zella Layne played the part of "Betty Crocker," the General Mills homemaking expert.

Eleanor Howe dispensed advice on *Eleanor Howe's Homemaker's Exchange.* Ed and Polly East entertained and enlightened their female audience on *Kitchen Quiz.* Allen Prescott conducted a popular program called *Wife Saver.*

Among the other leading personalities on women's programs were Adelaide Hawley; Alma Kitchell; etiquette authority Emily Post; Nell Vinick, who discussed good grooming and beauty tips; Edna Wallace Hopper (grooming and fashion ideas); Frances Scott—her program was called *It Takes a Woman;* Richard Willis, a charm expert who helped women to look their best through beauty and grooming advice on *Look Your Best;* and cooking experts Ida Bailey Allen and Mary Lee Taylor.

The Woodbury Soap Hour

Variety

Featuring: Bob Hope
Vocalist: Frank Parker
Orchestra: Shep Fields

The chief distinction of this variety program of the 1930s was that it served as an early showcase for Bob Hope's talents. (See also *The Bob Hope Show.*)

The Woody Herman Show

Music

Starring: Woody Herman and His Orchestra
Director: Chet Gierlach

Words and Music

Music

Narrator: Harvey Hays

The World Series

Sports

The first baseball World Series broadcast on radio was in 1921. Thomas Cowan re-created the action in a studio as the New York Giants defeated the New York Yankees five games to three. Among the sportscasters who handled the play-by-play descriptions in later years were Graham McNamee, Quin Ryan, Grantland Rice, "Red" Barber, Bob Elson, Mel Allen, Bill Slater, and Jim Britt.

The WSM Barn Dance: see *The Grand Ole Opry.*

X Minus One: see *Dimension* X.

Y

Yankee Doodle Quiz

Quiz

M.C.: Ted Malone

This quiz was first broadcast over ABC in 1943.

Yesterday's Children

Education

Hostess: Dorothy Gordon
Director: Charles Warburton

Yesterday's Children began over the Blue network in 1940. It presented famous men and women who explained why a particular book had been their favorite. Among the guests were President Franklin D. Roosevelt, Mayor Fiorello H. LaGuardia, Eddie Cantor, Helen Hayes, and Governor Herbert H. Lehman of New York. (See also *Dorothy Gordon.*)

You Are There

Drama

Creator: Goodman Ace
Director: Robert Lewis Shayon

Writers: Irve Tunick, Michael Sklar, Joseph Liss
Sound Effects: Jim Rogan

Don Hollenbeck and other CBS correspondents described re-enactments of famous events in history, using modern news-broadcasting techniques. Guy Sorel was the signature voice, and the only permanent actor in the cast; he played such roles as William the Conqueror, Napoleon, etc. The program had its première in 1947 and was originally titled *CBS Is There.*

You Bet Your Life

Quiz

Host: Groucho Marx
Announcers: George Fenneman, Jack Slattery
Orchestra: Billy May
Producer-Director: John Guedel
Producer: Harfield Weedin
Director: Bob Dwan
Writers: Bernie Smith, Hy Freedman
Theme: "Hooray for Captain Spaulding" by Harry Ruby and Bert Kalmar

Groucho would interview the contestants and then ask them the quiz questions. If any contestants said "the Secret Word" they received a bonus. "The Secret Word" was usually an everyday word such as "fence" or "chair"; it was frequently said quite by accident by a contestant in the course of the interview. The couple who won the most money in the quiz was eligible to win more in a final big-money question. Groucho often aided contestants who weren't doing too well in the quiz by asking an alternate question, such as "Who is buried in Grant's Tomb?" *You Bet Your Life* was first heard over ABC in 1947.

You Make The News

News

This program presented dramatizations of news events.

Young Dr. Malone

Serial Drama

CAST:

Dr. Jerry Malone	Alan Bunce
	Carl Frank
	Charles Irving
	Sandy Becker
Ann Richards Malone	Elizabeth Reller
	Barbara Weeks
Robbie Hughes	Richard Coogan
Alice Hughes	Nancy Coleman
Mrs. Jessie Hughes	Isabel Elson
Bun Dawson	Tommy Hughes
Mrs. Dawson	Fran Hale
Bun's friend	Frank Bealin
Dr. Copp	Ray Appleby
Mira Dunham	Jean Colbert
Dr. Dunham	James Van Dyk
Veronica Ferral	Helene Dumas
Mr. Wright	M. McAllister
Molly	Gertrude Warner
Eddie Blomfield	Bernard Zanville
Doc Harrison	Richard Barrows
Miss Burns	Katharine Raht
The lawyer	William Podmore
Mrs. Penny	Tess Sheehan
Ruby	Amanda Randolph
Daisy Matthews	Ethel Morrison

Marsha	Elspeth Eric
Jean Osborne	Naomi Campbell
Mr. Janac	Sellwin Meyers
Horace Sutton	Ian Martin
Shari	Joy Terry
Tony	Frank Ayres
Jim Farrell	Herbert Nelson
Ingrid	Eleanor Phelps
Dr. Axland	Arnold Korff
Dr. Kwan	Ray Hedge
Lucille Crawford	Janet McGrew
Dr. Sewell Crawford	Paul McGrath
David Crawford	Jack Manning
Christine Taylor	Betty Pratt
Marie Duncan	Pattee Chapman
Mrs. Morrison	Ethel Wilson
Roger Dineen	Barry Thomson
Phyllis Dineen	Joan Banks
Carl Ward	Larry Haines
Mrs. Hale	Ethel Everett
Malcolm Johnston	Lester Damon
Tracy Malone	Jone Allison
	Joan Alexander
	Gertrude Warner
Sam	Berry Kroeger
	Martin Blaine
Lucia Standish	Elspeth Eric
Gene Williams	Bill Redfield
	Bill Lipton
Lynne Dineen	Donna Keath
Dr. Ralph Munson	Larry Haines
Mother	Evelyn Varden
	Vera Allen
Jill Malone	Joan Lazer
	Rosemary Rice
Frank Palmer	Bartlett Robinson
George Fredericks	Robert Haag
Sandy	Tony Barrett
Dr. David Malone	Bill Lipton

Announcer: Ron Rawson

Producers: Basil Loughrane, Ira Ashley, Dave Lesan, Minerva Ellis

Directors: Walter Gorman, Stanley Davis, Fred Weihe, Theodora Yates, Ira Ashley

Writers: Julian Funt, David Driscoll, Charles Gussman

Sound Effects: Hamilton O'Hara, George O'Donnell, Walter Otto

Organist: Charles Paul

Young Dr. Malone made its debut over the Blue network in 1939. "Dr. Jerry Malone" worked at "Three Oaks Medical Center."

Young Hickory

Serial Drama

CAST:

Hickory	Raymond Edward Johnson
	Macdonald Carey

Also: Betty Caine

Director: Maury Lowell

Writer: Bill Murphy

Young Hickory proved to be the setting for a real-life romance; actor Raymond Edward Johnson and actress Betty Caine first met on the show and were married several months later.

Young People's Church of the Air: see *Religion*.

Young People's Conference

Discussion

This program featuring the Reverend Daniel Poling was first broadcast nationally by NBC in 1926.

Young Widder Brown

Serial Drama

CAST:

Ellen Brown	Florence Freeman
Jane Brown	Marilyn Erskine
Mark Brown	Tommy Donnelly
Marjorie Williams	Toni Gilman
Maria Hawkins	Agnes Young
	Lorene Scott
	Alice Yourman
Victoria Loring	Ethel Remey
	Riza Joyce
	Kay Strozzi
Peter Turner	Clayton "Bud" Collyer
Dr. Anthony Loring	Ned Wever
Hope Wayne Munks	Louis Hall
Yvonne	Lili Valenti
Mrs. Tyson	Irene Hubbard
Herbert Temple	House Jameson
	Eric Dressler
	Alexander Scourby
Uncle Josh	Bennett Kilpack
	Tom Hoier
Luke Baxter	John MacBryde
Mrs. Charlotte Brown	Ethel Remey
Dr. Douglass	James Sherman
Roger Power	Frank Lovejoy
Millie Baxter	Charita Bauer
Evelyn	Helen Shields
Miss Todd	Jane Erskine
Joyce Turner	Joan Tompkins
	Helen Shields
Frederick Nelson	Ray Largay
Hulda	Ethel Intropidi
Nelson Davis	Joy Hathaway
Jimmy Davis	Jimmy McCallion
Darius Boggs	Warren Colston
Peter	Alan Bunce
Martha	Florence Malone
Tug Baxter	Tommy Hughes
Olivia McEvoy	Bess McCammon
Norine Temple	Joan Tompkins
Mark	Dickie Van Patten
Mrs. Garvin	Muriel Starr
Judith Adams	Virginia Routh
Wayne Gardner	Robert Haag
Alicia Grayson	Eva Parnell
Barbara Storm	Arline Blackburn
Maggie Sprague	Athena Lorde

Announcer: George Ansbro

Producers: Frank and Anne Hummert
Directors: Martha Atwell, Ed Slattery, Richard Leonard
Writer: Elizabeth Todd
Sound Effects: Ross Martindale

Organist: John Winters
Themes: "In the Gloaming," "Wonderful One" (in the final years of the program)
Opening:

ANNOUNCER. Now it's time for *Young Widder Brown!*

MUSIC. *Theme up full*

ANNOUNCER. *Young Widder Brown,* the story of the age-old conflict between a mother's duty and a woman's heart.

The romantic interest centered on "Ellen Brown" and "Dr. Anthony Loring." She ran a tea room in "Simpsonville"; he interned at the local hospital.

Young Widder Brown was heard over NBC beginning in September 1938, following a brief run on Mutual. The program was originally titled *Young Widder Jones.*

Your Dream Has Come True

Audience Participation

Host: Ian Keith
Announcer: Verne Smith

Wishes from "The Wishing Well" were granted to lucky contestants on this program.

Your Family and Mine

Serial Drama

CAST:
Woody Marshall — Raymond Edward Johnson
Judy Wilbur, "The Red-headed Angel" — Joan Tompkins
Matthew Wilbur — Bill Adams
Winifred Wilbur — Lucille Wall
Millicent Pennington — Francesca Lenni
Ken Wilbur — Bill Lipton
Laura Putnam — Francesca Lenni
Barbara Putnam — Joy Terry
Donald Putnam — Maurice Wells
Arch Hadley — Carl Frank
Silas Drake — Arthur Maitland
Lem Stacey — Parker Fennelly
Dick Burgess — Peter Donald
Also: Frank Lovejoy, Morris Carnovsky, William Quinn, George Coulouris

---

Producer: Henry Souvaine
Directors: Larry Hammond, Harold McGee
Writers: Clyde North, Lillian Lauferty

Your Family and Mine had its première over NBC in 1938.

Your Happy Birthday

Quiz

The Birthday Man: Edmund "Tiny" Ruffner (6′7″ tall)
Vocalist: Helen O'Connell
Orchestra: Jimmy Dorsey

Your Happy Birthday was first heard over the Blue network in 1940.

Your Hit Parade

Music

Vocalists: Buddy Clark, Frank Sinatra, Bea Wain, Joan Edwards, Freda Gibbson (later known as Georgia Gibbs), Lawrence Tibbett, Barry Wood, Jeff Clark, Eileen Wilson, Bill Harrington, Doris Day, Lanny Ross, Kay Lorraine, Johnny Hauser, Kay Thompson, Margaret McCrea, Bonnie Baker, Dinah Shore, Andy Russell
Orchestras: Freddie Rich, Lennie Hayton, Johnny Green, Leo Reisman, Richard Himber, Ray Sinatra, Al Goodman, Axel Stordahl, Orrin Tucker, Carl Hoff, Harry Sosnik, Mark Warnow, Raymond Scott
Harpists: Verlye Mills, Lucile Lawrence
Also: Fred Astaire, Ethel Smith, or-

ganist; Lyn Murray Singers, Ken Lane Chorus
Announcers: Martin Block, Del Sharbutt, André Baruch, Kenny Delmar, Basil Ruysdael
Director: Lee Strahorn
Writers: Gail Ingram, Richard Dana, Bunny Coughlin, Tom Langan, John Henderson Hines, Jacques Finke, Paul Dudley
Theme: "Lucky Day"

Your Hit Parade presented the top popular songs of the week "as determined by *Your Hit Parade* survey, which checks the best-sellers in sheet music and phonograph records, the songs most heard on the air and most played in the automatic coin machines—an accurate, authentic tabulation of America's taste in popular music." There were also a few "Lucky Strike Extras," songs not on the charts at the time. The climax came when the number-one song of the week was announced—it was always the concluding number. Its identity was not revealed until the actual introduction of the song.

The program made its debut over NBC in 1935. In 1938 W. C. Fields appeared often as a guest, doing sketches with Hanley Stafford, Elvia Allman, and Walter Tetley.

Your Hostess: see *Interviewers.*

Your Lover

Music and Talk

Songs and conversation with Frank Luther were featured on this program.

Your Unseen Friend

Drama

CAST:

Your Unseen Friend, The Voice of Conscience — Maurice Joachim
Also: Mae Murray, Sydney Smith, *et al.*

These dramatic sketches, based on problems submitted by listeners, were heard Sundays at 5:00 p.m. over CBS. The series began in 1936. "Your Unseen Friend" interpreted the dramas to assist listeners in solving their personal problems.

Yours for a Song

Music

Starring: Jane Froman, Robert Weede
Orchestra: Alfredo Antonini
Producer-Director: Carlo De Angelo
Writer: Nora Stirling

Yours Truly, Johnny Dollar

Adventure

CAST:

Johnny Dollar, insurance investigator — Charles Russell
Edmond O'Brien
John Lund
Bob Bailey
Bob Readick
Mandel Kramer

Producer-Writer-Director: Jack Johnstone

Director: Jaime Del Valle
Writers: Gil Doud, Paul Dudley, Jack Newman, Sidney Marshall, Bob Ryf, Les Crutchfield

Yours Truly, Johnny Dollar began over CBS in 1950. The program always ended with "Dollar" itemizing his expenses, then signing off, "Yours truly, Johnny Dollar." Lund, Bailey, Readick, and Kramer played the role after 1950.

Youth vs. Age

Quiz

Host: Cal Tinney

This program was first heard over the Blue network in 1939.

Z

Ziegfeld Follies of the Air

Variety

Featuring: Guest Stars
Orchestra: Al Goodman

It was on this program, sponsored by Palmolive and heard Saturdays at 8:00 p.m. over CBS, that Fanny Brice introduced to radio audiences her characterization of "Baby Snooks." Jack Arthur played the harried "Daddy." Later the act appeared on *Maxwell House Coffee Time* with Jack Arthur, then Alan Reed (Teddy Bergman), then Hanley Stafford as "Daddy." Writers David Freedman and Phil Rapp are acknowledged to be the creators of the "Baby Snooks" character. (See also *The Baby Snooks Show; Maxwell House Coffee Time; Palmolive Beauty Box Theater.*)

Bibliography

Abbott, Waldo. *Handbook of Broadcasting.* New York: McGraw-Hill Book Company, 1941. A textbook for college-level radio students with an extensive bibliography.

Allen, Steve. *Mark It and Strike It.* New York: Holt, Rinehart and Winston, 1960. An autobiography with mention of Allen's radio career.

——. *The Funny Men.* New York: Simon and Schuster, 1956. An analysis of the techniques of sixteen prominent comedians with considerable reference to radio comedy.

Archer, Gleason L. *History of Radio.* New York: American Historical Society, 1938. The outgrowth of a lecture course, this book covers radio up to 1926.

Arnold, Frank A. *Broadcast Advertising.* New York: John Wiley and Sons, 1933. A book devoted to broadcast advertising and the role of advertising agencies.

——. *Do You Want to Get Into Radio?* New York: Frederick Stokes Company, 1940. A discussion of the employment opportunities in broadcasting.

Banning, William Peck. *Commercial Broadcasting Pioneer; The WEAF Experiment, 1922–1926.* Cambridge, Mass.: Harvard University Press, 1946. The story of the early days of the NBC flagship station in New York.

Barber, Red. *The Broadcasters.* New York: The Dial Press, 1970. A personal recollection of forty years of broadcasting by one of the most famous of all sportscasters.

Barnes, Pat. *Sketches of Life.* Chicago: Reilly and Lee Company, 1932. Reprints of broadcasts by Barnes in the *Jimmy and Grandad* series.

Barnouw, Erik. *A Tower in Babel.* New York: Oxford University Press, 1966. A history of broadcasting in the United States to 1933.

——. *Handbook of Radio Writing.* Boston: Little, Brown and Company, 1939. The techniques of writing for radio and markets for scripts.

——. *Radio Drama in Action.* New York, Toronto: Farrar and Rinehart, 1945. Radio drama during wartime.

Benét, S. V. *We Stand United.* New York: Farrar and Rinehart, 1945. Radio drama by the famous poet.

Berg, Gertrude. *The Rise of the Goldbergs.* New York: Barse and Company, 1931. Some early sequences from the long-running series.

Blair, Cornelia. *The Nora Drake*

Story. New York: Duell, Sloan and Pearce, 1950. A synopsis of the serial drama of the same title.

Bouck, Zeh. *Making a Living in Radio*. New York: McGraw-Hill Book Company, 1935. Mostly devoted to servicemen and engineers, but it does have chapters giving advice to announcers and actors.

Brindze, Ruth. *Not to Be Broadcast, The Truth About Radio*. New York: Vanguard Press, 1937. A discussion of the conflicts among government, advertisers, and broadcasters in the control of broadcasting.

Cantril, Hadley. *The Invasion from Mars, A Study in the Psychology of Panic*. Princeton: Princeton University Press, 1940. The script of the Orson Welles broadcast as well as an analysis of the public reaction to it.

Carlile, John S. *The Production and Direction of Radio Programs*. New York: Prentice-Hall, 1939. The details of radio production including hand signals, studio diagrams, etc.

Carpenter, H. K. *Behind the Microphone*. Raleigh, N.C.: 1930. A very early study of behind-the-scenes-in-radio.

Carter, Boake. *I Talk as I Like*. New York: Dodge, 1937. A discussion of the details necessary for a radio news broadcast.

Chase, Francis, Jr. *Sound and Fury, An Informal History of Broadcasting*. New York: Harper and Brothers, 1942. A light but complete coverage of broadcasting history up to 1942.

Cheerio. *The Story of Cheerio by Himself*. New York: Garden City Publishing Company, 1936. The broadcasting career of "Cheerio" is outlined.

Chesmore, Stuart. *Behind the Microphone*. New York: Thomas Nelson and Sons, 1935. An early behind-the-scenes book.

Codel, Martin (editor). *Radio and Its Future*. New York: Harper and Brothers, 1930. This book contains articles by various broadcasting authorities of the time.

Correll, Charles J., and Gosden, Freeman F. *All About Amos 'n' Andy*. New York: Rand McNally, 1929. The history of "Amos 'n' Andy" and excerpts from their radio broadcasts.

——. *Here They Are—Amos 'n' Andy*. New York: Ray Long and Richard Smith, 1931. Stories about "Amos 'n' Andy" taken from their radio series.

Corwin, Norman. *More by Corwin*. New York: Henry Holt and Company, 1944.

——. *On a Note of Triumph*. New York: Henry Holt and Company, n.d.

——. *Thirteen by Corwin*. New York: Henry Holt and Company, 1942.

——. *Twenty-six by Corwin*. New York: Henry Holt and Company, 1941.

——. *Untitled and Other Radio Dramas*. New York: Henry Holt and Company, 1947. These books by Norman Corwin are anthologies of his radio plays.

Coulter, Douglas (editor). *Columbia Workshop Plays*. New York: Whittlesey House, 1939. A collection of fourteen radio plays from the famous series.

Crosby, John. *Out of the Blue*. New York: Simon and Schuster, 1952. A collection of newspaper articles on radio by the famous critic.

Cuthbert, Margaret (editor). *Adventures in Radio*. New York: Howell, Siskin, 1945. This book contains articles and plays by such authors as Edna St. Vincent Millay, Arch Oboler, Archibald MacLeish, etc.

Daniels, Leslie Noel. *Dick Steele, The Boy Reporter*. Chicago: 1934. A mimeographed script of the program which was available from the sponsor, the Educator Biscuit Company.

Donaldson, Charles E. *Popular Radio Stars*. Washington, D.C.: 1942. Brief glimpses of the radio stars of the day.

Dragonette, Jessica. *Faith Is a Song*. New York: D. McKay Co., 1951. An autobiography with reference to her radio career.

Dunlap, Orrin E. *The Story of Radio*. New York: Dial Press, 1935. A history of radio with some emphasis on the technical aspects of broadcasting.

Edwards, Ralph. *Radio's Truth or Consequences Party Book*. New York: 1940. A game book for playing this popular radio game at home.

Eichberg, Richard. *Radio Stars of Today or Behind the Scenes in Broadcasting*. Boston: L. C. Page and Company, 1937. Glimpses of popular radio performers as well as the major radio stations.

Eisenberg, Azriel L. *Children and Radio Programs*. New York: Columbia University Press, 1936. A study of New York metropolitan area children and their radio listening habits.

Fitelson, H. William. *The Theatre Guild on the Air*. New York: Rinehart and Company, 1947. Radio plays as adapted and performed on the program of the same name.

Floherty, John J. *Behind the Microphone*. Philadelphia: J. B. Lippincott, 1944. A behind-the-scenes look at radio broadcasting.

——. *On The Air, The Story of Radio*. New York: Doubleday, Doran and Company, 1938. An illustrated description of radio broadcasting with some discussion of early television.

Flynn, Bess. *Bachelor's Children, A Synopsis of the Radio Program*. Chicago, Ill.: published by Old Dutch Cleanser, 1939. This book, available from the sponsor by mail, brought listeners up-to-date on previous episodes.

Folger, J. A. & Co. *Judy and Jane*. Chicago: 1930. This was a mimeographed script available to listeners from the sponsor.

Gaver, Jack, and Stanley, Dave. *There's Laughter in the Air*. New York: Greenberg, 1945. Biographical sketches of leading radio comedians as well as script excerpts.

Goldsmith, A. N., and Lescaboura, A. C. *This Thing Called Broadcasting*. New York: Henry Holt and Company, 1939. A history of radio broadcasting and some discussion on writing radio drama and comedy.

Golenpaul, Dan. *Information, Please!* New York: Random House, 1940. A book about the program, with quiz questions designed to "stump the experts."

Green, Abel, and Laurie, Joe, Jr. *Show Biz, From Vaude to Video.* New York: Henry Holt and Company, 1951. An extensive history of "Show Biz" compiled from the pages of *Variety*.

Gross, Ben. *I Looked and I Listened.* New York: Random House, 1954. Reminiscences gleaned from years of writing a radio and television column.

Gurman, Joseph, and Slager, Myron. *Radio Round-Ups.* Boston: Lothrop, Lee and Shepard Company, 1932. This book on radio programs covers some of the early days.

Harding, Alfred. *The Pay and Conditions of Work of Radio Performers.* New York: 1934. A study of the economics of a broadcasting acting career.

Harmon, Jim. *The Great Radio Comedians.* Garden City, N.Y.: Doubleday and Company, 1970.

——. *The Great Radio Heroes.* Garden City, N.Y.: Doubleday and Company, 1967. The titles are self-explanatory for the contents of these two recollections of radio.

Harris, Credo Fitch. *Microphone Memoirs.* Indianapolis: Bobbs-Merrill Company, 1937. Written by a radio station manager, this is a book of reminiscences about early radio days.

Hettinger, Herman S. *Radio, The Fifth Estate.* Philadelphia: American Academy of Political and Social Science, 1935. A discussion of the broadcasting field covering a wide scope.

Hickock, Eliza Merrill. *The Quiz Kids.* Boston: Houghton Mifflin Company, 1947. A book about the popular radio program of the same name and its stars.

Higby, Mary Jane. *Tune in Tomorrow.* New York: Cowles Education Corporation, 1968. An amusing account of her experiences in radio by the star of *When A Girl Marries.*

Hill, Edwin C. *The Human Side of the News.* New York: Walter J. Black, 1934. An account of Mr. Hill's career as a newscaster.

Husing, Ted. *Ten Years before the Mike.* New York: Farrar and Rinehart, 1935. An entertaining account of the author's experiences in radio.

Kaltenborn, Hans von. *I Broadcast a Crisis.* New York: Random House, 1938. A collection of broadcasts that Kaltenborn ad-libbed during the Czech-German crisis.

——. *Kaltenborn Edits the News.* New York: Modern Age Books, 1937. This book is a collection of news reports of the major events of the year 1936.

Landry, Robert J. *This Fascinating Radio Business.* Indianapolis: Bobbs-Merrill Company, 1946. A historical account of radio broadcasting and its stars.

Lass, A. H., McGill, Earle J., and Axelrod, Donald. *Plays from Radio.* Boston: Houghton Mifflin Company, 1948. An anthology of plays for amateur groups to perform.

Lawrence, Jerome. *Off Mike.* New York: Essential Books, 1944. A light behind-the-scenes study of radio.

Lazersfeld, Paul F. *Radio and the Printed Page.* New York: Duell, Sloan and Pearce, 1940. These are the findings of a Rockefeller Foundation research project regarding the preferences and conflicts between radio and the various printed media.

——. *Radio Listening in America.* New York: Prentice-Hall, 1948.

——. *The People Look at Radio.* Chapel Hill: University of North Carolina Press, 1946. The above two books are reports on surveys of radio listeners conducted by the National Opinion Research Center. Lazersfeld acted as analyst and interpreter of the accumulated data.

Lent, Henry Bolles. *This Is Your Announcer.* New York: Macmillan Company, 1945. An account of a radio announcing career.

MacLeish, Archibald. *The Fall of the City.* New York: Farrar and Rinehart, 1938. A radio play in verse by the famous poet.

McBride, Mary Margaret. *Out of the Air.* New York: Doubleday and Company, 1960. Miss McBride's account of her radio career.

McNamee, Graham. *You're on the Air.* New York and London: Harper and Brothers, 1926. A very early account of radio broadcasting by one of its pioneers.

Morell, Peter. *Poisons, Potions, and Profits, The Antidote to Radio Advertising.* New York: Knight Publishers, 1937. A further subtitle is: "An expose of fraudulent radio advertising and the harmful ingredients contained in nationally advertised products."

Morris, Lloyd R. *Not So Long Ago.* New York: Random House, 1949. Reminiscences of radio broadcasting.

National Broadcasting Company. *Alice In Sponsor-Land.* New York: NBC, 1941. This book, for the radio industry and advertiser, outlines the benefits of advertising on radio.

——. *Thirty-five Hours a Day!* New York: NBC, 1937. A publication for the trade about the amount of effort put into NBC broadcasts.

Oboler, Arch. *Fourteen Radio Plays.* New York: Random House, 1940.

——. (editor). *Free World Theatre.* New York: Random House, 1944.

——. *Ivory Tower and Other Radio Plays.* Chicago: W. Targ, 1940.

——. *Oboler Omnibus.* New York: Duell, Sloan and Pearce, 1945. The above four books are anthologies of radio plays written or edited by Arch Oboler.

Parker, Seth (pseud. for Phillips H. Lord). *Seth Parker and His Jonesport Folks, Way Back Home.* Philadelphia: John C. Winston Company, 1932. An account of how the *Seth Parker* programs came to be and how they were broadcast.

——. *The Seth Parker Hymnal.* New York: Carl Fischer Music Company, c. 1930. A hymn book containing many of the audience's favorite hymns from the *Seth Parker* radio program.

Ringgold, Gene, and Bodeen, DeWitt. *The Films of Cecil B. DeMille.* New York: Citadel Press, 1969. While primarily concerned with DeMille's films, this work contains a complete listing of DeMille's *Lux Radio Theatre* productions.

Saerchinger, Cesar. *Hello America.* Boston: Houghton Mifflin Company, 1938. This book tells of Mr.

Saerchinger's efforts in Europe to broadcast major events for American listeners.

Settel, Irving. *A Pictorial History of Radio*. New York: Citadel Press, 1961. A large photographic compilation of radio history.

Siepmann, Charles Arthur. *Radio's Second Chance*. Boston: Little, Brown and Company, 1946. A social criticism of the radio broadcasting industry.

Sioussat, Helen. *Mikes Don't Bite*. New York: L. B. Fischer, 1943. How to overcome "mike fright" and relax before the microphone.

Slate, Sam J., and Cook, Joe. *It Sounds Impossible*. New York: Macmillan Company, 1963. Reminiscences and anecdotes about radio's history.

Stedman, Raymond William. *The Serials*. Norman, Oklahoma: The University of Oklahoma Press, 1971. An accurate and exhaustive study of radio, TV, and motion picture serials with considerable material on soap operas and children's adventure series.

Summers, Harrison B. *A Thirty-Year History of Programs Carried on National Radio Networks in the United States*. Columbus, Ohio: Ohio State University Press, 1958. An extensive list of network radio programs for a thirty-year period.

Thomas, Lowell. *Magic Dials*. New York: Polygraphic Company of America, 1939. An illustrated story of radio history.

Thurber, James. *The Beast in Me and Other Animals*. New York: Harcourt, Brace and Company, 1948. One of the essays in this book concerns radio memories.

Treadwell, Bill. *Head, Heart, and Heel*. New York: Mayfair Books, 1958. The biography of "Uncle Don" Carney.

Tyler, Kingdon S. *Modern Radio*. New York: Harcourt, Brace and Company, 1947. An account of radio today and its future.

Van Loon, H. W. *Air-Storming*. New York: Harcourt, Brace and Company, 1935. Forty educational broadcasts by the noted author.

Waller, Judith C. *Radio, the Fifth Estate*. Boston: Houghton Mifflin Company, 1946. A critical account of radio and its relation to the other mass media.

West, Robert. *The Rape of Radio*. New York: Rodin Publishing Company, 1941. The misuse of radio and what it could be.

Woodfin, Jane. *Of Mikes and Men*. New York: McGraw-Hill Book Company, 1951. An account of radio history and the personalities involved.

Wylie, Max. *Best Broadcasts of 1938–39*. New York: Whittlesey House, 1939.

——. *Best Broadcasts of 1939–40*. New York: Whittlesey House, 1940. These two books contain scripts and comment on the broadcasts for radio programs in various categories such as comedy, drama, documentary, etc.

——. *Radio Writing*. New York: Farrar and Rinehart, 1939. A textbook on how to write for radio with much illustrative material.

[Anon.] *This Is War*. New York: Dodd, Mead and Company, 1942. This book contains radio dramas by Norman Corwin, William N. Robson, Maxwell Anderson, *et al.*

PERIODICALS, DIRECTORIES, AND ANNUALS:

American Broadcasting Company. *Blue Feature News.* New York: 1942.

——. *Blue Network Advance Programs.* New York: 1942.

——. *Blue Network Shows.* New York: 1942.

The Billboard. New York: 1894 to date.

Broadcasting. New York: 1931 to date.

Columbia Broadcasting System. *CBS Highlights.* New York: 1937 to 1942.

——. *CBS News.* New York: 1939 to date.

——. *CBS Student Guide.* New York: 1939 to date.

National Broadcasting Company. *NBC Behind the Mike.* New York: Jan. 3 to Dec. 13, 1940.

——. *NBC Blue Advance Program Service.* New York: 1939 to 1941.

——. *NBC Chimes.* New York: 1943 to date.

——. *NBC Digest.* New York: Oct. 1946 to Oct. 1948.

——. *NBC Red Advance Program Service.* New York: 1939 to 1941.

National Radio Artists Directory. Jan. 1940.

Radio Annual. 1938 to date.

Radio Best.

Radio Daily.

Radio Guide. Known as *Radio Guide* (1931), *Radio and Amusement Guide* (1932–33), *Radio Guide* (1933–40), and *Movie and Radio Guide* (1940–43).

Radio Life. 1940.

Radio Mirror. Also known as *Radio TV Mirror* and *TV Radio Mirror.*

Radio Personalities. New York: Press Bureau Inc., 1936. Edited by Don Rockwell.

Radio Row. 1947.

Radio Stars. 1932.

Radio Tele-News. 1945.

Sponsor. 1946 to date.

Stand-By. 1939 to date.

Tune-In. 1944 to 1946.

Variety. 1905 to date.

Variety Radio Directory. 1937 on.

Who's Who in T.V. and Radio. New York: Dell Publishing Company.

Writer's Radio Theatre. 1940 and 1941.

Index

'N